A BURGHER QUIXOTE

From a pencil drawing by A. S. Langley.

PAUL DU PLOOY.

A
Burgher Quixote

DOUGLAS BLACKBURN

INTRODUCTION BY STEPHEN GRAY

AFRICASOUTH PAPERBACKS
CAPE TOWN : JOHANNESBURG
DAVID PHILIP

AFRICASOUTH PAPERBACKS

This series includes important works of southern African literature
that are at present available only in hardback or are out of print or
not readily accessible or 'banned'; there is also provision for new
writing. The books chosen will be not only those whose worth has
become acknowledged, but also interesting and significant works
that need rescue from neglect. Among the titles contracted are a
number of books recently 'unbanned', after having been sent by
the publisher for review. Also included in *Africasouth Paperbacks*
are books from Africa south-of-the-Sahara, i.e. west, central and
east African works not before available in southern Africa in paper-
back, but of particular interest or needed for study purposes. The
first titles available in this landmark series are listed at the back of
this book.

First published 1903 by Blackwood & Sons, Edinburgh and London

Published 1984 in Africasouth Paperbacks by David Philip, Publisher
(Pty.) Ltd., 217 Werdmuller Centre, Claremont, 7700 South Africa

Text only reproduced facsimile from the Blackwood edition

ISBN 0 86486 025 0

© 1984 Introduction by Stephen Gray

Printed by Creda Press (Pty.) Ltd., Solan Road, Cape Town

CONTENTS

CHAPTER VI.

CHAPTER VII.

CHAPTER VIII.

CHAPTER IX.

CHAPTER X.

CHAPTER XI.

CHAPTER XII.

CHAPTER XIII.

CHAPTER XIV.

CHAPTER XV.

CHAPTER XVI.

CHAPTER XVII.

INTRODUCTION

Blackburn was a knight errant . . . a typical journalist of the old school, a brilliant writer, generous to a fault, and always hard up while in South Africa . . . His books rank with the very best South African novels, for Blackburn wrote of what he saw from his own viewpoint and that of no one else. May he rest in peace.[1]

The author of *Prinsloo of Prinsloosdorp* has given us another work, which will be read with entertainment by all who appreciate the best of fiction with a firm basis in fact. Among the scores of novels written in the late war the *Burgher Quixote* will stand out foremost in its power of literary expression and striking humorous portraiture.[2]

The father of the modern school of novelists.[3]

A new satirist has arisen, and, appropriately enough, from Africa, the home of surprises . . . he has given us . . . as brilliant and sustained an essay in political irony as we can remember to have appeared in the last thirty years . . . . It is enough to commend it to the reading public as a first-rate work of art, which deserves a permanent place amid the literature of social and political satire.[4]

We agree with the statement that Blackburn's aim is evidently 'to sketch for a younger generation details of a past or passing phase of South African life, rather than to write fiction, the result being an inside view of historical happenings, very useful to relieve and illustrate real South African history like Dr. Theal's.[5]

. . . absurd and humorous . . . shrewdly put together . . . .[6]

. . . many races and many methods of thought must be reckoned with in Africa. Nor is the slimness of the Boer character the least difficulty wherewith we are confronted. To understand a good man or a bad man is easy enough; but who should fathom the cunning of the half-wise and half-wicked? Such a book as Mr. Blackburn's *A Burgher Quixote* (Blackwood) is, indeed, a luminous commentary upon the hardship of our task. Who can cope confidently with the sly cunning of such a man as Sarel Erasmus, the central figure of Mr. Blackburn's admirable story? . . .

Now the book, which is written without the smallest trace of bitterness, is proof enough that Lord Milner has to deal with 'slimness' of a very special sort. Men like Sarel Erasmus, who are clever enough to hoodwink Joubert and Viljoen, will easily deceive the British officials who are sent to govern them. And the worst is that, being unconscious humorists, they prefer to turn their very great gift of cunning to the worst possible account. All these things are clearly presented in the *Burgher Quixote,* a book which, nevertheless, we value more for its admirable qualities than for the interesting facts which it sets forth. In the first place, it is a model of irony, simple and sustained. Nowhere is there any faltering, nor any forgetfulness of the method employed. And how great this achievement is will be understood if we consider how few ironists that our literature may boast. To the ironist one temptation is constant: he becomes so earnest in his desire to prove his point that he drops into argument, or even into morality. Of this cardinal sin Sarel Erasmus is always guiltless. He never knows, what is patent to the reader, that he is a sorry scamp who consistently shows the white feather. He preserves from beginning to end the beautiful appearance of simplicity, which makes the most dastardly of his actions seem respectable. It is true that Mr. Blackburn had already shown how great is his power of satire. But his *Burgher Quixote* will manifestly increase his reputation, and we recommend this masterpiece of irony to our readers, not merely because it will teach them a profound lesson of South Africa, and show them the reverse of the medal which has for its obverse Lord Milner's report, but because it is packed with amusement, and prompts a smile with every page.[7]

In the Sarel Erasmus series, Blackburn contributes two more books with a political background. *A Burgher Quixote* (1903) describes Sarel's misadventures during the South African War, and *I Came and Saw* (1908) is an account of Sarel's visit to England. These two books have the failings of their predecessor, *Prinsloo of Prinsloosdorp,* with regard to loose structure, and Blackburn's humour begins to pall on the reader who has learned by now what is to be expected of Sarel. Blackburn himself, however, seems to have developed an interest in his rogue, and his humour is more sympathetic when he sees the absurdity of some English customs through Sarel's eyes.[8]

To Milner, civilisation in the backward parts of the earth such as . . . the Transvaal, came with irrigation works, railways, schools, agricultural improvement, veterinary science, police, roads and telegraphs—in short, with regulated order. On this level, the imperial mission was akin to advanced estate management of a paternalistic nature; it was the plain duty of an advanced people to elevate those lower on the rungs of civilisation.[9]

Krugersdorp, 22nd (Special)—At the Police Court this morning Mr. Douglas Blackburn, editor of *The Transvaal Sentinel,* was charged with assaulting Doctor A. Lachmann.

The evidence of the complainant was that, on the previous night, Blackburn had summoned him from bed and charged him with calling a certain lady a liar. The doctor asked the name of the lady, and on receiving it, denied having used the language alleged. What he had said was in German, which would be less offensive than if the same had been said in English.

Blackburn then gave him five minutes to write an apology, which he refused to do, upon which Blackburn assaulted him with an oak stick, causing severe wounds on his body and head . . .[10]

He was quite a rascal in his younger days. Quite a character, a leg-puller. You couldn't always tell if he was serious when he was telling a story.[11]

The air is pregnant with inspiration, and I am laying it under contribution and endeavouring to crystallise it in the pages of my long-promised sequel to *Prinsloo of Prinsloosdorp,* which will see the light as soon as the public require a relaxation from the absorbing but exhausting records of the Coronation.[12]

Mr. Blackburn, we understand, is an invalid who lives in Basutoland. He used to be a journalist in Natal. One can only regret that his newspaper training did not give him a better conception of South African life.[13]

He was . . . smallish, stooping somewhat, with a face tanned to a uniform pale brown by South African suns. He wore an old blue serge suit, shiny with age and dusty with ash from his cheroots, and a clean starched collar which contrasted with his shabby tie and battered straw hat. He looked raffish and poor and fond of a glass, all of which he was. He looked like a retired adventurer, a man who has seen monstrous things in remote places and now found himself in this backwater which suited him as well as any, a man content to remember and talk. All that he was. He was also a professional writer.[14]

He served during the Anglo–Boer War with the Volunteer Ambulance and was wounded at Pieter's Hill. He was a noted student of calligraphy and gave evidence on handwriting on many occasions in Natal and Transvaal courts.[15]

Lord Roberts heralds the invention of the shrapnel bomb, an innovation that will 'utterly destroy all living things within the ground they swept'.[16]

Jan had seen Krugersdorp and Johannesburg, and Pretoria; he knew the world; he was at Krugersdorp when Dr. Jameson made his raid . . . . He was very handsome now; not tall, and very slight, but with fair hair that curled close to his head, and white hands like a town's man. All the girls in the countryside were in love with him. They all wished he would come and see them. But he seldom rode from home except to go to the next farm where he had been at school. There lived little Aletta, who was the daughter of the woman his uncle had loved before he went to the Kaffir war and got killed. She was only fifteen years old, but they had always been great friends. She netted him a purse of green silk. He said he would take it with him to Europe, and would show it when he came back and was an advocate; and he gave her a book with her name written on it, which she was to show him.[17]

Colonialism, in its best sense, is a natural overflow of nationality; its test is the power of colonists to transplant the civilisation they represent to the new natural and social environment in which they find themselves . . . .

   Aggressive imperialism is an artificial stimulation of nationalism in peoples too foreign to be absorbed and too compact to be permanently crushed. We have welded Afrikanderdom into just such a strong dangerous nationalism . . . The injury to nationalism . . . consists in converting a cohesive, pacific, internal force into an exclusive, hostile force, a perversion of true power and use of nationality. The worst and most certain result is the retardation of internationalism.[18]

Not the least extraordinary result of the war in South Africa has been the quantity of literature to which it has given birth. The bulk of this literature has described the operations from the British standpoint. This was only to be expected, since the Boers are essentially a pastoral people, without art or literature, and apparently devoid of that temperament which is a fertile bed for intellectual progression. But considering the descent of which they are so proud, it is a curious trait in their national character that they have retained few of the refinements of their ancestors. Consequently, such literature as voiced their view of the late struggle, which was given to the public before the termination of hostilities, came from the pens of aliens who had served for a time in their midst. For the most part this was of an ephemeral and worthless nature,—some of it so partisan and violent as to suggest the labour of the mercenary. One or two of the younger generation of Boers, town-bred by reason of the new-found wealth of the Republics, essayed when in exile or captivity to write the story of their experiences . . . . With the termination of hostilities has come a new craze for war literature—a demand for the personal stories of the leaders of this pastoral people, who, for the last three years, have presented to the world the anomaly of a tiny nation maintaining armed defiance to one of the Powers of the world.[19]

> Take up the White Man's burden —
> And reap his old reward:
> The blame of those ye better,
> The hate of those ye guard.[20]

Like Mr. Blackburn's other books, it is in a different class to anything else in the way of South African story-writing since Olive Schreiner's early work.[21]

Didn't I tell you, Don Quixote, sir, to turn back, for they were not armies you were going to attack, but flocks of sheep?[22]

THE AUTHOR

Douglas Blackburn was born on 6 August 1857, in Southwark, the son of Elizabeth Blackburn, née Ward, and George Blackburn, a journeyman leather-dresser in the abattoirs of south London. At 23 he became the editor of the *Brightonian,* an independent newspaper of liberal opinion in Brighton, which exposed corruption in civic affairs and was bankrupted and closed in 1884. Then on Fleet Street he was a drama reviewer for a decade, and came to the Zuid-Afrikaansche Republiek in that capacity for the *Star.* With the Jameson invasion of 1895, he moved to Krugersdorp as the independent editor–proprietor of the *Sentinel,* a weekly newspaper, polemically anti-jingo and pro-republican in its policy, which exposed corruption in high places. With the *Sentinel* liquidated in 1898, he returned to Johannesburg to write and edit his one-man satirical paper, *Life: A Subtropical Journal,* which revealed corruption in high places. From here he published two anonymous novels, *Kruger's Secret Service* and *Prinsloo of Prinsloosdorp,* of the latter of which *A Burgher Quixote* was the sequel.

With the outbreak of the war, Blackburn rode with the Boer commandos as a correspondent, was deported to Moçambique by his friend of Krugersdorp days, General Ben Viljoen, for unknown reasons, and repatriated himself to the British forces, facing his republican comrades over the battle line in Natal as a correspondent. Wounded during the skirmish of Pieter's Hill near Colenso, in December 1899, he was hospitalised, and collated the *Times of Natal* history of the first phase of the war from Pietermaritzburg. Recuperating in Loteni Valley, during the second, guerrilla phase, he wrote *A Burgher Quixote,* which ran into three impressions within the year of its publication (1903). It was his first work under his own name.

The novels *Richard Hartley, Prospector,* about the Z.A.R.'s last days, *Leaven: A Black and White Story,* about labour relations in Natal, and the last of the Sarel Erasmus trilogy, *I Came and Saw,* were to follow by 1908, the year of his return to London. Besides writing fiction, Blackburn contributed copiously to the *Daily Mail* in London and the socialist weekly, the *New Age.* The experience of close on two decades in South Africa is summarised in his joint-autobiography with W.W. Caddell, *Secret Service in South Africa.*

In Edwardian London Blackburn lived off his wits as a cryptographer and a pioneer of short-hand techniques, but on Easter Monday, 1916, retired from the war-torn city to edit his last one-man weekly (exposing corruption in places), the *Tonbridge Free Press,* in Tonbridge, Kent. There he died of lobar pneumonia on 28 March 1929, aged 71, his last column for the paper appearing posthumously. He is buried there in an unmarked pauper's grave.

Rest in peace.

THE WAR

The Second Anglo–Boer War—call it the Boer War, the last of the Gentlemen's Wars, the Tweede Vryheidsoorlog—was declared on 11 October 1899, two days after President Kruger's ultimatum to the British to remove troops from the Natal border. In that last year of the century the Transvaal Republic comprised 80 000 Boer men, women and children, 124 000 Uitlanders, and 645 000 blacks, and was 190 000 square kilometres in extent. With its ally the Orange Free State (80 000 square kilometres with a total population of 207 000), the Boers could muster 20 000 Burgher commandos.

After thirty-one months of action, peace was declared on 31 May 1902. The death count: 27 000 Boer women and children died in concentration camps, then known as relocation centres, their dead menfolk unnumbered; 21 000 British dead, buried in marked and unmarked graves; 14 000 blacks dead, on both sides. The estimated cost: £200 million.

Rest in peace.

The Transvaal and the Orange Free State joined British South Africa, which included the Cape, Natal, the Kingdom of Basutoland, Griqualand West, Zululand, British Bechuanaland, Bechuanaland Protectorate, Transkei, Tembuland, Pondoland, Griqualand East and the British South African Charter territories (Rhodesia), an area of 1,9 million square kilometres with a population of some 2,5 million. This, in turn, was part of a total worldwide empire of over fifty colonies of 13 million square kilometres with a total population of 248 million.

For this market some 350 novels were written in English about the war.

Blackburn's royalties on *A Burgher Quixote* kept him for about eight months and were sufficient to pay for an operation to remove a bullet from his left kidney.

Loteni P.O.A.
via Nottingham
Natal, SA
Sep 29, 02

[To William Blackwood, Esq., Edinburgh]

Dear Sir,—I have to thank you for your letter of Aug 22, which, with one from the Editor of the *Spectator,* has reached me . . . I will forward you the M.S. of my new book which I hope may justify the kind and almost enthusiastic appreciation bestowed upon my *Prinsloo of Prinsloosdorp* by the *Spectator* reviewer.

Although I have followed up the new line I created in *Prinsloo,* and though the new work is strictly humorous, I have been very careful to keep as my objective throughout my desire to interpret and convey to English readers that strange mental attitude of the Boer which is always so great a puzzle to the newcomer, and leads to so much misunderstanding. I think I am justified in saying that I am accepted by South Africans as the leading literary exponent of Boer character. I have made a careful study of him for ten years, and have watched him in the Dorp, Veld, City and Battlefield, and I think I know him well, for he has been a delightful study. I have been on commando with him in two Kafir wars and had the special-ly good fortune to be the only English correspondent on the Boer side up to Elandslaagte, where I was at the request of certain Hollanders put under arrest and conveyed over the border to Delagoa Bay, and later I went to the front on the British side and was badly wounded at the Battle of Pieter's Hill. Since then I have been recuperating in Natal and writing the present book, which as an old journalist—I think I am senior acting pressman in the Transvaal—is a successful attempt to present the Boer as he is, with due regard to his good as well as bad points and his limitations . . . .

My absence from home in Krugersdorp renders it impossible for me to act upon the suggestion of the Editor of the *Spectator* by sending you a copy of the long and flattering review of *Prinsloo* which appeared in that journal in Aug 1899 but I may state that the opinions expressed were endorsed by the entire South African Press, who recognise that I have founded a style in South African literature, which it is my earnest desire to maintain and improve; and if the work has the good fortune to meet with your approval, I can answer for the South African Press and reading public, to whom I may say without egotism I am a very familiar figure. I mention these facts as a business man, for when one has been writing for thirty years the sentimental gives place to the practical. At the same time I feel justified in admitting that I regard this book as the work of my life and shall be quite prepared to stand or fall by it. The M.S. runs to 100,000 words, and in lieu of a better title I have called it *A Burgher Quixote,* but in matters of detail such as this your opinion is of more value and I should of course gratefully accept any suggestions.

I may explain, in conclusion, that although the scene and period of the story are mainly of and in the recent war, it is *not a war book,* but essentially a work of humour and analysis of Boer character under very striking and interesting conditions

> Faithfully yours
> Douglas Blackburn

> November 17, 1902

[To W. Blackwood, Esq., Edinburgh]

Dear Sir—I send by this mail a registered parcel containing the M.S. of my Afrikander novel, *A Burgher Quixote,* in accordance with my letter of Aug 25th . . .

I have spared no pains to make the book real and a standard. The characters are not creations but actual portraits of common types; the incidents are, without exception, actualities of the past three years, and the style is an exact replica of that affected, in writing English, by the priggish half educated young Afrikander of the Government office.

But my earnest desire has been to open up an entirely new literary field and this I have done so far as material goes, for no other writer has handled it.

The accompanying drawing is the very best and only accurate picture of a Dopper Boer I have ever seen, and was specially drawn. Could it be used?

The dedication I intend as a public compliment to a Scotsman—

an Edinboro man—who has done much for literature in South Africa, and who is known and esteemed by every Scot in the land.

> Awaiting your verdict,
> I am, yours truly
> Douglas Blackburn

FURTHER READING

Blackburn, Douglas. *Prinsloo of Prinsloosdorp: A Tale of Transvaal Officialdom,* reprint. Cape Town: South African Universities Press, 1978.

Blackburn, Douglas, and W. Waithmann Caddell. *Secret Service in South Africa.* London: Cassell, 1911.

'Douglas Blackburn: Journalist into Novelist'. *English in Africa,* Grahamstown, March, 1978, pp. 1-47, Blackburn issue including a selection from the *Sentinel* and the Blackburn–Blackwood letters.

Gray, Stephen. *Douglas Blackburn.* Boston: Twayne, 1983.

Maxwell-Mahon, W.D. 'Douglas Blackburn'. *Dictionary of South African Biography,* vol. 4. Durban and Pretoria: Butterworth, 1981.

Nagelgast, E.B. 'Johannesburg Newspapers and Periodicals, 1887-1899'. *Africana Byways,* Anna H. Smith, ed. Johannesburg: Donker, 1976.

Nathan, Manfred. *South African Literature: A General Survey.* Cape Town: Juta, 1925.

Viljoen, General Ben J. *Under the Vierkleur: A Romance of a Lost Cause.* Boston: Small, Maynard, 1904.

Stephen Gray
Johannesburg, 1984

NOTES

[1] William Hills, obituary, 'Douglas Blackburn: Some Personal Recollections', *Star* (3 April 1929).

[2] 'New and Recent Books', *Natal Witness* (4 July 1903).

[3] Stanley Portal Hyatt on Blackburn, quoted in A. St. John Adcock, 'The Literature of Greater Britain', *Bookman* (Sept. 1912), p. 248.

[4] Anonymous review of *Prinsloo of Prinsloosdorp,* in *Spectator* (26 Aug. 1899), pp. 288–90.

[5] John Forrest, 'South Africa's Writers', *African Monthly* (Feb. 1907), p. 377.

[6] Sarah Gertrude Millin, on *Prinsloo of Prinsloosdorp,* 'The South Africa of Fiction', *State* (Feb. 1912), p. 137.

[7] 'Musings without Method' column, *Blackwood's Magazine* (June 1903), pp. 854–6.

[8] J.P.L. Snyman. *The South African Novel in English, 1880–1930.* Potchefstroom: University of Potchefstroom, 1952, p. 55.

[9] G.H.L. Le May. *British Supremacy in South Africa, 1899–1907.* Oxford: Clarendon, 1965, p. 8.

[10] *Standard and Diggers' News* (24 May 1897).

[11] Interview with Eric Maskell, an apprentice to Blackburn on the *Tonbridge Free Press* in the 1920s, Tonbridge, Kent (13 June 1976).

[12] Douglas Blackburn, 'The Marvels of Loteni: A Voice from the Dead', *Natal Witness* (19 June 1902).

[13] 'The Problem of Black and White: How a Novelist would Treat it: Hysteria from Basutoland', *Cape Argus Weekly Review* (21 October 1908).

[14] Rupert Croft-Cooke. *The Altar in the Loft.* London: Putnam, 1960, p. 124.

[15] 'Death of Douglas Blackburn', *Star* (30 March 1929).

[16] *Star,* South African Republic (16 Nov. 1898).

[17] Olive Schreiner. 'Eighteen-Ninety-Nine'. *Stories, Dreams and Allegories.* London: T. Fisher Unwin, 1923, p. 38.

[18] J.A. Hobson. *Imperialism: A Study.* London: Nisbet, 1902, p. 6 and p. 10.

[19] Review of Christiaan Rudolf de Wet, *Three Years' War,* in *Blackwood's Magazine* (Jan. 1903), p. 21.

[20] Rudyard Kipling.

[21] Review of *Richard Hartley, Prospector,* in *Star* (28 Nov. 1905).

[22] Cervantes.

NOTE

THE few words of the Taal introduced into the narrative are essential to give force to the dialogue, as they are of frequent recurrence in conversation, and have no English equivalents. The phrase *oprecht Burgher* is much on the lips of Boers. Its strict interpretation is "upright," but it conveys much more, being used to differentiate sharply between the Burghers who are such merely by right of citizenship and those to whom burghership is a serious obligation. It is always used in the spirit in which an Englishman would speak of a God-fearing earnest man.

The adjective *slim* implies smartness and cunning, not necessarily of an objectionable type; its converse being *schelm* (skellum), a low, unprincipled, blackguardly person. *Oom* (uncle), *tante* (aunt), are terms used in addressing elderly people familiarly, who respond with *neef* (nephew). Men of equal age speak of one another as *coos* (cousin). A colloquial peculiarity of the Taal is the tiresome frequency with which a speaker introduces the name of the person addressed.

It should be remembered that in the Taal the final *d* is always *t*, *v* is *f*, and *w* is *v*; hence *veld* is pronounced "felt," *Van der Merwe*, "Fonder Merva." The *a* is always very broad, particularly in names such as Dahvid, Ahbel, Sahrel, Erahsmus.

Indaba is a much-used Zulu word, meaning a serious conference; *schrick* (skrick), a sudden fright; *vrachter*, really! truly! A *voorlouper* is the Kafir boy who leads the oxen; *tronk*, the jail; *Rooinek* (red-neck), a contemptuous name for Englishmen; *Taakhaar* (long-hair) *Boer*, a Boer from the remote districts, shaggy and slovenly.

A BURGHER QUIXOTE

———•———

CHAPTER I.

*Shows the beginning of the Erasmus family, and my
reasons and fitness for my mission.*

It is not without great and careful thought that I
have decided, boldly and honestly, to put my full
name and district to this truthful story of the struggles
after righteousness of a once oprecht Burgher of the
late South African Republic, with a full account of
the temptations that assailed him at the hands of
the clever and educated wicked, and in the end brought
about his fall.

Since the introduction of many newspapers into the
country, I have, both as a private person and in my
capacity as public prosecutor, seen how great is the
mischief that arises from persons writing grave ac-
cusations without affixing their names and districts,
thereby often causing innocent people to be suspected,
on no better ground than that they are able to read
and write,—a reason perfectly justifiable a few years
ago, but not to be admitted in a court of justice
to-day, when it is impossible to enter a farmhouse,
even in the most remote districts, without seeing
accounts and letters pinned on the wall, awaiting the
time when a neighbour who can read writing shall
come along. Only a short time since, they would

have been kept till the quarterly Nachtmaal, when the predikant would have to interpret them.

But it is not alone that I despise the man who would write that which he dare not own to. I hold that just as no man has a right to preach unless he be a qualified predikant — by which it will be seen that I have no part or lot in the Dopper Church — so a man who stands up among his fellows and speaks or writes for them should prove his right; and that I fearlessly do, for as public prosecutor of Prinsloosdorp and one time smallpox tax-collector and marketmaster, I have been placed most favourably for knowing that side of the characters of my late countrymen which they are most often anxious not to have revealed.

Of my educational ability I need say no more than this, that long before I held any Government office I was well known for my learning, and whenever I trekked through any district, even in the Orange Free State, my fame as a reader of difficult letters in the Taal, Hollands, and English, and particularly summonses and legal papers, was so great, that as soon as it was noised abroad that Sarel Erasmus was on trek, the farmers would come in to my outspan from miles around, bringing letters for me to read, or summonses to advise on, until one might think that the Government vaccination officer was making his half-yearly visit. I need hardly remind any one who reads that I am the writer of the famous life of my late father-in-law, Piet Prinsloo of Prinsloosdorp.

It appears even now passing strange to my mind that an Erasmus should have to explain to the world who he is before beginning to tell of his doings. Time was, and that not many years ago, when my father and I, on riding up to a farm in any district, would have no need to tell our names; but so vast has now become the inhabitants of this country, that a man may be excused for not quickly realising to which branch of the Erasmus family a Sarel belongs; and I fear this ignorance will increase now that so many strangers have come into the land who do not even know the name, and much less recognise the great likeness we Erasmuses all bear to our common ancestor. This was the case when I arrived at Maritzburg as a prisoner of war.

"What name did you say?" asked the British officer who received me.

"Sarel Erasmus."

"How do you spell it?" was the surprising answer.

"Sir," replied I with great dignity, "I am a descendant of that Erasmus who translated the first Greek Testament and taught you English true religion."

"Sorry I have not the pleasure of the gentleman's acquaintance," said he, haughtily, the foolish fellow being plainly ignorant that that Erasmus lived nearly five hundred years ago; and I had to pronounce the name several times, and even write it before he could recognise it.

This brings me to another of the good reasons that have weighed on my mind in deciding to tell my strange and pathetic story.

It is a common reproach among Englanders that we Transvaal Boers are ignorant. When I hear this remark from an educated Englander I always reply "*tu quoque*," which, educated though he is supposed to be, he rarely understands, but thinks it is the Taal, or what he ignorantly calls "Dutch." Without any desire to be considered biassed or unmannerly, the truth to which I am pledged compels me to say that the English are ridiculously uninformed on South Africa, and the recent war has proved this to an extent that has amazed me. How common is it, for example, to find the grossest misspellings of South African names in the English papers, mistakes that would not be made by a Boer schoolboy. Although geography is supposed to be learned in British schools, few officers knew what a kopjie, drift, vlei, or krantz was, and this despite the fact that these names abound on the map of South Africa.

I am not of those who ridicule Englanders for not

being able to pronounce our Taal, nor do I laugh when I hear them talking of being "on" the veld, which last word they speak so strangely. The reason I do not smile is that I see in this a great and providential design and meaning. The inability of Englanders to pronounce the *g*, *d*, and *v* properly was designed, like the word "shibboleth," which the Ephraimites could not pronounce, to enable us to recognise our natural enemies; for many Rooineks, especially Scotsmen, learn the Taal so quickly, that if it were not that they stumble over these words for long after, many a Boer would be deceived and not see that he was having dealings with a Rooinek, and perhaps miss a chance to make profit out of him.

Although I am naturally proud to be descended from the original Erasmus of Rotterdam, I am equally proud that I am not, as so many Afrikanders are, ashamed of my Hollander descent, particularly since I read in a book, which I do not quite believe, that a Jewish musician named Meyerbeer was the original of "Les Huguenots," as they are called in France. But whether true or not, it has always made me feel great contempt for the du Toets, de Villiers, du Preez, and Viljoens, who never miss the chance to explain to Rooineks that they are not Hollanders but Huguenots. I make only one exception, and that is for my old friend Paul du Plooy, of whom I shall have much to say in this book. I gravely suspect he was of Huguenot descent, but he did not know it, being very unlearned; therefore out of kindness of heart, even when most angered by him, I never told him what I suspected about his Jewish origin, for he was ever sore against that nation, and used to make a long discourse wherein he showed that the Jews who come to this country could not be Bible Jews, for they would not fight Kafirs, and knew nothing of cattle, of which the real Jews of the Bible possessed great herds.

The first Erasmus who came to Cape Colony was predikant on a Hollander ship of war, which was wrecked in Simon's Bay coming from the East Indies; and for that reason he called the first son he had born in the land Paul, because that great Bible man was once shipwrecked.

I am not given to boasting, and, least of all, of my forefathers; for I hold that if a son will not take blame for the misdeeds of his father, neither should he take credit if his parent never got into jail. Therefore if I appear to put great weight on my good descent, it is not out of unseemly pride, but for the very sufficient reason that I am writing not only for South Africans, but for uninformed Englanders; and I find that it is usual for them to set great store upon, and make much explanation as to their ancestors, as we found in the early days of Cape Colony, when every runaway sailor or soldier who tramped to an up-country farm always told the Boer that he had great and rich relations at home, and that he was related to dukes, lords, and governors; whereby many Boer maidens were falsely persuaded to marry these men, who would after a time say that their parents had cast them off for marrying Boer girls, and the Boer father had to support them both.

When I look back on the work I have done,— being yet only twenty-eight years of age,—I can see that people who put importance on good breeding have much good cause, for all the Erasmuses, with a few exceptions, have been marked by great qualities above their fellows, and all of them have done something out of the common, even the bad ones being horribly and unusually clever in their wickedness. It would seem that the family was destined to be, even as the original Erasmus was, teachers and instructors of their fellow-men, for the stories told of my ancestors in Cape Colony are largely made up of records showing their superiority. It was an Erasmus who first made up for a bad grape harvest by putting Cape gooseberries with the wine, which has since been the universal habit. Another Erasmus discovered the Dassie serpent—that great snake with the head of a rabbit and body of a reptile, only seen about the season of Nachtmaal; though there be those that say my ancestor came upon a puff-adder that was just swallowing a rock-rabbit. But those that said this did not stand well in the kerk, and afterwards were proved to be infidels.

A third Erasmus discovered a way to make medicine for smallpox and scurvy out of a prickly pear of a particularly malignant and fast-growing kind, that was making the best ground on his farm useless. There happened to be in Simon's Bay certain British ships visited badly with both these diseases. My ancestor offered to make large quantities of the medicine if the captains would let their sailors dig up all the prickly pear roots, which they did. But when some of those who took the medicine got worse, the captains said that it was a trick planned by Erasmus to get his farm cleared cheaply, and they tried to make the Governor of Cape Colony order that the work be paid for; but the ships being English, and the governor a Hollander who hated Englanders, he refused, and there was nearly war between the two countries.

The cause of the dividing of the family into two branches was the unrighteousness of a cousin of my grandfather—Gert Stephanus Erasmus. When the British Government bought out the slaves of the Boers, this Gert, having the same name as my grandfather, wickedly took the money that was rightly his, and refused to give it up. But he gained little thereby, for, believing the foolish report set about that the British had no gold to pay with, he gave an order for seven hundred pounds in exchange for a gold watch that stopped almost before the Jew had left the farm, and turned out to be brass. Ever after, my branch of the family cut off all connection with the Gert Erasmuses. My grandfather solemnly called every one to witness that never would he have in his family a child bearing any Christian name borne by the offspring of this Gert Erasmus, and he kept his word, though he could little foresee how much trouble the cunning of an evil-minded man would cause him; for when Gert heard of the resolve, he planned a great and wicked revenge. Shortly afterwards his third boy was born, and he immediately gave him ten Christian names. Not content with this, he got the predikant to show him how he could add other and fresh names to the children already born; and this was done, using up near sixty good names. And as each child was born, he gave it ten and even twelve names, so that when my father came, his parents were sorely perplexed for a name for him, Gert having used up all the best, leaving only those that were foolish, or favourites with Christian Kafirs. What made the choice more difficult was the objection of my grandmother to the names borne by the children of one Frikkie Smuts, who, after promising her marriage, had cast her off for another girl; and as the Smuts had now a large family, the finding of a name became so hard that my father had to wait nearly a year before one could be found that was not disgraced by Gert Erasmus.

Then Gert, in pursuance of his viciousness, persuaded his two brothers to follow his evil example in wasting names on their children, so that the three sons and two daughters who followed my father were destitute of Christian names for long, and all got to be called "Nick," for when asked what their names were they had to answer "Nix," which is Taal for nothing. But of course this could not go on, particularly when marriage-time came; and often names were not given them until they were in the kerk, when the predikant would have to find one in a great hurry. Being a godly man, he wanted to give Bible names; but all the good ones had been purposely and viciously used up by Gert or his brothers, and the predikant had to use names that were strange in the land, which is why so many of the good Erasmuses have names like mine, while when you find one with a Bible name you can always know that he is a schelm. It is through there being so many such that the name of Erasmus got into evil repute, getting many of those who bore it into tronk in the Free State and Rhodesia, where the landdrosts are much against an Erasmus, even arresting me at Bloemfontein on suspicion of horse-stealing, a scandal for which the landdrosts and police had to make apology and pay my hotel bill.

I got my taste for high education from that Erasmus who was the first to use himself, and show other Boers how to employ, a ready reckoner in calculating the price of his wool, such a thing not being before known in the land. But it brought him trouble, for the slim buyers at Port Elizabeth once refused to accept the reckoning as correct, because they said the date on the book showed it to be last year's reckoner; and Piet Erasmus could not satisfy the foolish Boers that age does not affect figures as they believed it did, though the real cause of their mistrust was that the book had been printed in England, and had one or two real blunders made by the printer. In the end they lost in their selling, as the ignorant ever must when dealing with the educated, as the painful story of my dealings with Andries Brink will show.

And this brings me to a matter which I fear will be misunderstood and put to my discredit by English readers, who are ever high in praise of education. This history shows plainly how dangerous a thing it may become, for nearly all the misfortunes that came to me were caused by too much learning on the part of those I had to deal with,—just as the Boers in the Transvaal have suffered through the educated Hollanders, who have robbed the true sons of the soil of their birthright by taking to themselves all the offices best paid, and selfishly keeping out oprecht Burghers by making Paul Kruger believe that it was necessary for all officials to be able to read and write; which is as foolish as to say that no man should be allowed to drive a waggon till he can build one. It is true that many of the early officials in the Transvaal were educated, but that was because so many Burghers had made their sons predikants that there were not enough kerks for them; and as a predikant is fit for nothing else he was made a Government man, like some of the judges, who could not drive an ox-team even if they were given the waggon and cattle for doing it.

I have never been quite able to decide firmly whether education is altogether good, since I have, as public prosecutor, seen so many cases wherein educated Kafirs use their learning to forge passes for liquor or staying out late, and white men for writing false things about Boers. But I do hold that it is the educated man who wins until he meets another who is yet more so. Being educated is like being the only doctor in a district. He makes all the money till another doctor comes and takes away his people. So one educated man in a district is great and looked up to so long as there is none other; but when reading and writing grow common he is held in small esteem, and his chance of profit grows less. This is particularly the case when, as generally happens, he has told wrong things that the new-comer finds out and exposes to the neighbours, as was the case with young Piet de Villiers, of the Rustenburg district. He had a learned book from which he made medicine for gallsick for cattle, and heart disease in men and women; but a French Roman Catholic priest passing that way saw it, and knew it as a Latin book which is used in the churches to say Romish prayers out of. The Boers, not loving anything Romish, were angry with de Villiers, and he sold no more medicine. This case gave rise to the proposal of a member of the Raad that there should be only one educated person allowed in a district, at which the Rooinek papers made great ridicule. I myself think it was not a wise proposition, for our laws were strong enough to punish people who used their learning wrongly, though through mistaken mercifulness they were not used as much as they might have been.

As I got my love of learning from my grandfather, so I got my legal instinct from my father, and I fear I also got with it that kindness of heart which made him as unsuccessful in law matters as it made me, judging from the money point of view, which is the only way one can tell whether law be good or not.

The way my father came to mix up in law was this :—

When I was a very small kerel he once had six loads of forage that he could not sell, there being much that year. Hearing that a law-agent in the dorp six hours away wanted forage, my father loaded up two waggons and trekked. The agent, whose name was du Preez, said he had just sent to the Paarl for forage, which was not true, but, said he, rather than my father should have the trouble of taking it back, he would buy it, but only on condition that he had all six loads at half price, to which my father agreed; and within a fortnight the whole of the forage was delivered. But when it came to paying, the agent said he had no money, and that my father must take payment in law, which was a thing that up till then he had no use for. Not being pressed for money, he foolishly consented to the arrangement, and went home to think how he could get back the value of that forage.

As ill-luck would have it, the district landdrost, an old friend of my father, had applied to the Government to give him a better paid office ; but they had replied that he had not enough experience of civil cases, which was true, for the people in our district were very peaceful, and only used the magistrate for having their Kafirs punished. The landdrost was telling all about it to my father, who in the goodness of his heart did a foolish thing. "Daniel," said he, "I have a lot of money owing me by law-agent du Preez. I will make him give me law for it, and you can practise on me," and he went to the dorp and told du Preez that he must have either money or law, but preferred law.

"Have you any children who want marriage-contracts drawn up," asked du Preez, "or people who owe you money and whom you hate and would put to trouble?"

My father thought over all his wrongs, but except the family hatred of Gert Erasmus there was nothing strong enough to make a law case out of, till at last he remembered that his next neighbour had dammed the river above him, making him sometimes short of water.

"That's it," said du Preez; "we will apply for a summons against him for stopping your water," and my father went home well pleased in his heart that he could now do a good act to the landdrost and get more water for himself.

In a few days the law-agent sent a letter asking for ten pounds for office fees, for, said he, "the English Government will not take forage in payment of court fees as the old colonial Hollander landdrosts would."

My father saw the landdrost, and tried to get him to take forage instead of money, but he replied that though his heart was good enough to do it, the law was stronger than his heart. So my father had to pay in good gold. Nor was this the end, for hardly a week passed without du Preez sending for more money. My father would have stopped the action, but the landdrost pointed out that it would not be fair to him, and in any case my father would have to pay the other man's expenses without having any fighting for it. So the money was paid to du Preez, my father secretly thinking that it was only lent; for the landdrost, being his friend, was certain to give judgment in his favour, which he did. But the other man took the case to the Supreme Court at Cape Town, and the judgment was reversed; so that in the end the law-agent not only got the six loads of forage, but the waggons that rode them and the land it grew on, for my father had to pass a bond over part of his property as security for the costs.

This it was that made him always want me to be a lawyer, for, "Sarel," said he, "there is a lot of money in the law. I know, because I put it there."

It was ever a great grief to my father that he could

not afford to have me taught law properly, as the
attorney wanted a very high premium; for, said he,
"Young Sarel is so clever that if I teach him law he
will soon take away all my clients, so I shall want to
be well paid for teaching him to supplant me."

It was because I could not learn law in the usual
way that I married the daughter of Piet Prinsloo, for
next to being in the office of a lawyer, the best thing
is to be married to the daughter of a landdrost who
knows no law, and get made public prosecutor in his
court; for an intelligent man must learn much by
noticing his mistakes and reading the remarks made
by the judges of the High Court when they reverse
his decisions, which was how I learned law.

I think it only right to explain, that although I am
what is called a lawyer, I was never a proper one,
being only a law-agent, which is not so high as an
attorney, and requires only that one pay fees but pass
no examination. This in the old days was quite good
enough; but since the Uitlanders got so strong in the
Transvaal, they set such weight on examinations that
the judges at last shut us out from all courts except
the landdrosts'. But even then much money could be
made by a law-agent who had good ways with Kafirs,
for they were always in trouble and paid well to be
defended.

Of my six years' experience as public prosecutor in
the court of my father-in-law I will not occupy time in
saying much, for if I once began to say all that I
might, I should fill many chapters, as there is much
in my career that needs explaining, especially to those
who know not the ways of the officials of the Transvaal. It is sufficient that I should say that being by
nature honest and kind-hearted, I was never properly
understood or appreciated. I confess that I now and
then made mistakes, for having to learn my law as I
went on from a landdrost who knew none himself, and
having to fight clever advocates from Johannesburg
who knew more law than all the landdrosts and public
prosecutors of the land, it was not to be wondered at

that my law was not always of the best quality. But it should not be forgotten that my salary was not large, and even then, I was much more successful in getting convictions than my father-in-law was in having them upheld on appeal.

As is usual with public prosecutors, my most successful and profitable work was in breaking down in my cases, which was done by purposely putting in a wrong date or name in the summons and not defending it when the lawyer for the defence objected; for I hold with the great English lawyers who say it is better that fifty guilty men escape than that one innocent man be convicted. Therefore I could never see wrong in taking a reward to see the weak and merciful side of any case for the prosecution. I am not wishful to take part in the great and long discussion on the morality of officials who take payment from the public, for I have long since agreed with that Transvaal judge and the late President Kruger, who declared that it is neither wrong nor is it bribery to give a reward to an official for paying special attention to your case, any more than it is unrighteous to give a policeman a few shillings for keeping an eye on your house while you and your family are at Nachtmaal. Such a reward is but an inducement to further vigilance; and I freely confess that I have often been able to see the weakness in my summons when I have been promised a reward if the accused should be acquitted. Otherwise I might have been careless and got a conviction that would have been upset on appeal, causing unnecessary expense, and making both my father-in-law and myself appear ridiculous,—a thing no man who values his professional reputation can afford.

I could, if necessary, give many very excellent reasons in defence of my habit of never pressing a prosecution too hard. In the first place, the jail at Prinsloosdorp was very small, and could not accommodate all who should rightly have been in it, and if we flogged all guilty Kafirs, the landdrost got a name for cruelty with the Rooinek papers, and the

Government would not pay all the fees of the jail doctor who examined the Kafirs for flogging; so there was nothing for it but to fine them what money they had, except when labour was much needed for the roads, when of course they were always sent to jail without the option of a fine. But it was in dealing out justice to white people that my father-in-law and I found it so difficult. Now and then there would be such a flood of crime that the court had to sit all day, and the sum collected in fines became very large. But it made us very unpopular; for not only was the man fined strongly against us, but his friends joined him, and it often happened that more than half the white inhabitants of the dorp would not invite us to their houses or even speak to us, or if they spoke, it was very offensively. So having so few friends, my father-in-law and I used to go very often to spend our time in Johannesburg, where we were not so well known, which generally ended in my father-in-law doing something foolish that got him into the Rooinek papers and brought strong criticism on him and landdrosts and other officials.

These things made the life of a public prosecutor so full of thorns, there was no alternative but to make money as quickly as possible, so that the position might be given up; and the holder was often driven to go into the Raad or some other Government office where money could be made without so much overlooking on the part of the Rooineks and jealous Afrikanders.

Looking back upon my public career, I can now see that often, without knowing it, I was a great and useful agent for bringing together the two races, Englander and Afrikander, for whenever I could find it in my conscience, I never pressed charges against Rooineks. When prosecuting miners for drunkenness I always tried to find out how much money they had spent on drink in the dorp, which was often the whole of their monthly cheque; and in stating the case I would mention that the prisoners had spent so much, instead of doing as some did, go to Johannesburg and squander their money there, only coming back to finish their drunkenness in the dorp on credit. My father-in-law always favourably considered such cases, and made the fine no more than the prisoner had left. Naturally this good nature was made matter for spiteful comment by the Rooinek papers, which went so far as to state that my father-in-law was interested in canteens in the dorp, when as a matter of fact he was only part owner of one; while the 'Critic' actually declared that he issued permits for drunkenness, an utterly false charge, seeing that there was no such printed form issued to landdrosts.

But while I have just cause for feeling aggrieved at the treatment I have received at the hands of Englanders, it is against my late countrymen that I feel the greatest anger; and that I have reason, the story I have embarked upon telling will clearly show. As it is skilfully and truthfully unfolded, there will be revealed the picture of a just and well-meaning Afrikander struggling to free himself from the bondage placed upon him, and fighting hard, and not always successfully, against the temptations of the worldly-wise, who were prompted by no nobler feelings than jealousy, greed, and cowardice. I tell my story—foolish though it may sometimes make me appear—because it is not only my own. The records of the treason courts show that there are now in prison men as good as myself whose struggles against the ignorance and superior strength of their countrymen have been misunderstood, and ended, like mine, in disaster. But I do not repine in an unmanly way, for my superior education and reading show me that it is only by the sufferings of others that the good of the world is advanced. The mistakes I have made—and I admit they are many—will help the world to know the real character of many of my countrymen, among whom I have been as a Don Quixote, fighting on behalf of Great Britain against the folly and ignorance that have caused such loss and suffering.

I know it may be said that in denouncing and exposing my late countrymen I shall be false to that Christian spirit which was planted in my heart when a deacon of the Dutch Reformed Church, and particularly by my present residence in jail. But I hold it to be my duty as a loyal British subject, although I have not yet been able to take the proper oath of allegiance, to do all that in me lies to prevent Great Britain being again deceived by those who would perhaps form another corrupt Boer Government in some other part of South Africa, as is vainly imagined by many, and for which some thought I was fitted for first President, though I now know this was but said to flatter me and keep me on commando when I secretly wished to surrender, being quite content to fill a position for which I might be less well fitted, but wherein I should be more free from the evil planning and plots of the wicked. And that position I sincerely say should be that of my old profession of public prosecutor, but in a larger and better-paying dorp, where my superior knowledge of my late countrymen would ensure that they do not escape the just punishment for their crimes.

CHAPTER II.

Shows how I was made to be an oprecht Burgher against my conscience, and reveals the inwardness of a dorp in war-time.

WERE it not that I now hold in abhorrence all that pertains to the manners and customs of predikants of the Dutch Reformed Church, with a few exceptions I would follow their pattern, and begin this work with a thoughtful dissertation on the wondrous way in which accident directs a man's steps, even as it did in the days of the Great Trek, when a lion chased my grandfather, causing him to turn into the way that led to the finding of that spring that directed his choosing the spot for his farm, whereon was later found the gold that made his sons rich but unhappy.

In the events that I have set out to tell in truth and plainness will be seen how many errors that I have made have been the following on of accidents that I could not foresee or prevent; and this I commend to those who would blame me for the part I took in the war.

I had been farming with my cousin, Chris Vermaak, in the Newcastle district of Natal over a year after leaving the Transvaal, as I had hoped for ever, when I received an urgent message from my brother Jan to go to Vrededorp and help him smooth certain difficulties, he having been wrongfully, and in mistake, arrested on a charge of horse-stealing.

I was very grieved when I received his letter, not only because I did not wish again to cross the Border, but for the reason that Jan had once before been

wrongfully charged with the same crime in the Orange
Free State, and unjustly convicted. Knowing so well
the landdrost at Vrededorp, I feared much that he
would allow that almost forgotten circumstance to
prejudice him, especially as Jan was my brother, and
the landdrost a great believer in the Bible doctrine of
visiting the sins of the fathers upon the children or
of brother upon brother. But knowing all this, I
foolishly consented to go, not even yet having learned
the folly of doing a kind act when it causes the doer to
run a risk.

"Jan," said I, when I saw him in the tronk—for
they would not allow him bail—"Jan, you have been
very foolish to get caught; but did you really steal
the horse?"

"Sarel," answered he, "have you seen it?"

"I have," said I.

"Then how can you ask me that question? Isn't
he a beauty? How could an Erasmus help jumping it,
if he found it alone?"

I rebuked him sternly, but told him that, as his
brother, I thought it my duty to do what I could to
save him from just punishment. So I went and saw
the public prosecutor, young Hendrik Kemp, who had
been smallpox tax-collector during my time at Prinsloosdorp, where I often had to show him how to
prepare his books for the office inspector, and more
often lend him money to make his accounts come out
right, which lending was very dangerous if the inspector took it into his head to look at my books on
the same visit, as he at last did.

"Hendrik," said I, after we had talked over the
case, and he had shown me the summons, which made
it very bad for Jan, "how are the accounts? Can you
now keep proper books to please the inspector?"

"Ja, thanks to you, I have had very little trouble
lately."

"And is it true that half your summonses are dismissed on exception, through your mistakes in drawing
them?"

"Not half, coos, but nearly half."

"Then, Hendrik," said I, "let me draw this one for you, for I fear I shall lose my skill for want of practice."

He was at first fearful, but when he saw ten five-pound notes on his table, and remembered how much he was short in his fine account, and how near was the inspector's visit, he relented, and allowed me to help him.

When the case came on next morning, the attorney I had engaged for the defence took exception to the summons in that it made out that the offence took place on the 29th February, there being no such date in any almanack, English or Dutch, for that year, and outside the jurisdiction of the Court. Hendrik not making any objection, but putting the fault on to the Hollander clerk, the accused was dismissed, though the landdrost spitefully refused to do what Jan's attorney asked, that he might say that Jan left the Court without a stain on his character.

I am proud to be able to say, as his brother, that Jan did not attempt to leave the dorp until he had given me the £50 I had paid to Hendrik Kemp,—an evidence of the kindly feeling that has ever existed in my branch of the Erasmus family, the brothers never robbing one another, even when the temptation was great and the opportunity very present.

And here I have to tell of that strange and unwelcome accidental shaping of a man's path to which I referred at the beginning of the chapter.

Just as I had said good-bye to Jan, who should come up to me but Hans Potgieter, landdrost of Prinsloosdorp.

"I am glad, coos, that, like the oprecht Burgher you are, you have come back to do your duty to your land. It is troublous times, Sarel, and the rifle and saddle must be ready."

"Coos," said I, "I must go back to Natal, for the cattle are sick,"—which was true of two of them.

"Nay, but you must not. You must come with me to Prinsloosdorp, where I return to-night."

I confess that I did not like the way Hans spoke,

nor the way in which the Burghers standing round looked and smiled. There was something unpleasant behind it all; so I thought to gain time, and told him how we had rinderpest on our farm, and that I was the only man in the district who knew how to inoculate cattle.

Hans laughed as he asked, "Are they your own cattle, Sarel?"

Now if I told the truth and said "Yea," and that I had got them away from the Transvaal secretly, it would make it appear true, as was said, that I had gone for good. So I lied, and answered "No."

Then said Hans: "If they are your cousin's cattle, let him look after his own. Are they Natal cattle?"

"Yes."

"And many of them sick?"

"Yes, half of them."

"Then it is a judgment of the good Lord that sickness should be among the cattle, and if you are a good Burgher you will let them die, so there will be less to draw the cannon and waggons of the Rooineks when the war comes."

My heart gave a great thump, for I now knew what all the riding between the Transvaal and Natal Boers meant, which was that war was truly coming. Before I could ask more, Hans went on—

"Sarel, you must come and fight for your land. If you don't come cheerfully you will have to come as a prisoner, for there is a warrant out for you for stealing Government money."

Immediately a great sickness came over me, not of fear but of the heart, for I was sick and sad that the Government I had served so well should be so ungrateful as to want to punish me for no wrong-doing beyond being short in my cash through ignorance of accounts.

"Hans," said I, "I will go with you as I intended to, but do not think I go because I fear the warrant. I go because I wish to do my duty and bleed for my country."

So we went on by the next train, Hans keeping close to me when we got out at the stations to drink coffee, as though he feared I should run away, which I could not, even if I would, for I knew that the telegraph would stop me before I could get out of the Transvaal, which is one of the drawbacks to that otherwise useful invention.

On the way up Hans told me it was planned to have war, and drive the Rooineks into the sea at Durban and Cape Town; and he showed me a little pattern of the new flag that was to take the place of the Vierkleur. He told me of the great rewards in farms and cattle that would come to the oprecht Burghers when Paul Kruger was President of all South Africa, and I was glad that war was to come.

It was now the middle of September; and when we reached Prinsloosdorp I found the Burghers already making ready to go on commando, and war in the mouth of every one, especially those who in the old time had been most friendly to the English. I also found that Hans was right about the warrant; but, as he told me when I was safely arrived in the dorp, it was only issued that my services might be secured for the Government, which, as he pointed out, was to be taken as a great compliment rather than a slur, showing that the State did put great value upon my help. So I accepted that very satisfactory explanation, and consented to remain and give the Government of my great knowledge.

A few of the more unchristian Burghers, and particularly the Hollanders, were inclined to say hard things of me, and would ask, in a sneering way, Had I gone to Natal to learn to keep accounts? But others thought none the worse of me for being posted in the 'Staats Courant' as a thief; which is one of the good sides of the Boer, for he is ever kindly disposed towards officials who have made mistakes in their accounts, so long as it is only the Government or a Rooinek who has suffered. So, though the field-cornet would not give me the post I was best fitted for,—the serving out of rations and money to vrouws of Burghers going on commando,—he gave me work of another kind that was not without profit, and greatly atoned for my having to leave Natal.

I worked very hard in the office of the field-cornet, and made myself very useful, being the best-educated official in the dorp; so that there was small chance of my being sent on commando, a thing I did not desire, for I could not find it in my heart to go and shoot English after the kindness I had received in Natal. But, to make certain, I got a certificate from the district surgeon that I was suffering from an internal complaint that might prove fatal, not merely if I got into fighting, but even, as the doctor told me privately, if I got near to where danger was. That paper served well for some time, for even Hans Potgieter could not refuse to believe the written word of his own medical officer. But I was near coming to sorrow over these certificates, for one day, when a Burgher whom I much hated for having said hard things of me brought a doctor's certificate to excuse him from going on commando, I foolishly said such things could be had for the asking, and meant nothing.

"Then why did you get one?" asked the Burgher.

"I did not ask," said I, "except to go on commando; but the doctor asked me to stay, saying I should be useless in the veld."

"That proves that the doctor knows what he is saying," answered he, but I did not reply to the insult.

At the risk of being thought disloyal to the English, I cannot help saying that my anger was raised by seeing how many of them in the dorp tried to get permits to remain instead of being sent away like their fellows; so I bethought me of a way to punish them for their cowardice and want of patriotism to England.

"Hans," said I one day, when a dozen of these fence-sitters had been begging him to recommend them for permits, "these men are cowards, but they will be more use to us than they will to their own side. I have a plan for punishing them. Let me tell

them I can get them permits to stay if they pay me
£10 each. Then after a short time you can obey the
law and tell them they must go, and that I had no
right to issue a permit, being only a subordinate."

Hans at first did not quite see with my eyes, for
it was only a short time before that he had got into
the papers for taking money to let a Rooinek remove
infected cattle contrary to the law. But when he had
counted up how much it would be worth in cash,
"Sarel," said he, "why did you run away? Had you
been here before we might have made much money,
for you are very slim and know all the rascality."

This flattered me, and I weakly agreed to his plan,
which was that I should issue permits to stay for £20
apiece instead of £10. Even then we soon found
that we had made a great mistake in fixing the sum
so low, for we could easily have got £50, as I know
Hans did later on from several Rooineks, though he
did not tell me or give me my full share as agreed.
Once or twice I felt sorry that Hans had agreed to
my plan, but he smoothed me by saying, "Coos, this
is a great plan for punishing cowards. If they will
not fight for their own people, let them be fined like
other wrongdoers. Besides, it will be the last chance
we shall have of getting any milk from Rooineks for
some time."

I was glad that when the time came for these
Rooineks to be sent away, as they were later, both
Hans and I were out of the dorp, for I hear they
made a great noise; but as we had given them no
receipt for the money they could prove nothing, which
made their punishment the more severe.

There were among those who paid to stay, but
were sent off, some for whom I felt very sorry, they
being good and upright Rooineks, although not
Burghers, and I had promised to stand their friend.
But my sorrow ceased when I learned that one of
these, for whom I felt the most, proved in the end
a great scoundrel. He was an apothecary, and stood
well with the Burghers because he always gave big

doses of physic in large bottles, instead of the small quantities which the other apothecaries sold at such high prices, besides speaking the Taal very well for a Rooinek, and giving long credit.

The Burghers had heard much of the great English explosive called lyddite, and feared it even more than the long knives of the lancers, particularly as many of them had been in Johannesburg at the time of the awful dynamite explosion. Therefore it is no marvel that when they heard how this lyddite turned kopjies into kloofs and valleys, and killed hundreds by shock alone, they were filled with fear, which brought out many old complaints that they thought had been cured, and gave the district surgeon much trouble in writing certificates.

It happened that this apothecary, knowing he would be turned out of the dorp, wickedly went to old Piet Faurie, a Boer standing well in the district. "Piet," said the apothecary, "you are going on commando, and may be killed by lyddite. I should be sorry, Piet, if you should be killed, for you owe me more than any other Boer in the district. So, if you will give me your word that you will not say where you got it, I will give you a medicine that will make lyddite of no use."

Now it happened that Piet had been in the great dynamite explosion at Johannesburg, and was stunned speechless for three days, besides being turned green all over; and his one great matter of talk ever since was dynamite, whereby he was listened to as the only man learned in explosives. The apothecary made plain to him that lyddite was just one hundred times wickeder than dynamite, but that if a man's head could be made soft there would be no shock,—which Piet could quite understand, for he had suffered in his head ever since he was knocked off his waggon by the concussion. So the apothecary gave Piet a large bottle of a dark and sticky medicine that had to be rubbed on to the head night and morning, and even oftener if he was going into fight.

Piet, being foolish, thought it must be good medicine because it had a dreadful smell, being what is called assafœtida. Piet took a very large quantity with him when he went with the commando to Sandspruit, and at first caused great trouble, for the Burghers would not have him in any tent because of the odour, until he told them it was a cure for lyddite, when they all begged some, and rubbed their heads so many times a day that the Kafir servants could only be got to come near them with the sjambok. But the cruel part of the business was that the stuff was no protection at all, as was proved very soon, for the very first Burgher killed by lyddite had not only rubbed his head, but his body, and had been living alone in the veld for a week, as the others would not have him with them.

When the Burghers found how cruelly they had been deceived, they sent back two of their commando to wreck the apothecary's shop; but he had already sold the business to a Burgher, and been sent over the Border.

In like ways did many unworthy Rooineks take advantage of the faith of trusting Burghers, thereby bringing the name of Englander into evil repute, as in the early days in the Colony and the Transvaal.

The predikant took the subject for his sermon one Sunday, and used words of wisdom when he made plain that while it was only right and godly to spoil an enemy, as did the Israelites the Egyptians, yet it was sinful to ride upon the ignorance of a Burgher; and he read the story of hairy Esau stealing the birthright of his brother and deceiving his father, for which he was justly punished by being made the servant of servants, as the British would be to the Boers whom they had so greatly deceived. The sermon had a very comforting influence, being preached on the Sunday after the battle of Elandslaagte when the people were beginning to doubt all that had been said about the Lord being on the Boer side.

I shamefully confess that my anger was much raised

by the same course—the bad lyddite medicine and Elandslaagte; and being now acting field-cornet in charge of the dorp by reason of my internal disease and the laziness of the proper field-cornet, I punished such Rooineks as remained by commandeering £10 worth of goods or money from each of them, and ordering them not to leave their houses after dark to play whist, which was their common and regular habit, even when bad news had come in. I also made some of them close their stores, until the Boer vrouws made a great outcry thereat, the closing not suiting their convenience.

These same vrouws were a continual thorn and weariness to me, all the men being away except about 200 of them who had doctors' certificates, which they did not deserve.

When the news of the battle of Elandslaagte was posted outside the telegraph office they broke the windows, and frightened the operator so much that he dared not leave the office to go home to supper; and I only got them to promise not to hurt him by making him give a speech from the window, where they could not reach him, explaining that the wires had been tampered with by the British, who had sent false news.

Next day the Government sent from Pretoria a stern rebuke to the operator, forbidding him to frighten the women by posting bad news. Henceforth we only told them of victories, which had a very peaceful effect except upon the Rooineks.

Another great weariness to me was that fifty women of the dorp had been made nurses to attend any sick or wounded that might come in. By a foolish mistake, the district surgeon appointed as head over them a young Hollander woman because she was what is called a "qualified nurse." This rightly caused great discontent, and the women held a noisy meeting, and appointed, instead, Mrs Van den Berg, who had great experience in curing rheumatism and pains in the legs and back with a medicine she had got from her grandmother, who got it from a Hottentot in Cape Colony. They also made me send away all women who had not good Boer names, whereby perhaps we lost some good nurses; but it was well that the staff was made smaller, as the first case that came in showed.

He was a Boer despatch-rider who had fallen from his horse and hurt his leg. When he was brought to the hotel we used as a hospital, thirty-nine women nurses came in and quarrelled as to who should bandage his leg, making the old Burgher so scared that he became really sick, and his leg was not bandaged at all, Mrs Van den Berg saying that bandages would stop the medicine from flowing properly through the blood. Then she made him swallow her rheumatic medicine, and rubbed him hard with it, all against the will and knowledge of the doctor. The rubbing took nearly all the night, the women taking turns, till the old Burgher cried and begged them let him sleep. When Mrs Van den Berg came at six in the morning to rub him again and give more medicine, the old man was gone; and after a long search the Kafirs found him hiding in the stable, where he said he wanted to be quiet and have no medicine or rubbing.

This caused more trouble, and Mrs Van den Berg came no more to the hospital, she telling the Burghers that the wounded man had left the hospital because there were Hollander and English nurses, when the truth was that he only feared her and her medicine.

The next case we had gave me even more trouble. It was a young Burgher having something internal like fever or measles or perhaps my disease. Then it was that every old vrouw in the dorp wanted to try her own pet medicine upon him; and although the doctor sternly forbade them, they would not take nay, but secretly physicked the boy with twenty different kinds of certain cures. In a week the boy was dead, and each of the vrouws said it was because of the medicine given by the other. Whereupon the district surgeon gave orders that no more women were to be admitted to the hospital, and ordered me to keep them out. I might as well have tried to keep out the air, which was even easier. Not only did they come in as often as they pleased, but they petitioned the Government to remove the district surgeon for giving the order, saying it was his secret aim to get the Hollander and English nurses back. This I did not mind, for the district surgeon had told people I was now well enough to go on commando, but when the women told the field-cornet that if he did not send me on commando they would sjambok me, I saw that they are right who would keep women out of politics.

But the great blow came when the vrouws sent for Katrina Bester, who was with her mother in Pretoria, and bade her send me to fight. Katrina came to Prinsloosdorp, and my heart was secretly sad, for she is a bitter Boer vrouw with a rough tongue, and a great sorrow that she had no sons to send to fight the Rooineks. But there were other reasons why I did not wish to see Katrina. She was too ready to get married, for it was she who first asked me, and not I her, which fact I would have borne in mind by those who may, as usual, misjudge my later doings. It was useless my asking her to wait until I got a higher salary.

"I have a thousand pounds," said she—"take it and buy cattle, which will make us rich sooner than if you keep on sitting in the police court making enemies by prosecuting your friends," for at that time the Rooinek papers had made great fuss because no Burghers were ever convicted at the Court at Prinsloosdorp; and we had to convict the next guilty ones by order from Pretoria, and this had made great discontent.

Much against my will I took the money to buy cattle with, but they being dear because of rinderpest, I did not then buy any, but put the money into gold shares in Johannesburg, which will some day be worth very much.

As soon as I had done this Katrina wanted to marry, but I asked her to wait until my first wife had been dead a year, to which she agreed. But before the year was up came the trouble that caused me to leave the Transvaal for Natal, and no longer having any salary, and Katrina's money being in the mine, I could not then marry. Katrina was all against my leaving the Transvaal, for, being a woman, she could not understand things properly or see that an honest man could not stay to hear his good name despoiled.

"If you must go away, why not go to the Orange Free State, or the Old Colony where your Boer kinsmen are, rather than to English Natal?"

This was what she preached, being strong in her hatred of all things English, and not knowing that in times gone by, before I knew her, I was cruelly assailed by jealous enemies in both those countries, and had even more unjust charges made against me there.

Almost the first words Katrina said when she saw me at Prinsloosdorp were—"Why are you not fighting, Sarel?"

"Katrina," answered I, with great feeling, "if you love me, why would you have me go away when I am dying from an internal complaint?" and I showed her the doctor's certificate.

"Must you then die soon?" she asked.

"Ja, certainly; I am a dying man."

"Then why not die fighting instead of being sick in the house, causing trouble and expense, and having no wife to look after you, as you might?"

I was much pained at this cruel speech, and cried much that night instead of sleeping, for though I did not wish to marry Katrina, I was angry that she should care so little for me as to wish to see me dying from lancers' knives or perhaps lyddite.

"It is not that I want you to be killed," said she next morning, when I told her how much I had cried at night; "I want you to live and be a commandant, and get more cattle and money and things."

It was the old story. Again and again had she made my life a burden by whipping me with her tongue to go faster and be higher, she not being content that I was public prosecutor.

"Why not be landdrost?" she would say, "or even judge,"—she in her foolishness not knowing that such places were only for those high in favour in Pretoria, and that some judges were expected to know law. But Katrina could never forget that her sister Lizbeth had spurred on her man to be great in riches in Pretoria, when he only wanted to sit on the stoep and smoke and drink coffee; and ever since she had tried to spur me.

For a whole week she stayed not her tongue. "Go fight, and be a man," was the psalm she sang day and night, for she was always at my house with her aunt, who took care of me.

It was of no avail that I showed her I was of more use in the field-cornet's office, because I could write and spell well.

"Do you write and spell better than I?" she would ask, and I could not say nay, for Katrina was clever above Boer women, having a clever sister who had taught her.

This daily striving made me sick and weak, till one day I was really and truly too ill to go to the office.

"I shall go and tell the field-cornet you are sick," said Katrina; and I was pleased, for it was the first time she had been kind since her return. Besides, I should have peace in the house while she was gone, which I had, and rejoiced that it was noon before she came back.

"Sarel," said she, "there is no need for you to go to office any more. I have learned how to do your work, and the field-cornet will have me do it while you go to fight."

And so it was. The hand that pushed me into danger and wrong-doing was that of my intended wife, for she herself filled in the form ordering me to join the commando under my old enemy, Ben Viljoen.

It was known throughout the dorp what Katrina had done, and women watched the house to see that I did not get away. But it was not needed, for Katrina never left me, talking all the time and making me swallow large quantities of medicine for my internal disease, till one night she gave me medicine so strong to make me fit for fighting that I was really sick, and the doctor said I must stay in bed.

Never did a sick man have so many visitors or a sweetheart more attentive. Katrina stayed by me all day and most of the night talking war, and feeding me with every awful physic that any old vrouw brought and advised her to try.

On the third day Mrs Van den Berg came in with her rheumatic physic, and remembering what happened to the Burghers at the hospital, I got out of bed, saying I was quite well and ready to go to fight, which was untrue; but I resolved that it was less suffering to fight Rooineks against my conscience than to be physicked by all the vrouws in the dorp, and have to bear Katrina's tongue all the time.

It happened that only half an hour before Mrs Van den Berg came in I had swallowed some of her medicine, Katrina telling me it was something else. I thought the old woman would go mad with joy. She kissed me, and made me listen to all the cases that had been cured by her physic, mine being the quickest; and then she went to the hospital and insisted that the two sick Burghers there—both bad with fever—should take some of the physic that had cured me so well and quickly.

If I had changed my mind and wanted to go back to bed it would have been impossible, for Katrina had got everything in readiness, even to the exact time the train would leave,—a most unusual thing for a Boer woman, who never believes time-tables,—and next morning she went with me to the station.

Nearly all the women of the dorp were there, and six other Burghers who, like me, had internal diseases and doctors' certificates, but wives who loved war.

The predikant, too, was there, and made a prayer so long that the train would have gone without us had not Katrina told the driver to wait.

"Good-bye, Sarel, and don't come back till you have shot a hundred Rooineks," were her parting words, making my heart sore at her unchristianlike cruelty. But I would not let her go unpunished. As the train went slowly out of the station—

"Good-bye, King David," I said.

"What do you mean?" asked Katrina.

"Go home," said I, "and read in the Bible what happened to David when he put Uriah in the forefront of the battle."

"You are not Uriah," said she, "you are the ewe lamb," which caused great laughter against me, the six Burghers making jokes about ewe lambs for a long time, till I stopped their mouths at one station by buying whisky.

Sometimes on the journey I would get out of the carriage, and I noticed that the other Burghers never let me out of their sight.

"Are you sent to watch me?" I asked at last; "and do you think I am not going the journey with you?"

"Nay," said they, "we do not think that. What we fear is that you, knowing Natal better than we, will get farther into it, and that would make us jealous."

"Certainly you would be jealous if you could not get away," I said, and with that cutting answer I took away the whisky and spoke no more to them till we reached our station.

CHAPTER III.

Shows how the wicked and envious conspired against me, but were put to shame by the Solomon-like judgment of Piet Joubert.

I HAD been ordered to join the commando of Ben Viljoen, who had just returned, having fought well at Elandslaagte and gone on to Johannesburg, where he was presented with a gold watch and made much of by the Burghers who had contrived to stay out of the fighting. Ben was a proud and haughty man, and puffed up with pride in that he had been raised from lowliness to greatness in a small space, and certain that he was better fitted to command the Boer forces than "Slim" Piet Joubert. Ben was exalted in his own esteem because General Joubert had at last taken his advice, and invaded Natal against his own wish and judgment. But at the first war-council held at Sandspruit, Ben, who had a slippery tongue, had so worked on the feelings of the younger commandants that they had passed a resolution to cross the Border. It was only by crying great tears, and asking the old Burghers if they meant to despise him for a young kerel like Ben, that they reconsidered the plan, and by a majority of two votes undid the resolution they had come to, and decided to be guided by the old man. But Ben never ceased to work until he had his way, and the Border was crossed. This success pleased him very much, for he was a young man who had had much to do with Rooineks, and did not care to read in his Bible how pride goeth before a fall. "Nay," said he, when an old Burgher named Paul du Plooy read him this, "I believe that part which says the first shall be last and the last first, and the humble shall be exalted. That's me. So now go on horse-guard and take your Bible with you, and read it closer before you throw it at my head again."

This Paul du Plooy had been a Dopper, but did nothing but study the Bible and quarrel with the deacons. He next went over to the Dutch Reformed Church, where the predikants are more college-learned; and they confuted old Paul so often that he left them and had a Church of his own made up of his family, though he was always trying to get Burghers to join, and did not even mind having Rooineks and Germans and a Jew, who only pretended to agree because Paul sold him tobacco cheaper than any one else, whereby the old man lost money.

When I heard Ben use these jeering words, and saw how abased the old Burgher was, I felt sorry for him; but before long I learned to mitigate my grief, for old Paul proved a great depression in the laager. He would come half-a-dozen times a-day to Ben or the General, carrying his Bible and pointing out some verse which showed that the Boers were either in the right and were going to smite the Rooineks hip and thigh, or if we got a reverse it was a punishment for not holding more prayer-meetings, at which Paul did all the praying. As Paul always had a verse to prove what he said, and could talk more persuasively than an auctioneer, much time was wasted in listening to his discourses, which gave many Burghers an excuse for not fighting.

At last Ben Viljoen made an order that no more verses were to be shown him or the Burghers unless they encouraged fighting, and then they were not to be discovered until they had worked out true,—an order that puzzled Paul deeply, and for a time checked the output of prophecies.

I think it proper to say so much about Paul du Plooy,

for the reason, as will be seen, that the old man did much to guide my steps both for right and wrong later on.

Ben Viljoen was not pleased to see me, for I doubt not he feared me as he did General Joubert and Louis Botha, he being highly jealous of both of them.

"So you have come, kerel, to finish the war," said he sneeringly, when I reported myself. "But I fear there are not many towns left in Natal that we can call after you until we get to Durban. While I am finding one, you may translate and make copies of these letters and telegrams that we have found in the post-office at Newcastle, for I know you are the only man in the Transvaal who can spell properly."

"I have come to bleed for my country," said I with great dignity, "and not do the work of a post-office clerk."

"I know that," said Ben; "that is why I want you to do something useful first."

Ben has a biting tongue and hates his enemies with great bitterness, and I knew that sooner or later he would have me put in the forefront of the battle, as Katrina would. This thought made me change my resolve, and decide to translate the papers properly, and not as I at first intended, in a way to deceive Ben and help the British, for I remembered that Ben was proud of his knowledge of English, and was certain to examine my work very carefully, on purpose to find mistakes by which he could make me look foolish before the Burghers. So I translated with truth, making the work last as long as possible, so that I might not be sent to fight the English. But, put the skid on as hard as I could, I could not make the work last out till the commando had gone. It was not till two days after I had finished that Ben began to call names for a small commando to go out towards Ladysmith.

Just as I was fearing to hear my name called, a thing happened which, but for what afterwards came, might have made me feel grateful that whisky was invented. We had in our laager ten Irish Boers and some who said they were Irish, thinking it was a nation that escaped commando, like Germans and Frenchmen. The news came that the Johannesburg Irish Brigade under Colonel Lynch had laagered ten miles away and had brought much whisky, being presents made them by admirers before leaving Johannesburg. As the train which brought them had made a quick journey, they had not had time to drink more than two or three bottles a man, so there was plenty left, as the Burgher who brought the news explained. As soon as this was known, all the real Irish Boers in our commando were off at a gallop to the Irish camp, whereat Ben Viljoen swore so terribly and got so wrathful against whisky, that the predikant called a prayer-meeting at which the whole commando turned up, for they ever preferred praying to fighting. Ben stood on the outside fringe and swore quietly; but he dared not stop the praying, for it was fast becoming an open secret that Ben was an infidel, not caring whether he went to the Dopper or the Dutch Reformed Kerk, but preferring neither, and scoffing at predikants who did; and when the Burghers wanted to pray and sing psalms he generally pretended that the English were coming, and that we ought to prepare to meet them. Just as President Burgers in the old days lost his fights with the Kafirs through his want of religion, so did Ben Viljoen lose us Elandslaagte, as I heard before I joined the commando, and saw the truth of afterwards.

Had he not been so hardly encased in sin he would have seen how he was punished that very day, for the British came into our laager at night, wounded six of our Burghers, and drove us out, the predikant himself being badly hurt by falling down a krantz while running away.

Next day we formed another laager near the Irish Brigade, which was bad for our commando, as the Irishmen still had plenty of whisky and winning ways, that seduced the young Burghers of our commando into drunkenness and irreligion to such an extent, that when the predikant called a prayer-meeting that night the Irishmen held a smoking-concert a few yards off. It was sad to see the young Burghers one by one cease to sing psalms, which they knew well and could voice properly, steal furtively away to the smoking-concert, and raise their voices in profane choruses that they did not know. What made it worse was that the songs were all English, there being no good ones in the Taal. Ben Viljoen, with his usual godlessness, refused to stop the smoking-concert, and laughed loudly when the Burghers sang a psalm and were drowned by the choruses from the concert. I was not surprised that we were again driven from our laager by the shell-fire of the English next day, and I read it as the work of Providence that my horse was killed, as it made my going to fight less probable, for we were very short of horses just then. But my joy became sorrow in the morning, for Ben Viljoen came to me.

"Sarel," said he, "you want to bleed for your country, don't you?"

"Certainly, commandant; that is why I came."

"You know this district, too, eh?"

He said this sneeringly, for he knew that I had come into Natal to escape the injustice of the office inspector; so I very discreetly answered, "Not much."

"But," said he, in a manner that forbade my saying nay, "did you not tell Hans Potgieter that while you were in Natal you were always riding round to stir up the Natal Dutch?"

I had said that much to Hans, but it was not true, and only said to make my path smooth.

"Did you ride or did you not?" asked Ben with fierceness.

I could but say "Yes," or appear a traitor and dissembler.

"Then you are the man we want to show where our friends' places are. You must ride with thirty Burghers and bring in all our friends who are yet on their farms, and do as much damage to the Rooineks as you can. Do you understand?"

My heart went sick, but I dared not say nay, being but one to a thousand. Just then the comforting words of the Bible came to me, "Be ye wise as serpents, but harmless as doves," and I resolved that while I was wise with the Burghers, I would be harmless as a dove to the British and kill none.

"Commandant, if I do not great things you may say I am no oprecht Burgher," which would be the truth, and would do me no harm if he did say it after I had got away, as was my intent.

"Perhaps I shall say it in any case," said Ben; "but meanwhile ride, and remember that your great actions will be watched. And don't forget that you have to kill one hundred Rooineks for Katrina."

This speech showed me that Ben had been told of Katrina's conduct, and my anger rose high; but I was comforted by the blessed thought that she only made come true the words of Scripture which say, "A man's foes shall be those of his own household."

As I rode out with the Burghers on our wicked work I thought much on these things, and how strangely these happenings were making me believe more than ever how true and comforting the Bible was, for one passage kept ringing in my ears, "Come ye out from among them; Come ye out from among them." The hoofs of my horse said it quite plainly, and the squeaking of the saddle echoed it, while the wickedness of the talk of the Burghers, and their jokes about me and Katrina, commanded plainly that a God-fearing man like me should not sit in the seats of the scornful, but come out from among them. These solemn and righteous thoughts kept me quiet for a long time, which the Burghers remarking, some of them asked if my internal complaint was coming on badly,—a question to which I did not answer, for something told me that I should leave the punishment of those who mocked me to Providence; and I did, little thinking how soon I was to be avenged upon them.

About sundown we came in sight of the farm which I thought to be that of Gert Jansen, a Transvaal Boer, but lately come to Natal. I had not seen or spoken to him, but when I was cross-questioned by Hans Potgieter as to what I had seen and done in Natal, I said I knew that Gert was a friend, guessing it only because I had heard he had been born in Rustenburg, Paul Kruger's own place.

"That is Gert Jansen's place, is it not?" asked the Burghers.

"Yes, and he is one of us," I answered.

"Then shall you ride up alone to see if all is safe," said they; and with a sore and fearful heart I rode up alone, expecting any moment that a shot might come, for we had seen signs that the British had been hereabouts. I had a large white handkerchief in my pocket, which I intended to wave if I saw any khaki men, and ride up and surrender. But no sign did I see either of khaki or of Gert Jansen. There were no cattle in sight, nor Kafirs nor kitchen smoke,—and, above all, no dogs barked, the surest sign that a Boer farm is deserted.

When at last I got up to the homestead I saw marks of a great and recent trek. All the waggons were gone, and perhaps Gert had gone to join the British, which thought made me feel sick, for it would make my story a lie, and cause them to doubt me. But again Providence helped me, for when I went into the sitting-room I saw on the table an account-book and papers, and at once a thought came how I might save myself. I took a pen and wrote in a disguised hand: "I have been carried off by the Rooineks. I will escape and join the Boer commando.—GERT JANSEN."

I went over the house, but found no sign of anybody alive, so rode slowly back to the Burghers and told them what I had seen.

As I expected, they began to say hard things, and asked if all my friends in Natal were like Gert, some of the younger Burghers saying Gert had learned to run from my example. But I said nothing till we reached the house, when I pretended to find the book and showed them the writing, which closed the mouths of the scoffers.

But their punishment was close at hand. One of them found a bottle of whisky, and soon they were all drinking, but offered me none, which in one way proved fortunate, though in another it told against me, as the sequel will show. Some were for burning the place, saying that Gert must be with the British as a friend, or why had they not looted his place when they carried him away? a thing that weighed with the corporal of the party, who was for burning. But just as they would begin, more whisky and Dop brandy were found, and they sat down to drink, doing no damage beyond cutting open the stuffing of the sofa and best chairs to look for any money that might be hidden, and throwing the empty bottles through the glass of the windows. There might have been more damage, but some of the Burghers said they were tired and sleepy; and soon half of them were lying about the house, after much quarrelling who should be on the beds, which they settled by getting as many on each as could lie straight, for they had not seen a bed for many weeks.

Seeing so many asleep, and others getting drunk, I began to think I might get away from them; so I went outside to mark how the road lay before it got too dark, and to pick a good horse, my own being but poor.

As I was looking at the horses, old Franz Lieben-berg touched me on the shoulder.

"Are you in a hurry to go? or is the internal complaint bad?" he asked sneeringly.

"Yes, coos," I answered boldly. "It is the internal complaint; but it is not I who have it, but the kerels inside," meaning that those in the house were drunk. But I did not see how that speech was going to rise up against me in the aftertime.

I went inside the house, and was trying to move one Burgher who had fallen into an uncomfortable position, when he awoke, and, seeing me, exclaimed, "You schelm! you have poisoned the drink!"

My heart gave a thump as the others took up the saying, and as many as could stand crowded round me. At that moment Providence again helped me, for one of the Burghers who was not drunk came running into the house shouting, "The Rooineks are coming!"

We ran out to see, and on a kopjie about a mile away saw khaki men riding towards us.

Never did men get sober more quickly. Some who a minute before were groaning that they were dying rushed to their horses, and before the khakis were come two hundred yards nearer we were off. They fired, and some of us fired, but no one was hit; and when after an hour's hard riding we stopped in a donga and counted, there were six Burghers missing, and them we never saw again.

"It was a trap, kerels," I said. "The verdomde Rooineks poisoned the whisky and left it for us."

But I could see that some did not believe me because I had run away from the Transvaal, which again showed the truthfulness of the Bible, which says, "having once put your hand to the plough do not go back," for going back had caused all my pain of mind and the mistrust of my fellow Burghers.

After this bad fright the Burghers were in no mood for going to look for other places, but were all for returning; so by a long and troublesome path we got back to laager.

Ben Viljoen was away when we arrived; and, fortunately for me, Piet Joubert was there, and, thank Providence, in a good humour, for news had just come in of a defeat of the British and the capture of many horses and oxen and several Kafir runners with important letters on them. But I knew, for I could feel it, that trouble was coming to me for the mishap. I sat on a stone and smoked, and tried hard to think of what I should say to defend myself; but my years of experience as a public prosecutor made me see only what I should say if I were prosecuting myself, and a bad case mine was.

Most of the drunken Burghers having been made sober by the schrick given them by the khakis, had now time and inclination to get sick again; and those that had been most drunk were now telling the whole laager about the fight, and lying wickedly of the number they had killed. Presently I heard old Carl Vollmer, who had been the first to run, boasting loudly of his great deeds.

"I dropped two with one shot at 800 yards," said he.

"Nay, Carl," I broke in, "there were three; did you not see the third—a little man—crawling behind an ant-heap?"

Carl looked at me sideways a minute before he answered—

"Nay, coos, you are wrong. I got that fellow with my trial shot, and only hit his leg."

"But he was an officer," said I, knowing that this would please Carl, for it was ever the delight of a Boer to shoot an officer.

He looked very pleased; so, knowing he was a Burgher of influence, with a son a commandant, I made haste to follow up my wise policy—

"It was you, Carl, who stopped the rush and saved us, for so many of the other kerels were too full of whisky to shoot."

This was a bold saying, but I remembered that Carl was a teetotal Boer and always against whisky, and being on the Licensing Board at Prinsloosdorp, where he ever said Nay to granting a licence, unless very well paid to say Yea.

The Burghers began to come up to listen, so I made haste to agree with my adversary while he was yet in the way. In a loud voice, and pretending not to know that those of whom I spoke were listening, I went on—

"There was some good shooting by Phanie van den Berg. I saw him drop three khakis." And thus I went on, skilfully but dishonestly praising those Burghers who I thought were likely to be most against me if trouble came, yet all the time secretly knowing they were great cowards, who thought more of riding than shooting. At the same time, I knew they dare not deny my stories about them.

"But," asked one who had not been at the fight, and a Hollander, a race that is always hard to convince of the truth, "if you shot so many, why did you not stay and finish them?"

"Man, but they were like the locusts for numbers, and had lances and lyddite, and were round us on every side," I answered.

"But if you were surrounded, how did you get away?" the troublesome Hollander went on.

"It was the Lord's doing," said old Paul du Plooy. "He opened a path, as he did for the children of Israel through the Red Sea. Was it not so, Sarel?"

"It is quite right, Oom," said I, pleased to find the old man my friend. "It all came to pass as you said it would. Man, but you are wonderful with that Bible of yours; you can read all that is coming like an almanack, but these young kerels will not believe, and so are punished." And then I told them how the six Burghers whom we had left drunk had been scoffing at Paul, and saying how glad they were that he was not with them to preach tribulation. They had not said anything like this, but I was making friends with the old man by being wise as a serpent but harmless as a dove.

Just then a Natal Burgher who had been listening gave me a great shock.

"I know Gert Jansen well," said he, "and I know that he is as much against whisky as Carl Vollmer. How, then, did the whisky get into a house like that?"

"It was a trap of the Rooineks," I said.

"But khakis don't carry whisky in big bottles. They carry it in small flasks, and leave the big bottles in camp. Have we not found them ourselves at Dundee and Newcastle? The only man likely to keep whisky is Andries Brink. Are you sure it was not his place you were at?"

My heart gave a great thump, for since I had had time to think it over I had begun to have doubts whether it was Gert Jansen's place we had been to.

The Natal Burgher went on. "Andries has willows all round the kraal, and plenty of wire-fencing, but Gert Jansen has neither trees nor fence."

"Then it was not Gert Jansen's, and Sarel is a liar," broke in a young Burgher, who was angry because I had not included him among those who shot well.

"But what about this?" and I showed them the leaf I had written and torn out of the account-book.

"Let me see it," said the Natal Burgher. When he had read it he laughed. "These Rooineks are wonderful," said he, "for they have taught Gert to write. When I knew him two months ago, he made a mark for his signature."

Then all the Burghers were very quiet, and looked very serious. The writing was passed from hand to hand and closely examined, especially by those who could not read.

Old Paul du Plooy came to my help again,—

"Man, but you don't know what a kerel will do when he is sorely scared. May it not be that the khakis stood over him with their lances and long knives and made him write? A lame man would jump at such a time."

And then Paul told them a long story of how, when he was a boy, in the Ventersdorp district an angel appeared to a man named Coetzee while he was herding sheep, and taught him to read and write. Paul had a lot of these stories, which often came in very usefully, as this one would, had not the Hollanders and younger Burghers begun to ask questions, that showed how greatly the infidel religion had been imported into the country by the Hollanders, and, I fear, also by Johannesburgers. It is true that I myself do not believe that angel story, but it has been told so often since I was a boy that there may be some truth in it.

When old Burghers set to discussing a puzzling subject, time is going to be cheap; so when they started on trying to settle whether the farm we had been to was Gert Jansen's or Andries Brink's, I went away, for my legal knowledge had taught me that the less an accused person says the better. So I went away, and tried hard to think out a plan for my defence against the trouble that I knew was coming, though I felt that by my superior cunning I had made my path much smoother than it seemed at first.

My greatest enemy in the laager after Ben Viljoen was Harry Otto of Prinsloosdorp, who had learned much wickedness in Johannesburg, where he had been a detective, and was so full with it that there was no room for more, though he was in that matter like a sponge which, being full, has yet room for more. He was bitter against me because I was the only official in the dorp who would not shut my eyes to his wickedness when he took money from illicit liquor-sellers not to report what his eyes saw. Several times, when I was prosecuting these men, had he spoiled my case by his lying evidence; but in the end I made him look foolish by proving that he had taken bribes. It was true I obtained a conviction; but I was sent for to Pretoria, and severely rebuked by the Government for my over-zeal in making an official appear bad. I knew, therefore, that if Otto could injure me with Ben Viljoen he would, and for that I was now preparing.

Ben did not return till next day, and his coming brought more trouble than I had expected, for with him came this same Otto whom we had left in the farmhouse. He had been sleeping off his drunkenness in the stable, where he was not found by the khakis, nor had we missed him. He told a story to Ben that was not in my favour, and I was not a bit surprised when a little later I was told to prepare to be tried for leading the Burghers into a trap.

It was Paul du Plooy who brought the news.

"I think they are going to shoot you, Sarel," said he. "But you have got to die of something, perhaps that internal complaint, which will be very painful, or perhaps shot or lanced by khakis. Much better be shot by people who know you than by khakis who don't. The predikant says he won't read any service over your grave; but never mind, Sarel, I will do it, and make a nice prayer that I have invented. And I'll make the speech that I made over the grave of my second wife. I've only got to alter the names."

And then the old man read great chapters out of the Book of Job, because he said I was like him, having an internal complaint. The parts he read were very gloomy, and made me out to be a very wicked man. When he had read six or seven chapters very slowly, because he could not spell all the words,—

"Oom," said I, "you read and talk as if you thought me guilty. Do you?"

"Sarel," said he, "I am an old man, and have seen many strange things both among Kafirs and white men and wild creatures, and I know that when any of these are in a corner they do the best thing that can be thought out to destroy their enemies and get away safely. Why should you not poison those who would destroy you? I would do the same to the vultures that would destroy my sheep; and are not your enemies seeking to destroy a ewe lamb?"

"But I have an answer to all their charges; and being clever in law, I will defeat them and make them ashamed."

"Nay, Sarel, this is war-time, when we have no law, only justice," said he.

I was afraid it would be so, but I had hoped my long practice at drawing summonses might show me how to upset this one against me, and I told Paul so.

"You are very ignorant, Sarel, for you do not know that they only hold a court-martial on people they know to be guilty. Your only chance is to trust to the Lord and me, or else do as Lieutenant Tossel did—get the case sent to Pretoria to be tried, where there will be no witnesses against you, and no trial will come. Besides, there will be no chance for you to play lawyer tricks, for there will be no summons, and I heard them say they would not let you defend yourself, for, being a lawyer, you might trick them into believing you innocent."

Then for the first time I saw how the wicked had encompassed me about to work my ruin, and I saw that Paul was right in reading all the dreadful parts of Job that fitted only the guilty and the dead.

" Paul," said I, " it seems that you might well read my burial sermon now."

" I will do it with pleasure," answered he ; and he would have begun if I had not gone away.

That afternoon two Burghers came and told me I was a prisoner, and would go before the Court at sun-up next morning. They made it so early because I was to be shot, they said, before the commando broke up laager, which was to be at seven o'clock.

They made me sleep in a waggon that night with two Burghers, and at sun-up next morning the Court sat in the open, General Piet Joubert being President. The others who had the judging of me were Ben Viljoen, Commandant Schoemann, and four other commandants whom I well knew as unrighteous. Old Paul came and sat on the ground behind me to give me courage, as he said, though the remarks he kept making for my ear alone were not comforting, being such as: " That is very bad, Sarel. He is lying, but they believe him." " That is worse and worse, Sarel." " Never mind if you are shot, Sarel, the Lord will punish these wicked false witnesses," and so on, all of which was kindly meant, but did not help to give me courage, as Paul intended.

A Burgher who acted as Clerk of the Court read out the charges, which were :—

(1) That I had led certain Burghers into a trap by taking them to a certain farmhouse, well knowing that the English were there in ambush.

(2) That I poisoned or drugged certain whisky, with the object of making the Burghers sleep while the English came upon them.

(3) That I tried to desert from my fellows while they were asleep.

(4) That I had confessed to Franz Liebenberg that I had made the Burghers sick.

(5) That I had told Paul du Plooy that I was guilty and ought to be shot, and had asked him to read the funeral service.

As this last was read out Paul cried, " You lie! you put falseness on my words," and got up to snatch the paper.

The President begged him to be quiet, but he said he would not, and they had to let him make a long speech, which was not much good to me, for he explained that what he had said was that he thought me guilty, and wished to read the funeral service, and not that I had said so.

When Paul had made an end of speaking, which was not for some time, for the old man would say many times the same thing, the President asked me if I were guilty.

"Certainly not, Piet," said I with great boldness. " But let me hear and see the witnesses who say I poisoned the whisky and did the other things."

So they called up one after another the Burghers who had got drunk at the farm, and they all told in exactly the same words how I showed them the bottles of whisky, but refused myself to drink.

" How do you know it was poisoned? " I asked the first witness.

" Because it tasted like poison, and made me sick."

" What poison did it taste like? "

" Cyanide."

" When did you ever drink cyanide? "

" Never."

" Then how do you know it was cyanide? "

" Because that is the only poison I know except sheep dip. When I lived near one of the Rand mines I had a cow die through drinking cyanide water."

Ben Viljoen looked wrathful and swore, and the General laughed right out.

"Who carried the corkscrew to open the bottle?"
I next asked.

"We had no corkscrew, but broke the necks of
the bottles."

"Would not the corks come out easy without a
corkscrew?"

"No."

"Why not?"

"Because they were covered with silver."

Like a clever lawyer, I did not make any remark
on this last point, but asked all the other witnesses
about the corkscrew, as if I wanted to make out that
they were lying when they said they broke the necks.
They all told the same story in the same words, but
they did not reckon on my great skill at cross-examina-
tion, and could not see that if there was still the lead
capsule over the cork I could not have drawn it to
put in the poison.

I could soon see that neither General Joubert nor
even Ben Viljoen believed the poisoning story, so feared
no more from that, though one of the witnesses made
a great point against me; for when I asked him, as
I had asked all of them, how he knew he was poisoned,
he turned up his trousers and showed a big red mark
on his calf, where he had once been bitten by a puff-
adder.

"Whenever I am poisoned, that mark gets red and
full of pain, as it is now," said he; and as all Boers
believe in such things, this testimony did me great
damage.

Franz Liebenberg next told how he had caught me
trying to run away from the farmhouse while the
Burghers were suffering from the poison, and that
when he reproached me I told him I had poisoned the
whisky and was going to run away.

I made Franz look very foolish by insisting that he
should repeat my very words frequently, which he did,
always in a different way. But the Court called six
other Burghers to whom Franz had told the story.

Of course I objected that hearsay evidence was not

proper, but Ben Viljoen angrily interrupted—"We want the truth, not lawyer monkey tricks,"—and each man told his story word for word, which I could not make them tell differently; and the case looked black against me, old Paul meanwhile whispering verses from the Psalms about my enemies having triumphed over me, and suchlike, till I grew angry and kicked him hard in the ribs with my heel, at which he shouted out as he picked himself up after rolling backwards down the slope of the bank on which he was sitting, "And now I'll unsay all I told the Court."

"General," said I, "do you hear that? Here is the most godly Burgher in the laager now going to belittle himself and eat his words because he is kicked. Let me kick the other witnesses, and perhaps they will do the same."

I saw a smile begin to grow round Piet Joubert's mouth, and I was comforted, for I knew that when Slim Piet smiled there was no bite in him.

"Is that the sort of evidence you would convict a public prosecutor on?" I asked. Then I demanded to see the *corpus delicti* of the poisoned whisky, and "Where are the corpses?" I asked.

"Five Burghers lie dead in the farmhouse poisoned by you. I saw them myself," said Harry Otto.

That lie did me much good, for Harry had forgotten having told Ben Viljoen and other Burghers that he was not in the farmhouse, but had escaped through being in the stable, where he was looking for incriminating documents, as all detectives do.

I made the most of this in my speech, which lasted over an hour, and was very eloquent and convincing, and the best of all the good ones I ever made, though I had great work to explain why I did not partake of the whisky, I being wrongly supposed never to miss the opportunity to drink.

When I had finished, the General said the Court would go to breakfast and consider. I also went to breakfast, but could not eat, for Paul du Plooy kept on saying, "Eat, man; you will be braver when you are dying if you are not hungered. Men who are going to be hanged always make good breakfasts."

When the Court came out of the tent I saw that General Joubert was trying hard not to smile, and my heart thumped as I watched his mouth to see if the smile grew large and ugly, for then I knew I was safe.

"Sarel," said he, "the Court find you innocent; but there is a grave doubt, so we will think over the proper punishment. Meantime, you will be made chief commissariat corporal of the commando you rode out with, and have the serving out of the rations and the whisky, so that if anybody dies of poison all doubt will be removed, and we can shoot you with a clear conscience."

It was worth all the soreness of mind and heart I had gone through to see the faces of the Burghers when they heard the sentence. Paul du Plooy came up to me looking very sad,.for he was one of those who would have to get his rations from me.

"Sarel," said he, "don't forget that I was your friend in the hour of trial, even though you did kick me."

It was not till long after that I learned it was Piet Joubert who had been my friend, and that he was against believing the false charges against me; but knowing the wickedness of the hearts of the Burghers, and being wise as a serpent and well called "Slim Piet," he made a plan that I should be tried, so that the Burghers could not say that he shielded me, while in his heart he meant that I should be proved not guilty. By putting me to give out the food he punished my enemies after the manner that would have been done by King Solomon, whose photograph is very like Slim Piet; for they would all the time be in great fear lest I should poison them, as was the case, for they made great outcry, and went hungry for some days. But the General would not listen to their complaints, saying, "You want the man to be shot; then what better cause shall we have than if one of you die from his poison?"

Thus was I, like Joseph in Egypt, made great in the land, and triumphed over my enemies. Like him, I had it in my power to prepare for a time of famine, for I sold privately the food that the frightened Burghers would not take at my hands.

But my greatest triumph came when large stores of whisky and brandy were captured from the English convoys and brought in to laager. The General gave an order that I alone was to have the giving of it out, for, being slim, he saw in this a great plan for keeping the Burghers from getting drunk, as they always did when such drinks came in.

" Who wants cyanide ? " I would cry in derision ; but few would take the bottles, so I kept them to give to those who had befriended me in the hour of my trial. But they being few, there was much left on my hand, which, when the fright of being poisoned had died away, I sold for large money.

At last the young Burghers who had learned to drink whisky in Johannesburg and at Krugersdorp, and were thus poison-proof, being, so to speak, salted, came to me, not being able to hold out any longer in the sight of so much good whisky lying in the cases unopened.

" Sarel," said they, " we will drink the whisky ; but you must first drink, as the Kafir chiefs do before they pass the beer, to show there is no poison."

At first I refused ; but as that made them think the charges were true, I had to drink a large tot from each bottle I gave out, and even the tinned beef and biscuits I had to eat of, which in time made me very sick, for the Burghers were not content that I should open a tin of biscuits or jam and taste a little in proof that all was good, but they made me eat of every man's portion, so that I did nothing all the morning but eat and drink till I was drunk, and could take no more. Then the Burghers would lay me on a piece of cor-rugated sheet-iron in the sun, and watch to see if I died, for some one had said that hot iron always brought out poison quickly, which was why doctors put hot pokers on snake-bite wounds, though they did not want to cure me as hot pokers did, but to bring the poison out, so that they would have proof that it was inside me, and then be able to shoot me.

I had been baked every day for nearly a week, and was almost beginning to hope they would find poison in me, when there came to me Pat van der Murphy, an Irish Boer who had married a Van der Zyl, and had taken part of her name to show how much he hated England.

"Sarel," said he, "it makes my heart as sore as your body must be to see you drinking so much and being baked all for doing your duty. I know how whisky should taste when it is not poisoned, so as I like you much and we both have calves from the same bull, I will take the risk of dying to show these Burghers that you are a true man and no poisoner. I will taste the whisky when it is given out; but as I never could eat biscuits, they being too dry and making a great thirst, you must go on eating them."

"Van der Murphy," I answered, "you are a kind-hearted man, like all your race, though you do make trouble in your own land and sing profane songs instead of going to prayer-meeting. But you know that Ben Viljoen will not let you have more than six soupies of whisky a-day, lest you talk politics."

"That is from jealousy, for he knows that we Irish-men fight like devils when we are full; and he wants to finish this war by himself, so that he may have all the glory."

I knew this was mostly true, so, "When will you begin to taste?" I asked.

"I'll take a bottle now of each brand that you have got, and if I am alive in the morning I will come and taste some more in the presence of all these dis-believing kerels."

That was a generous offer, so I gave him four bottles, being persuaded by his smooth words to give him two of each brand instead of one.

Next morning Van der Murphy could not get up,

being very sick. And the word went round the laager that I had poisoned the Irish Burghers, and there was great trouble; for, said they, if whisky will make an Irishman sick it must be poisoned. And they went to Piet Joubert to make complaint against me.

Then came Piet to the laager, looking dark and wrathful, and ordered all the Burghers to stand up before him.

" How many of you have drunk whisky ? " he asked.

None of them would speak, and there was a long silence till up spoke old Paul du Plooy.

" Piet," said he, " you know that I am an oprecht and sober Burgher of the land, but last night I drank a whole bottle, as did many of these kerels who are afraid to speak. I am well and strong, and I will drink another to show that it is good whisky, and not poisoned."

Then, one by one, about twenty Burghers, mostly young ones, confessed that they had been over-persuaded by Van der Murphy to drink the whisky and give what was left to him if they felt ill, as all of them now said they did.

Then said the General to me, " Sarel, make out a list of all these kerels who say they drank and feel ill, and so long as they are in the laager they are to have no strong drink."

And these Burghers went away with sore hearts and ashamed.

Thus did Slim Piet Joubert show that he was verily a Solomon in Israel.

CHAPTER IV.

I am given a mission that is brought to nought through the bloodthirstiness of a Dopper.

MY position being made strong by the word going round the laager through Paul that Piet Joubert was my friend, I became more happy; but never did the sound of the Bible words leave my ears. All day they rang plainly, "Come ye out from among them," and every hour gave me fuller reason for obeying. But I had less travail of soul now that Ben Viljoen was gone away, as were many of my worst secret enemies; and as no one had died in my corps, the Burghers began to have more faith in me, particularly those that loved whisky, among whom, to my great surprise, was old Paul du Plooy, who never let me forget that he had saved my life by making himself a drunkard.

"But," said he, when I reproached him for dancing to the music of an accordion when very full of whisky, "did not David drink wine and dance before the ark?" and he sat by me and read all the Bible stories he could find about wine; and after reading and expounding them to fit his own case,—which somehow he always contrived they should,—he drank more whisky till he cried, and began to tell me all about his first wife,— as men who have married two or three ever do,—and about his boy who had been taken prisoner by the British, making the story very long, till he fell asleep sobbing; and the young Burghers came and finished what was left of a nearly full bottle, making him believe when he awoke that he had drunk it all alone.

Paul, being old, had got himself made corporal of the laager, which meant that he had not to go out with the commando, but helped me in giving out the rations and took charge of the horse-guard; though at this latter he was little good, for he always took his Bible with him, and read it instead of watching the Kafirs, finding verses to read to the young Burghers, who, he said, were accursed through dwelling in the tents of the unrighteous Rooineks in the days when they were in Government offices at Johannesburg and Pretoria. And Paul used to make prophecies of evil to befall them, which did not come true until young Gert Keet got shot in the mouth by his own mauser going off. Now it happened that young Keet was very profane, knowing all the swearing words and songs of the English. Having his teeth and part of his tongue shot away, Paul pointed to it as a great judgment, and read so many verses to prove it that for some days afterwards we had more prayers and psalms than smoking-concerts, and there was a holiness in the laager like to a great Nachtmaal, for the Burghers always preferred praying to fighting, and Ben Viljoen being away, there was no let or hindrance to godliness.

Just at that time there happened a thing that made me change my mind very much on the wisdom of having too much Bible when out fighting, though I would not have it thought that, like certain godless commandants, I would put obstacles in the way of those who would rather sing psalms than fight.

One day, when Paul was out on horse-guard, one of the Kafirs came to the laager saying Paul wished to see me secretly, and that I was to bring a bottle of whisky. This last pained me much, for after my serious talk Paul had agreed not to take more than two soupies of liquor with him. But I thought it better to take it, as it would show him I had as much faith in him as I wanted him to have in me; besides, I need not leave it with him if I found it dangerous. So with great scheming, for my movements were ever closely watched, I contrived to get away from the laager to the kloof where Paul was supposed to be bossing the Kafir horse-guard. I found him very full of something on his mind.

"Sarel," said he, "I have done something that would make my name great in Israel were I not a godly and oprecht Burgher. I have to settle in my heart whether I shall obey the Bible or Ben Viljoen, and I think I shall go on the Bible. What say you, neef?"

"If it were the Bible against Ben out of war-time, I should go on the Bible," said I; "but in war-time a commandant like Ben Viljoen is greater than the Bible."

"Suppose, Sarel, you had got a khaki colonel with a lame leg that knows the Bible well, what would you do?"

"What does the Bible say?" I asked to gain time, for I did not want to advise without knowing Paul's opinion.

"There is nothing about khaki colonels in the Book, but there is about the Gibeonites, and the colonel I have got is one of them,—at least his name is Gibbons, which he tells me is Rooinek for Gibeonite."

"You talk in clouds, Paul; tell me all about it."

And in many words he told me how, while sitting reading the Bible, he lifted up his eyes and saw a man in khaki crawling to cover in a donga. Fearing that it might be a trap, he sent a Kafir, who came back saying a lame khaki lay in the donga. Paul took his rifle, and going up carefully, found that the words of the Kafir were true, for there lay a khaki crying out for water.

"Are you alone?" asked Paul in English.

"Quite alone, lost and wounded, and a friend."

Paul, still keeping his rifle pointed, went up and talked, when the khaki told him he was a colonel sent by General Buller to ask General Joubert what terms he would give if the English gave up fighting and left the country; but his horse had bolted and thrown him, hurting his leg, and, what was worse, carrying away in the saddle-bags the letter he had brought for the General. "And now," said Paul, "he is afraid to come into the laager, for he has nothing to prove that his story is true, and he fears to be shot as a spy."

"Let me see him," said I, but Paul would not let me go to him till he had read in the nineteenth chapter of Joshua about the Gibeonites who came into the Israelites' laager and obtained a league by craft.

"That story should make you very careful, Paul, for this may be a crafty Gibeonite," said I, feeling that out of his own words I had confuted him. But no lawyer was ever more clever at making his bad case seem good than Paul.

"He is no doubt a Gibeonite, for his name says so, and he may be crafty; but does not the Bible story tell how, despite their craft, they became servants to the Israelites?"

I could not answer to this, so we went to the donga, and there found a young khaki with K.R.R. on his shoulders, and speaking like an Irishman in the Boer Irish Brigade.

"Are you a colonel?" I asked, for I had seen one in Maritzburg before the war, and he was old and grey, while this one was quite a boy, as I told him.

"That is true," said he; "but you would not be surprised if you knew how you Boers have killed off our colonels. The British have no colonels left, and have to make them from privates."

"Of course he is a colonel," said Paul; "look at his shoulder—'K.R.R.'—Colonel Rooinek Rifles. Is not that so?"

"Certainly," said the khaki, who looked faint, and sat with his back against a boulder. "Have you brought the whisky?"

"Can you drink it?" I asked, for he looked so faint and ill that I feared it might hurt him.

The Colonel smiled as he answered, "I'll try," and he put the bottle to his mouth and kept it there long. When he had finished, he was much stronger, and talked with a free tongue.

"Why has Buller decided to give up?" I asked.

"Because he has been sent for to go and fight the Chinese and take his army with him. England is in a bad way, what with France and Russia and America all wanting to help you, to say nothing of old Ireland."

"Has Ireland risen at last?" I asked, for I had heard Pat van der Murphy often say that this war would mean Ireland's chance.

"Risen is it?" said the Colonel. "The Irish have captured London, and the Parliament House is full of Irishmen; and the Dubs are going to join the Boers, and the Irish Rifles as well; and as General Roberts is an Irishman, and nearly all the Highland regiments are chock-a-block with Paddies, the best of the British army will be with you, and there will be very few left to fight the Chinese. So they are· going to chuck this job and get out of the country. That's why I'm sent to see General Joubert. But I dare not go without my credentials, for the news is so terrific he wouldn't perhaps believe me. You seem good kind Boers, so if you will help me to get away, I may find my horse and the letter, or go back to my camp and get a fresh one, and so stop this awful war before you wipe out the British army."

"But if you are lame, how can you travel?" I asked.

"Oh," says he, "the whisky is a great healer, and I am nearly well, and if I have some more of it, with some rooti and beef, I shall be all right."

"Sarel," said Paul in the Taal, "I can see a great plan to make you and me great in the land. We will get this khaki away to fetch the letter, and then you will have a dream that you saw a Gibeonite, and I will interpret it to the commando that Buller is going to send in to make peace, and when this kerel comes back and the commando finds it is all true, you and I will be prophets in the land and wax great."

"If we let you go to-night, when will you come back?" I asked the khaki.

"I shall come back in two days," said he.

Paul and I talked it over in the Taal. I liked the

thing much, for I saw in it a way to get the goodwill of the Burghers and make us both in high esteem, and particularly Paul, who was much given to prophecies that did not come true; but as he had stood my friend I wanted much to help him. So I agreed to what Paul proposed, and having shown the khaki the best way back to his camp, I returned to the laager and sent back the Kafir with more whisky and bread for him, telling the native I would shoot him if he told any one what he had seen.

An hour later Paul came to the laager saying all was well, that the khaki had gone away happy and full of whisky, so that he feared he might not remember the password or the advice Paul had given him about the road.

Paul then told me what I was to dream that night, and how I was to tell it at breakfast in the morning, when the Burghers were listening.

"It is a great plan," said Paul, "which I learned from Paul Kruger, who is great on dreams, which made him famed in the days when he was not even a field-cornet."

Next morning, over the coffee, when most of the Burghers were in hearing, I told Paul that I had had a Bible dream, wherein a man wearing a strange dress came to the laager and asked to see Joshua, and I put in many things that Paul had read to me out of the chapter in Joshua. Now, all old Burghers put much weight on dreams, and they all began to listen very closely and to ask me questions, and tried to interpret it in their own foolish ways. But Paul, after they had all tried to find the interpretation, gave his, which was that a messenger would come from the Rooineks offering peace, even as the Gibeonites did, and that we Boers should come out as conquerors and make the Uitlanders hewers of wood and drawers of water, as Joshua did the Gibeonites. And Paul read the chapter, at which most of the Burghers were greatly pleased.

Then Paul and I waited patiently for the coming of the messenger from Buller.

As the days passed and he came not, I began to fear what had several times been in my mind—that the khaki was no colonel; for I remembered afterwards that the English do not spell colonel with a "k" as we do, neither do they send messengers to laagers alone. When I told Paul what I thought he was very angry.

"Sarel," said he, "you have become like to the Englanders and Hollanders for unbelief. Did not the Bible come true in your case? and were not your enemies made to be a reproach while you were exalted?"

And thus would he talk always, till one day a party of Burghers, who had caught a British convoy and some prisoners, brought in newspapers; and in one of them was a story how a private in the King's Royal Rifles lost his way, and walked on to a Boer picket, whom he befooled into letting him go by a story that he was a messenger from Buller to Joubert come to beg for peace; and the whole story was set out in print, making Paul and me look so foolish that for a time I was very wrathful with the English. But I was glad that the Burghers did not know who the "two simple Boers" referred to were.

But Paul, with his great slimness in turning misses into bull's-eyes, said, when the story had been read—

"Kerels, has not my interpretation of Sarel's dream come true? You hear what the paper says, how a messenger was sent. It is no doubt that his heart failed him, and he went back and told this lie to cover his failure."

And many of the Burghers saw it as Paul wished them to, and his fame as an interpreter of the Bible was increased.

A few days later came another thing that made Paul rejoice, and claim that his prophecy was coming true in so far as I was to be exalted over my enemies.

Piet Joubert wanted to send a message to a commando of Free State Burghers, telling them to come to him over the Berg. Now it happened that all the

Natal Burghers, and those who knew the roads and passes, were away fighting, and there was left only me,—for I had lost no chance to make everybody think that I knew Natal as well as I knew my own district of the Transvaal, for I was always hoping that I might some day be chosen to go on some such expedition, which would give me a chance to obey the voice that was ever calling me to come out from among them. So my heart thumped with joy when the General sent for me and told me he had a great thing for me to do.

"You know, Sarel," said he, "you are suspect for running away, and Ben Viljoen and some of the commandants who know you best would have that you do not leave the laager. But you are too clever to keep shut up in a kraal. You say you know this country?"

"Well, General; for when I was away from the Transvaal I was learning it."

"Let me hope it is truth," said he, "for I am going to believe you. Take two good Burghers whom you can trust, and find the commando of Heilbron Burghers somewhere between Harrismith and the Berg. Give this letter to the commandant—Birkenfeld is his name, I think—and come in with them. You will be back in a week. Do this well, and you shall be made a corporal; if not, you will have me on the side of Ben Viljoen."

"General," said I, "this is what I have been waiting for." And I went away with a light and cheerful walk.

I was sorely troubled as to whom I should take, for, excepting old Paul, I trusted none, and him I feared because of his Bible-reading and his prophecies; but he settled it as soon as I told him what the General had said.

"I must go with you, Sarel," said he, "for the prophecies are meant for both of us, and we stand or fall together."

Paul chose the other Burgher, a young kerel fresh

from his father's farm at Rustenberg. I know Paul chose him because he used to listen to the old man's Bible-readings without wanting to go away as the other youngsters did; but Paul said he took him because he had no wiliness, and could not be troublesome. I was for taking Van der Murphy, as he had been so kind to me in saving me the pain of tasting whisky; but Paul would have none of him.

"He is not quite a Boer, although he has a Boer wife," said he; "and if we should meet an Irish regiment he will surely join it, for these Irish would drink with Satan if he came from anywhere in Ireland and carried whisky."

So we saddled up; and with a Kafir and a packhorse carrying some extra food and our blankets, we left the laager at sun-up next morning. I was full of joy, for I had obeyed the voice and come out from among them; but I dared not tell Paul that was why I was so happy and sang English chorus songs.

We had no trouble in getting across country to the edge of the Drakensberg, for the British were not in that district; but as we turned southward we ran greater risk, for we had had no news of khaki movements for some time. We came to a deserted farm about sundown, and sent the Kafir on to see if khakis might be there, but he reported all safe. The place had been deserted long, and though we searched well we found nothing, either open or hidden, that we could eat or drink, but we did find something that gave us a great schrick.

Paul was going into the stable thinking to find something, as Boers are fond of using these places to hide things, when he came out with a run, looking very scared. Before he could tell me what was the matter, two big baboons came out and got away. This proved the hand of Providence, for the monkeys were hunting for hens' eggs, some of which we found, the fowls being too wild for the owner to take away with him.

We found one good bed left, and Paul and I slept in

it; but he would not take off his clothes, being an old Burgher, not used to the effeminate ways of the new generation. I wanted him to take off his boots, or at least his spurs; but he would not, but instead preached a long sermon on the foolishness of these new ways of sleeping, telling me that he had not taken off his clothes except to change them for the quarterly Nachtmaal for fifty years, for once he was foolish enough to take them off for sleeping, and caught a cold that made him deaf for years.

When we left in the morning, Paul was for setting fire to the place, for, said he, "Did not the children of Israel destroy the dwellings of their enemies with fire?"

"Yea, Paul," said I; "but the smoke may bring up the khakis."

This made Paul change his mind, and not a godly desire to do what was right, as was my case. But I was not angry with him, for I knew that he had been led away from righteousness by the predikants, and he was too old to become just and Christian-like like me.

But I did not reckon on the cunning of old Paul and the wickedness of the boy Van Niekerk. Before we had been riding a mile,—

"Look!" said the Kafir.

We looked back, and saw smoke and flames rising from where the farmhouse stood.

"Why did you do that wickedness?" I asked of Paul.

"It was not I, but the boy here," and he called young Van Niekerk names.

"But you bade me do it," said the lad, making Paul look very foolish.

I did not say more, lest Van Niekerk should talk about it when we got back, and I did not want to have it said that I had burned English places; so I only said it was a pity, as the place might be useful when we returned, because of the eggs.

For many miles Paul talked of nothing but the

doings of the children of Israel, and how they smote their enemies hip and thigh, and destroyed their flocks and herds.

"I feel I have done a great sin, Sarel," said he, "in not destroying those fowls; but let us hope that the fire will have devoured them."

And thus this bloodthirsty old man talked and quoted the Bible, always to the end that he might have justification for destroying his enemies.

Towards sundown we came to the edge of a spur of the Drakensberg, and, looking down the steep sides, I saw something that made me feel sick all over. Riding on the level ground right below us were eight khakis, whom we knew not to be Colonial volunteers by the way they rode — with a long stirrup, and straight up in the saddle. They had seen us against the sky-line, and most likely had heard Paul shouting all the vengeful verses of the Psalms, which he did as other men whistle or sing as they ride. Presently they all stopped and got together in a bunch, which was foolishness, seeing that they thereby made a mark that even a Kafir could not miss, for khakis at this time did not understand how wrong it is to keep close together like frightened sheep when fighting Boers.

I was for getting behind the hill again; but great bloodthirstiness had come upon Paul through thinking and talking of the children of Israel, and he was all for shooting, as was also the boy Van Niekerk, who had only just joined the commando and had killed no Rooineks.

Had I been alone with Paul I should have had my way and gone in peace; but I was afraid of what the lad might say about me when we got back to laager, for he was a fierce young kerel, after having listened with both ears to all that Paul had been saying. So we put our horses under cover, well behind the ridge, and planned to play a trick that has always puzzled khakis.

We separated about fifty yards apart and fired after

each other, running a short distance to fire the next
shot, thus covering a long line and making it seem
that there were many of us. It is a great and excellent plan when there are only few; and in the
Natal papers we often used to read how the British
had been attacked by hundreds of Boers when we
knew that not more than a dozen had been within
twenty miles.

The khakis, still keeping together, kept on their
horses, and shot in the direction they supposed us to
be. But their bullets fell short, for they cannot judge
distance in hilly country; and even if they could,
they would not have hit us, for there was nothing
of us to be seen except Paul's hat, which he set on a
stone in a place where he was not, after the Boer fashion
of making Kafirs fire away their shots for nothing.

I might have killed every khaki, being a splendid
shot, and knowing the range as well as if I had
measured it; but though I fired often, I was careful
not to take aim, for I was resolved not to have it on
my soul that I had killed a Britisher.

After we had fired about twenty shots apiece, the
khakis galloped off, leaving a lame horse, which Paul
said he had hit, though I believe it was the young
kerel who did the work; but Paul was ever vain of
his shooting, and would not admit that a boy could
do as well as he. So, much against my conscience,
I agreed with Paul that he had shot the horse, which
I could see made the young kerel very bitter against
Paul, at which I was secretly glad.

We waited till the khakis were out of sight behind a
ridge, then went on, keeping well on the under-side of
the hill. After riding till far into afternoon, a thunderstorm gave signs of coming, so we rode for a kloof
that, being full of thick thorn-bush, would give us
shelter. When we got into it we found many caves,
large and small. We off-saddled the horses, and got
into one of the holes just as the rain came down, as it
only does in this hilly land in summer.

While we were eating some biscuit and drinking

whisky, the Kafir signed to us to listen to something. Above the noise of the rain we heard the clatter of horses that were shod, proving that they had no Boer or Colonial riders, and, looking through the thick bush, we saw the khakis we had shot at, come for shelter like ourselves.

"Let us shoot them, Sarel," said the bloodthirsty Paul.

"Nay, that would be foolishness, for they are eight and we but three, and no doubt there are a thousand not far off."

I did not believe what I said, but I was resolved not to shed innocent blood if it was British.

"Let us go deeper into the cave," said I, and, much against their wills, Paul and the young kerel came in with me. The cave was long and narrow, and so dark that one standing at the entrance could not see into it many feet for the blackness.

"Where is the Kafir?" presently asked Paul, and I saw that he was not with us.

"He will be hiding under a bush," said I, knowing how these Dutch-bred natives fear the khakis.

It was more than an hour before the rain ceased, and during all that time we had heard the khakis laughing and talking about twenty yards from our cave. I had great work to prevent Paul from talking Scripture, for our being in a cave reminded him of the Bible story of the Adullamites, which he would tell me till I got angry.

"What is the good of telling these stories if they do not show us how to get safely away?" I asked in anger. "What happened to these Adullamites?"

Then Paul reproached me for my ignorance of the Bible, and made a long discourse on the evil that came to young Burghers through living in towns with Rooineks and Hollanders.

"But," said I at last, wishing to stop his preaching, "you don't tell me what became of the Adullamites."

Paul thought hard for a minute. "It is too dark to see, or I would read it," said he.

" Nay, but tell me."

" But I forget," answered he. And then it was my turn to reproach him ; and I should have preached an even longer sermon on the folly of old men pretending to know what they did not, had not a serious thing come to stop me.

The young kerel, Van Niekerk, had grown tired of hearing so much Bible talk, as youngsters do, and had crept out to see what the khakis were doing, as he had not heard them for some time, and the rain was nearly done.

He came back looking scared.

"Oom," said he, " the khakis have gone, and I cannot see our horses ; but by the spoor I think they have got them."

We ran out of the cave, having no thought of bullets in the face of this great calamity.

It was true. The khakis had gone, and there in the mud were plainly the tracks of our horses, which we knew through their being unshod, while those of the khakis were, like all Rooinek horses, shod, which was why they could not gallop over rough country after us Boers.

" Paul," said I, " you don't know what happened to the Adullamites in the cave, but I do know what has happened to us. We shall have to walk back to the laager, and perhaps die of hunger before we get there."

And Paul and young Van Niekerk sat down and wept, after the manner of tender-hearted Boers in great trouble.

I would not say a word till they had finished weeping, for it is not good to stay a Boer when his tears and groans are coming fast. When they had both ceased,—

"What shall we do, Paul?" I asked. " Let us follow and shoot them,"—for even my righteousness was not strong enough to stand the loss of my horse, which is only nature in an Afrikander.

" Sarel, you now say shoot when it is too late. If we had shot before we should not now be in this trouble," and the old man assailed me bitterly, so that I went out of the cave to escape his angry words and to get my rifle; but, lo! it was not where I had put it in the mouth of the cave, neither were there any saddles. Then I saw in a moment that that scoundrelly Kafir had taken them away.

"Who was that Kafir? Was he not caught with letters from the English?" I asked.

Paul remembered that it was so, and then we knew how we had been betrayed.

It was a sad party that left the kloof and climbed the hill to get back to laager, for a Boer cannot walk like Rooineks, although his feet are larger, but being born to the saddle he must ride.

When we reached the top of the ridge, falling often on the wet and slippery rocks, we saw far away the khakis leading our horses, and leading the pack-horse was our Kafir, carrying a rifle, which no Boer allows a Kafir to do.

"Look at that, Sarel," said Paul; "they steal our horses, and insult us by arming a Kafir in our sight! And these are the people that you would not have me shoot! It is a righteous judgment on you."

"And what about you?" I asked in anger.

"And on me for listening to the voice of the tempter."

It was quite fifty miles back to laager, over mountains and rough country full of rivers we did not know, and could not cross without horses, for this being the rainy season, the rivers were all very full. What was worse, there were no farms where we could get food, the very few there were being deserted. We dared not go into Kafir kraals unarmed, for all Natal Kafirs hate Boers, and would kill us or bring the khakis upon us.

When I thought on this, there came on me the wickedness of Paul in burning the farmhouse; and it became my turn to reproach him and make a Scripture discourse, which was not strong, however, for hunger was making me weak, and the thought that I should be more hungry still made me yet weaker;

but I could not help agreeing that all this suffering was a judgment for burning the farm.

How can I fully tell the misery we went through on that awful trek? It rained again that night, and became very cold, and we had no cave to shelter us. The boy crawled into an ant-bear hole, and came near to being drowned by the water that ran in, while Paul got bad rheumatics in the back, so that he could only groan and cry, while his Bible was wetted till some of the leaves fell out, which he took as a very bad sign.

At sun-up we passed on, very stiff and weak, and after an hour or two we saw a Kafir kraal of six huts, with mealie gardens and a few peach-trees. We lay down in the long grass and made a plan, for we were so hungry that fear of the Kafirs was nearly dead; and had we had the strength, we should have gone down and taken food by force, for we had eaten nothing but a biscuit the previous day, being anxious to find a good sleeping-place before we ate, which plan was upset by the appearance of the khakis.

We could see no men about the kraal, only a few women and very young children, for the men were perhaps all away with the British, who were ruining them by great pay, good food, and little work, which the Kafir in his heathenism loves.

We waited and watched, hoping that the rest might make us stronger, and that the women might go out of the kraal to the river for water, or to look after the cattle we could see grazing about a mile off. Then, if they left the kraal, we might go down, for there was certain to be mealies and perhaps milk, for we could see two cows with the cattle. But the women did not leave, so we sat on, very sick, and scorched by the sun. It was the longest day I ever knew, and the suffering was made worse by Paul's groans, and his reading all the doleful psalms with a jerky voice, stopping at every line to groan, while the boy Van Niekerk cried.

At last the sun went down, and in the fast-growing

darkness we crept with pain and fear towards the kraal, hoping at the worst to find some green peaches on the trees, it being yet early summer. And perhaps the Kafirs might be kind, if I told them I was English, I being often mistaken for one; but I feared for Paul, who was the roughest Taakhaar Boer that ever came out of the Waterberg.

We got among the peach-trees, and had begun to eat the hard green fruit, when the dogs scented us, and came barking furiously. Then followed the women and children with knobkerries and axes and sickles, and among them a very old man with an assegai.

Now the Natal Kafir cannot speak Dutch, the Natal people foolishly learning the Kafir language, instead of doing as the Boer does—make the Kafir learn the Taal. Therefore I could not speak to them, but only point to my mouth and say, "Niko mena skoff," which is kitchen Kafir for "Give me food," and with the exception of a few words of abuse, was all of the Zulu language I knew.

At first the women seemed afraid of us, and kept a short distance away, but when the old Kafir came up and talked to them, they came up to us, pushing and pulling us about.

I tried a few words in English on the old man, which he seemed to understand, for he answered, "Ikona Inglish; dam Dutch, where is your pass? come to tronk," and he led the way to the kraal, the women—as is always the case when there is trouble— making the most noise, and treating us most roughly. He led the way to the cattle kraal, and signed to us to lie on our backs, which we quite understood, but refused to do until the women pulled us down. Before I could quite understand what they were going to do, the women had put a big bamboo pole across our necks as we lay on our backs, and tied our wrists and necks to it, so that we could not move without great pain, for the plaited grass-rope and bits of hard leather reim they used hurt us much.

When we were all tied up, the women felt in our pockets and took our knives and other small things. But they did not find the General's letter, that being between my waistcoat and shirt; neither did they take Paul's Bible. Then they went away, a young girl throwing mealie cobs at our faces, and putting the dogs to bark at us.

This action of the girl set me thinking sad thoughts of Katrina, as but for her I should not be in this wretchedness; and I renewed my resolve never to go back to her again, though I feared she would not let me leave her, particularly if I became great,— though so far I saw no sign of that greatness that Paul had prophesied for me, and for once I was glad that his prophecy did not seem likely to be true.

My anger against Katrina became very hot, and I think I might have followed the pattern of young Van Niekerk and cried, had not the groaning and lamentations of Paul turned my wrath to him.

"What about your Bible now, Paul? will it show you how to cut grass-rope without a knife?" I asked in my anger.

"The Bible says nothing about white men being tied up by Kafirs," answered he, always ready to make his case good by Scripture. "The Bible tells us to destroy Kafirs, and if we had obeyed it, we should not now be tied up like oxen in the yoke, for we should have no Kafirs in the land except those that were our bondsmen; and now, instead, we are theirs."

I answered something very sharp and clever, for which I was afterwards sorry, for even while I spoke a great miracle was happening.

I have said that the dogs stayed behind to annoy us. Among them were two puppies, which had been for long quarrelling which should pull the bit of harness-strap with which my right hand was tied. They pulled and bit at it, as puppies will, until it got loose, and by much painful striving I contrived to get my right wrist free, and very soon both my neck and those of Paul and the boy were out of the yoke; and in half an hour we were more than two miles from the kraal, the dogs, however, following us and barking all the time. The Kafirs did not follow us, being, as we supposed, busy drinking Kafir beer.

We were still very weak, not so much for want of food—for he is no Boer who cannot go sixty hours without biting — but from the travelling afoot, to which we were not used, and the heart-soreness that comes of shame and anger; and puzzling all the time what story we should tell when we got back to the laager, for we dare not say we had been tied up in a cattle-kraal by Kafir women.

We came to the burned farm before sundown, and went up to it, hoping to find we knew not what; but the fire had done its work well, leaving little but the stones and iron-work. But in the stable, which had not been burned, we found that which again made Paul rejoice, and reproach me for my want of faith in the Bible; for we found why the baboons went there, it being not for hens' eggs, but to milk a cow, which, with her calf, had been overlooked in the trek, and was in the habit of coming to the stable at night. We got a little milk from her which strengthened us, and made us look more brightly at the future.

"We must take this cow and calf back to the laager," said Paul. "It will show that we have done something, even if we have lost our horses, and we shall at least have milk to keep us from dying on the journey."

So after a good night's rest in the stable, where we found a few mealies and contrived to boil them, we set out for the laager, driving the cow and calf, fearing all the time lest we should fall in with khaki scouts, for the country was more covered by them than I had thought. We travelled ten miles that day,—which was good, considering we had to drive the cow and calf,—slept that night in the grass, and reached the laager safe, but heart and body sore, about noon next day.

General Joubert had gone to visit the camps around

Ladysmith. Ben Viljoen was also away, and, fortunately, many of the Burghers who had been most unfriendly to me. Still there was a sufficient leaven of them remaining to influence the others, and Paul and I came in for much ridicule, which even the cow and calf did not appease, but add to. This treatment decided me to get away again as soon as I could get horses. The Van Niekerk kerel was too sick with fear to come again; but old Paul was quite willing, for, said he, "If wonders keep on happening as they have, you will soon begin to believe that I can interpret Scripture properly."

"Ja, Paul," I answered; "I do begin to see that you are not as other men; but you must burn no more farmhouses."

So with good horses, and a Kafir we could trust,— he having been in jail in Natal, and therefore hating the English,— we set out again next morning, my heart feeling light that I had not had to face General Joubert or Ben Viljoen, and deliverance from the bondage of the laager being in sight.

CHAPTER V.

*I redeem the errors of a bad start, and meet a girl and
a man who enter into my life.*

KNOWING the road now the better for the first journey,
and our Kafir, having been born in the north of Natal,
knowing the short paths, we made good travelling
towards the Berg, so that we were an hour on the
other side of the burnt farmhouse before we had to
off-saddle for the night. Paul was for going on to
the native kraal, shooting all the women, and burning
the huts by way of punishment for their treatment of
us; but I was afraid that by this time they might
have sent word to the British, who might be on the
look-out for us, so, Paul agreeing, we kept well away
and left vengeance to the Lord, which, as the end
showed, was wisdom,—though, when we were too far
away to return, Paul, as was his custom—which I
think he could not help—began to bewail that he
was not acting as the Bible told him he should with
the children of Ham and heathendom. His anger
became even greater when we saw, about two miles
off, a troop of cattle on the march, driven by four
Kafirs without rifles. Paul, being a true Boer, could
never see cattle not his own without wishing that they
were, and planning to get them; and he was for
shooting the Kafirs and hiding the cattle in a kloof
till we could come for them on the return journey.
It was a sore temptation even to me, and we discussed
it hard for half an hour. I was about to give way to
oblige Paul, when there came out from behind a kopjie

an escort of twenty khakis, who were following at a
foolishly great distance.

"Paul," said I, "where would we have been had
I listened to your words? I will put my law-learning
against your Bible, and always come out best," which
saying made Paul very angry, for, like all old Boers,
he could not see that young men could be wise and
know things unless they were predikants or doctors,
and sometimes lawyers; but I, not having been to
college, and being only what is called in the Transvaal a law-agent, Paul would never give me credit
for being learned in the law, for he did not know that
less than half the appeals against my cases were upheld by the High Court. But, being without education, he could not put proper value on this, and held
my judgment in light esteem. Therefore was I
always joyful when it happened, as it did just then,
that my way of thinking and of reading signs proved
more correct than his. But, for fear of making him
angry, I did not rejoice much over my victory, and
only kept it in mind to tell him when his opinion was
contrary to mine.

While we rode, a great purpose was being brought
to ripeness in my heart. I was thinking, first whether
I could get away safely to Maritzburg without Paul,
or, secondly, whether I could persuade the old man
to come with me; for in my secret heart I liked him
more than I disliked his preaching, and he being rich,
with only one unmarried boy who might be killed or
die with the British, and having three six thousand
morgen farms in the best part of the Waterberg and
nearly a thousand cattle, I hoped to keep him from
danger of being killed till I had persuaded him to
make a will, which he had not done for Bible reasons,
which was foolishness.

Now Paul had great notions on the strength of the
Boers, and was satisfied, both from the Bible and
from his own conceit, that the British would be driven
into the sea, as I shamefully confess I, in my deep
ignorance and through the deceit of those who misled

me, at first believed. But when I saw how fresh khakis rose from out of the sea to take the place of those we had killed, I began to feel uncertain. If, thought I, I can get Paul far enough into Natal, and let him see for himself that the khakis are as plentiful as mealies in a forage store, he will come to my way of thinking and save his life. But the great thing was how to get him away without his guessing my object. I dared not talk in a way to make him think I was not the oprecht Burgher I said I was, and the way he kept close by me when I went out of the laager, made me think he might be set to watch over me by my enemies, and particularly by Ben Viljoen, of whom he had great ideas, even to the extent of being a nuisance; for he carried with him printed copies of Ben's manifesto called "God and the Mauser," which he would read in full to those who could not get away from him. At Prinsloosdorp, before he went on commando, he did nothing but carry round and read this manifesto, holding men in corners till he had finished. Before long, his passing down the street was like to the passage of the small-pox ambulance, for when the Burghers saw him coming they turned back or went into the canteens, leaving the street quite empty. Therefore it will be seen I had a great trial in Paul, and his conversion was the greatest task I had ever begun, for I was sore afraid that he would convert me instead, as he could talk much faster and longer than I, and when out-argued, always fell back on the Bible, from which it was hard to move him, as the predikants had found, when he criticised their sermons and quoted the Bible against them, as was his happiness and undoing in every kerk to which he had belonged.

Now I have seen in my passage through life that good fortune cometh most to the man who, seeing a sign of good, follows it up, like one who, searching for lost cattle, follows every spoor till he comes to the right one. My many good fortunes have all been brought about by doing this, though it is only those who have superior education and sharpness who can know which is the right spoor to follow.

It happened, as if it had been arranged by Providence, that we should come upon a Zulu witch-doctor hiding in the long grass in the veld as we passed. We stopped and made him strip, thinking to find letters from the British, which, if we had discovered, I quickly planned to deceive Paul upon, reading them to the advantage of the British. But we found nothing but Kafir medicines and the many childish trifles these heathen carry, and among them was the *dol oss*, or bones with which they read fortunes, find lost cattle, and tell the future. Herein was one of those spoors that I have spoken of, and being superior in education to Paul, I used it to my advantage.

"Oom," said I, "as we are on a great venture, let us make this witch-doctor throw the *dol oss* so that he may read the end."

I knew that when on his farm, Paul, being a Waterberg Boer, was certain to have used these Kafirs to find his lost cattle, so what I said fell on fruitful ground, particularly as the Kafir spoke the Taal.

"Good," said he; "let us ask the Kafir if we shall get fortune and greatness out of this journey."

I put the questions, and the Kafir threw the bones and noted how they fell upon the ground, and after great thought read the answers, which for the most part were such as Paul wanted, and pleased me, for they fitted in with my plan.

Now it happens that there are often among Kafir witch-doctors impostors, even as there are among white doctors, and I could see what Paul could not, that this Kafir was not a qualified witch-doctor, but had that cunning which enabled him to see quickly the sort of answer that was wanted to the questions, a gift he had in great abundance; so I planned to use it to my own profit, being skilful in the art of putting artful questions through my training as public prosecutor.

When it came to my turn to put questions, Paul having had the asking most of the time, I asked—

"Will the old baas stay with me all through my passage?"

"Ja," said the Kafir.

"Will my plans come out to my good?"

"Ja."

"Will it be good for the old baas to listen to my words?"

"Ja."

"Always? even when his words are not as mine?"

"Ja; always."

And so I spoke in this strain, generally getting the answers I wanted. Then, having got enough, we took an English sovereign which the Kafir had sewed up in his blanket, telling him that it was wrong not to carry Kruger money, and having given him some tobacco to make snuff, we ordered him to follow behind us, lest he should see khakis on the way he was going and give information against us. He made a great outcry, but the sight of our rifles and sjamboks made him cease complaining and follow us silently, being thereby rightly punished for his pretending to be a qualified witch-doctor, I being always strongly against such when I was public prosecutor.

But although I could see that Paul was much worked upon by the prophecies of the witch-doctor, he was not altogether satisfied, and I felt it would be wisdom for me to make my case stronger if I wanted to get the mastery over Paul. So I considered carefully as we rode, and at last thought out a great plan.

It was the custom of Paul when in doubt about a thing to open his Bible at random with his eyes shut, and opening them quickly, read the verse on which they fell, a habit he had learned when on commando with Paul Kruger in the early days. It was on this I planned to work. So when we had off-saddled in the heat of the day, and Paul slept under a thorn-bush, I secretly got his Bible, and with great pains and much searching found the verse, "Out of the mouths of babes and sucklings shall come forth wisdom," which in the High Dutch of our Bible reads very much stronger than in the English. Then I took a big ant, which is a Bible insect, being well spoken of by Solomon, and putting him on this verse, shut the book and crushed him, so that his body lay on the verse. Next I put a piece of twig between the leaves, so that when Paul took the book it would most likely open at that spot.

The plan worked with great smoothness as I had hoped, for when Paul awoke he saw the Bible lying by his side and took it up, when it fell open where I had marked it. Paul first tried to rub off the mark, then read the verse to himself.

"What is that mark, Paul?" I asked.

"It is a dead ant."

"And what is the verse he lies on?"

Paul read it.

"Is not that strange? what does it mean?" I asked.

The old man did not answer for a little while, then he said—

"It means, Sarel, that I should keep the book in my pocket."

But for all his short answer I could read that the seed had been sown on fruitful ground, and would bring forth a hundredfold.

There was another matter that filled my mind much on the journey, and that was to know what was in the letter I was carrying. There was always smouldering in my breast a secret fear that Paul was watching me on behalf of Ben Viljoen, who had never forgiven me for escaping the court-martial. If I could know the inside of that letter much might become clear that was now dark; and further, it would make me of more importance in the eyes of the Free State commandant to whom I had to deliver the letter if I could let him see that I was so far in the secrets of General Joubert as to know the inside of secret despatches. I had often looked close at the large envelope, but it was not easy to open, although there was no wax seal upon the flap,

as would have been the case had it been written in a
Pretoria office. I thought very much on this letter
that night while Paul was sleeping, and a providential
chance gave me the opportunity to satisfy my desire,
for, quite by accident, I left it lying outside my blanket.
By sunrise the dew had wetted the gum so that it
opened easily.

I read it over several times before I could fully take
in the joy it gave me. After giving the Free State
commandant instructions to make a diversion into
Natal and destroy the farmhouses of certain Natal
Boers who had not joined the Transvaalers, as they
ought, being Burghers of the Republic, the letter went
on to say that I, the bearer, being a great friend of the
General, he wished the commandant if possible to give
me something to do with his commando, and to see
that I had a chance of doing good work.

These kind words from Piet Joubert made me feel
sorry that I had planned to leave his commando, and
I rode lightly and brightly the rest of that morning till
Paul asked me what made me so happy.

"It is a good dream I had, Oom. I dreamt that,
like Joseph in Egypt, I was set in high places, and "—
this I said to please Paul and keep his friendship—" it
all came through your riding the same path as I."

"And what like was the dream? because, you know,
Sarel, dreams are strange things, and it is not given to
all young men to interpret them properly, for there are
more wise old men than wise Josephs."

Now I had not prepared this dream, and not being
ready at lies like most Afrikanders, I could not plan a
good one quickly.

"It was not a Bible dream," said I.

"But how do you know? Any dream may be made
a Bible dream if you know how to interpret it, as I do."

"It was cloudy and misty, as one sees the Drakensberg at sunset."

"But with a good glass one can see the snow and
the krantzes, and even the baboons; and I have such
glasses here,"—and he touched the Bible which he

carried in his coat side-pocket. "Tell me your dream, Sarel. You say I am in it; let me see for myself."

I could not get away from this, therefore I began to invent a dream, telling it slowly, as if I was loth to make myself appear as great as the dream made me, but really to gain time to build it up nicely.

"I dreamt that I was a young ox that had lost my herd, and after much wandering in strange veld, I found it. But when I wanted to graze with them the other cattle horned me, and drove me out of the herd, saying that I made the grass bad for them and had brought the rinderpest and red-water from the strange veld in which I had been grazing; so I had to hide in the kloofs and dongas, and eat the sour grass all alone."

"That is a Bible dream so far," said Paul; "for was not Nebuchadnezzar driven out to eat grass for his sins?"

"But the Bible says nothing about sour grass, nor had I done any wrong to the rest of the herd," said I.

"Go on telling, and let me be the judge," said Paul.

"While I was in misery, there came up an old trek-ox which had pulled in the same span for many years."

"That's me," said Paul.

"And this ox took pity on me, and made me feed near him; and when the other oxen would drive me away, he fought them, and made them so afraid that they left me alone. And I grew fat on the good grass, till the Boer who owned the herd made me after-ox with the old one who had stood my friend, and we pulled together in the same yoke."

"That's all right so far, go on."

"One day we were pulling the waggon over a very bad place, and even the old ox grew tired; but I pulled so hard and well that the waggon was lifted out of the rut. The Boer was very pleased, and said to the voor-louper, 'This is a good after-ox. I shall put him in the span only when the waggon comes to a bad place; till then he shall always be a led ox and do no hard work, for he is too good to spoil.' And the Boer did this, and I grew fatter and stronger."

"And what became of the old trek-ox?" asked Paul.

"I looked after him, and when I had to pull in the same yoke with him, I pulled doubly hard; and when the nights were cold and the wind high, I lay on the wind side of him and kept him warm."

Paul rode along some time without speaking, only smoking hard. When he broke silence he said—

"Sarel, that was a very good dream; but you see the old ox was the better ox, otherwise the farmer would not have kept him always in the yoke both for the good roads and the bad. The young ox was not put on the trek-chain except when the road was bad; so some day, when he knew that a bad piece of road was coming he would take advantage of being loose and run away into the veld to escape hard pulling, and when he was caught, as he would be, he would be kept always in the yoke and have no more light work."

I did not like this interpretation, but Paul ever read dreams to suit himself; so I would not talk against him, but I could not but be unhappy over the ending that Paul put to it, and I rode on in silence.

While we rode, we suddenly sighted a farmhouse on the low ground a mile away, with Kafirs scattered about, by which we knew that the farmer had not run away. We off-saddled and lay in the grass while we sent the Kafir ahead on foot to find out all he could, and if it would be safe for us to go on. He had been gone fully an hour, and Paul and I were nearly asleep in the hot sun, when the sound of horses' hoofs cantering towards us made us reach for our rifles, and look out through the grass without showing ourselves. There came over the ridge a young girl on a Basuto pony, riding on a man's saddle with one stirrup crossed over, as women ride when they have no side-saddle. She was about eighteen, and a Natal girl, for she had nothing of the Boer maiden about her except the clear complexion our missies have till they get married. Besides, she was dressed in clothes that had been made for her and not bought out of the store window, and wore gloves, which no Boer girl does; and when she spoke, it was the Taal as is spoken by girls who live in Natal or have been to school at Bloemfontein or Johannesburg.

"I see you are oprecht Boeren," said she; "I am Charlotte Brink, and my pa is Andries Brink of Sterkfontein. He is sick in bed and cannot go on commando, though his heart is there. Won't you come to the house? There are no rooibaatjies nearer than Mooi River and Ladysmith."

"How did you know we were here?" I asked.

"An old Kafir witch-doctor came to our place this morning. He threw the *dol oss* for you on the road."

"Shall we go?" I asked Paul.

"Ja; Brink is a good name. All the Brinks are good, as the Coetzees are bad. There was never a bad Brink nor a good Coetzee."

Suddenly my heart gave a thump, for I remembered that Brink was one of the names of the renegade Natal Boers mentioned in the letter I carried; and I felt sorry that I had not told Paul that I had read it, for I did not know whether we could trust Andries Brink after this.

"If your pa is an oprecht Burgher, why have the English not driven him away?" I asked.

"Ach, man, pa is too slim. He tells them he is a loyal Natalian, and they are such fools they believe him."

Just then our Kafir returned with a message from Andries, saying all was safe, and we were to come and drink coffee, so we rode with the girl to the place.

As we came in sight of the front of the house, I saw a big man go quickly off the stoep into the house.

"You have other men there," said I to the girl.

"Nay," answered she, "only pa."

I did not say what I had seen, though I thought it strange, and I could not get close enough to tell Paul what I had seen. When we reached the house we found Andries in bed, but looking not a bit sick, and having his clothes on, which I did not put much weight on, knowing that old Boers do not always undress when they sleep.

He made much of us, telling us all the war news, but I noticed that he did not ask us whence we had come or where we were going, as a Boer always does before he begins to talk of other things. Later on he spoke in a way that showed that he knew much about us and the commando we had left, all of which was a great bewilderment to me at the time.

"You know much for a sick man who cannot ride out," said I.

"Ja," answered he; "four of my trusted Kafirs are running despatches for the English out of Ladysmith, and they mostly come off the road to this place, so that I can read all the letters. I copy them and send them to Kemp's and Schoeman's commandos."

This surprised me, but it explained why he stayed here instead of going on commando.

"Are you very sick?" I asked after a bit.

"Ja. I have an internal complaint that keeps me from riding; but good cometh out of evil, as the Bible says, for I am more useful to our people here than I should be on commando. My eyes are also bad, so that I cannot shoot."

As Andries quoted the Bible, I saw Paul's face light up. He had been very quiet through all the talk, saying but little, but all the time watching Andries as if to read him. But so soon as he heard that bit of Scripture I could see his heart open to Andries, and he began to talk, and it became my turn to listen and watch. Before six cups of coffee had been drunk and his pipe filled twice, Paul had told all that he knew of the doings of our commandos, till I was surprised that he knew so much, for although I had been in the laager with him, I had not heard a quarter of what he told, which showed me that the old man must be deeper in the secrets of the commandants than I. The thought made me angry, and in my wrath I did as men who are angry often do, I said a foolish thing, for I asked, "Are you sure of all this?"

Then it was his turn to be wrathful and foolish, for he turned on me, and with the manner of a man who has been doubted and is anxious to convince one that he knows much, he told me many things of the secret doings of the commando, and of his friendship with Ben Viljoen, finishing every story with the words, " Would they tell that to a young ox? " by which I saw that my dream had greatly angered him. Sorely was I tempted to answer something about old oxen being often too foolish to know enough not to eat the poison tulp-weed in the veld; but I feared to make an enemy of him, for I could see that he was already jealous of me, and should it happen that Andries was the important man he made himself out to be, Paul might damage me in his eyes, and I had not forgotten the affair of the poisoned whisky and the court-martial. So I kept my tongue in the yoke, and went outside, that my anger at his looseness of speech might not provoke me to further indiscretion.

Now while I walked about at the back of the house, I looked about me to see if our horses were being cared for, but I could see neither them nor our Kafir. I thought nothing of that at the time, knowing how Kafirs, as soon as they get to a farmhouse, go to the kitchen or the quarters of the kitchen boy. So, instead of seeking farther, I went back to the room, thinking after all I had better stay to keep a check on Paul's slippery tongue.

When I reached the front of the house, Paul was standing in the bit of garden. " Sarel," said he, " we have done well in coming here. Andries is an oprecht Afrikander, and can help us to greatness, for he is giving us copies of the Ladysmith letters to take back, and a lot of good secrets that will make Piet Joubert rejoice."

" Paul," said I, " you may be old and wise, but you have also the foolishness of old men. How know you that Andries is oprecht? "

" Because I have looked through him, and he knows the Bible."

"But many schelm Burghers know the Bible well."

"Ja, Sarel; but I know when a man reads his Bible for wisdom, and not for the ears of the predikant. Andries is meek also, and knows when he finds a man who reads the Bible better than he does himself, like me. He has but just now told me I ought to be predikant."

"Paul," said I in anger, "you are easily verneuked. You do not know as I do that Andries Brink is no oprecht Afrikander but a renegade Transvaal Boer, and he has deceived you with his Bible language."

"Sarel, you are still only a young calf, or you would know that Ben Viljoen and Commandant Kemp do not trust men without reason, and Ben trusts me, while Kemp trusts Andries."

"And a greater than they trusts me," I answered in triumph.

"You speak foolishness," said Paul, and he laughed a scornful laugh. "I suppose it is Piet Joubert and Paul Kruger."

"It is Piet Joubert."

Again Paul laughed saying, "Sarel, your dream has filled your head like whisky."

"What would you say if I could show it you in his own handwriting?" said I, my anger roused at the unbelief of the old man. Paul only laughed again and turned to walk away. I went after him and shook him by the arm.

"You must know it," said I, "for you know all the secrets of Piet Joubert." This I said with bitter sarcasm.

"I know that you are a suspect, and that I have to watch you that you do not run away," said he, still more sneeringly.

Then my heart thumped, and the red blood came before my eyes.

"You schelm! you traitor! I will make you a liar by the General's own words," and I put my hand to my hip-pocket to get the letter. It was not there, and after a moment of fright and heart-thumping, I remembered that I had put it carefully in my saddle-bag.

"But you have not seen the inside of the letter," said Paul.

"I have; the General showed it to me."

"You lie; show it to me," answered Paul.

"It is in my saddle-bag; come and see," and together we went to search for the horses and our Kafir.

As before, there was no sign of Kafir or horses, so I found the Kafir house. There on the floor lay our boy, Sixpence, stupid, sleepy, and drunk. I kicked and sjamboked him till he sat up.

"Where are the horses and the saddles?" I shouted, but he could only mutter and fall back with eyes closed. I sjamboked him till I cut the shirt off his back, and then only partly awakened him, so deeply had he drunk of the Kafir rum out of the bottle that lay empty on the floor.

The screams of the boy brought out other Kafirs, and presently Charlotte came riding up, her horse wet and distressed with hard riding.

"We want our horses and saddles, for we must go," said I firmly.

"But the horses are in the kraal," answered she.

"Nay, we have looked there; but where are our saddles?"

The girl spoke to one of the Kafirs in Zulu, who answered her.

"The horses have gone to graze in the vlei; I will send for them," said she, and she sent a Kafir off.

"But where are the saddles?" I asked.

Charlotte said she would find them, and, dismounting, went to the stable, Paul and I following. When I reached the door, the girl was uncovering my saddle from a heap of forage. I rushed at it, and took out the letter from the saddle-bag, joyful to find it safe. After abusing the Kafir for causing so much trouble by covering the saddles with forage, the girl went into the house.

"Now, Paul, read that, and say whether you still

think me a calf and a liar," and I handed him the letter.

Never did I see a man's face change so quickly.

"Sarel," said he, "this is a great stumble we have made. Let us get out of this sluit before we get further stuck. Do you think the girl has read this?"

That was my great fear, and I knew not what to say. Before I could make up an answer, Charlotte came to the stable and told us her father wanted to see both of us, and we all went to the sleeping-room of Andries.

A Kafir was there, taking out from his blanket pieces of paper curled round very small, others from the hollow quills of the feathers in his head-dress, and out of the curled wool of his head—in short, from all sorts of strange hiding-places about his person. The last he brought out was from the handle of the little wooden snuff-spoon that Kafirs carry through the hole in the lobe of their ears, the handle being purposely made hollow to receive it.

Andries took up some of these little letters and, unrolling them with great care, gave them to me to read. They were written very small on thin paper, and were hard to read; but I made them out to be letters from English people in Ladysmith to their friends in Durban, Maritzburg, and other places in Natal.

"Now you see how I get my news," said Andries, and my suspicion of him faded away, for if he were a real friend to the English, and not an oprecht Boer, why should he open their letters?

"Charlotte will copy all of these that are of use, and you can take them to General Joubert," Andries went on; "she is very clever, and can read the secret writings such as this one," and he showed us one letter that was all figures and strange words and signs, like the shorthand writers make, only not so elegant. I knew it for what is called cipher, having seen such in the office at Pretoria.

Having read all the letters and put on one side those that he thought good enough to copy, Andries began to tell us the many good services he had done the Boers; and he talked so long and made himself such a good oprecht Burgher that Paul began to be quite friendly again: but all the time I was impatient to get the old man away, that I might talk to him and have this matter settled, for his words about my being a suspect that he was watching had come as a great blow, and I felt like one who being innocent is accused of crime, and knows not what to answer.

Often I said we must be going; but Andries was ever ready with some delay, such as, the boy had not yet found our horses, or Charlotte had not begun to copy the letters for us to carry back, talking so much in the intervals that the time passed quickly. Then he got out some brandy, which at first I would not touch, until Andries said if I did not drink with him he would begin to think I was no oprecht Burgher, or I would not insult another by refusing to drink with him in his house, especially as he was sick.

After such words so plainly put I could not refuse, but I was careful to drink very little, and to put in plenty of water when I found that the room began to turn round, which was not for nearly three hours. As for Paul, he had no such discreetness, but drank all that Andries poured into his glass, and his tongue ran loosely and so fast that I had no time to stop him. Suddenly a bright thought struck me, which I put into words—

" Are you the only Brink hereabouts ? "

" Nay," answered Andries; " there is my cousin Jan Brink at Braakpan; he is a great schelm, for he is with the English, and people who do not know me mix us up."

" I told you you were mistaken," blurted out Paul, and the foolish old man told Andries what the letter had said about him being a renegade whose farm was to be burnt.

Andries said bluntly that we were making fun of him, and that he did not believe there was any such letter, and he made so much of this that much against my will I showed him the letter of General Joubert. As he read it, it somehow seemed to me that his manner was that of a man who read a thing knowing what was coming.

"It is my cousin Jan the General means," said Andries quietly, when he had read the letter very carefully. "I am glad that his place is to be burned, for it serves him right."

"Where is his place?" I asked.

Andries told us it was about twenty miles off our road towards the British lines.

It was well on into afternoon before the Kafir had found our horses. Andries tried hard to get us to stay the night, and Paul was quite willing, for I saw he had fallen under the spell of Andries and supported him in all he said, till the brandy having reached my old complaint, and I feeling very giddy when I tried to sit in the saddle, I at last gave way and consented to rest on the sofa till I was better, which I did, waking up to have some supper, and find Andries, Paul, and Charlotte talking and laughing gaily. Feeling better I got up, and had some more brandy, and I remembered no more till morning, when Paul came to tell me it was time to go. So with a farewell drink of brandy, and taking the copied letters in my saddle-bag, we rode off towards the Berg, which we reckoned to reach well before sundown.

CHAPTER VI.

*Shows how I skilfully evaded having to slaughter Britishers,
and am shown the path to fortune.*

As soon as we had got well out on the road I opened
up with Paul on the subject that was making my heart
sore. He had been talking fast on other matters, as
one who tries to put off a man who would come close
with unpleasant truths.

"Paul," said I, quite calmly, "what did you mean
by saying that I was suspect, and that you were
watching me?"

"Ach, Sarel, did I not say there is little wisdom in
young men? I said only what was talk in the laager,
for you make me angry when you decry the wisdom
of men old enough to be your grandfather. In the
old days of the Great Trek they would have tied you
to the waggon-wheel for being only half as pert. I
remember——" and then he told a long story of a
young kerel who would not listen to the words of
the old men and got eaten by a lion.

"These be children's stories," said I, trying hard
not to be angry. "Tell me truly, are you watching
me for Ben Viljoen?"

"Sarel, if you were suspect, would the General trust
you with his letter, and let you know beforehand what
was in it? And why should he give it to you and
not to me if you are suspect?"

That was the great difficulty that was making me
think the story of my being watched was false, and
immediately the dust fell from my eyes and the

hardness went out of my heart, and in my gladness
I told Paul that I believed him, and would not again
think him a liar.

" And do you believe that Andries Brink is an
oprecht Burgher ? " he asked.

" Ja, for the matter of those letters show it," said
I, " even more than his soft speech, for any man may
say he is your friend, but not all can prove it by
deeds." And at this speech Paul was very pleased,
for his belief in Andries was very great.

Just then I turned to see how our Kafir was riding,
for he was not yet sober, and very sore from the rebuke
I had given him with the sjambok. As I looked, my
eyes saw a strange sight, for about five miles away,
going towards where Andries had shown us the
English pickets, was a girl on a very fast horse.

" Is that Charlotte Brink, Paul ? "

He looked hard for some time, and then looked at
me without speaking. When he answered he said, as
one who does not believe his own words—

" She is after the cattle."

" What are Andries' cattle doing five miles from his
farm in war-time ? " I asked.

Paul was again quiet, so I followed up what was in
my mind.

" And what was sick Andries doing on the stoep
when we rode up, if he was too sick to get out of
bed ? " and I told Paul what I had seen, but still the
old man was silent.

" And what about his cousin ? Did you ever hear
that he had one ? "

" That you should answer," said Paul, " for were you
not in Natal more than a year finding out and stirring
up the oprecht Afrikanders ? "

This was meant as a sneer at my absence from the
Transvaal, but in his ignorance Paul did not see that
he had made a great point for me.

" Certainly," said I ; " it is because I have been in
Natal looking for oprecht Burghers that I know
Andries has no cousin hereabouts, and that it is he

against whom the General makes warning. That is why he did not think it needful to put the full name. If there had been two Brinks near one another, he would have said which was meant. Besides, is it not strange that the General did not tell us to visit Andries and learn things from him?"

"Nay, Sarel, his place is far out of our road, and we should not have seen it if the girl had not met us," said Paul.

"And she came on purpose to trap us and find what we were doing," answered I.

"Why did you not say all this sooner?"

"What was the use, when you had put your Bible faith in Andries, and had told him all there was to tell? Vrachter, Paul, but he turned you inside out and sucked you like an orange—and you a wise old trek-ox!"

Then up sprang Paul's wrath, and he re-said nearly all the offensive things he had before mentioned regarding me, except that he did not say that I was suspect.

When he had made an end of his abuse, he checked his horse and followed on slowly.

"Paul," I shouted, "you need not come on, for it will only make your heart sore to see my advancement! Go back to your friend Andries."

Now, as I have before said, there comes in the lives of all men who take up great and serious things, certain sudden diverting of the path, which if properly followed leads to success. Such a case came upon me just then, a beautiful diversion that placed in my power the man of whom I was most in fear.

As I galloped away, half in derision, and half in hopes that Paul would take me at my word and think that I meant to leave him, I came upon the edge of the hill, and saw within an easy range below, about thirty khakis, riding so loosely that at first I took them for Colonial Volunteers, who ride much like Boers. I signalled to Paul and the Kafir to get back, while I turned below the ridge to get out of sight.

But Paul being naturally pig-headed, and hating to take even a life-saving warning from a young man, came riding up to the edge of the ridge and saw what I had seen.

" Let us shoot," said he, jumping off his horse, and leading it back out of sight.

" Nay, Paul, they are too many," said I.

" But they cannot see us, nor can they climb the ridge because of the stones."

I moved away without answering.

" Go, schelm suspect! go join them, and I will shoot!" shouted Paul.

I rode fast away, not being sure whether he meant to shoot me or the khakis, for he was full of pale wrathfulness. Next moment there came the sound of Paul's mauser.

" He has killed a khaki, baas," said the Kafir, who was looking over the ridge.

Nine times did Paul shoot, and the Kafir called out as a man was shot till four were hit—and three horses, while the rest were riding hard out of range, seeing nothing to fire at in return. They rode in a line with the foot of the ridge, and as they came past where I lay I heard words in the Taal, and looking closer, my heart gave a thump, for I saw they were Boers in khaki.

Quickly I mounted and rode up to Paul, who was seeking another point to fire from.

" You foolish old schelm, it is your own people you are killing," said I, and just at that moment, as if to help my words, we plainly heard a Boer lying wounded below the ridge call out in the Taal, " Come and stop my bleeding, kerels, or I die."

Paul stood as one drunk and dazed. Before he could say a word I began—

" And now, you old fool, listen to the bleatings of a calf. If these Boers find that you shot them you are a dead man. Now do as I tell you. Fire slowly, as if you are shooting at khakis running away; then, when we have shot enough, we will go to these wounded men and tell them we have driven off the British, whom we saw attacking, and you will be saved. But mind, Paul, if you talk loosely or drink whisky, or do anything I tell you not to do, I shall tell them what you have done, and our Kafir, Sixpence, will bear me out."

"You have learned wisdom from the old ox," said Paul, his pride even in calamity not letting me have credit for doing anything clever without his help.

So we fired several shots slowly, as Boers shoot when sure of their aim, and then went down to the wounded men below, telling the Kafir as we went what our plan was, for he had seen Paul's great blunder, and promising to kill him if he said otherwise.

We found two Boers dead, one dying, and the fourth shot through the fleshy part of the neck, but not dangerously. All four had been hit on or near the head, and I called Paul's attention to this.

"Man, but I am a great shot!" exclaimed the foolish old fellow, whose pride was consuming him. The wounded man, whose neck I was bandaging, heard Paul's boast.

"What means he?" he asked; "how came he to shoot?"

"You misunderstand," said I; "he means that he is quite as good a shot as these British, for the last khakis he shot were all hit as you are."

Paul was going to say something, but I signed him to be quiet, and I think the wounded Boer was satisfied. At any rate Providence came to the help of the foolish old man, for at that moment the blood rushed badly from the wound, choking the man, for he died in a minute, and we were spared the trouble of carrying him away.

The other and more wounded Boer was being helped by Paul. He was also dying fast, but he could not forget his family.

"Paul," said he, when he had asked the old man his name and district, "there are twenty-five sovereigns in the pouch of Sannie Plessis lying dead there.

Take it, and send it to my poor wife if I die; if not, you and I will divide it."

Paul answered that he would do this, for he himself often had tender thoughts for his own family, and would not go to fight Kafirs for fear of leaving his son an orphan.

I had sent the Kafir after the retreating Boers to bring them back, and very carefully they returned, making the Kafir ride well in front, with their rifles pointed at him so as to shoot if he were a false Kafir.

When they found all as he had said, they told us they were part of a Johannesburg commando, and were looking for British transports. Their commandant was one Frikkie Snyman, a big blustering town Boer, who talked all the time of the khakis he had killed and the great things he had done.

"Before you came up," said he, "we had killed twenty of these khakis, and we should have finished them if you had not come and interfered by driving them away. We were going round the kopjie to cut them off, as we could not ride up it."

"Won't you go back and see if there is anything worth taking off the dead bodies?" I asked.

"Nay, it is not worth it: those khakis have nothing we want, and no money. At the last fight we had yesterday, we wasted an hour in going over one hundred dead bodies, and found not even a Bible."

"I think you are right," said I, "for the bodies look only fit for the vultures. It would be waste of time to go to them."

Snyman looked at me sideways, as if he guessed I was secretly laughing at him for a great liar; then, without any remark from me to start him, he said very roughly if we joined his commando we could not have any share of the loot.

It was time for me to show this vain and boastful creature that I was of equal importance with himself. So I showed him the envelope of the letter I was carrying.

"Ach, man, but why did they not send a Kafir with

it ? " he answered. " They know the country, and can even get through our lines into Ladysmith."

" General Joubert does not take Kafirs into his secrets, although some commandants may," said I, with great bite in my words and manner.

Snyman turned on me as if he would have killed me, for I did not then know how hard I had hit him by my sarcasm, he being one of those low Afrikanders who had once taken a Kafir wife, and was held in low esteem therefor throughout his district. I believe if he had not been made afraid by the sight of the letter I carried he would have shot me on the spot. But I could see that his commando loved him little, and were secretly glad that I had sneered at him, so I felt no fear.

" Good-bye, commandant. How many khakis shall I tell the General I saw you kill? Better go up and count them." And Paul and I rode off, expecting every moment to find a bullet following us.

" He is a nice fellow to be commandant, when there are men like you and me, Paul, who are not even corporals."

" Ja, Sarel ; and now I shall punish him, for I shall not send that money to the wife of the dead Burgher, but you and I shall divide it," and he took out the purse, which was covered with blood.

There was in it twenty-five pounds.

" Have you half-a-sovereign, Sarel ? " asked Paul, when he had counted the money.

" Nay."

" Then must I give you thirteen pounds, as I too have no half-sovereign."

Now this was only a small thing, but it was as a feather showing the way the wind blew; for had he not been afraid of me, Paul would have kept the thirteen pounds and made me take the twelve, I being the younger. So, feeling I was master, I followed him up to make my mastery felt.

" I wonder what Snyman would have done if he knew you shot those Burghers," said I.

Paul answered nothing.

"And what a good thing it was he was not there when you so foolishly boasted about your good shooting."

Again Paul kept silence. After a bit he answered very quietly, looking at me sideways the while—

"Sarel, is it not more likely that he would have believed that the shooting was done by one who was not an oprecht Burgher—say one who had tried to run away?"

It was my turn to say nothing, but to think, for I saw by that answer that Paul was even yet unrepentant, and did not mean what he had said when he professed sorrow and promised not to believe that I was a suspect. And these thoughts made me again hear the secret voice bidding me come out from among them. So I planned to speak no more, as if to show my mastery, but to wait until we met the Free State commando, when I would take my fate boldly in my hands and let Paul see who was the real master, for I feared him little in the face of General Joubert's letter.

That evening at sundown we met the pickets of the commando, and an hour later were in their camp. Their commandant was Johannes Birkenfeld, an educated Free Stater who had been in the Free State Raad, and was opposed to the war from the first. When he had read my letter, he replied angrily—

"It is the old story. You verdomde Transvaalers mean us to do all the voorlouping, while you ride on the soft mattresses in the waggon. And now Piet Joubert wants to make cattle-thieves of us. Are there not men in your commando more fitted for the work?"

"Sarel is," put in Paul; "he is an Erasmus, and they are very good judges of horses that belong to other men."

When I afterwards rebuked Paul for saying this, the foolish old man said he only meant to put in a good word for me.

Somehow I did not like Birkenfeld. I did not like
the haughty way in which he spoke, nor the way he
dressed, which was more like a rich Burgher going to
Nachtmaal in a town than a commandant in war-
time; for he was very clean, as if he washed every day,
and wore new clothes, and rode a horse that I could
see had been cleaned and combed. Most of his
Burghers, too, were very clean, and rode horses that
were fat, and they regarded Paul curiously, never having before seen a real rough Taakhaar Boer perhaps,
for the Free Staters are vain and look upon themselves
as very superior to Transvaalers, because they can
mostly read, and put much thought and care on good
dressing for themselves and their children.

After a time, when we had had coffee, Birkenfeld
grew tamer, and asked many questions quite civilly
about General Joubert, and Ben Viljoen, and other
commandants, most of whom it seems were strangers
to him; for much as he prided himself on his superior
knowledge of things, he had never yet been in Pretoria,
and only once in Johannesburg, so that in truth he
was most ignorant.

" So you know all these renegade Burghers, Sarel ? "
he asked.

" Ja," said Paul, always ready to answer for me, as a
parent answers for his child.

" Then must you guide my commando, for we start
at sun-up to-morrow, and you must show us all these
places."

This was not what I wished, for it meant that I
should have to conspire against the English.

When we were alone, I reproached Paul for having
said what he did, when he made the stupid answer I
have already recorded,—that he did it to advance me,
when I well knew it was to expose my ignorance of
the thing I had made my boast; for it was vain to
keep Paul from seeing that I knew very little of Natal,
at least of the part we were now in.

That night I had my revenge, for when Paul got out
his Bible and wanted to read aloud I said, " Kerels,

he should not be called Paul, but Jeremiah, for he only
foretells misfortune," at which the Burghers all laughed,
and would not hear him.

But Paul never let any one else have the last word.

"Ja, kerels," said he, "I am indeed like Jeremiah,
for he was always warning the children of Israel against
the false prophets who would lead them astray."

"And who is the false prophet?" I asked, rather
foolishly.

"Have you not read of wolves in sheep's clothing?"
answered Paul; and I was silent, for I had a fore-
warning that his words might come true sooner than
he expected, as, after the unfriendly words of Commandant Birkenfeld, I had secretly planned to do all
I could to put a skid on the looting of farms, whether
of renegade Burghers or Natalians.

Next morning at sun-up the commando was on the
way, nearly 400 strong. We took a roundabout route
to avoid the khakis, who were not anywhere near, for
Paul and I had to tell the story of the affair of
Snyman, lest the commandant should hear of it
from other lips. Paul and I got great credit for having driven off the British, but stupid old Paul could
not keep to the right number. We had arranged
between us that there were ninety-six khakis, but Paul
could remember only the nine, so that sometimes it
was ninety-six, then sixty-nine, and once nine hundred
and six, which made him look very foolish, and most
of the Burghers began to have doubts.

It was nearly noon next day when we came in sight
of Andries Brink's place, I having led the commando
that way quite against my intention. When I saw
where we were I began to feel anxious, for I wondered
what Andries would do and say in the presence of a
big commando and a man like Birkenfeld, who was
not easily deceived.

While I was thinking over this, Paul called to me,
"Here comes Charlotte," and right into the commando
rode the girl on a big black horse. She came close up
to where I rode, but took no more notice than if I had

been a stranger as she asked of the next man, " Who is your commandant ? "

Paul, with his usual officiousness, was going to answer, when I signed him to quietness, and the commandant coming up, there was no need for a guide.

" I am commandant," said he ; and Charlotte put into his hand a letter, and without a word or sign to me or Paul, galloped off.

" Sarel," said Birkenfeld, when Charlotte was well away, " here is a letter from a man named Andries Brink, who tells me that there is a British patrol at his cousin's place, and that you, Sarel, can lead me. Who is this Brink ? "

" An oprecht Burgher who stands well with General Joubert," answered Paul, always ready to talk, though I could not understand why he should speak up for Andries after all that had occurred. I was also puzzled at the letter, and wondered how Andries knew I was here. I was also greatly troubled by the words of Birkenfeld, for I did not know where this place of Jan Brink's was ; indeed, I was not sure that there was such a place. But I dared not show my ignorance, not even to Paul, so I led on in the direction I supposed it might be. Good fortune was my friend, for, to my great surprise, after three hours' riding we came upon a farmhouse which, without asking me, the commandant made sure was the place we wanted. So, after the manner of Boers out fighting, the commando took cover some two miles from the place, and, much to my regret, the commandant sent me with two Burghers to reconnoitre.

We soon saw signs of life on the farm, and a dozen saddles lying opposite the door showed that Andries' information was correct. But there were other signs which I did not like. There was a great quietness over the homestead, and for a great distance around, while the way the wild birds would suddenly rise and cry showed that they had been disturbed by something we could not see. A Hottentot Kafir who was with us said he could smell many horses. These Hottentots are very clever at reading signs in the veld, much better than Basutos or Zulus or Griquas, who can find only what they can see plainly, and would tell you a waggon was near only by falling over the trek-chain. But a Hottentot is different, being as clever as he is small and dirty. If Paul had been with me, he would no doubt have been prophesying disaster in a loud voice, but for once I was free to work without him. So we lay down and watched for an hour, when I sent the Hottentot back with a message that there were twelve khakis in the farmhouse, and perhaps more camped elsewhere, for I thought it safer to be cautious, and my superior intelligence proved again triumphant.

The commando scattered widely, so as to surround the homestead, which, like all Boer and most old colonial farmhouses, was low down, to be near the water. I chose for myself a nice bit of cover in a bushy kloof, where I intended to wait until the danger was past, or at least until the commandant should find me and make me do something. It wanted only a few minutes to sundown, so that anything we might do must be done quickly, for Boers do not fight in the dark. I had the Hottentot back with me, and a young Free Stater who had not yet seen fighting, and was sobbing quietly, as most boys do when danger is drawing near.

Presently there was the sound of distant horse-riding, and the Hottentot pointed through the sugar bush.

"Look there, baas!" said he, very excited.

I looked, and saw coming fast over the rising ground opposite, and riding hard for the homestead, a crowd of our men. In a flash I guessed the truth. While we had been surrounding the homestead, we had ourselves been surrounded by the khakis, and I knew what the stillness and the shrieking of the wild birds had meant,—the veld was full of khakis!

Next moment came the crack of Lee-Metfords, but not a Mauser replied, the Free Staters riding hard for the cover of the farmhouse. They were within three hundred yards of it, when a great volley came crashing out, and the Burghers crowded together like frightened sheep; they could neither advance nor retreat, for they were doubly surrounded—khakis outside, and khakis inside the ring. I led my horse farther back into the kloof, and the Free State lad and the Hottentot followed with their horses. I could not well send them out, though I much wished they were not with me, as I had a plan I did not want them to know; but if they had gone out the khakis would see them, and, thinking more were here, might fire into the kloof.

All the time the firing became greater and quicker, the English, as is their custom, firing faster than the Boers, not staying to take aim, thereby wasting hundreds of bullets in what they call volley-firing.

I sent the Hottentot up the kloof to see if there was a path by which we might get away, and asked the Free Stater to go with him, secretly hoping they might find one and get off, leaving me to carry out my plan. But the lad was too frightened to leave me, and the Hottentot came back, saying that the place was no kloof, but a valley that narrowed like a kloof, and that even if it did not lead right beyond the khaki circle, it was so thick and rocky that we might be hidden there for days. At this the Free Stater said he would go, which he did, he and the Hottentot leaving me at the mouth of the kloof, while they went up, and I never saw either of them again.

It was not till some days afterwards that I found how true my reading of the position was, for, like most people who take part in a great fight, I saw very little of what was passing, and knew less.

After half an hour the firing grew fainter, and I knew that the Boers had managed to find some way out of the ring, as they generally do, and had got away. It was nearly dark by this time, and I was just making up my mind to carry my plan out, which was to ride up to the farmhouse and surrender to the khakis, when I heard a party of mounted men passing the mouth of the kloof. By their talk I knew them to be Natal

Volunteers. I did not wish to be taken by them, as it might happen that there were among them those who knew me, and the story I had prepared to tell might not be believed by them. Besides, they were carrying two or three wounded comrades, and by their talk were very bitter against the Boers; therefore I thought it an improper time to surrender. So I lay quiet and heard them pass on to the farmhouse, when lanterns and fires began to show, proving there were many khakis there. I got a great fright once, for I saw a lantern coming towards the kloof, and heard men marching. They came up to within twenty yards of the kloof entrance, and I heard what I rightly guessed was the placing of sentries. Two men were left; and so quiet was the night that I could hear most of their words, from which I gathered there had been a great fight, both sides having lost several men. Any thought of surrender I may have had was driven away by the talk of these two sentries. They were what are called Tommies, only just out from England, and full of thoughts of fighting. They were very angry at the Boers for not standing up to shoot, calling them cowards for lying behind stones.

"That big man on the white horse must be Kroojer," said one; "I knew him by his whiskers."

"Nay," said the other, "Kroojer don't fight. He is a downy old cove, and keeps in his palace in Johannesburg, drinking champagne, you bet."

There followed a long dispute on this, one holding that he had seen Paul Kruger on a white horse; the other, who was better educated, ridiculing the idea. Then they fell to discussing what they would do if they caught Kruger, proposing some most unchristian schemes of revenge. Suppose they caught me, I thought, they would give me no chance of surrender, for I had grown a big beard since I had been on commando, partly because it was not always easy to shave, but mainly that I might not be reproached for being a Hollander, which was a favourite taunt against such of us as, having been Government officials, were supposed to have made money by learning from Hollanders how to steal.

I began to fear greatly as these men talked, for it was clear that if they should by a mischance find me, they would do to me what they had prepared for Paul Kruger; so I sat and thought out plans, the chief and best of many being to get back to the place of Andries Brink, for I worked it out by logic thus: If he should prove to be a true and loyal Afrikander I should be safe, as he believed me to be one also; and, if the commando should find me there, it would not look as if I were trying to escape. If, on the other hand, he turned out to be a renegade and with the British, I would attain my heart's desire, for he would assuredly help me to join those with whom I had greatest sympathy, because their cause was just.

So, full of these thoughts, I carefully led my horse up the kloof; but the night being very still, the sentries must have heard his hoofs, for, being a town horse, he was shod.

"What is that?" I plainly heard one Tommy say in a frightened voice. I also heard what made my heart thump—the cocking of a rifle. But my presence of mind and coolness did not desert me, for almost without thinking, I used an old Boer trick, and made a noise like a baboon, which I can imitate to perfection. But I had forgotten that I had heard there were no baboons in England, not even in the open country, so that these Tommies might be more frightened still by the noise I made; and such proved true, for as I grunted and chattered and shook the boughs of the thorn-bushes, a pair of large white owls flew out with a noisy whirr. Bang went a rifle, and as I tried to hurry away,—which was difficult because of the dark and the thick bush and rough ground,—I could hear the Tommies running towards the farmhouse, and the khakis coming out of it, talking loudly and shouting orders and advice, and altogether there was great tumult for a time, more like a Boer laager when a shell falls into it than British soldiers.

I remained quite still, lest the sound of my horse's hoofs should betray me and the khakis follow me into the kloof, though I knew that the darkness would keep them out; for it is one of the most blessed inventions of Providence for war-time and similar dangers.

Things happened as I hoped and thought, for when the Natal Volunteers heard the story of the sentries they knew at once what had happened, and I could hear their loud laughter, the Natal Volunteers being ever glad of a chance to make fun of a Tommy; and they seemed to get much enjoyment out of these sentries mistaking the grunting of a baboon for Boers.

Gradually all grew quiet again, and then I cautiously groped my way up the kloof till I came out on the rising ground, where I had a good look round for more khaki sentries, but saw none; so I set out towards Andries Brink's place, knowing the way fairly well now, although it was dark. I struck a Kafir path, which I followed, and about midnight it brought me to the boundaries of Andries' place, which, like most Natal farms, was well fenced with barbed wire, and covered some ten square miles.

I pulled up at the drift, whereby I knew my position, intending to give my horse a drink and myself time to think out my plans as to what story I was to tell Andries to account for my coming.

As I dismounted, there happened one of those Providence-sent little things that, as I have philosophically remarked before, do so much to direct a man's way when he has sense enough to use them. I stepped on to a loose round stone, and came near spraining my ankle. As it was, the wrench caused me great pain, and made me feel sick; but it did more, it put a great light into my soul. Why not tell Andries I was wounded in the fight? It would give me a double excuse,—first, for coming to the house; secondly, for not going away again.

I was secretly sorry that my sprain was not worse, except for the pain, for Boers go much on things they can see, like swellings and cuts and blood, but

I had none of these things. If I could but show a wound it would help me much. I took out my knife, and, turning up my trouser leg, tried to find a place that, if cut, would bleed much, but be neither serious nor painful.

I tried several places, but the knife being blunt, the pain of cutting was so great that I had nearly changed my mind, and made shift to be content with the sprain, when, sticking the knife hard for the last time and drawing it quickly across my calf, I was pleased to feel the warm blood coming plentifully, and more pleased that the pain was not so great as I had feared, as is ever the case if men will only face danger and difficulty with bravery.

I waited till the blood had soaked and smeared well over my leg and trousers, so far as I could judge in the dark, and then I tied it up with the white hand-kerchief I had carried as a precaution in case I had to surrender, and set out towards the farmhouse, thinking all the time what Katrina would say if she could see me, for vrouws are not quick at understanding diplomacy, and she would have been certain to put a different and false meaning on my cleverness. Thus often do thoughts of a woman who has no sympathy with her man hold him back from doing great and profitable deeds!

There was another matter that troubled me much. I remembered that I ought to look pale, as wounded men always do, the more so as I have a good ruddy English complexion, very superior to that of a Boer; and this was always against me when I was ill with my internal complaint at Prinsloosdorp, some of the vrouws saying I could not be ill if I looked so red and rosy. The only way I knew to make my face white was to hit myself hard in the stomach, as an Englishman once did to me in the dorp because I would not reduce his bail-money; but the memory of that blow was so painful that I dared not try it, but rode on, relying on my good fortune and my bleeding calf.

As I neared the house the dogs came barking at me,

and I saw the light in the sitting-room suddenly go out, putting the place in darkness. While I tried to quieten the dogs, I heard the voice of Charlotte on the stoep, asking in Dutch and English, " Who comes there ? "

" It is I, Sarel Erasmus," I answered. " I have escaped being killed by the Rooineks, and am badly wounded."

" Stay there, Sarel, or the dogs will bite you," answered Charlotte, and there came a long silence.

At last the girl spoke again.

" Are you alone ? " she asked.

" Ja, quite, except for my pain."

" Sure ? Before God, Sarel, you have no khakis with you ? "

" Charlotte, why do you think I would do so wicked a thing ? " I answered, yet secretly sorry that she should not want to see khakis.

" Then off-saddle, turn your horse loose, and come in," said she, and I did so.

When I got into the sitting-room, where the lamp had been again lighted, I saw a sight that I think made me turn pale.

Four khaki men were in the room with Andries Brink, Charlotte, and a Boer whom I afterwards knew as Carl Uckermann, a Natal Burgher.

" Just look this way, Mr Erasmus," said a voice at the dark end of the room, and, looking that way, I nearly fainted, for a revolver was pointed at me by a fifth khaki.

" You must consider yourself our prisoner, so please lay your revolver on the table, with the muzzle pointing towards yourself," said a voice behind the pointed revolver.

" I have no revolver," I answered, which was true, and my mauser I had put against the wall on the stoep.

" Feel him, Jack," said the man with the revolver, still pointing, and I felt hands going all over my body.

"He's all right, captain," said the voice of Andries Brink. "Now you can sit down, Sarel, for Englishmen don't hurt their prisoners, so don't look so frightened. They have caught me in the act of passing despatches, and have kindly promised not to shoot me or burn the place if I give up all I have, and I have done so," and he pointed to a heap of papers on the table. "If you have anything, I advise you to give it up."

"I have nothing, and can tell little," I answered. "If I had, I would give it up willingly."

"That's spoken sensibly, Sarel," said Andries. "There's no good in a man saying he is innocent when the blood is on his hands. I am caught, and I don't try to deny it, and I would rather be caught by the English than by your people under the circumstances. Wouldn't you, Sarel?"

There was something in the manner of Andries' speech as if he wanted me to say hard things of the Boers. I did not answer for a time, which, Andries noticing, he put more grass on the fire by saying, "They treated you badly enough at the laager, eh, Sarel? Nearly shot you, simply because you did not stir up rebels in Natal, eh?"

It was now clear to me that either Andries was a great dissembler, or he was trying to deceive the khakis. What was the right thing for me to do? In a moment I decided to throw in my lot boldly with the British.

"Ja, Andries," said I; "I am glad I am captured, for I am sick of it all."

"I knew you would be, so you must do as I have—take the oath of allegiance. It's a better oath than the Transvaal one, and those who take it now will have the first pick when the farms are given away. You might have Hans Potgieter's farm at Potchefstroom for your share, eh?"

This was the first time I had heard that Burghers who took the oath had farms given them; but, thought I, this has been told Andries by these khakis.

"I would take twenty oaths to get that farm," said I.

"One is enough," said the captain of the khakis. "And now, Andries, let's get on with the letters, while Sarel looks to his hurt."

Charlotte signed to me to follow her, and went into the kitchen, where, without saying much or asking any questions, she put a chair for me, and set before me food and coffee. Then she asked me about my wound, which, until the khaki captain spoke of it, I had wellnigh forgotten, being so filled with surprise at all that had happened.

"I was run through by a lancer," I said, in answer to Charlotte's question as to how I got my hurt.

The khaki captain burst out laughing, for the kitchen door being open, he could hear all that was said.

"But I thought you killed all the lancers at Elandslaagte?" he asked.

"Nay, captain, they killed us. The way they ran through us was like fire in the grass on a windy day."

"How many were killed?"

"I saw about a hundred."

"Boers or English?"

"Boers; I did not see a khaki killed," said I, which was true, as I was not there; but I felt it would be diplomacy to say these things to please him. He laughed again, and said something about Falstaff and his man Buckram, which I at first thought referred to some English officers who were fighting at Elandslaagte; but later on, when I had thought a bit, I remembered that it was something from Shakespeare, for Charlotte, who was highly educated at Bloemfontein, laughed much, making me ask the reason, to which she answered, "You have not read Shakespeare, Sarel," and laughed again so heartily that I was angry, and the anger made me remember I had read of Falstaff, and I saw that the khaki captain was making ridicule of me, though I foolishly did not put proper weight on it at the moment, or

I would have shown him I was no man to laugh at. But the pain of my wound kept other things out of my mind, and I began to make the most of it, nursing my leg and groaning much.

"Does it hurt much?" asked Charlotte, "for I noticed that you walked quite well."

"Ja, Charlotte; but men do not show when they suffer. I only want you to do something to prevent it getting so bad that I cannot fight for the British," I answered boldly, and loud enough for them to hear in the sitting-room.

"But if you can walk well you can also run," said Charlotte, who was laughing much, as if she could not forget the captain's jokes from Shakespeare.

"I shall not run," I answered with real anger.

Then said Andries, "You will be of little use to us, for the captain here wants you to run despatches, as I told him you were good at that."

"Certainly I am," said I, secretly thankful to Andries for helping me over a bad place, and more thankful that Paul was not present, for he would have quoted the Bible to my discomfiture.

Just as Charlotte began to wash and bandage my wounded calf, one of the khakis came into the kitchen and sat down.

"Excuse me," said he, very politely, "I am only doing my duty in watching that you do not run away before you have taken the oath. You are too good a man to lose."

"That is what General Joubert said," I answered, "and I am wondering what he will say when he knows that I have left him for good."

"Good riddance—I mean, that he will no longer have any fear that you will be captured with important despatches on you."

This answer of the khaki made me the more angry because Charlotte laughed much at it. I could see, also, that she admired the khaki very much, he being young and nice-looking, and having what all women love to see—new uniform.

While she bandaged my leg a great thought came to me. Why not be revenged on this khaki by making love to Charlotte? It would punish him, and at the same time her friendship would be very useful to me. She could know nothing about Katrina, unless old Paul had told her at our first visit; and even if she did, she would be pleased to take me from her, for next to getting a man who is free, Afrikander girls love most to take a man from the girl he has promised to marry, which is why when men lose their wives they generally marry their first sweetheart, in order to fulfil their broken promise before it be too late. As I watched Charlotte and the young khaki, the resolution to take her affection from him grew stronger in me; for loyal though I was to the British, it did not seem right that while war was going on between the two races, a Boer girl should show preference for a man of the enemy, and this as much as anything else determined me in my plan. I had always been a great favourite with the vrouws and young girls, for, owing to my superior education and my acquaintance with Hollanders, I knew how they should be treated, which is with respect, though not as with the English, as if they were so very superior, which makes them conceited before marriage and expensive in their habits afterwards. Having resolved on my plan, I began very carefully.

"I am sorry to give you all this trouble," said I; "but when a man has no wife or woman to care for him he is always the more thankful for kindness like yours."

This, thought I, would soon show whether Charlotte knew anything of Katrina; but she only answered, "Ja, men are very feeble and foolish things when they are sick."

"Foolish, Charlotte! how foolish?" I asked.

"You were foolish in mistaking a bayonet-prick for a lance-thrust, and yet more foolish for being on the Boer side after they had treated you so badly."

"Quite right," said the khaki, as if he knew all

about my story, though I afterwards saw that he only said it to agree with Charlotte. This made me determined to agree even more with her than he did, so I answered, "Ja, Charlotte, you are quite right; I was foolish, but after your kindness I shall fight only for the British."

"Perhaps," said she, in a meaning sort of way, "it may be long after the war is finished that you will be fit to fight, for this wound is poisoned. I know, for I have been in the hospital at Maritzburg."

This gave me a great surprise and fright, for I feared that my knife, being dirty, might have caused the poison, as I had known such things.

"How do you know it is real poison?" I asked.

"Are you sure it was done with a lance?"

"No; it may have been a bayonet."

"That settles it," said Charlotte, "for you do not know that Coos Brink and his men caught the first khakis that went to his place, took their rifles, and poisoned the bayonets, and when the khakis got master again they used the bayonets, not knowing they were poisoned. It is one of these that has made your wound."

"You are quite sure, Charlotte, that the wound could only have been made by a poisoned bayonet?"

"Quite," answered she; and then I secretly rejoiced, first, that there was no cause for my fear; secondly, because my skill in laying traps in cross-examining witnesses had proved so great and useful. Besides, I saw in it a great opportunity to make a good effect upon the khaki captain and his men; so I said in a voice loud enough to be heard by them in the sitting-room, "Charlotte, I am glad that I am poisoned, and I hope that I shall die; for if I do, then will the righteousness of the British appear in making war upon and expunging from the earth a people who will use poisoned weapons as if they were Bushmen."

"You are a brave fellow!" called out the captain from the other room, and he and the others came into the kitchen and shook hands with me, and gave me whisky to drink, filling up my glass again and again; while Charlotte sat by me and kept asking very tenderly if I felt the poison throbbing, and whether it hurt me much, and sometimes filling my glass with whisky till I felt no more pain in my leg, but got so well and strong that I sang English songs, including " God save the Queen," although I only knew part of one verse; and altogether the evening was most cheerful and happy, and I regretted very much when Charlotte and the captain insisted that I should go to bed lest the poison worked too quickly. They laid me on a sofa in a spare room, and kindly and thoughtfully put chairs against it so that I might not fall off, Charlotte saying that poison made people jerk and writhe through its great torment.

So I went to sleep, rejoicing greatly that I had become a loyal Britisher.

CHAPTER VII.

Reveals the character of the slimmest schelm
in South Africa.

I DO not know how long I had slept—for I had omitted
to note the time when I went to the couch—but when
I awoke I felt seriously unwell, and began to fear that,
after all, Charlotte might be right, and that I was really
poisoned; for my head was aching and I was very
giddy and thirsty, which are always signs of poison.
In my fright I got off the couch, and, opening the
door, found that it led on to the front stoep, or, as
they call it in Natal, the verandah.   There was a
light still in the sitting-room, and on looking beneath
the edge of the blind I saw the khaki captain, Andries,
and Charlotte—in fact all the company—just as I had
left them, and the little clock on the mantel-shelf
told only a little past eleven.   Though the blinds were
down, the window was open because of the warmness
of the night, and I could hear what was being said
quite plainly, the talk being in English.

Now there is a saying in that language that listeners
hear no good of themselves, which may sometimes be
true; but it is of equal truth that a discreet listener
may learn much that may be of use to himself, as it
proved in my case.

As I looked through the window I noticed with some
surprise that Andries, who during the evening had been
too sick to get out of his chair, was skipping about the
room as lightsome as a two-year-old, thus giving me
my first easily read spoor on which to follow up my

track, for it was now plain to me that his sickness was like mine, only part of a great plan; but what that plan was I had yet to find. Another thing that caused me great wonderment was this. I have a wonderful memory for voices, though not for faces, which comes no doubt through my having to study the manner of witnesses to find the truth when cross-examining them as public prosecutor. When first I heard the khaki captain speak a memory went over me, but I was too agitated to give it much thought. As I now watched him, I recalled the Market Square at Johannesburg, where I could see and hear this same captain making bids for horses one day three or four years before. It was his peculiar laugh, which he put in at the end of nearly every sentence, that seemed so familiar to me; and as I exercised my memory I seemed to recall his sandy moustache and steely eyes; but beyond that all was a mist except that the Market Square was plainly before me.

I have often read in books how that people listening, like myself, hear all they are wishful for, and in a very short time the speakers saying just what is wanted; but it was not so in my case, for the talk was of a kind that gave me no knowledge, but only brought up still plainer memories and sounds of the Market Square, and the sales of horses and cattle going on, for all of them were talking of the price of oxen and horses as if they were cattle-dealers,—even Charlotte now and then joining in by telling what she had seen at Maritzburg, or other down-country places, in the way of cattle-buying and selling. Then Andries would mention a neighbour, and say what had become of his cattle; how that So-and-so was riding transport for the British with so many waggons and oxen; how that he thought he would take that or the other road, and so on, till I grew more puzzled than ever. While I was trying to build an explanation in my mind I got a great start, for the captain suddenly mentioned my name, though I did not hear all that he had said, but Andries' answer was very plain.

"You need not be anxious about Sarel," said Andries. "Charlotte has got him fixed up. Her medicine is wonderful stuff, and holds young kerels like birdlime, doesn't it, Charlotte?" whereat they all laughed.

"But if he is one of these talking fools he will be more dangerous than useful," went on the captain.

"He doesn't meet Charlottes every day," answered Andries; and then they began to talk of cattle again, and I had time to wonder what was meant by Charlotte's medicine, also to try and remember what I might have said to cause the captain to speak of me as a "talking fool."

I listened long afterwards, but they did not again speak of me, and I went quietly back to my room, feeling like one who is invited to have a soupie of dop when the man finds he has none left in the flask. They had given me only the desire to drink more, but had not satisfied it.

I did not rise next morning till I had seen Charlotte and Andries, for I wished to make out that I was yet very sick. Charlotte was very kind, and anxious about me, and would not let me get up till she had again dressed my wound, which, I was very sorry to see, was healing fast, and did not look at all bad. She, however, to my surprise, said, "Sarel, I was wrong yesterday when I said your leg was poisoned. You were lucky in not getting a poisoned bayonet; you have only a bad flesh-wound."

"But," said I, wishful to see how far she was deceiving me, "may it not be that the poison is in the bone, for the pain is very great?"

"No, Sarel, there is no poison, and all you want is rest, which you must have, for the khaki captain has something for you to do that he may feel sure that you are as friendly to the British as you said last night you were."

"Charlotte," said I, "tell me truly—are you with the Boers or the British?"

"Which are you?" was her answer.

"I am afraid to speak till I know where I stand."

" Do you then mistrust me and my father ? "

" These are mistrustful times," I answered, with great diplomacy.

" But you say you want to be with the British and leave the commando, where you are already suspect."

" Who told you that ? "

" Have you forgotten the talk you had with me in the kitchen last night, when I had dressed your leg ? "

A great feeling of fear and shame came over me, so that I could not speak,—fear, lest I might have said something about Katrina ; shame, that I had been made to talk without remembering what I had said. And again came fear lest Charlotte might have put some poison in my whisky to make me talkative, as I have known done in Johannesburg and Pretoria by men who were seeking to learn gold secrets from those who had found mines, but would not tell where they were.

All these thoughts passed over my brain while I sat wondering what answer I should give Charlotte. Presently it came upon me how to speak with care and wisdom.

" Charlotte," said I, " after your great kindness and care I cannot but do what you wish. If you say I am a Boer, I am one ; but if you say I am a Britisher, I am that and more so."

" That is well spoken," said she, looking very pleased. " When you have eaten I will come and talk again, and tell you what we want you to do," and she left me wondering greatly whether I had made another mistake.

I had not much time to consider or to make any further resolutions or plans, for a few minutes after came the khaki captain, with Andries and the other khakis. The captain seemed very kind, and asked how I was, saying he hoped I should soon be well, as he had great work for me to do. Then he came to business.

" So you want to take the oath of allegiance like Andries, and be a good Britisher ? " said he.

" That is why I came here," I answered, that being

a diplomatic answer, in that I did not commit myself by saying a plain "Yea" or "Nay."

"You quite understand what you are doing, and that if you break your oath you will be shot?"

I could not think of any answer to this straight question except, "I have myself put men on oath thousands of times," which was the truth.

"Then," answered the captain, "there will be less excuse for you if you break it."

He then gave me a small English Bible, which he took from the bookcase, and I repeated after him the words of the oath, to which were added, "and I promise to obey Andries Brink," which words I knew did not belong to the oath; but I said nothing, but resolved to meet cunning with cunning, for when he said "kiss the book," I took care to kiss my thumb and not the Bible, so that my conscience would be at peace if it happened that I had to break the oath. For, first, he did not know that we Afrikanders do not kiss the Bible when we swear, but raise our right hands, so that I was doubly safe; and further, the Bible was an English and not a Dutch one, which was as if a Chinaman had been sworn upon it instead of a saucer,—all of which precautions on my part show how valuable knowledge and education can be to those who have the sense to use them, for I was now quite safe if I had to deny having taken the oath.

"And now," said the captain, "Andries will tell you what we expect of you. All you have to do is to take your instructions from him, and if you acquit yourself well you will have no cause to regret what you have done."

He then wished me good-bye and good luck, and shortly afterwards went off with his men towards Mooi River.

As soon as I got the opportunity, I opened up with Andries the matter that was on my heart.

"This is a great game you are playing, Andries," said I; "are you sure that it is safe?"

Andries lit his pipe before answering, and sat down beside me on the stoep.

"Sarel," said he very quietly, "this is a great game *you* are playing. Are you sure it's safe?"

"If those I play with are oprecht men, yes; if not, no," was my ready answer.

"Quite right, Sarel; it was because I knew you were oprecht that I told the captain to trust you. He was at first against you, but Charlotte and I made it smooth for you. You will find you have done the right thing when the end comes."

"But, Andries, how do you manage to run with both without danger?"

"By making both believe in me. I run straight with both, so that whichever side wins I shall be on it. That is what you must do."

"Do you mean that you show the Boers the British despatches, and the Boer letters to the British?"

"Certainly, if it suits me, and if the despatches suit too. If they don't, well, Charlotte alters them till they do; she is a slim girl is Charlotte."

"But is there not one side that your secret heart favours most?"

"I am an Afrikander, Sarel, and I love money and cattle, and like men who have plenty of both."

"Which means that you favour the side you get most out of?"

"You are a clever lawyer, Sarel, to see things so plainly. I see it is useless to hide anything from you."

"But how can you tell which side will pay you best in the end?" I asked, not appearing to feel flattered by his great compliment.

"I cannot tell; I am content with the side that pays best for the time."

"Do the British pay well?"

"I pay myself, and I am fairly liberal in my payments."

"But how?"

"With cattle. I have many hidden in safe places along the Drakensberg."

" Whose cattle were they ? "

" Some have the brand of my English neighbours, some of my Boer friends, and many more, especially the horses, *had* the British army mark."

" But suppose the Boers should find their cattle in your hands ? "

" Then I tell them I have been taking care of them till the war is over, and shall take part in payment for my trouble and kindness."

" A dangerous business, Andries."

" For a fool, yes ; for a sensible man, nay."

Andries did not speak for some time, but sat smoking and watching my face. After a bit, when I was trying to think whether I ought to trust him, he said, " Sarel, a war like this comes but once in a man's lifetime, and he would be a fool who did not make the most of it. If you are the man I think you are, you and I can plan so that it matters nothing which side wins in the end. All we have to do is to keep in the middle till it is over. I am going to give you a grand start. You must go back to your commando."

This speech did give me a start, though not the kind that Andries was thinking of; for if there was one thing that I had no wish to do, it was to rejoin my commando. Andries must have seen that I was not pleased, for he said, " Yes, you must go back; but it is to say good-bye. You will take with you things that will establish you so strongly in the favour of Piet Joubert, that you will have no cause to fear or envy any one. You shall take back British letters and despatches and information—some good and true, some not—which you shall say you captured on a despatch-rider; and then you are made, for all will trust you."

" But, Andries, this may be all very well for the things that are true, but what about those that are not, for they must soon find they are false ? "

" Do you not know, Sarel, that men are ever ready to believe what they wish to believe, and if only you hit sometimes they will take no regard of the misses, but will say ' He is wrong here, but he was right there,' and they soon forget the wrong in the right."

" You are a slim kerel, Andries, and I am glad I came to you; but what must I do in the laager?"

" Learn all you can of what is moving, particularly cattle and horses, and get them as near the Berg as you can, when I will do the rest."

" But, Andries, the Boers will not move cattle without strong guards. How can I bring them alone?"

" That is what you have to learn. If any fool could do it I should not be here to-day, nor should I want the help of a slim kerel like yourself. Do you not see, Sarel, that you must be clever, or I would not take all this trouble with you. It is not that I want to make you rich, but myself, and I can do it quicker and better with your help than with any one else's, and that help I shall pay well for."

Now if Andries had talked for a year he could not have won my heart better than by that speech, for it showed me that he was a true and oprecht man; if he were not, he would have tried to make me believe it was out of love for me that he wished to have me work with him. He was looking hard at me as if to see how I took this; so I kept my feelings close, and did not put into words what I felt. His next speech was one that called for all my astuteness and guard over my face.

" Where did you leave your vrouw?" he asked.

" In the cemetery at Prinsloosdorp," I answered, making my voice sad.

" But you wear no crape, so you are taking another, eh?"

" Men cannot buy crape on commando."

" Nay, but they can bring it with them. But have you no next vrouw, Sarel?"

" Mine has been dead only two years."

" Two years is long enough to be a second time a widower." Then, without waiting for me to speak, he went on: " Charlotte likes you, Sarel. I shall tell her you have no vrouw, and are a free man."

"Why?" I asked, pretending I did not understand.

"But, man, you must know that girls always take more interest in a free man than a married one, unless they want to spite his wife. Yes, Charlotte likes you, and all that is good in this business will be of her doing."

I was of course very pleased to hear this, but not surprised, for I am ever successful at being a favourite with women, knowing, as I have said before, how they should be treated both before and after marriage, and particularly after.

"Is it her wish that I should return to the laager?" I asked.

"Sarel, did I not tell you two things—first, that Charlotte is very slim; secondly, that she likes you? Would a slim girl want a man she likes to do a thing that would not benefit him?"

"Ja, she is slim," I answered, not knowing exactly what to say. "Education is a good thing sometimes even for women, and Charlotte has it."

"Ja; I spent much money on her at Bloemfontein and Pretoria, and now I am gathering the harvest."

"I see you have plenty of books," I said, taking one from the bookcase, for we had come in from the stoep to drink coffee. As I opened it to read the title—which, being a man of education, I naturally did first, not opening it in the middle like ignorant Boers—I noticed an English name written in it. I took up another book, and the same name was there.

"Who is this John Wilson?" I asked.

"I bought those books on the market at Maritzburg," answered Andries, and with that answer I was content, until, walking round the house later, I saw certain old packing-cases marked "John Wilson, *viâ* Mooi River," and an old Scotch cart marked "John Wilson, Ross Castle," on the name-board. I was greatly perplexed, for I did not then know that I had discovered one very good reason why Andries had no fear of losing his farm if things went wrong, for it was not his, but one deserted by the owner.

This and other things made me feel uneasy about Andries, for it was certain that he had not told me all. When, therefore, we were again alone, I made another effort to get more truth out of him. So I spoke out boldly.

"Are you not foolish," said I, "to tell me all that you have, not knowing whether I may not go to the commando and tell them that you are playing double?"

"Nay," answered Andries very quietly, "you would be the last man to do that, for you dare not. First, they would not believe you, you being already suspect; and secondly, as the predikants say, I have something I have only to show General Joubert to make him sorry he trusted you."

"What is that, Andries?" I asked, feeling very uncomfortable.

"Nothing particular; only a copy in your own handwriting of the despatch you carried to the Free State commandant."

My heart gave a great thump, for I had not remembered making a copy of that despatch, and, least of all, had I any memory of having given or shown it to Andries, though I had a slight recollection of intending to do it for my own use, so that I might quieten any one who, like Paul, doubted that I was in the confidence of the General.

"What do you think would happen if I sent that to Piet Joubert, saying I had captured it on a khaki, who said he had bought it of a man very like you?"

When I got over my first fright I saw that Andries was so strong that he could make me do what he willed, so, making as though I cared nothing, I said—

"You are right, Andries; but do you not think I trusted you before I gave you that copy?"

"Certainly, Sarel, for you are a good judge of men, as a lawyer must be."

And though this speech pleased me, showing as it did that Andries had a good opinion of me, yet I was unhappy, for I was not satisfied that I had given Andries a copy of the despatch, though I was discreet in not letting him see that I had forgotten it. As we sat in silence, smoking and drinking coffee, there came into my heart a great distrust of old Paul, who might have given the despatch, though, as he could not write, the matter still puzzled me. It was also true that I had drunk freely on that day; but my brain was clear when we left, for I well remembered that I nearly fell over in getting into the saddle, and I also recall that the Kafir laughed and said something in English, which surprised me at the time, for it is not usual for a Kafir on a farm to speak that language in the presence of Boers, however well he may know it. My remembering all these things proves that my brain was clear, and that the brandy I had drunk had not made me forget so great a thing as copying an important secret despatch, and giving it to Andries.

Andries must have read my thoughts, for he came up, and putting his hand on my shoulder said—

"Sarel, you must not funk things. You have a great chance now of getting even with your enemies. You trust in me, and do what Charlotte and I tell you, and you will come out on top. The letters you are carrying will put you in high favour with Joubert and even Ben Viljoen, and you will be trusted, so that you can do as you wish and soon be rich, so that you need not care which side loses. Now, get up your heart by eating, and make ready to leave to-morrow by sun-up."

"But my wound, Andries." I felt sorry after I had said it, but the hatred of the thought of the laager and commando was strong on me.

"Your wound is like mine, Sarel, just as we are both alike in our slimness, eh?"

And I saw that I had not been able to deceive him in the matter of my sickness, and that there was nothing for it but to do as he wished, for he was strong, and, like all wicked people, clever, while I, though equally clever, was not prepared for such wickedness, and thus fell easily into the snare of the fowler. So far I had prospered exceedingly, but I was yet only on the edge of the road that was to lead me on to success,

and I liked not the idea of going back to the commando,—even Andries' advice to me not to funk having
little effect, for it is easy for a man to advise another
to be brave. Indeed, I have found that people generally give two kinds of advice,—one like that given
me, to be brave, which is, as I say, easy; and the other
that is unnecessary, and only given because the person
offering it has not read and studied the true character
of the one advised. Of such was the remark made by
Andries as I helped myself to a soupie of whisky.

"Sarel," said he, "you are a slim and clever kerel,
and there is no end to the good you may do both of us
if you will talk and drink less."

This, being so baseless, made my anger rise, so I
answered with great dignity—

"Why do you say these hard things? Am I not
ever careful what I drink?"

"Ja, you only drink the best, I know; but being a
man with a great and sensitive brain, you are speedily
knocked out. Take my advice; there is no liquor in
the laagers good enough for you, so don't drink inferior
stuff. Great and clever men only drink the very best,
or none. Now let us talk of the trek, and count the
cattle we are going to get."

This last speech watered down my wrath, for it
showed me that Andries could see the real reason
why liquor, when bad, affected my brain, which con-
firmed my belief in his great far-seeingness.

We then sat down while Andries read the letters I
was to carry to the laager. They did not tell much,
being mostly from people shut up in Ladysmith, who
were writing to their friends through the Kafir runners.
Those that did seem of value to a commandant were
plainly written for the purpose of deceit, perhaps by
the khaki captain, perhaps by Charlotte. But, as
Andries said, it mattered nothing to me whence they
came. I was to tell Piet Joubert that I had shot a
British despatch-rider and found them on him; and
to help out this story the letters were put into a
British saddle-bag. Andries then gave me further

advice as to keeping my eyes and ears open to find what ·had become of the cattle taken from Natal farmers, and to learn all I could of the movements of transport, both British and Boer. He added to it much information which will be given out in its proper place in this story of the doings of a great rascal. Then Charlotte bound up my leg to make it look as if it had been very bad, saying meanwhile several kind things that made me feel sure she wanted much that I should come back with success; and when I tried to kiss her she was not angry, but only said, "Wait till you come back, Sarel."

We had a pleasant evening, for I felt very happy, though the thought of the laager did now and then come like a sudden pain in the heart, and before sun-up next morning I was away.

CHAPTER VIII.

*I become commandant; but learn that being exalted
does not always bring happiness.*

As I rode, I fell to looking back over what I had so
far accomplished, a habit I had learned when, as public
prosecutor, I had finished drawing up a summons,—a
practice that is very necessary, as it helps one to
remember any untruth one may have been compelled
for usefulness' sake to tell. If the public prosecutors
of the Transvaal had followed my example more, and
had looked over their work before going into court,
instead of louping about the dorp bragging how strong
was the case they had against a prisoner, in order to
frighten his friends into arranging with the public
prosecutor, there would not have been so many break-
ings down of prosecutions so soon after the case had
opened.

The case for myself, as I arranged it in my mind
while I rode along, stood thus:—

1. I was under suspicion with the Burghers of my
commando through having left the Transvaal before
the war and dwelt in Natal.

2. I had a strong enemy in Ben Viljoen and other
commandants, who were jealous of me, and sorry that
I had come back, and were waiting for an opportunity
to discredit me.

3. I had been wrongfully charged with leading my
Burghers into a trap and poisoning whisky, but had
been triumphantly acquitted, and given the confidence
of the greatest man of them all—General Piet Joubert.

4. I had been sent on a confidential mission, had fought and bled for my country in the calf, and was now going back with important letters and information that would prove I had been a very oprecht and useful Burgher, and had done what few other Burghers could have accomplished.

5. I had made a friend of Andries Brink, who sat well between both parties, so that whichever won I should be safe; and, above all, Andries had promised to show me how to become rich.

6. I was now going to do my part of the business by learning where to find Boer cattle, and, as it were, to claim the reward for which I had been working so hard, all of which was making for my advancement and triumph over my enemies.

I made a quick and good ride to the laager, seeing nothing of the British, and hearing only the boom of the guns at Ladysmith. I had gone over the story that Andries had invented to explain my absence, and there seemed no weak place in it, so that by the time I reached the laager I felt strong and bold.

The Burghers seemed surprised to see me, and I thought some of them looked as if they did not care whether I had returned or not, so soon are a man's acts forgotten if he leaves his people for any time. Old Paul du Plooy alone came to greet me as if he meant it.

"You are not lanced or lyddited, Sarel?" he asked cheerfully.

"Yea, Paul, lanced in the calf; but the steel let in much more knowledge than it let out blood." I said this loudly, so that others could hear, and they stopped as if they would learn more; but I hurried to the tent of General Joubert.

I found him looking very dark and unhappy, for things had been going badly of late. He was reading letters, and did not look up when I went in.

"General," said I, "throw all those papers away till you have seen what I have brought."

He looked up and frowned, as he always did when surprised.

"Ah, neef, so the khakis have not got you?" said he, kindly.

"Nay, General, but I have got them. Look!" And I poured out all the letters I had in the saddle-bag, telling him as I did this the story Andries had made for me.

The General said no word, but looked long at the letters, for he read English very slowly, and I sat on the ground and smoked, waiting for him to speak. At last, after he had looked at nearly every piece of paper, making as if to read it, he spoke.

"Sarel," said he, "I have never yet made a mistake in a man. I knew that a young ox that had fallen at a bad place in the road would go very carefully next time, that is why I gave you this chance, and I can see you know how to profit by experience. Now go away while I have these letters translated, and if the Burghers want to know what you have been doing, tell them you have been doing work for Piet Joubert, and that he is satisfied. Don't leave the laager till I have spoken with you, for I shall want you again."

I went away light as air, and purposely put myself in the way of such Burghers as I knew were not friendly towards me; but they were not so curious as I had hoped, for I was ready to crush them with my replies.

"Been a prisoner?" asked one.

"Lost your road?"

"Changed your mind about deserting us?"

"Been to learn how to poison whisky?"

These were some of the questions asked by the younger Burghers, who were not worth triumphing over; so I held my peace—a calm and holy peace, for I felt that the hour of my glory had at last come.

I went to where old Paul was living in a long hole under a sheet of corrugated iron, where he used to lie at full length on his stomach all day reading the Bible, his feet alone showing at the end of the tunnel. So I sat down by his head and prepared to tell him my good fortune.

"Well, Sarel, and has the young ox come back to the yoke?" asked he.

"Nay, Oom; he has come back to be a led ox, as the dream said."

"But what does the Boer baas say?"

"He says the same. But wait a bit, Paul, and you will see my dream come altogether true," and I told him all that I had done—that is, I told him the story according to Andries; but I was careful to tell him the exact words spoken by General Joubert, for I did not know how far Paul might be in the confidence of the General.

"Go slow, Sarel, go slow," was all the old man said at the end of my talk, and he shook his head as if he had doubts.

I felt my anger rising that the old man should doubt me, but I kept it under and went away, putting myself in front of certain Burghers; but they did not ask any questions, because I was ready with cutting answers. Had I not been so prepared I should have had many things asked of me, as I have frequently noticed through life, and particularly when I have prepared answers to any objections a defending attorney might make, for he never made them if I was ready.

An hour later I was sent for by the general. "Sarel," said he, "I am making you a commandant. You must pick three hundred good men, and when you have got them, come again to me."

I could not speak for joy, which Slim Piet saw, for he said, "Say nothing now, Sarel; but have your men ready by sun-up to-morrow, and be ready to ride at noon. Take this and go."

He gave me a letter written by the adjutant appointing me commandant, and signed by himself.

I went straight to old Paul in his hole. "Oom," said I, "the young ox *is* the best in the span. Look at this," and I showed him the General's letter.

Paul read it slowly, then, crawling on all-fours out of his hole, said, "Sarel, I must be with you. You will never do any good without me."

"Ja, certainly," I answered angrily, but with bitter sarcasm; "you helped me get the despatches, did you not, and you kept me from shooting Burghers, eh?"

"Sarel," said he quietly, "we will say no more about that; it is buried with the poisoned whisky. What I mean is that you will want me to show you what the Bible would have you do in the day of victory."

"But I can read, Oom."

"Ja; but there is reading and reading. Nay, Sarel, I will come with you and be chief of commissariat. I am getting too old to be of use in the laager, for I soon weary. Besides, old men must have time to read their Bibles."

"As you put it in that way, Oom, I shall be glad to have you," said I, with the air of one having authority. "Now go and tell the Burghers that a new commando is in making."

It was a delightfulness that paid me well for all the sneers I had had to put up with to see the faces of the Burghers when I read the authority of General Joubert, and in a voice of masterfulness told them I was going to pick my own Burghers. It was the custom to ask for volunteers for a new commando; but I feared that if I did that, few only would offer, which would make me look foolish. Therefore I said plainly that the work I had been given by the General required only the very best men, for I have found in my passage through life that it is useless to make a thing appear cheap and free. Make it seem only a gift for the few, and all will want it. This was the idea I kept uppermost in my talk to the Burghers.

Now I cannot miss again pointing out how all things work together for the good of those who know how to take advantage of them, by which I mean those who have the sense to see when a spoor leads to the game. As I was repeating the announcement that I wanted only the best men, a young kerel who had often sneered at me, being ready with the tongue through having been a clerk in the post-office, where they are always practising smart sayings on the customers, asked, "Will there be plenty of whisky?"

This made the Burghers laugh, which I was afterwards glad of, for that laugh raised my wrath; so remembering that this young kerel had only recently been well thrashed by a young Burgher not nearly so big as he, I went straight and boldly up to him, and with my closed fist hit him, English fashion, on the point of the chin, knocking him down. He was stunned and surprised, for Burghers are not used to this sort of fighting. Before he could get up, "Do you want any more of my whisky?" I asked, "for I have plenty left;" and to prove it I punched him while he sat on the ground, saying with each punch, "Have a soupie of whisky, have a soupie of whisky," which made the Burghers laugh. This made my victory complete, for the kerel called out, "No more whisky;" so I kicked him hard, and, turning to the Burghers, asked, "Does anybody else want whisky?"

They were silent, and though some of them were angry at my having struck a Burgher, most were secretly pleased, especially the older men; for this young kerel had often used his slippery tongue to make them seem ridiculous in the eyes of the young Burghers,—which is an abomination to old men who have fought and bled for their country before those who laugh at them were born.

"Now," said I, "those who wish to join me may speak to Paul du Plooy. You will have a good commandant and——" here I made an impressive pause —"and whisky." And I walked away.

Before I had gone ten paces, Van der Murphy and all the Irish Boers in the laager were after me.

"Sarel," said he, "you are the commandant we want, for you have pluck, so we will join you."

"Saddle up and get over the spruit there and talk to Paul," I answered, with great dignity, for I had resolved to be firm, like an English officer, and not too familiar with my Burghers, like General Joubert, of whom all were rightly afraid. I also planned not to answer when spoken to, like him, for not only does it give you time to frame a proper answer, but it makes the person who speaks feel foolish and nervous to be kept waiting for a reply. I went to the adjutant to arrange about provisions and other things, and took care to keep away from the Burghers as long as I could, to give them time to make up their minds. When I went back an hour later I met Paul, who looked very serious.

"How many have saddled up?" I asked.

"Nearly all you want—in number."

"And what are they like?"

"You may well ask, Sarel. Man, but it's well I resolved to come with you. You have got all the wickedest young kerels, and all the laziest old fellows in the laager. And, God help us, Sarel! all the Irish Boers have joined, and they are fighting over who is to be their corporal. We have got the husks after the winnowing; but, Sarel, I shall be as a holy scourging wind, and supply the leaven of righteousness."

I saddled up and rode over to the spruit where they had assembled. Paul was right. I had got the husks of the laager, and most of the swine that ought to have fed on them. They received me with laughter, and cries of "Good old Sarel!" "Where's the whisky?" "Sing us a psalm, Paul." Then they crowded round me, all clamouring at once. One wanted a new saddle, another a horse, another a water-bottle, clothes, or bandolier, till I was dazed, and forgot my resolve not to answer at first when spoken to, but expressed myself in the language of a compound manager on a Rand mine when the Kafirs are troublesome.

"Tell Paul all you want," said I; and I rode off, leaving the old man like a sheep among jackals.

I was very sore at heart, and tossed about as to what I should do: for if I were severe and did all I had the right to do as commandant, I should lose all my Burghers; and if I were kind they would do as they liked, as they did in the only Kafir campaign I

went on,—the Magato war,—when they refused to
fight, but held prayer-meetings and sang psalms and
drank German beer instead; and when the commandant tried to break up the psalm-singing they tied him
up to a waggon-wheel till he sang with them.

While I was walking full of these sad thoughts,
another of those wondrous small chances came my
way. One of my Burghers, a big heavy man, carrying
double his proper number of blankets, with a mackin-
tosh and several bundles, all on a very small horse,
passed me.

"Neck," said I, "if you are going to catch cattle
and bring in loot, you won't have much for your share,
for you cannot carry it."

"Cattle and loot, is it?" answered he.

"Hush! not a word," said I, as if in great fear lest
he should mention it to the other Burghers, while I
went away to prevent further questioning.

In ten minutes the word went round that my commando was going after cattle, and in half an hour I
could have had every Burgher in the laager.

"I have said nothing about cattle and loot," was
my answer to those who would know more; but I was
careful to say it in such a way that, as they say in
English, a man could read between the lines, and that
is the way they mostly took it.

"Don't shout too loud or you will scare the game,"
was my parting words to them as I rode off to the
General to take my last instructions.

"You have all the Burghers you need?" he asked,
when I had reported my commando as quite ready.

"Ja, General, and more."

"I am glad, Sarel," said he, "for I feared they
might not want to go with you. It shows me that
you have the goodwill of the Burghers, but "—and here
the old man smiled his dreadful smile—"don't forget,
Sarel, that there are many wild things in the veld."

I did not quite understand him then, but I soon did.

Then the General gave me my orders, as an English
soldier would say. But we Boers on commando do

not take orders; we call it advice. I was to go as far south of Ladysmith as I could, and cut off transports with supplies for the British troops, who were trying to relieve the town. I was to work with any Free State commando I met, and generally to keep in check any attempt of the British to get round between Ladysmith and the Drakensberg, which was then the most exposed part of Natal, and the only direction from which the British could advance without being seen plainly.

If I lived to be President of United South Africa for my reward, I would say "let me die" rather than pass another day such as that on which the commando left the laager. Up would come Burghers to complain that Paul had not given them this or that, or that he had favourites, and gave the best saddles and boots to them, even when they did not need them. As I did not wish to rebuke Paul before the Burghers, I put them off with a promise that I would see them righted, and waited till I could get word in private with the old man.

"Sarel," said he, when he had heard what I had to say, "you know the greed and wickedness of good Burghers, but you do not know what this span of wild oxen is like. I am a scourging wind to them, so leave me to blow on them if you have any faith in me. If not, do the blowing yourself."

Half an hour later Paul was lying under the shade of a thorn-bush reading the Bible, while great business was doing at the waggon that had the stores.

"How came you away, Paul?" I asked.

"I have appointed the man who said he could give out stores better than I," answered he.

A few minutes later there came to me a Burgher full of wrath against Paul.

"I gave him two pounds to make me corporal of the commissariat," said he, "and I find another Burgher in my place."

I sent him away with the promise of putting him right, and went to Paul.

" How could you do this foolishness ? " I asked him.

" Sarel," said he, "you are like all the Burghers; you think you can do a thing better than the man who is doing it. If you want to find out how clever you are, go to the waggon and try to give every Burgher all he thinks he ought to have. You will soon do as I have done—appoint another."

" But you have appointed two."

" Most likely. They drove me so mad that I did not know what I was doing; perhaps I have appointed a dozen."

" But you were not too mad to forget to make them pay you two pounds."

" Of course not. They were all so anxious to help that they did not mind paying me to be allowed to do so."

" But there will be trouble."

" There is always trouble in a commando."

" But suppose these Burghers demand their money back ? "

" They have done so, and have not got it."

" Then will they go to General Joubert ?" said I.

" Nay, Sarel. It is plain you do not know your Burghers. A man who will pay two pounds to be allowed to make money by giving out stores will not lose his chance of making loot by quarrelling with his commandant and getting left behind. Sarel, you were very slim in talking about loot. These Burghers would rob a predikant of his cattle."

" But, Paul, these Burghers want their two pounds back. If they come to me again what must I do ? "

" Take them aside and talk about loot. Tell them I shall be the man who keeps account of all cattle brought in."

Thus did this old man try to corrupt me to injustice for the sake of a few pounds, though, as he afterwards explained, by taking the money he rightly punished them for their greed in wanting to make profit out of the State.

Next morning at sun-up I had the commando ready

to trek, and I went to say good-bye to General Joubert. He was very kind and in good spirits, for things had been going well again.

"Be an oprecht Burgher, Sarel, and keep out of danger," said he.

"I will do that, General," said I.

"Then can I send a good report of you to some one."

I thought he meant Oom Paul Kruger and the Executive at Pretoria.

"Then I stand well there now, General?" I asked, remembering how angry the Government had been at my leaving the Transvaal.

"Ja, Sarel; and I hope to see you living together as man and wife should. Good-bye," and he went away before I could ask what his strange words meant.

When I got word with Paul I told him what the General had said, asking him how he interpreted such language.

"Katrina has written to him asking him to keep an eye on you," was his reply.

"How do you know that, Paul?"

"You are not the only one in the secrets of General Joubert," said he.

The thought that this might be true made me very sad and full of shame that I should be written about as if I were a young kerel whose mother was not near to watch him. I was also sore that Paul should know more than I did of my own affairs, for it gave colour to my fear that he was, after all, only a spy set to watch over me, and perhaps help me to get a fall; and I began to regret that I had brought him with me, for I could see great trouble in front of me from this cause. Yet I dare not quarrel with him, for I knew not how strong he really was; and even if I told about the shooting of the khaki Boers, he would perhaps be slim enough to outwit me. So I was as a man who knows there is a snake in the bedroom, but dare not get out of bed to kill it lest he tread on it in the dark.

Then it was there came to me great sorrow that I was not quick in thinking clever and proper answers to speeches at the moment they were most wanted. It is true that I could always make good and sharp replies, but I was too careful about making them good, which took time to think over, and was like fixing the sight of your rifle while a buck was running away. But so many things had happened unexpectedly to my good that I was in hopes an accident would happen that would rid me of Paul. Therefore I made as if I knew quite well that Katrina had written to Piet Joubert.

"Ja," said I, "Katrina and Slim Piet have ever been good friends, and it has been well for me."

"Then why did you run away from the Transvaal when your figures would not add up properly, if Piet were your friend?" asked Paul.

"I said he was Katrina's friend."

"But are not a wife's friends her husband's also?"

"Sometimes he is glad they are not," I answered, making at last a good and sharp answer at the right time, for it was well known that the family of Paul's third wife had been a great trouble and expense to him.

Paul was silent, and I went off before he had time to shoot back an answer; and the trouble and rush of getting the commando away drove all thought of this matter out of my mind, for Burghers have not yet learned, as the English have, to ride off at a word, but must make a very long business of starting, leaving their places to go back for a pipe or a pair of boots, or coming up to tell me not to start for a quarter of an hour. Then some of them would not saddle up till they knew who was to be their corporal, and if they had chosen one they would want to choose over again. So to stop trouble I made appointments which, being made in a hurry, were not always good; and some of those I appointed would not take the work, and I had to persuade some one else. All this took much time, and it was nearly noon before we got away,

the General sending a messenger to say that if I could
not start my span he would send another driver, at
which the Burghers laughed, for the messenger, being
one of those who had a spite against me, shouted his
words.

Paul rode with me, and talked as boldly and master-
fully as if he was commandant, and not I. " We
shall off-saddle there, and water there, and sleep at
So-and-so," he went on, till I had great work to keep
my tongue from slipping, and telling him that I was
commandant and had the ordering of these things.
But I restrained my words, knowing that the time
must soon come when I could put my heel on his
neck.

I was distracted from further unhappy thoughts by
the Irish Boers coming up and wanting to be made
corporals, and generally offering to take all the offices
that had no fighting attached to them. Paul was for
putting them off; but for that reason, and to show
my authority, I made Van der Murphy a corporal.
This brought up old Hendrik Keiser, a German Boer
who spoke the Taal so badly that few could understand him, but for all that he was a great stickler for
the use of that tongue.

" I object to having a corporal who not only does
not speak the Taal, but who talks Irish, which no
one can understand," said he; "and what is more,
if I hear any more of this bastard English-Irish, I
shall leave the commando. It is neither the language
of monkeys nor Hottentots."

" What's that you say ? " asked Van der Murphy.
And then came great tribulation, for becoming a
Burgher does not make an Irishman love fighting less.

Now it happened that Van der Murphy was very
strong in his feelings against Germans ever since a
German manager was put over the mine where he
had a contract for riding transport from the railway-
station. This manager had reported Van der Murphy
to the directors for staying on the road and drinking
whisky, and talking of England falling, while the

mine was waiting for the dynamite he was carrying, whereby Van der Murphy lost his contract and had great difficulty in getting another, because he talked so much politics to the miners. The result of his losing the contract was a fight with the manager, and I, as public prosecutor, had to prosecute Van der Murphy, and get him bound over to keep the peace against all the Germans in the dorp, because he had said he would kill them all to be revenged on Germany. Although I made it as light and easy for Van der Murphy as I could by keeping back the most damaging evidence, the landdrost fined him ten pounds for the assault, for the Germans were the best customers of a beer-hall that belonged to the landdrost, and, as he said, he could not have his trade spoiled by a wild Irishman because he had taken a Boer woman's name. Then, again, Van der Murphy only drank whisky at the English canteen, which, as the landdrost said, showed that he was no patriotic Burgher, or he would have drunk dop or German beer,—all of which small things always weighed with our landdrost in giving judgment against wrongdoers who were not thoroughbred Boers.

All this was well known to Van der Murphy, and it rankled in his heart; and as Irish hearts are ever sore, this kept his raw and sensitive, and he was always bitter against anybody with a German name. As many good Boer names are also German, it led to many mistakes on his part, and numerous fights, both in the dorp where he lived and in the commando. Whenever he met a German, or one whom in his ignorance he took for a German, Van der Murphy would talk at him to make him fight, which generally took a very long time, for both Irish and Germans are ready with their tongues, and can say bitter and cutting things. When old Hendrik got angry he would talk fast in English, German, and the Taal, being a good swearer in all three tongues; and as Van der Murphy knew only two of them he always got the worst of it, for Hendrik got in three blows to Pat's one. Then Hendrik had the best through being, like all Germans, better learned than Van der Murphy. He had read a book about Ireland which was full of abuse of Irishmen, and Hendrik would get it out and read long passages to Pat, just as old Paul read his Bible to confute the Burghers. What with his funny way of talking the Taal, and his serious anger against Irishmen,—who, he said, should all be in tronk, as the book showed,—Hendrik made the Burghers laugh exceedingly; and they would all pretend to agree with him, so that he might go on abusing Irishmen. After a time the Burghers would look to these quarrels for their amusement, as they did the psalm-singing; and when they were dull, one would go to Hendrik and tell him something bad that Van der Murphy had said about Germans, and then they would stand round and smoke and laugh while the two quarrelled. And often, when I wanted them to go look for khakis, they would start the two quarrelling, and say they could not leave until they had seen the end of the fight. It was fortunate that Paul had told me of this, for as soon as the quarrel began I rode the Burghers hard, and steadfastly refused their requests that we should halt to see the end. The two, finding they had no audience, soon ceased to stand and abuse one another, but did it as they rode.

"You'll ride the horses down," said Van der Murphy as he came up; "but I suppose you know where we can get plenty more."

"Commandant," said Hendrik, "you must make an order that all Burghers speak the Taal; I cannot understand what these Irish Burghers say."

"Then how do you know I was abusing Germans?" asked Pat.

"By your looking so ugly."

And then the two went at it again, only Hendrik spoke German and his shocking Taal, and Pat quarrelled in Irish-English, which is a language so strange that even I, who wield the English with admirable fluency, found it difficult to understand him.

At last Van der Murphy said some very severe things of Germans in the Taal, when Hendrik, coming up nearer to me, said—

"Commandant, will you interpret for me the Hottentot language of this wild whisky man?"

"You can't understand any language," answered Pat.

"Yours is no language," said Hendrik.

"My proper language requires educated men to understand. It is a learned language, and was spoken by the kings of Ireland."

"And your kings were all murderers. No wonder your English Government won't allow it to be spoken."

"But it is spoken all over the country," said Pat.

"Ja, by the pigs."

This made the Burghers laugh, and Van der Murphy, although very angry, was fond of a joke and laughed too, for he saw that old Hendrik had put a cartridge in his mauser, as he generally did when he had said such stinging things that Pat talked of murder.

This talk of what was the proper language to use on commando kept up for long, for a talkative Dane, who was learned in languages, made rude remarks about the Taal because there were so few words in it.

"You see," said he, "that even Hendrik, although he is all for the Taal, has to use German to get angry in. There is no tongue like English for good swear-words. It is a fighting language."

This brought up all the foreigners in the commando, and there was babel broke loose, for my Burghers were English, Scotch, Irish, German, Hollander, Danish, Russian, French, Peruvians, and many other nations not found in any postal directory. And all had something to say in favour of their language, till Paul du Plooy put on the skid beautifully.

"Kerels," said he, "you may fight and quarrel in any tongue you like, but you will have to get your rations in the Taal, for a commissariat corporal who is an oprecht Burgher knows no other tongue."

"Then," said Van der Murphy, "I can talk my native language when I want my rations, for there is no name in the Taal for whisky except the proper one."

This language business was not the only trouble I had. When the Burghers were at head laager they were kept in fairly good order through fear of General Joubert, for they knew that the troublesome ones were always sent where there was danger of fighting, and this had a wondrous result on their conduct. But now that they were free, they behaved like children home from school. They gave their rifles to the Kafirs to carry when on the trek, went off in threes and fours to shoot buck whenever they pleased, and quarrelled with me if I would not wait for them; and when I reproached them for leaving the commando when khakis might be about, they said they had gone to look for cattle and horses, as I was no good at finding where they were. When I asked Paul what I should do, he only said—

"Sarel, you are like Moses with the children of Israel in the wilderness. They are discontented and rebellious, and the false gods they worship are cattle. But I am Joshua, and you know that he was oprecht, and made the paths smooth for Moses."

We had been riding three days and had seen no cattle, when the Burghers came to me and said—

"We have been in this wilderness now many days, and see no cattle. Let us make a laager and go out in small parties, for a great commando is seen a long way off by the Kafirs, who give warning to the khakis, and get away with their own goats and cows. We will draw lots to see who shall go out, and the rest shall stay in the laager to fight khakis when they come."

I could see that the real reason was that they might stay idle in the sun all day to smoke and drink coffee, and do other things the existence I knew not of at that time. But as the plan would suit me, I told them I agreed with them. I was very anxious to see

Andries Brink, to learn how I was to make the profit he had spoken of, for so far, although I had been made commandant, I could not see that it profited me much, unless trouble and tribulation were profit. I was like a man with a new gun of a pattern to which he had not been used, and knew not how to load and shoot it. Therefore was I glad at this plan to go out in small parties, for I would offer to make one, and, leaving Paul in charge of the laager, I could ride to see Andries and get wisdom.

When I told Paul what I had resolved he was glad; for although he was always telling me not to give way to the Burghers, when he found he was to be left in authority he said I had done right in listening to what they said. For Paul loved authority, which had caused him to be thrown out of all the churches he had joined.

I stopped the commando and told them my plan. They were to make a laager, and throw lots to see who should go out and bring in cattle; but, said I, "remember that all cattle must be brought into laager, and, when sold, the price equally divided among all."

This was the beginning of trouble, for those on whom the lots fell to go out said they would not have all the danger and trouble of finding cattle if they were to share equally with those who stayed safe behind in laager,—and this after they had agreed to the plan. But each man thought the lot would be in favour of his staying.

While they quarrelled, a great and clever plan came to me, giving me my much-wanted excuse for getting away as nearly alone as possible.

"Kerels," said I, "you are afraid of the danger. Of course there is very great danger,—that is why I chose you. Now, to show that I would not ask any Burgher to do what I feared to do myself, I am going to a place where I know the khakis are waiting and watching, and I shall bring away good cattle. Who will go with me?"

As I hoped and expected, there was no answer. I

waited a minute or two, fearing some Burgher whom I did not want might offer,—for the wickedest are often the bravest,—but no one spoke. So I told them I would take only Kafirs, and leave them to settle among themselves who should go out looking for loot. I chose two who spoke very little Dutch, so that they might not hear too much, and giving my last instructions to Paul for the sake of keeping up my authority, although I knew he would pay no heed to them, I rode off to Andries Brink's place, distant about six hours, or by English way of reckoning, about thirty-six miles.

"Well," said Andries, before I could tell him anything, "you have got your commando, and a fine lot of winnowings it is. Never mind; we don't want Burghers too oprecht for our work."

"But how do you know about my commando?" I asked, much surprised.

"Do you think my commando sits drinking coffee and playing cards all day?" he answered.

"Do my Burghers play cards?"

"How many Jews and Johannesburg Burghers have you, Sarel?"

"About twelve," said I, after thinking.

"Then you have twelve card-parties going on night and day."

"But my Burghers are mostly kerels who can't play cards Rooinek fashion."

"Of course not, that's why the good kind Johannesburg Burghers are teaching them."

Andries then, after his quick abrupt fashion, changed the subject. "You must be up and doing, Sarel. There are transport waggons coming up from Mooi River, by way of the roads between Estcourt and the Berg. As they do not expect to meet any Boers there, they will have a very small escort. You must take care of those waggons, Sarel."

And then he told me his plans,—where and how I was to hold them up, and where to take the cattle and horses. He was to send a Kafir with me who knew the country, and who would show me a place where he could hide half the horses in the British army, and no one be able to find them without a balloon.

"But," said I, "my Burghers are lazy, and will not fight even for cattle," and I told him about their forming laager and sending out only those chosen by lot.

Andries thought and smoked some time before he answered.

"Sarel," said he, "I must ride with you to the laager and stir these rascals up. I will make them pull together the way I want them, like a span of old trek-oxen; but I must wait till Charlotte comes."

"Where is she?" I asked, for I had wondered I had not seen her.

"Charlotte is about her father's business. She is a good and loyal Colonial girl to-day, and is at Estcourt. How do you think I should know all about the convoys but from her? The only thing I fear is that she will get engaged to too many British officers. She already has one at Maritzburg, one at Mooi River, one at Estcourt, and two at Durban; and she tells me the hardest part of her work is to remember which engagement-ring to wear."

"I wonder she did not engage herself to me," said I, half in fun, half in earnest.

"She might have accepted a ring, but she would not take a man who already has a sweetheart who can use her tongue, pen, and sjambok equally well," said Andries.

"How do you know this?"

"Man, but you must think me a calf! Does a man start as a waggon-maker or blacksmith without tools?"

I saw what he meant, but I did not quite understand the remark about Katrina using her pen.

"Katrina writes well, does she not?" said I, by way of finding what Andries knew.

"Ja; a nice plain hand that an old General who is nearly blind can read easily. But, Sarel, never mind about Katrina; she is looking well after you. Make money; that is what vrouws like."

"Then Charlotte knows about Katrina?" I asked.

I must have put much feeling into my question, for Andries looked hard at me.

"Charlotte does not know everything," said he, and again changed the subject; neither dare I ask more, for I did not wish that Andries should see that he knew more than I of the work going on behind my back. So we talked of other things till supper-time, and went to bed early.

CHAPTER IX.

Shows how the wisdom of a commandant and the slimness of a whole commando are as clay in the hands of a clever potter.

CHARLOTTE did not arrive by mid-day as Andries had said she would; but a Kafir came in very early, bringing a letter which, I suppose, held some of Andries' secrets, for he rode off with the Kafir, not telling me anything except that he would be back by sundown.

During his absence I tried to find out something more about this strange man, for I thought it my duty to know all I could of one who held my life in his hands as he did. Therefore I tried several drawers and boxes, but all were locked, showing great caution on his part. I satisfied myself, however, on one thing, which was that the farmhouse was not his, but belonged to one Wilson, who had deserted it early in the war, and it had been taken possession of by Andries, so that if anything went wrong, and the place were burned or looted, he would be none the worse off. I found this out by talking to the Kafir servants, one of whom had been working for Wilson. They had been warned by Andries to say nothing, but they were no match for me, who had had such experience in cross-examining lying witnesses who sought to hide the truth. But beyond this I found nothing that enlightened me as to this man, of whom I had a strange fear, yet wanted to trust, for he was a very slim and bold man, and I felt that whatever happened it would be better to have him for a friend than an enemy.

During the day two other Kafirs arrived at different times, but would say nothing to me about their business when they found that Andries was not at home. This made me admire the man more, for it is not every white man who can make Kafirs so loyal and clever as those about him seemed to be. These two boys had plainly travelled far, for they had their blankets and food with them, and I doubt not were some of the native runners who were carrying letters in and out of Ladysmith. Cleverer Kafirs I never met, for they pretended they knew neither English nor Taal, though afterwards I found they knew both well.

Andries came back before sundown, as he said he should, but before he said a word to me, he had long speech with the Kafirs, seeing each separately in his bedroom, but sitting with the door wide open, so that he could see if any one came near. When he had done his talking with them, he told me that he should not wait for Charlotte, but would ride with me to the laager early next day.

An hour after leaving the farm we saw a party of khaki scouts, and this made us lose time by riding out of their way several miles, so that it was nearly seven hours before we reached the laager. Not a man, not even a Kafir, was on sentry, and Andries and I rode to within fifty yards of the camp before we were noticed. Then one or two Burghers came idly up and asked me, " Where are the cattle ? "

" Where is Paul du Plooy ? " I asked.

" The scourging wind is being made into a calm," answered Van der Murphy, who came up at the moment. " You will find him under his roof."

I rode up to the place where Paul had made his rest —a thorn-bush covered with an old blanket. There sat the old man, with his legs tied to the trunk of the bush.

" What's the meaning of this, Paul ? What is the scourging wind doing ? " I asked.

" The scourging wind has been abased by the hot blasts from hell," answered he, sadly.

I got down and cut the rope, which had been passed through the prickly branches of the thorn so cleverly that he could not reach the ends to untie them, and the Burghers had taken away his knife.

"Sarel," said he, rubbing his ankles, "you have all the sons of Belial in this laager."

"But how came you here?"

"They tied me up because they hated righteousness."

"That means you preached too much?"

"Ja; but I did more—I overturned the money-changers' tables."

"What do you mean?"

"Sarel, even as the Pharisees of old sat at the receipt of custom, so have the Jews and Uitlanders from Johannesburg sat ever since you left, playing with three cards and spoiling our people, for they have now all the money of the oprecht Burghers, and those that have no money to pay have given 'good-fors.' Everybody lost except Van der Murphy, who fought them till they gave him his money back; and now he is one of them, and helped to tie me up. Man, but the lust of greed is over them all."

When Paul had had some whisky he told Andries and me all that had happened since I left the laager; how, as soon as I had gone, the Jews and Johannesburgers brought out cards, and taught the young Burghers a game called "Seven up," or "Under or Over Seven," and "Find the Lady," both of which I remembered through having to prosecute certain Johannesburgers at Prinsloosdorp for taking the money of the deacons of the Dutch Reformed Church during the Nachtmaal week. I was, therefore, not surprised to hear that when the young kerels had lost their money, the old Burghers who were looking on at the games got angry that the young ones were so stupid as not to be able to win when it was so easy, and showed them how it was done. In the end they lost their money also, and then blamed the young kerels for encouraging them to play. Some of them then went to Paul and asked him to stop the playing. This he tried to do; but

as they took no notice, he upset the boards with his
sjambok. On this the young kerels turned on him,
saying he had prevented them getting their money
back, as they were just beginning to regain some of
their losses. The one who made the most outcry was
Van der Murphy, who, having, as I have said, become
one of the thieves, encouraged the young kerels to tie
up Paul, as I had found him.

Andries laughed much as Paul told his shameful story.

"You see, Sarel, I knew better than you what was
doing in the laager. It was time that I came to make
the rough places smooth."

"How many have been out after cattle?" I asked
of Paul.

"None; they love cards better than work."

"We thought you were bringing in the cattle," said
Van der Murphy, who was full of whisky.

"Ja; where is our cattle that Paul promised us?"
asked several Burghers.

"Paul never promised you cattle," I answered
angrily.

"Ja, Sarel, I did," said Paul hastily and sadly.
"You see, when I upset their tables, much of the
money was lost in the scramble, and they would have
sjamboked me if I had not promised to make it good
when you brought in the cattle. They took all the
money I had, and made me pay back what I had
received for appointing corporals to serve out stores."

"Ah, and who is serving out stores now?" I asked.

Van der Murphy answered for Paul. "We don't
want any one to serve us; we serve ourselves. But
there is little now left to serve. When do we get more?"

"Sarel," said Andries, "Paul is right; you have all
the sons of Belial in this laager. Let me show you
how to tame them." Then he added in a whisper,
"Don't look surprised at anything I do."

He stood up on an ant-hill, and in his big voice
called out, "Burghers, come for your loot-money."

Within a minute every man in the laager was
standing round us.

"Burghers," said Andries, taking a big official envelope out of his breast-pocket, "I have certain money here which the State Treasurer has given me to pay to those to whom it is due, being their shares of the cattle-money."

The Burghers crowded round us, and a pleased and hungry look came over their faces. Andries looked at a paper writing very deliberately.

"Jacobus Gert du Preez, sixty pounds," he read out, and looked round the crowd. There was a silence, for the Burghers were puzzled, not quite understanding this thing; neither did I.

"Come forward, du Preez," said Andries, taking from his satchel a big handful of bank-notes. Still no one answered.

"I don't know any Burgher of that name in the commando," said I.

"Then, Paul Kestern, ninety-four pounds," Andries went on, again looking round, as if expecting some one to step forward; but no one did, and the Burghers looked still more dazed and puzzled. After waiting a minute Andries said—

"Burghers, it seems I have made a mistake in the commando. I am Andries Brink, assistant to the Treasurer-General of the Loot Fund, and I have over a thousand pounds here in notes and Government orders to pay to Burghers who have been sending in looted cattle. I was told I should find the commando about here, but it seems this is not the right one. But perhaps some of you may be fathers or brothers to Burghers in the other commando, and would take the money for them."

"Have you anything for Patrick van der Murphy?" asked that wicked man.

"Is it Van der Murphy of Prinsloosdorp?" asked Andries with a very straight face.

"Ja, coos."

"Have you a brother named Mike Murphy, without the 'van der'?"

"Ja, that's he."

"Then I have his name. Are you sure he is your brother?"

"Well, as he is not so much a Burgher as I am, I suppose he is now only my half-brother, but he used to be my full brother."

"But have you full authority to act for him?"

"Certainly; what's his is mine, and what's mine is his."

"Right," answered Andries; "then hand me over the two pounds he owes to the corporal of commissariat of his commando for whisky."

This made all the Burghers laugh, and put them into good humour, which is a difficult thing to do with old Burghers on commando, and the man who can do it is sure of being held in high esteem. But the laughing of the Burghers made Pat angry, and it was some time before he got back his good temper sufficiently to say that there must be some mistake about the two pounds, as his brother was a teetotaller.

Then answered Andries, ever ready to turn speech in his own favour—

"You are right, Pat; there must be a mistake, if this brother of yours is a teetotaller. It is a pity, for I have five pounds for Mike Murphy, and it would have been twenty if he had not been too lazy to go out for cattle, but prefers to stay in laager and talk Irish and English politics. Anyhow, Pat, I will give you the money for him," and he handed Van der Murphy a five-pound note.

At this the Burghers opened their eyes, for it is one thing to hear money talked of, but quite another to handle it; and this they did, passing the note from hand to hand. Then the Burghers began to follow the example of Van der Murphy and ask where the commando was, if So-and-so was entitled to money, and many others.

"Before I answer," said Andries, "I will read through my complete list; and if any Burgher recognises a relation and will promise to give up the money to him when he sees him, I will hand over what may

be due, for I cannot go riding all over Natal to look
for a missing commando."

Then he began to read names. There was great
silence while eight or nine were read out, till he came
to " Piet Coetzee, twenty pounds."

Immediately a dozen Burghers shouted out, " He is
my brother ! " " My cousin ! " " My uncle ! "—till there
was a babel. But Andries kept quite cool while the
storm lasted, and the Burghers quarrelled with each
other for claiming relationship.

"Now, kerels," said he, slowly counting out twenty
sovereigns, " I cannot say which of you are the real
relations of Piet Coetzee, but I do know you are
oprecht Burghers, or you would not be in this commando. So I will give this twenty pounds to the
Coetzees to keep for Piet ; and if you have to give it
up to him, you may keep five pounds for your trouble."

The ten who claimed relationship with Piet Coetzee
rushed forward, and Andries, with a great show of
carefulness, asking many questions as to the exact
relationship, gave each Coetzee two pounds.

"Now, kerels, hear what I have to say," said Andries,
and he made a speech that set the laager on fire. " I
hear some of you say," said he, "that you did not
know about this looting fund. Of course not. How
can a man expect to know what is going on, if he
spends his time in playing cards and lying in the
shade when his name is called for commando ? Did
not your commandant tell you when he was made
commandant that he was going on important duty,
and would pick his men ? If the General had made
it known in all the laagers that Burghers were wanted
to make money for themselves, not a man would have
remained before Ladysmith. You are the chosen
people. Commandant Sarel Erasmus chose you, and
if you treat him kindly and do as he wishes, you will
all go back rich in money or cattle, and perhaps both.
Now, Burghers, throw away your cards and prepare
to saddle up by sun-up to-morrow, for the good Lord
is giving the enemy into your hands. A convoy of

twenty waggons is on the road with only a small escort, and it is yours for the taking, if only you will do what Sarel tells you, for he has all the plans in his head. Will you be oprecht Burghers?"

"Ja!" they shouted in chorus.

"Then two days hence you will have twenty pounds a man. Now go; look to your horses, clean your rifles—which I see have been left to clean themselves. Think of the good things that are to come, and repent that you tied up the only man who tried to keep you from your evil ways."

At this old Paul, who had been listening, came forward and began a speech; but the Burghers would have none of him, but called to Andries to go on, for they love to listen to men who can talk with a loose and quick tongue, as is seen by the way they were led astray by slippery tongues before the war; and Andries was clever above men with his, besides having a cheerful countenance.

Paul looked very disappointed that the Burghers would not hear him, but I whispered him to wait a bit, when Andries would get him a hearing; so, with much grumbling, Paul gave way, and Andries continued to speak.

He exhorted the Burghers to keep secret from any other Burghers they might meet the fact that they were making large sums of money, and, above all, he spoke good words for me, telling them I had planned hard to get this commando for their benefit, and altogether made it clear to them that they could do nothing without me, but everything with my help, which was the best reason why they should be kind to me.

I was so joyful that I could have kissed Andries, and made up my mind to do to him as he wished the Burghers to do to me, which goes to prove how even intelligent and educated men are won over by the flattery of a skilful dissembler such as Solomon warns against.

When he had done with me, this clever man gave

Paul a good word that made the old man cry with pride.

Said he, "I appoint Paul du Plooy to represent me, who represent the Government. He will keep account of all the cattle brought in, and I shall come to the laager to get that account and pay out the money, and to hear Paul's report on those who have done the best, by which I mean those who have not set up their foolishness against the wisdom of those appointed to lead them. I have full authority in this matter from General Joubert, and if Paul or your commandant report any Burgher as unworthy, he shall have none of the money."

As he spoke these words he took from his pocket a large official envelope and waved it; but I noticed that he did not offer to read it, neither did the Burghers ask him so to do; for when the glitter of gold is in the eyes of a Boer he can see no more than an owl in the sunshine.

"Now, Burghers," said he in conclusion, "make ready for to-morrow, when you will, under the guidance of your commandant, put in the first seeds of what is going to be a bountiful harvest that will feed you and your children for the rest of your days."

If Burghers had the custom of cheering, as have the Rooineks, they would have cheered loudly; but instead, they crowded round Andries, shook his hand, called him "Coos," and made much of him, till I got him away to my part of the laager, where the Kafir had made us some supper under a waggon. Andries being gone, they turned their praises on old Paul, shaking hands and making much of him, particularly those who had been against tying him up, as they had no money to play cards with. And they took him under the shade of a Cape-cart and begged him to read the Bible to them; which he did, not needing any pressing. He read nearly the whole book of Job, till those who had not slipped quietly away fell asleep over their pipes.

For the first time there was no trouble about

sentries at night. It is true I heard high words from a few Burghers; but when I demanded, with great authority, to know what it was, they answered that the quarrel was that all wanted to go on watch.

When Andries and I were alone, which was not until we had let Paul make a long discourse and read a long chapter of prophecy, showing that it was right to spoil an enemy by taking his cattle, I said to Andries, "Is it right about the Burghers' money?"

He laughed as he answered, "Sarel, money talks. That twenty pounds to those rascally Coetzees, and the fiver to that wild Irishman, talked louder than all the speeches ever made in the Raad."

"But have you authority for paying, as you say you have?"

"Sarel, I have lived in the Transvaal, where the motto is, 'Nothing for nothing, and very little for a shilling.' These Burghers are now satisfied that they are going to make money, for they have seen it paid out freely. Twenty pounds in their hands is worth twenty hundred in the Treasury. It is only the price of a couple of oxen, and for it we ought by this time to-morrow to have twenty spans of good oxen to our account, to say nothing of horses and stores."

There was still much in this matter that was cloudy to my understanding, and I was resolved that I should know all that could be learned for the asking. So I said, "But about the money. Do the Government pay for oxen they capture?"

"Sarel, you must not try to learn too much at once. No trade is learned in a day. Look at that; feel it— count it," and he threw me a big bundle of what appeared to be every kind of bank-note used in the country from Cape Town to Pretoria. "Is that money, or is it not?"

"It is," said I.

"Then, you doubting Thomas, do you think it falls from the skies, or is brought by the ravens? No, I earn it, and some of it is yours if you are not a fool."

"I fear that twenty pounds will not reach the

Coetzee it belongs to," said I, not knowing exactly what to say in the face of this great puzzle.

"So do I," answered Andries.

"Then why did you give it to them? Surely you know the Coetzees are a bad lot?"

"Sarel, you should have stayed in the laager and learned that little game with the three cards that cleaned out the Burghers. It is a great educator."

All at once a great light filled my soul, and I saw clearly what before was strangely perplexing.

"Andries, you have salted a mine!" said I.

"Say rather treacled; that's what they call it in the Transvaal. Treacle attracts flies, and, what is more, keeps them sticking where you want them."

And then I saw the great skilfulness and wickedness of the man, and admired him more than was good for me.

"Andries, it is you who are commandant, not I," I said in my joy and admiration.

"Exactly, Sarel. That is where brains are so useful. I do the thinking and planning, and you do the work and have some of the treacle. And now let me tell you another thing, for you have much to learn. You have got these Burghers tied to you by the strongest reim ever made—greed. I have tied them to you; do not loosen the knot. Keep away from them, and don't talk much to them except about loot and money. To-morrow, before we start after these waggons, I will show you how to untie another kind of knot. You have too many sea-lawyers in this commando, Sarel."

"Nay, Andries; I am the only lawyer, and I am only a law-agent."

Andries laughed. "Ja; but there are other agents—agents for mischief. Are there not in the commando some great rascals who would do you harm, and of whom you would be glad to be rid?"

"There are such," said I; "but I fear that now that they have smelt gold they will be like thirsty cattle at a water-hole—very hard to drive away."

"Tell me their names," said Andries.

I easily thought of many, but I told only about twenty.

"Now go over them again and tell me the worst of all these."

I could not reduce them by more than five, and Andries wrote them down.

"Now tell me," said he, "who among these are the slim kerels, for bad men are not to be feared if they have not brains."

I could think of only two or three among them.

"That will not do, Sarel," said Andries. "You are too short-sighted. It is not wisdom to deny cleverness in your enemy or to think that you are cleverer and slimmer than he. You have named all but the right ones. I have been in your commando only a few hours, but I know who are the slim kerels; so does Paul. Call him."

"Paul," said he, when the old man had sat down under the Cape-cart with difficulty because of his tallness, "I want the names of all the slim and wicked Burghers in the laager."

"Write down the whole roll and you have them," said he, "for they are the wickedest Burghers ever corrupted by Rooineks."

"Nay, Paul, you are sore because they will not listen to your preaching. Tell me the names of those who would put you and Sarel out of the commando."

"Put down every name except ——," and here Paul gave the names of the six Burghers who had hypocritically asked him to read the Bible to them under the cart, although their names were among those I had given Andries as the worse.

After a long indaba Andries made out a list, Paul being most careful to see that the names of those who had mistreated him were on it. But Andries would have no advice or help from Paul, and made the list as he himself thought it should be, after he had heard what Paul and I had to say about each man. When at last it was finished it had but six names, and

Andries added to it Pat van der Murphy, whom neither of us had given.

" But he is not wicked when he is away from the whisky," said I. " You have left out the names of twenty men who are ten times wickeder than he."

"Sarel, he is a Murphy by birth, and he has put a Hollander 'van der' in front of it. The two are bad enough by themselves, but when they are mixed they are dynamite. Now leave me here alone till I call you, and see that no Burgher comes near me for an hour. When I want you I will call you."

When Andries called me it was to tell me to bring up Pat van der Murphy privately. I did so, and Andries being satisfied that no one was listening, said in a low voice, " Pat, I am going to do something to show how much we Afrikanders appreciate you Irishmen for helping us. You have heard me say I have a lot of money belonging to the Burghers, due to them when they bring in loot cattle. Now as I shall have to go to other commandos, and do not know when I shall be back, I am going to leave the money here. The Burghers will be told that their commandant has it. Now, Pat, you know there are scabby sheep in most flocks, and such may be here, and who knows but that the commandant may be robbed ? Therefore I have selected you to carry it, and when you give the money up, you will have twenty pounds for yourself. Keep a still tongue, and let no one share your secret."

Van der Murphy made a speech in which he said he was the only man in the commando fit to be trusted with the money, which, he said, showed how skilful a judge of good men Andries was ; and he was going on to tell all sorts of things about the other Burghers, when Andries cut him short by taking a heap of notes from a big envelope and asking Pat to count one thousand pounds, which he did, taking a long time and making many mistakes.

When Pat at last said he was satisfied the count was right, Andries put the notes into a large envelope, sealed it, and gave it back to Van der Murphy, talking fast all the time, telling him what not to do and not to say. Suddenly he said, " Give it me back. I must tie it up. Pat, open that haversack behind you and give me a bit of string you will find there."

I was about to do it, when Andries waved me back in a meaning manner.

After looking for some time, Pat said he could find no string.

" Never mind ; stick this on the flap and write your name on it," said Andries, giving Pat some gummed stamp-paper.

Van der Murphy did as directed, writing the words " One thousand pounds," at the suggestion of Andries.

" Now," said he, " I don't want you to talk about this ; so while it is fresh on your mind, saddle up and ride away towards Spion Kop for an hour ; and if the Burghers want to know where you have been, say you have gone scouting," and Pat went off with the parcel in his inside breast-pocket.

When he had gone from the laager Andries told me to call up Gert Coetzee, whose name was on the list of six, and to him Andries, to my surprise, made exactly the same speech as he had to Pat, going through the same business of bidding Gert look for string, and finding none, the envelope being sealed with stamp-paper and signed. Gert was also sent to ride, but in the opposite direction to Pat. Then came the remainder of the six, one at a time, and to each was made the same speech ; each was bidden to search for the string that was not, and to each was given a sealed envelope in the same way, and instructions to ride off scouting, but all in different directions.

" Now, Sarel," said Andries when the last had gone, " your sea-lawyers are all settled."

I did not quite understand, but said, " Ja, that's so," for I did not wish that Andries should think I was slow at seeing through smart things, which usually I was not ; but this man worked so strangely that

there was no shame in any one, however well educated, not keeping pace with his cleverness.

Before we slept that night we had made full arrange-
ments for the morrow. All the commando was to go
excepting a guard of fifty that were to remain in the
laager under Paul, whom I made acting commandant,
which pleased the old man hugely, and suited me,
for I did not want him with me to preach disaster at
the most important event of my career. Andries also
decided that Van der Murphy and the other rascals
who had charge of the money should remain, he telling them each privately that it was too risky that
they should go fighting; and with that arrangement
they all readily agreed.

CHAPTER X.

*Shows how I gave myself to the tempter, but lost
the wages of my iniquity.*

IT was wondrous how quickly the Burghers got
through their breakfast and were saddled up next
morning. Long before sun-up they came to me in
twos and threes to tell me it was time to trek; but
I remembered what Andries had advised, and was
short, sharp, and dignified in my manner towards
them, and made my breakfast with great slowness,
just to show them how cool and unconcerned I could
be in time of great strife and seriousness. When at
last I gave the word to ride, they were off without
asking a single question, and not a Burgher had to
go back for anything he had forgotten, the most
truly marvellous thing I had ever seen in any commando.

As we rode, Andries told me about the transport
we were to cut off and capture. It consisted of
about twenty waggons, made up of parties from Mooi
River, Estcourt, and Maritzburg, travelling together
for safety, and taking by-roads over the desolated
country between the railway and the Drakensberg
mountains, so as to reach and supply that part of
General Buller's army scattered between Estcourt
and Ladysmith, then in the sixth week of its siege.

Andries had well thought out his plan, showing me
that he was a skilful man, who could see a very long
way in front of him. He knew exactly how many
waggons there were, whom they belonged to, and

whether the oxen were good or otherwise. " There are," he said, " three waggons belonging to Smith of Sandvlei, all good ; then there are three of Bush of Belmont, all poor. Bush is one of those Natal loyalists who are always abusing the Boers ; but when he heard the British were commandeering waggons and oxen, he sent all his best away to the most distant part of his farm, leaving only poor cattle to be hired at two pounds a-day. I am sorry that the British will have to pay a schelm like him for the oxen he will lose to-day."

And so Andries talked on, showing me how well Charlotte and his spies must have done their part of the work. He had also got all the details ready for the capture. " We shall sight them," said he, " as soon as we get on the top of yonder rise, just as they are preparing to cross Bokman's Drift. The road there goes down a steep hill, turns sharply up a deep kloof, and back on the opposite side, going up one side of a V and down the other, so that we shall have them in a narrow hole below us. We shall leave our horses on this side of the rise, and line the top of the pass, lying among the boulders, which are big and many. No khaki scout will ride among them to look for us, as they have been told at Estcourt there are no Boers in this part of the country. Now, Sarel, halt your schelms in that kloof and tell them what I have just told you ; it will satisfy them that you know all about the country, which they have doubts on so far."

I made Andries repeat all that he had said, so that I should make no mistakes, then halted the commando in the kloof and sent six Burghers ahead to spy out what was doing over the rise. While the scouts were gone I made a speech to the Burghers, describing all that Andries had told me. I was glad to see by the look on their faces and the remarks I heard, that they were surprised that I should know so much about the country and the proper way to attack a convoy. But they did not like the fighting, I could easily see, for nearly all the commando were fresh, having remained in the dorps and on their farms as long as possible, where they had done nothing but talk, and abuse the Burghers for being beaten at Elandslaagte. The only ones who had seen war had been at that great and bloody fight, and were never tired of telling about the lancers, and the Scotsmen who wear kilts and do such awful things with their bayonets, till the Burghers would go to sleep, feeling all the internal complaints for which they had got doctors' certificates.

In less than an hour the scouts returned and brought good news, except that the waggons were not as many as we had thought, being only sixteen; but there were three spare spans of sixteen to help pull over the bad places. There were about a hundred khakis as escort, and one of the scouts had recognised them as belonging to a regiment only just out from England, who would not know how we should attack,—for in the early days of the war the khakis always crowded close together when fighting, making it easier to hit than to miss them. But as they got wisdom they did as the Boers did—scattered widely, and ran away when they could fight no more, which is much more sensible than standing up to be killed.

"Are there any lancers?" asked a dozen Burghers of the scouts.

"Not one; nor are the bayonets in the rifles."

Immediately the anxious look on their faces faded partly away.

"There may be lancers behind," said Andries; "but they ride slowly, and will not get up till the business is all finished."

The serious look came back to the faces of the Burghers, and I began to marvel that Andries should say such a thing, till I remembered that he never spoke a word without having some good reason for it. As the Burghers began to look very thoughtful and ceased to talk much, as if thinking of their farms and their vrouws, I hurried them to take up their positions on the top of the rise before they had time to get more frightened. Andries gave good advice in the matter of taking cover, as so few of the Burghers had fought white men. They were more anxious to find spots where all their bodies were hidden than positions that enabled them to see what to shoot at. Most of them, too, began to light their pipes and place their hats on stones far away from them, as is the custom when fighting white men or Kafirs with guns; but Andries stopped this.

"These khakis," said he, "are not yet good shots, and if they fire at the hats they are more likely to hit you," on which the Burghers put their hats on very quickly. There was no lack of Burghers ready to stay with the horses below the rise; but as we had plenty of Kafirs to do this, I made them all go among the stones, which they did very slowly until Andries shouted, "Here come the khakis!" and they were out of sight instantly.

Truly the trap had been well planned; for when once the waggons had got down into the V-shaped gully they would be at our mercy, for we had two hundred and fifty Burghers, well covered, lying all along the edge, and commanding every bit of the road. Even if the khakis proved good shots, they would have no chance of hitting our men, for they would have to fire upwards—a very difficult thing when one must keep the body covered from an enemy who is looking down. Neither could the waggons go back, for the road ran along the steep side of the mountain, and was only just wide enough for one waggon, and easy enough for a careless driver to send oxen and waggon crashing to the bottom.

The advice I gave was that, at the word, the Kafir drivers and voorloupers who lead the oxen were to be shot. The waggons would then have to stop, for no Britisher can drive an ox-waggon without years of practice. The Burghers at the coming-out end of the valley were then to fire, to give the khakis a chance to run back, which was the thing Andries was most uncertain about, knowing that in their stupidity khakis will not run away, but stay to shoot, even when they can see nothing to shoot at. I also was secretly in hopes that when they found they could not go forward they would run, for I did not want to have it on my mind that I had shot any British; and least of all did I want them to stay and use their bayonets, which is a thing no Boer can stand, and, with the lances, ought to be forbidden in warfare as dangerous and painful.

We could hear the waggons and the cries of the drivers long before they began to descend the steep roadway, and the sound made my heart thump, for I could not help fearing that just as wealth was close to my hand I might get a bullet, though I got some consolation from remembering that the khakis are not, like the Boers, more keen on killing officers than privates; but then I knew that even the kindest khaki could not always be certain where his bullet would go. These thoughts must have been written in my face, for Andries, who sat near me, spoke sharp words to me as if I were in fear, not knowing that mine were only the proper thoughts that should be in a man's heart at such a time. I noticed, too, that when the young Burghers heard the sound of the waggons they began to grow restive, and talked and whispered until I had to call silence. Some of them handled their rifles in such a nervous manner, that I began to fear they would do as old Scheepers did at the Queen's Battery when the Jameson raiders were riding along all un-suspecting,—fire in their excitement and discover our ambush. I whispered my thoughts to Andries, who, being a fearless man, called out, "I'll shoot any man who fires before the word is given."

One of the Burghers answered, "Who are you to talk thus?"

Andries moved towards the man, with his sjambok raised, at which the Burgher took fright.

"All right, commandant," said the man; "I thought it was Jan Meyer," which was a lie, for the voices were very different.

Presently, after what seemed a long hour's waiting, we saw on the crest of the ridge two mounted khakis. They were the advanced scouts, and should have been at least a mile in front of the main body, but foolishly believing what they had been told at Mooi River about there being no Boers in this part of the country, they rode only about a hundred yards ahead of the first waggon, and on the road, instead of well on either side, where they must have seen some sign of us. But they did not, and rode into the trap, smoking and talking as if passing through the street of a friendly dorp. Next came the first waggon, with a few khakis on it, and others walking at the side, carrying their rifles slung or at the slope; and here and there a mounted transport-rider or owner of the waggons, swearing at the Kafir drivers and making a great show of doing something to earn his two pounds per waggon a-day. But never a one went off the track to see what might be behind the boulders that filled the valley and covered both sides of the mountain.

The first waggon had reached the bottom of the descent, crossed the drift, and rounded the corner for the upward journey, when just what I had feared happened. A mauser shot was fired by one of our Burghers lying in the line about midway along the road. Andries swore as no man who reads his Bible as he pretended to ought; but all his swearing proved vain, for before he had let out a dozen words the reports of rifles made it hard to hear a man speak. The Burghers were blazing away from both sides and front, and the khakis were unslinging their rifles and standing at the ready, looking for something to shoot at. But our men lay flat, and except for a hat falling here or there, or the barrel of a rifle showing above the stones as it was brought to the aim, there was nothing to make a mark. Three of the Kafir voor-loupers had been hit, and were howling and crying out as Kafir boys do when frightened and hurt. I saw some of the Kafir drivers throw down their long whips and crawl under the waggons, of which there were now six in sight, all in great confusion, some stopped. In others the drivers were whipping up the oxen, as if trying to pass the waggon in front, while in each span there were oxen hit and lying struggling in a heap, on to which other cattle were continually falling. Two young khaki officers were running among the men shouting out orders, and very sorry I felt for them, though at the same time I was angered by their folly in not getting under the waggon; and I was not surprised soon to see one give a jump and fall against the waggon, and almost directly afterwards the other sat down, but still kept shouting out directions, though I could see he was hit in the leg. Four or five khakis were also hit, and then the others very wisely took cover on the opposite side of the waggons; but though they fired rapidly, none of our men were hit. Presently three khakis fell at the same moment.

"Tell them to surrender," I shouted to Andries, who was watching the business through a pair of field-glasses.

"All right," answered he. "I don't want to appear if I can help it, so send a Burgher to tell them to put their hands up."

"Nick Grobbelaar," I shouted to the nearest Burgher I could see, "call out 'hands up!'"

But never a word from Nick. I called to him again.

"Nay, commandant, I have a vrouw and twelve children. I am not going to be shot because these khakis won't know when they are finished. Tell them yourself."

I called to three or four others, but none would speak, being fearful of drawing the bullets upon them; so, disguising my voice, I called out, "Surrender, and your lives will be spared. You are surrounded, and we only want your oxen."

"Come out, you cowards," was the only reply I got, and with it a volley in our direction, which showed that the Burghers had good reason for not obeying me.

Just then I saw a strange thing. The old German, Hendrik Keiser, stood up without his rifle, and, holding both hands high above his head, ran down the rough side of the valley, calling out in his funny English, " Don't shoot, *Zhon Bool* ! "

As soon as the khakis saw him they ceased to fire, only a few shots going off at intervals from both sides. The officer with the wounded leg got up with great difficulty and limped towards him.

" Do you surrender ? " he asked.

" Vy, no, I am knock in de shest, and de bullet make me run or fall on my face, so I run."

" Then come here," said the officer, and the last we saw of Hendrik was his fat body being pulled under the waggon, he talking fast in English, German, and Dutch. We could hear him plainly say, " You are dam fool Englishman. We are tousands and tousands. Why don't you run hard ? "

But the khakis did not run, but got closer under cover of the waggons and fired whenever they could get a mark, which was not often. The Burghers, too, began to shoot more slowly, for they were wisely fearful of hitting the oxen, which were now mixed up so much that it was impossible to hit a man except through a carcass.

" What shall we do ? " I asked of Andries, for I could see that if the khakis got behind the oxen we could do nothing, for our Burghers were firing less and less, the shots dropping in ones and twos, with long pauses between.

Before Andries could answer, a shouting came from the waggons highest up on the road, and, looking up, we saw our Burghers running up to the waggons, and the khakis standing as if uncertain what to do.

" Come on, kerels, they have surrendered," said Andries, getting up from behind the stone where he had sat all the time; but I, more discreet, did not move, and was rewarded, for a bullet took Andries in the hand, making him swear and yell as a wound there always does any man, even those who would not cry out if a bullet went through their bodies, as I have seen. When he had made a finish of swearing, Andries ran towards the waggons, shouting, "Stop it, you fools! we are too many for you," and one of the transport-riders took up the cry.

The khakis stood dazed and uncertain, while the Burghers walked up with no great haste until all the firing was finished; but before the smell of gunpowder was gone out of the air they were drinking beer with the khakis and making friends.

I never learned properly how the surrender came about, but from what I could see and heard, it was a case of mistake on both sides. Old Keiser had been hit, as he said, and did as men often do when shot—rushed forward; and as the ground sloped very greatly he could not stop himself, and so ran on on to the waggons. This was seen by both khakis and Burghers, and before it was understood, the fighting had stopped; the khakis seeing no officers, but hearing the transport-rider calling out "Stop," concluded that the order had been given to them to surrender.

There had been wondrous few hurts, considering that the khakis had so little cover. Both officers, a captain and a lieutenant, were hit, but not seriously. All the Kafir drivers were hit, and two voorloupers killed; but of the eight khakis only one was badly hurt, for which I was secretly very thankful.

"I thought you Boers were such fine shots," said a Tommy. "You had us in a box, yet only scratched half-a-dozen of us."

"We were merciful," said a Burgher, "for you did us no harm; you hit only one of our men."

"We could not see you," answered the Tommy, "but I can see you now. Take that for your mercy," and he hit the Burgher between the eyes, and knocked him down as if he had been shot. "Come on," shouted the Tommy, taking off his tunic; "come on. If you can't fight better than you can shoot I'll take on the whole bloomin' Boer army, Kroojer thrown in. Come on!" and he began punching every Burgher standing within reach of his fists.

He had knocked down three and driven the rest

before him, when a little sergeant came up. Although nothing so big as the fighting Tommy, he ordered him to put on his tunic and go behind the waggon, which the Tommy did in the most meek and obedient way. The Burghers would have run after him, but Andries called them back, saying, "Go, collect the rifles from the khakis and stack them here. Sarel, go you and talk to the khaki captain, and tell him he may march all his men back, as we only want the oxen and stores."

I found the young captain sitting under the waggon nursing a broken leg, and in great pain.

"I'm sorry you are hurt," I began; but he stopped me with "Damn your sorrow; go and find my sergeant-major, and ask if he has any medical comforts, and find out how many of my men are hit."

I went and inquired for the sergeant-major, and found him, like the captain, nursing a wounded leg. I told him what the captain had said.

"We have no medicine-chest," said he; "and as to the wounded, you can count them yourself, for you did it, not we."

I went the round of the waggons, and found the number of the wounded as I have mentioned, and went back to the khaki captain and told him. He swore a bit; then, speaking with as much authority as if he were master instead of me, said, "You want the oxen, do you? Well, I'm sorry I can't prevent your taking them, so take them and your damned rascals off as soon as you can, and leave us to go back in our own way; otherwise my men will start again, for they consider they have been had. The order to cease firing was given by one of your damned colonials. Why don't you come out and fight like men?" he went on, his anger rising, for he was suffering great pain from his leg, therefore I was not annoyed at his manner.

I was tempted to answer that we did not come out and fight because we were not fools; but there was before me the thought that I might soon be on the English side, and I did not want any unwise speech to come up against me. So I did not answer him in anger, but, instead, spoke cheerfully and friendly, saying there was no disgrace in his being defeated, for a young officer must be naturally ignorant. I meant nothing offensive, but he took it as if I did, and said some very severe things about Boers which I would not stay to hear.

While I had been talking with the captain, the Burghers were opening some of the cases on the waggons and helping themselves to the good things they found in them, particularly the wine and tinned things. At that time our Burghers had all they wanted in the way of food and clothes, for the stores commandeered in Johannesburg came down to the laager by the waggon-load, so they cared more for what the English called medical comforts—which is champagne and brandy—than food-stuffs, except of course jam and sardines, which a Boer would sit up in his dying bed to eat.

"Come and have some champagne, Tommy," said a Burgher who had opened a case.

"You are pretty liberal with other people's liquor," said Tommy.

"But it belongs to us now," answered the Burgher.

"Well, that alters the case, so I don't mind if I do," said Tommy, and he drank, and a dozen others with him.

"You are a rummy lot, you Boers," said one Tommy. "How the thunder do you come to speak English and look so white?"

Before an answer could be given, Andries came up and hurried the Burghers to outspan the oxen. They were not inclined at first to leave the drinking, till he whispered in the Taal, "Remember the poisoned whisky and the lancers."

This made them start, and most of them helped to get the cattle out of the yokes.

When we were ready to move on, Andries said to the khaki captain—

"Send a mounted messenger back to Mooi River,

telling them what has happened, while your men remain looking after the wounded. If any Boers turn up, tell them that General Joubert and Commandant Ben Viljoen are very strong against Natal Burghers who lend their oxen to the military, and have been here to take them away."

"Where is General Joubert?" asked the captain.

"Here he is," answered Andries, pointing to himself.

The captain took a long look at him, and smiled, answering—

"Well, General, I'm glad to have met you, and am only sorry that we have not changed places. But I did not know that Boer generals went out cattle-stealing. I suppose your friend there is Commandant Ben Viljoen?"

"He is. Come here, Ben."

I went up.

"Allow me to introduce you. Captain——?"

"Walker," said the captain.

"Captain Walker—Commandant Ben Viljoen,—the brains of the Boer army."

The captain said, "How d'ye do?" carelessly, smiling all the time.

"And now, captain," Andries continued, "let me give you some good advice, for you are a plucky chap, and if you take pains you may get a Victoria Cross yet. Next time you are in charge of transport, don't believe what the stay-at-home staff officers tell you about there being no Boers in the country, but send your scouts well in front and on both sides. And when it comes to fighting, make your men lie down, and set the example yourself, for a wounded officer is not much use. You fellows look very nice standing up waving your sticks, but my photographer is too busy taking the pictures of prisoners at Pretoria to be here to-day."

I did not catch the full reply of the captain, and if I had I do not think it would look well in print.

We then went away. As we passed the stack of captured rifles, Andries stopped and looked at them.

"There should be nearly a hundred here, but there are less than fifty," said he. "Where are the others?"

A young lad who was sitting by eating sardines, and drinking champagne out of a broken bottle, answered—

"All sold, coos."

"Sold! what do you mean?"

"Gert Smit was in charge of them, but he has sold them back to the khakis for a shilling each."

Andries burst out laughing.

"Sarel, they must have winnowed the jails to make up your commando," said he. "Never mind; fifty rifles won't hurt us. Let us get off with the cattle," and with much coaxing, bullying, and swearing we got most of the Burghers away from the waggons and the company of the Tommies, who were fast making them drunk, and had already made Franz Liebenberg sing "God save the Queen," and were starting a smoking-concert under the shade of one of the waggons, and drinking champagne and brandy as if it was milk. If we had not started then, there would not have been a sober man in the commando. As it was, half of them were getting foolish, and were shaking hands with the Tommies and drinking healths as if they were old friends met after a long time.

We got away at last, with about three hundred oxen and eight good horses—a very nice capture, worth in money at least three thousand pounds.

After about two hours' trek we came to a kloof full of thorn-bushes, where we off-saddled, and turned the cattle into a hollow, where the Kafirs kept them herded well together, while the Burghers finished the bottles of champagne and brandy and other things they had brought with them.

"Come with me, Sarel," said Andries, leading the way up the kloof out of hearing of the Burghers.

When we were quite safe from listeners, Andries unfolded to me his cunning plan.

"We have," said he, "over three thousand pounds worth of cattle, and now you must help me put the money in the bank."

I did not understand him, but not liking to show my ignorance, I answered that I should be glad to do so.

" I am going to ride back towards the waggons," he went on. " Half an hour later I shall come riding in as if all the devils were behind me, shouting out ' Lancers ! ' The rest will be quite easy. The Burghers will leave in a great hurry, and you with them, but not in front. After a bit you will hear a rifle-shot and fall off your horse, saying you are wounded, but telling them not to wait for you, which will not be necessary, but it will sound well. When they are out of sight you will come back to the kloof and help me bank the money."

It was a great and clever plan, and immediately I saw as through a mist when the sun and wind begin to melt it away. After a few more words of instruction from Andries, I went back to the Burghers, while he took his horse and went away quietly.

The Burghers were all lying in the shade, many of them asleep, for it was two hours past noon and the sun very hot. I sat down and waited, with my heart thumping forcefully, watching the Burghers, and wondering what would happen should the plan miscarry, though I could hardly believe that the name of " Lancers " would not prove of mighty effect; for not even the news that the Kafirs were making a night-attack during the Magato campaign produced such fear as the name of these British soldiers with what the Burghers, in their ignorance, called "long sticks with knives," just as they always miscalled swords "long knives." It was a long wait, as ever half hours always are when one waits for serious matters. I could hear Andries' horse many times before he came, so that when at last he really did come, I was hardly certain about it.

" *Pas op*, Burghers ! Lancers ! Lyddite ! " he shouted, riding right among the drowsy and half-drunken bodies.

Never have I seen men move more quickly ; never

were horses saddled faster; and, quick as they were, they would have been even quicker, but in their hurry and fright they picked up each others' saddles and bridles, a thing a Boer rarely does, for he knows his saddle as he knows his oxen and even his children. Most rode off before they had their feet in the stirrups, and more than one fell off because he had not properly fastened the saddle-girth. All the time Andries was dashing about wildly, shouting and exciting them to speed by crying in his big voice, " Back to the laager! Lancers! Lancers! Lyddite - guns coming! " So natural and serious did he look, that I began to think that, after all, it might be really true; and I should have believed it had not I noticed that he was driving the Kafirs back to the cattle, and striking hard and often at them with his sjambok.

" Now go, Sarel," said he to me, when the last Burgher was away. " Fall off when you hear the shot, and scream out loud as you know how."

I rode off; but, fast as I went, I could not catch up the main body, who were half-way up the farthest ridge. Just as I had got abreast of three or four of the rearmost, bang went a rifle-shot, followed quickly by three or four. I shouted out, " I'm shot! " reined in my horse, and carefully slipped out of the saddle, making a great groaning and sobbing, as Burghers do when hit. The Burghers nearest looked round over their shoulders, but before I could say " Ride on— never mind me," they had lashed up their horses and were out of hearing. So I lay still, holding the reins of my horse, and wondering what was to be the next part of this exceedingly cunning business.

A few more shots were fired from the direction of the kloof, and then I heard a horse coming towards me. I turned and looked, and my heart thumped, for I saw a khaki with helmet, and it came to me that, after all, the lancers had come. In my surprise I stood up, when the voice of Andries said, " Lie down, you fool, you are badly wounded; the fools may be looking from the kopjie."

I lay down, and carefully felt myself all over to make certain that I was not really wounded, so naturally did this clever man speak and act.

Andries burst out laughing. "You are not very badly hurt, Sarel; I could see that by the careful way you fell."

When I looked round, I saw to my surprise that not only was Andries in khaki uniform, but that four Kafirs with him were also wearing British uniforms.

"What is the meaning of this?" I asked, very much puzzled.

"Only part of the business. We are the lancers," and he laughed again. "Now get up as if you were really hurt, not as nimbly as you did when you got the lance in your calf. Lean on me as we walk back to the kloof, for the schelms are certain to be watching us from the kopjies. They'll think you are taken prisoner."

We walked slowly over the five or six hundred yards between us and the kloof, keeping on the higher ground, so that the watching Burghers could see well.

"You did that much better than you did the first wound you had, Sarel," said Andries, when we had got to the cover of the kloof. "Now we will drink success, for the schelms have been good enough to leave some champagne."

One of the Kafirs in khaki picked up a bottle and handed it to me. As he did so I recognised in him the Kafir I had seen at Andries' place with the letters from Ladysmith.

"So you had your boys with the transport, Andries," I said.

"I have my boys wherever they are most useful."

"What do we do next?" I asked, when we had finished the very good meal we made on the things left by the frightened Burghers.

"As soon as it is dark we go to the bank," answered he.

I asked no more, for I knew that whatever this clever man had planned would be done in his own time, and

I did not wish to say anything that would make it seem that I mistrusted him; and particularly was it important that I should not let him think that I was slow of comprehension, for a Boer can never resist taking advantage of one whom he believes to be less far-sighted and slim than himself, a habit they have learned from the Rooineks and Hollanders.

While we were eating, the Kafirs were cutting down big thorn-bushes, to be drawn by the rearmost cattle to cover up our tracks, which is an old Boer trick that is very successful when white men or Transvaal and Natal Kafirs have to be deceived, but is useless against Hottentots, who are so marvellously clear-sighted that they can tell the age and almost the colour of an ox by its spoor. But the Natal Kafir, having been spoiled by the treatment he gets from the whites, has lost what cunning he had, and uses his cleverness only to write forged passes to get drink.

We had, with the two Kafirs who had remained behind from the runaway commando, eight, which was not too many to drive three hundred cattle in the dark; but as we had horses enough for all of them, this did not matter so much. Besides, all the oxen were used to the trek, so they gave very little trouble, keeping close together and following the leading oxen, though the after-animals did not at first understand having to pull the thorn-bushes, and kept going off the track.

We left the kloof just as it began to get dark, first going back on our tracks towards the waggons, then turning towards the Drakensberg, which was in the opposite direction to our laager.

The bushes dragged behind acted wondrously well in smoothing and hiding our tracks, for while they laid the grass in one direction, making it look as if blown by the wind, they also raised the dust in the sandy parts, so that it fell again and covered the hoof-marks, till only a Hottentot tracker could see that a herd of oxen had passed.

We made good travelling, and within two hours had entered a wild and mountainous country, so full of kloofs, valleys, and broad and deep hollows, that an army as big as the British could hide for days without being seen by white scouts such as they used. The Kafirs seemed to know the road well, for they went on without pause or uncertainty, even when it grew so dark that we could not see two horses' length in front of us. The moon was due to rise at eight, so we halted for an hour till it was well up, when we got on again, the way being up the sides of mountains, along Kafir tracks so narrow that only an African horse could ride them without slipping. Now and then we passed over wide flat mountain-tops giving splendid grazing, but in winter-time covered with snow, as Andries told me. It was quite nine o'clock, and the oxen were showing signs of weariness, when I heard the lowing of oxen some distance to the right.

"We are near the bank," said Andries, as we began to climb a path so steep and stony that it seemed only goats could pass up it. As it was, the oxen often slipped, and one fell down the steep sides into the valley below, where we could hear its moans for some time.

When I had grown tired with the climbing, often being on my horse's neck or lying back on the crupper, we came out on the top of a mountain, which I could see in the moonlight was a great basin-shaped pan or hollow, perhaps more than a hundred acres in extent, and full of small wide gullies and little valleys that seemed made for hiding cattle. As far as I could see were beasts standing or lying down, till it seemed there was hardly room for our big herd. I afterwards learned that they numbered near a thousand oxen and horses, and all got as we had got these. A few old tents and Kafir grass-huts stood about, and into the largest hut Andries went as soon as he had dismounted, I following. It was kept for him, I could see, for there were a bed, table, stools, and the other things one would expect to find in a white man's place; also several wooden packing-cases that served as cupboards. From one of them Andries took out plates and knives, and other things needed for eating with, and we made a good meal on tinned provisions such as are served out to soldiers. There was also wine and spirits, which Andries offered me; but knowing that, as a man with an intelligent and active brain, spirits always does quicker work on me than on ignorant and unintellectual people, I felt fearful of taking it, though secretly I knew that my body required such support. Besides, I felt that now the time had come when I was to learn more than ever of the way I was to go to make money and keep safe with both sides.

" I do not think I will drink, Andries," said I, " for the champagne we had in the kloof has not yet left off its work in my head."

" Quite right, Sarel; men who have great things to do must keep away from the bottle, or they will get the worst of bargaining with men who know how to leave it alone."

This speech made me feel great faith in Andries, for it showed me that he had no desire to take advantage of me through my having a delicate brain.

" I suppose we have a settlement to-night," said I, encouraged by his honesty over the liquor to say in words what had been all the time in my heart.

" Ja, Sarel, we will have a settlement, for you have done your part well; but it is only the beginning of even greater things which you must learn to do without my help, for you must know I have other commandos helping me besides yours, and I cannot always be with you."

While he was talking, Andries went to a corner of the hut and moved away a box, showing a little hole in the ground, and out of that he took a small book.

" This is my private ledger. It is safer to keep it here among Kafirs who cannot read, than to carry it among those who can, eh ? "

While I smoked, Andries sat looking at the book and making calculations on the bare table. Presently he said, " Sarel, you have helped me get three hundred oxen and eight horses. They are worth, at present prices, let us say twelve pounds apiece all round, which is three thousand six hundred sovereigns. Now if your men had not run away and left you to bring the cattle without their help, half that money would have been divided among them, giving them five pounds apiece, and your share as commandant would have been perhaps twenty pounds. Now I am going to be liberal; I am going to give you fifty times that, which is a thousand pounds."

My heart gave a great thump of joyfulness; for though I had expected a good bit of money, I had not thought of so large a sum, for something had made me think that Andries was too fond of money to share liberally with others. Still I would not put my thoughts in words, but only said, "Yes," quite carelessly.

Andries took it as I secretly hoped he would—that I was dissatisfied.

"Man," said he, "how long would you have to be robbing the Government before you could make so much? With all your cleverness it took you five years to rob them of fifteen hundred pounds."

This reference to the affair at Prinsloosdorp angered me, because it was not true that I had had nearly so much, and I was going to explain, when Andries stopped me.

"Never mind how much you might have taken," said he. "It is enough to know that you have made a thousand pounds in a day. The question is, How shall I pay you? I have not a thousand pounds in notes here, nor do I think it would be wise for you to carry so much."

"But why cannot I take it from the money you left with Van der Murphy and the other Burghers?" I inquired.

"There are reasons," replied Andries, in a slow and meaning sort of way.

"Do you think he will go off with the money?"

"If he has not done so already I have made a great mistake in him."

"And the Coetzees—have they also gone?"

"They are on the way to the Transvaal by this time."

"Then why did you give them the money, knowing they were not oprecht Burghers?"

"I thought you wanted those men out of the way?"

"Yes; but there was a cheaper way of getting rid of them."

"Not much cheaper, Sarel."

"But a thousand pounds each is not cheap."

"How do you know they had a thousand pounds?"

"I saw you give it them."

"Which shows how clever I am as a conjuror, for if I could deceive a clever man like you I could take in a Hollander accountant."

I was astonished at what this speech revealed; but before I could say anything Andries went on—

"You saw me put the notes in the envelope?"

"Certainly."

"Yet did not see me take them out again?"

"No."

"Do you remember how I made each man look for a piece of string in my haversack?"

"I do."

"And what was I doing while their backs were turned?"

"Taking out the notes?"

"Nay, doing a very easy conjuring trick—changing the envelopes. I had one full of notes, six just like it, only full of bits of newspaper."

"You are a wonderful man, Andries; but suppose they come back and tell what has been done?"

"Sarel, you are very simple for a public prosecutor. Is it likely that a man who steals a purse will come back to say there is not so much in it as he thought? Nay, Sarel, although you have had to do with Rooineks on the Rand, you do not know human nature. Besides, do you not see that I had a double-barrelled gun? Suppose that instead of running away your

Burghers had helped in bringing in these cattle, and had asked for their share of the money I had promised. I should have told them that the money was with Van der Murphy and the Coetzees, who had run away with it, and so much would have been saved. As it is, this explanation is not needed; but you see, Sarel, I leave nothing to chance."

" But supposing they had not run away ? "

" I should have called on Van der Murphy to pay out the money, and finding only bits of newspaper in the envelope, I should leave him to satisfy the Burghers that he had not stolen it, and by way of helping them to make up their minds I should produce the original envelope, torn and dirty, which I should say had been found outside the laager."

I could not say a word, so surprised and full of admiration was I at this truly wonderful man; and for the first time I began to have doubts whether he could be an Afrikander as he said he was, for such rascality requires great brains and much education.

" After what I have told you, I suppose you will look well into the envelope I give you," said Andries, laughing.

" Nay, Andries, I think you'll play fair with me."

" Certainly, Sarel; it pays to be honest in playing games like this, and it would not pay me to lose your help, though I am afraid your Burghers will take a lot of sweetening before they get over that lancer scare enough to go after more transports. Now, Sarel, I owe you a thousand pounds. I can pay you half in Standard Bank notes, which are good in Natal; but the thing is, What are you going to do with them ? If you carry them on you and get taken prisoner by your own Burghers—which is quite likely—they are certain to search you,—for remember, Sarel, this will be the second time that you and certain sums of other people's money have disappeared together. And then you have been a Transvaal official, and all of you are believed to have part of the Treasury sewn in your shirts. So, Sarel, you must trust me a little longer.

Take a hundred golden sovereigns, which is not too much to lose and not enough to cause suspicion, but just enough to be useful if you have to run away suddenly—as no doubt you will."

I was bitterly disappointed. For though I quite agreed with Andries as to the risk and danger of carrying so large a sum as a thousand pounds, my experience as an official had taught me the wisdom of always taking money offered at the time, for so many things might happen if one delayed; and I had secretly hoped that as soon as I got the thousand pounds I might contrive to get safely away to Delagoa Bay. For although a thousand pounds is not a great sum of money as we reckon in the Transvaal, it would be sufficient to enable me to lie quiet till the war was finished. Andries, as usual, was quick in reading my thoughts.

"Sarel," said he, "you are foolish to be greedy. Do you not see that it is I who have all the work and the risk, for it is easy enough to get oxen, but not so easy to turn them into money. It is like the gun-running business: you can get all the guns you want in Durban, but the real work only begins when you are running them through to the natives, and then you do not always get your money."

"But, Andries, I thought you told me the Government paid you for the oxen."

"So they do, indirectly. I sell to the speculators, and they sell at fancy prices to the British Government to feed the troops; so you see the money comes from them in the end."

This was so different to what I had thought all along that I began to wonder whether I had not misunderstood everything.

"But do the British know that you are getting these cattle from them?"

"Sarel, you are young, and have a lot to learn. If a man asked you to teach him how you made money as a public prosecutor and saved fifty pounds a-month out of a salary of forty, could you do it in a minute? No, Sarel; everything worth knowing has to be learned slowly, bit by bit. I began to learn my trade during the Zulu war, but it did not last long enough to make me a master of the game. You know what an apprentice is; well, that is what you are to me, with the difference that other apprentices get no share of their masters' profits, and you get a third share before you know half the trade."

I could not answer this, for Andries had such a masterful way of saying "This is so," that I always felt like a child when its father taught it. Still I was not satisfied, and my conscience began to tell me that I had given myself to Andries without sufficient thought, and that I truly knew little of the trade in which I had adventured, and was therefore bound either to follow it up with Andries as my master or go back to the Burghers, unable to give them anything either in guidance or money.

"Andries," said I, "suppose something should happen to you before I got all my share of the money. Should I have to go to the British for it?"

Andries laughed much. "Nay, Sarel; you would have what you lawyers call a lien on the cattle. You would go to the Supreme Court at Maritzburg and sue me for breach of contract,"—and then he laughed again in a way that made me feel that he was so much the stronger that he did not hesitate to treat me as a child, and I wished I had old Paul with me that I might consult with him, for it is good to ask advice, even if you do not act upon it unless it agrees with your own opinion and inclination.

"Do you go back to the laager with me?" I asked.

"Nay, Sarel, I have other work to do. You must go back quickly, and tell them how you were captured by the lancers, who got back all the cattle. You will have time to make up a good story as you ride. And it must be good, Sarel, for you have got to keep their courage up. I shall want them again very soon, I hope."

"But what shall I tell them about the money? They are certain to ask about that."

"Sarel, you are as a child that needs its mother with it all the time. Have you no wisdom to learn to walk alone? Go back furious with the Burghers for running away and leaving you. Tell them that, being without their help, you and I only got a few cattle away, making only two pounds for each man. Then you can make a speech, saying that, though they do not deserve it, you will keep to the agreement, and share fairly the money you alone have earned, though they deserved to have nothing. You then go to the cart to get the money, and find instead this torn envelope. Call for Van der Murphy and the Coetzees, who will not be there, and leave the Burghers to guess what has become of the money. Now do you see why I chose men with bad characters to take care of the money? Sarel, when you know how to use him, a schelm is as good as an oprecht deacon of the Reformed Kerk."

I did not like this plan at all. Andries might say I did not know human nature, but I knew Burgher nature, and I could see a mountain of trouble blocking my path, and even worse. Then I had to deal with old Paul. He would be very wrathful with me for trusting the money to Van der Murphy and the Cootzees instead of with him, and would side with the Burghers, and I should be undone. Altogether I was in great straits; but I did not like to let Andries think I was afraid, so I told him I thought his plan good, and that I would be off early in the morning.

We wrapped ourselves in our blankets, for it was cold so high up, and I tried to sleep; but between the coolness and my sad thoughts of the morrow I slept little, and was glad when the light came. I fastened the hundred sovereigns about me as Kafirs tie up money in their blankets, and after having some coffee, saddled up.

"Now, Sarel," said Andries, "don't be afraid of your Burghers. Be baas all through, and when you have had your way with them, come over to my place and tell me what you have done. By that time I shall be ready with my next plan."

He gave me a Kafir to show me the way, and I left, very sad, and finding no consolation in the memory that lucky things had always come when wanted, to help me out of trouble; for it is only after the good chance has happened that a man recognises it and is thankful. When trouble again comes in front of him, he is just as fearful as ever, and so it was with me; for even if I could in faith see the way out, there was always present in my heart the memory of the nine hundred pounds that I had left behind.

CHAPTER XI.

A woman in a laager.

THE Kafir Andries had sent to show me the way had
worked in the Transvaal, so spoke the Taal very well.
Being afraid of my thoughts, I let him talk with me
as we rode, of course making him keep behind. I
also thought I might learn from him something about
Andries that would help me to know this strange and
clever man better. But the Kafir either knew nothing,
or, knowing, would not say, for I learned little that
I did not already know; so I gave up talking, and fell
to thinking of Katrina, and, naturally, thoughts of
her brought up Charlotte, — though, since I had
reason to give up making love to her, and fearing
that she knew I was no free man, I had almost put
her out of my head. But as I thought on her bright-
ness and cleverness, I began to wonder whether she
might not help me somehow, for I was in that perplexed state when a man looks round for something
he does not expect to find, yet secretly hopes may be
at hand. I could not see how she could help me,
but the thoughts would not go away; and soon the
trip of my horse's feet began to say, " Go to Charlotte,
go to Charlotte," just as they used to say, " Come ye
out from among them."

Was it not strange, and part of the wondrous plan
of which I have often spoken, that when the Kafir's
time came to leave me he should say, " The road is
now plain and easy to the laager; but if the baas
loses it, the place of Baas Andries is over there,

and he can go to it, and the missie will tell him the way."

I had not planned to go to Andries' place, for it was quite an hour off my road; but after this wondrous thing I could not but go. Besides, I did not yet feel strong enough to face my Burghers, and the story I was to tell them was not so smooth as stories should be to have truth written over them, and I feared the searching questions that Paul was certain to put. So, quite carelessly, as if it were a matter of no importance, I asked the Kafir—

"How do you know the missie is there?"

"I know, baas, because when I come back from taking her there she bid me tell the baas she would wait till he came."

"All right," said I, "I am not going there. You may go," and he left.

When he was well out of sight, behind the corner of the mountain, I turned my horse in the direction of Andries' place. Even the animal's body kept tune with the words that came from his hoofs, for he cantered without my spurring him, and I found myself shaking hands with Charlotte long before I expected.

She was on the stoep when I rode up, sitting in a deck-chair reading letters, and dressed in a pretty white frock, just like the English girls you see at Maritzburg playing tennis. She had light hair, too, just like them, and looked so clean that any one could see she had the English custom of washing long before she got dirty, which is a thing our Boer girls cannot understand, and laugh much at.

"I saw you coming, and have coffee ready," said she, as if she quite expected me. "Did my father tell you to come and bring a message?"

"Nay, Charlotte; I come because I want some one who is clever and far-seeing to tell me what I shall do when I go back to my schelms."

And then, without further delay, I told her how I feared that things would not work out there as her father had prophesied, giving her a fearsome account of the wickedness of Van der Murphy and the Coetzees, which was not altogether true; then I told her of the wicked plans for my destruction that they might be preparing.

"But," said she, "you have to go back; why not get there before they have time to make plans? You are commandant; let them know that you are. Is it not war-time, when you can do as you like, for will not Piet Joubert see you come to no harm? If I were you I would tie up Van der Murphy, and give him twenty-five."

"Charlotte, you do not know my Burghers. If I were to try that, they would begin first on me. It is easy for a girl to tell a man what he should do; but what would you do with two hundred and fifty angry Burghers who did not love you?"

"I should make them afraid of me, as you must."

"I should like to see how you did it," said I; for though I tried to make her believe I truly feared to go back, I was not so much in fear as in hope that she might ask me to stay and take care of her out of sympathy,—for some women do not like to know that men are in danger, though there are others who are only happy when they know they have sent a man to death, as I had good reason to know. To my surprise and disappointment her reply was, quite coolly—

"I'm going to the laager, Sarel, so you may as well go with me."

"Do you mean it, Charlotte?"

"Ja, Sarel; I have a fancy to see your Burghers, for I do not want them to hurt you, and they will not do anything to you while I am with you."

This speech pleased me very much, for I felt there was truth in what she said; and it certainly would be good for me to have a woman with me as protection in case anything happened. So, hoping she would not change her mind, I told her that I would never let her run the risk of being hurt by my schelms.

"Sarel," said she, "it is you they would hurt, not me, and I go to take care of you."

This was said so softly and kindly that I was as surprised as I was pleased; for if she knew, as I feared and believed, that I was no free man, but tied to Katrina by a loan of a thousand pounds and a promise to marry her, it was very strange, for it is not usual for a young girl to show any kindness to a man she does not want to marry. For one pleasant minute I thought she must love me; but suddenly that thought was washed away by the memory that Charlotte had been taught among English girls, and they think on these things so differently to Boer girls. Still, it was much more agreeable that she should think me a free man; for women are never the same to a man with a wife as they are to one without, even the married women paying more attention to a bachelor, out of pity for his lonely state. So I planned to make such remarks and speeches to Charlotte as would lead her to suppose I was a free man, yet, by being careful never to say yea or nay plainly, I should have a door of escape when the truth came out.

We sat still on the stoep, for the day was very hot, and I had no wish to go to the laager. It was so much more refined to sit there and look at Charlotte, who was pink and white, and so clever in her sayings, that I felt as if I were with a predikant for goodness, and a Johannesburg gold-company man for slimness, instead of with a girl only eighteen and not long from school. She was as much my master as was her father, only she was more serious in her masterfulness, and had not his way of laughing when he had said a bitter thing, which took away the soreness. Charlotte said sharp things with thin closed lips, and looked as if she wanted to say more, even harder and sharper.

Neither of us spoke for some time. I was thinking out something to say to Charlotte that would draw out her true feelings to me; but her eyes were fixed on the veld, which she looked at without seeing, as one who thinks hard. She looked very handsome that way, for her grey eyes were wide open, and had a misty look that was very soft and tender; and I began to wonder why I had not before noticed how much more pleasant she was to look at than my fat, flabby-faced, big-voiced Katrina, whose frocks never fitted close to her as did this one of Charlotte's, and whose hands were big and red, and her feet flat and without shape. When I used to reproach her for her large feet she would repeat a foolish saying in the Taal about large feet proving a large heart; but when a man has seen Rooinek girls, he begins to admire other things than hearts, for those he cannot see, and knows not whether they are large or small. It is not so with other parts of the body, which are ever before him; and this is one of the drawbacks of being educated, for I have noticed that when a young Boer gets education he is more particular about having for a wife a girl who looks nice, whereas those who are not educated think only about the cattle she will bring him, which is one of the reasons why old Boers are so much against education, unless they are going to make their sons predikants or doctors, which is the only use they think learning is for.

These thoughts were passing in my mind while I sat looking at Charlotte, and marvelling at the difference education makes to a Boer girl, when she suddenly started, as if awakened from a half-sleep, and looked round at me.

"When do we ride, Charlotte?" I asked, wishful to say something soothing, as I could see she was confused by my hard looks.

"When we have eaten; the Kafir is now cooking," answered she.

"But the laager is five hours away, and my horse is done up."

"It would not do up your horse to ride the short distance you came this morning," said she.

"But I rode hard, being anxious to see you," said I, thinking that at last I had the chance to say a good thing.

"Ja; because the nearer me, the farther from your commando," was her cutting reply. "There is a good horse in the paddock, and you can ride him; but go to-day we must, for my father will be here to-morrow."

There was no way out of this; so, after we had eaten, we saddled up, and by an hour after noon we were on the way to my laager.

We rode in silence for some time, for I liked to look at Charlotte as I had never looked before. She rode a big roan mare, and sat very lightly and gracefully in the saddle, not like a heavy Boer girl does, who will give a horse sore back in a two-hour ride. She wore, too, a long black riding-skirt instead of a short frock, which makes the Boer maidens look so broad and bulky when they ride; and altogether she made a picture so pretty, that it reminded me of those I had seen in books. I was riding a little behind, that I might see her the better, when she checked her horse and waited for me to get beside her.

"Sarel," said she, very quietly, and without taking her eyes from her reins, "while you were away your Burghers did a very foolish thing."

"That is no news to me," I answered wittily.

"Nay, perhaps not; but it is a thing that will hurt you unless you help me to put it right. Will you?"

"Certainly I will. What have they done?"

"They have caught a khaki captain—one of the Britishers I get much information from, because he is in love with me. It was he who gave me those letters you took to General Joubert, which made you go high up in his favour."

"Is this, then, why you come with me?" I asked, feeling a little angry and disappointed.

"Ja, Sarel; while he is away he is no use to me, and by being useful to me he is also helping you, and it is you I wish to help."

My anger went down on this nice speech.

"Charlotte, you shall have him back; ride on," said I, and she thanked me with so much heartfulness that my mind misgave me; and almost before I knew what

I was saying I asked, "Are you quite sure that it is for me, and not for the khaki, you are going?"

"Of course it's for the khaki. I go for him, as I would go for my horse if it were impounded."

"And you don't love him?"

"Do you think me a fool, Sarel? This khaki is very poor. If I wanted a khaki husband I could have plenty of rich ones. I know dukes and lords; and one who wants me much to marry him has an uncle who is a lord mayor. These khaki officers have lots of money sometimes, Sarel; but I don't want them while there are good Afrikander kerels."

I was too pleased to say anything; I could only listen, hoping she would say something more, but plainer. But she was quiet, so I asked—

"What sort of man is this khaki captain?"

"The sort of man who tells a woman all about himself, and lets her do what she will with him."

There was something in her way of saying this that made me doubtful whether she meant that she approved such a man or whether she despised him; for I had told her much about myself, and perhaps Charlotte might think I would let her do what she willed with me, wherein she was greatly mistaken. Several times I tried to lead her to say things that would remove any doubt as to what she thought of me, but always she cleverly turned the subject.

"Have you good horses at the laager?" she asked; "because the captain and I must leave to-night, for we have far to go."

"That would not be possible, Charlotte, for if my Burghers have got your khaki, I must ask General Joubert's leave before I can let him go."

"What! are you commandant, yet cannot say whether a man shall come or go?" she asked in anger.

"I can say 'Go,' but my Burghers may say 'Stay.' What then shall I do?"

"Be baas, Sarel. What is the good of being commandant unless you are?"

"But the captain may have been sent to the head laager."

"Then I go to the head laager after him. Sarel, I want that khaki captain, and I shall have him; and you must help me, otherwise——" She stopped suddenly, and looked at me in a meaning way that made me feel what she would have said.

"Charlotte, I have said I will help you, and I will not go back on my promise. I will do everything you wish."

I did not want to say this, but her masterfulness overpowered me, and I could not think of the proper thing to say at the right time, so that I said more often what I felt than what was wise.

I was not sorry when the laager came in sight sooner than I expected. We rode right on to it before we were noticed, for, as usual, there were no sentries on watch. It was not yet dark, and the light was sufficient to show me that the laager was in a state of disorder. Burghers were lying about sleeping, but not the sleep of honest, respectable weariness, but of cheap liquor. Some were playing at cards, some quarrelling; but above all the noise I could hear the voice of old Paul droning a psalm, which was a pure sign that there had been trouble.

A strange waggon was outspanned in the middle of the laager, by which I knew that fresh stores had come from Johannesburg, which meant much whisky; and it was not needful that I should look at the empty bottles and open cases that lay all over the ground. But, saddening and ominous as this sight was, there was one even more so, one that made my heart thump, and in a glance upset all the plans designed by Andries and myself.

Standing against the waggon, breaking the neck off a whisky-bottle, was Van der Murphy; and the redness of his face and the wetness of his eyes told me what state he was in. While I looked he raised his eyes, and, seeing me, came running towards me, still holding the whisky-bottle, and both arms out wide. As he ran he shouted, in the Taal, "Burghers, the great miracle-worker has come; the schelm who robs Burghers of their loot-money is come!"

Next moment the laager was like an ant-heap that has been broken on the top. Burghers that I thought were asleep, kerels who were quarrelling over cards, even old Paul, who was singing to himself,—all came crowding round, and a babel of voices called out, "Where is our money, you thief? Where is the schelm Brink?"

My heart became fearful, not for myself, but for Charlotte; and I was quickly turning in my mind the speech I should make to them to move them to compassion, when there was a great distraction. Charlotte gave her mare a sharp cut on the flank, and rode him right into the crowd of Burghers, who were still pressing on from behind all around us.

"Who said Andries Brink was a schelm?" she asked fiercely, looking round the crowd.

"I did," said young Van der Merwe, the same young kerel who, when full of whisky and cigar smoke, was always ready to remind me of the poisoned whisky. He was standing well in front, and just at Charlotte's right hand.

She looked at him for a moment, from his boots to his hat, as women do when they are going to be spiteful to a man.

"You long-legged baboon! take that, and that," said she, and, quick as the rifle-fire at Colenso, came the whistle of her sjambok, cutting the kerel over the head and face. He stood still for a moment or two with his hands up, as if dazed, taking half-a-dozen cuts without moving; then he suddenly turned and ran, shouting out, "No, no; I was joking!" Charlotte followed, getting in several severe cuts, till he crawled under the waggon, where she could not reach him.

"Now, you baboon, you will chatter again, will you? I am Charlotte Brink; do you think you will know me next time you see me?"

It would be a long time before he could see her, for

the sjambok had cut his eyes; and two such cuts will put out any man's eyes, and one will mark him for life if put upon the face, where Van der Merwe got most of his punishment.

Charlotte leant far over her saddle and tried to get another cut at him, but, with a howl of agony, he curled up like a snake that is struck, and writhed to the other side of the waggon, at which the Burghers began to laugh.

Charlotte looked round suspiciously, as if she thought the laugh was at her, but quickly saw the truth.

"I suppose that's how he ran when the lancers were after him," said she. They laughed again. "Yes, and others of you too," she went on defiantly. "You are a nice crowd to talk about not getting loot-money, when you are too frightened to keep the oxen my father got for you. I have come to pay Burghers. Does any one else want paying by Andries Brink's daughter?"

No one spoke, but many looked very foolish. Charlotte went on, pointing with her sjambok at a young Burgher who had been laughing much, "How many cattle did you bring in?" The moment the kerel found that Charlotte was speaking to him, he stopped the laugh, put on the most scared look, and backed towards the waggon, falling in his fright over one of the whisky-cases.

"He is not the first Burgher that whisky has brought down," said Charlotte—a witty speech that, after a time, even the oldest Burgher saw through, and laughed much; for the longer it takes a Boer to see a joke the more he laughs.

One of the first to see it was Van der Murphy, who, being Irish, was ever ready to think things funny, even when they were just the opposite. He came up to Charlotte as respectfully as a half-drunken man often does.

"Missie," said he, "you are quite right about whisky downing a man. Just look round this laager and take notes of the harvest. But whisky never downed a man as you downed that insolent, ignorant, long-legged young baboon, Van der Merwe, who has had his head swollen by success at cards, and required the physic you gave him. Further, missie, allow me, on behalf of patriotic Burghers who were present at Elandslaagte, to enter a protest against your sneer at those who ran from the lancers. Allow me to assure your royal highness that if you had seen those lancers at business you would have wondered that a Burgher ceased riding and running till he reached his own cattle-kraal. I was one of the few who did not run. I lay in a donga and watched the circus from between the hind-legs of a dead horse, and, believe me, your majesty, there are worse places when the angel of death breaks loose."

This speech had been made in a most solemn manner, and in English; and as most of the old Burghers could not follow Van der Murphy,—who spoke very Irish - English, especially when full of whisky,—they thought by his seriousness, and the way he had of bowing with his hat and the whisky-bottle, that he was making a religious speech; and they were quite persuaded of this when he wound up by speaking of the angel of death, which they understood. So most of them took off their hats very reverently, and stood bareheaded.

The sight of this was too much for Charlotte, for she gave one sweeping look around at these stupid old men standing as if at a funeral, then burst into a ringing laugh, and, swinging her horse round, rode through the crowd, most of the younger kerels running aside with their arms protecting their heads, as if they expected her to repeat the Van der Merwe business. Van der Murphy followed her up, still holding the whisky-bottle in one hand and his shabby ragged smasher hat in the other.

"Your majesty," he shouted, "you said you had come to pay us. The money your esteemed parent left turned to paper."

Charlotte pulled up and faced him.

"How do you know? did you steal it? Do you
want paying?" and she raised her sjambok. The
Irishman turned and ran for the waggon, rolling
beneath it, and dropping the whisky-bottle. Charlotte
did not follow him, so, seeing this, he carefully reached
out his leg and drew the bottle to him, saying, as he
did so, "Burghers, you have had an old woman for a
commandant, now you have got a young one. You
had better stuck to the old one."

"Come out and say that again," said Charlotte,
riding up to the waggon.

"No, thank you; my friend Van der Merwe here
would like a drink," and Pat made a swinging wave
with his hat and disappeared.

By this time the Burghers were all laughing and
behaving like children, for neither Van der Merwe nor
Pat were much liked in the commando, and no one
was really sorry that Charlotte should have whipped
one and threatened the other. She was just about to
get off her horse and go after Van der Murphy, when
old Hendrik Keiser spoke up—

"Never mind him, missie. He is only Irish, and
does not know the meaning of any language. We do
not believe he had any money, for he only knows
enough of the Taal to use it for lying."

"It seems that money is all this commando thinks
about except whisky," said Charlotte. "What do you
do to earn it? I suppose you have robbed the khaki
captain of the five thousand pounds he had, and that
makes you hungry for more."

The Burghers, who listened to every word Charlotte
spoke, looked at one another in surprise; and I too
was astonished, for I had guessed nothing of this
money, and in a flash my jealousy of the captain
vanished, for now I saw plainly what it was that
Charlotte wanted.

There was another man surprised besides myself.
I had wondered why old Paul had not come forward
to greet me, and had thought that he was angry with
me, when he came up with joy on his face.

"It serves you all right," he shouted at the Burghers; "you would send him away because you wanted an excuse to go to head laager for whisky, and now the money that should be yours goes to the Hollanders. Sarel," he went on, coming up to me for the first time, "they are well punished, for they are a wilful and headstrong people, who will not listen to my words of wisdom. They have sent the khaki captain to the head laager, and now the Hollanders have that five thousand pounds."

Charlotte looked angry and concerned.

"Sarel," said she, "we must have him back. Take me where we can talk. Come to this tent."

I then noticed for the first time that during my absence tents had been put up, and many rough shelters of blankets and grass made the place more like a laager before Ladysmith, and showed that the Burghers had made up their minds for a long stay.

The tent to which Charlotte walked, after giving her horse to a Kafir, was a large square one. "This is yours, I suppose," said she.

"Nay," answered Paul; "the commandant is like me,—we have no tent. I lie under a bush. The schelms took all the best cover, and will not even let me lie under the waggon."

"I suppose you will have to go with the Kafirs, being only commandant," said Charlotte, a speech that made me angry, for no man likes a woman to think he is of no account.

"Who is here?" she asked, looking in at the tent, where I could see several Burghers sitting or lying on the ground. "Turn them out and take it," said she to me.

I should not have had the courage to do this, but as soon as they saw Charlotte the Burghers stood up, and looked as foolish as if they were young kerels caught stealing, for they all looked at Charlotte's sjambok very uneasily as they sidled out.

The tent had some furniture in it,—looted, as I afterwards learned, from a farmhouse near by,—and, besides a table and sofa, there was a piano, which was used for a saddle-rack by day ; but at night, Paul told me, smoking-concerts were held here, and English songs sung by the young Burghers, while the old German played, as most Germans do. We sat down in the tent, while Paul went away to get us something to eat.

"This is nice," said I, meaning that the tent was comfortable.

"Yes, it was very kind of them to allow you to have it. Sarel, you don't seem to be much of a baas here. If I had not come, you would be helping the Kafirs to look after the horses by this time, I suppose."

I had told her, on the ride, a little of the sort of men I had in the laager, by way of preparing her for anything that might happen. So far things had gone much better than I had expected, so I felt bolder, and rather angry that she should have so poor an opinion of me.

"They are like young oxen," said I, "who have to be humoured if you would drive them properly."

"Meantime they put the baas on the trek-chain and get on to the waggon, eh," and she swung her sjambok round to indicate the tent.

"You see, Charlotte, they are mostly old Burghers who have bled for their country, while I am young for a commandant. But I soon had them out of the tent."

Charlotte laughed an annoying little laugh of sarcasm. Paul just then came in, with a Kafir bringing some biscuits and tinned things.

"I am thirsty; bring me some of that beer I see yonder," said Charlotte.

"But the Burghers will not let me have it," said Paul; "I tried to get a bottle for you."

Charlotte said nothing, but got up and walked to the case which lay near the waggon. "Here, you kerel, bring me that beer," said she to a young Burgher standing by. He looked at her in wonderment.

"Quick, pick it up," said she ; and, as if in a dream,

looking hard at her all the time, the young fellow took up three bottles awkwardly, and followed her to the tent, where Paul and I looked on, marvelling at this strange masterdom of a young girl, so different to what he and I had ever known.

"Sarel," said he seriously, "there will be trouble. The Burghers are already asking what the girl does here. They do not mind the sjamboking, but if she is going to make a Burgher do a Kafir's work,—well, there will be shooting."

I thought the same, though I did not say it. Charlotte was right in whipping young Van der Merwe, but it was going too far to make a Burgher carry beer for her.

For once Paul's prophecy came true quickly. While we were eating, I saw the Burghers gathering round the young kerel who had been so disgraced and humiliated. They were sympathising with him as if he had been unjustly beaten, while he was half inclined to cry, and kept glancing at the tent with a dark and sullen look, as I have seen on the face of a boy who wants to fight another who has beaten him, but dare not.

Presently the Burghers, bringing along the lad, all unwilling, came towards the tent, Johannes Steenkamp, a godly and serious old Burgher from the Rustenburg district, being their leader and spokesman.

"Sarel," said he, when he had reached the door of the tent, speaking in a tone that meant anger behind it, "is it the wish of Slim Piet Joubert that a young commandant should bring an English missie into the laager to treat the Burghers as if they were Kafirs?"

Before I could answer, Charlotte had sprung to the door, pushing me aside, and holding me back with one hand.

"Is it in the orders that a dirty Taakhaar should call my father a thief—my father, who has done so much to help you lazy schelms, who are too cowardly to take cattle when they are thrown at you? Is it in the orders for a great lump of a kerel like that to stand and look on while a lady has to carry her own beer ? And why do you call me an English missie ? "

She advanced with her sjambok threateningly towards old Steenkamp, who had stood listening to Charlotte's rapid and angry talk as one dazed. He backed away as Charlotte advanced, saying meekly, " I am sorry; but we thought by the way you made this young kerel do Kafir's work, that you must be English."

" Nay, I am true Afrikander," said Charlotte, " and I am come to do what you lazy whisky-swillers should do—bring back a khaki who has stolen your money; but now that you have been rude to me you may get it yourself, which you won't, for the Hollanders have it."

At this talk of money the Burghers at once turned on old Steenkamp, and told him to go away, to apologise, and to do all sorts of things, till the old fellow waxed wrath, and, turning round, began to quarrel with those who had before agreed with him.

" Go away and leave us to eat," said Charlotte, in her masterful way,—and she turned back into the tent, while the Burghers abused and maltreated old Steenkamp, and called out to Charlotte to come and sjambok him while they held him, so soon do men turn on those who are foolish enough to speak for them.

" Now, Sarel," said Charlotte, " I must go, or I shall grow tired of fighting for you; you leave me to do it all," which, considering that she never gave me a chance to say a word to the Burghers, showed that after all her English education she was still a Boer girl.

" Where do you go ? " I asked.

" To General Joubert, to get my khaki."

" Nay, Charlotte, do not go; stay here and write a letter to the General."

" I never write when I can talk. Saddle up and come with me. It is only six hours, and there will be a moon all the way."

" But you have not rested, and the horses are done up."

"If you do not wish to help me, be an honest man, and say so. Your excuses are childish. There are three hundred horses here. Get two of the best and come, or I go alone."

"But what will the Burghers say?"

"They may be your masters, but they are not mine. What will the Burghers say? Do you care more for what they say than for what I may say?"

I could not think of a proper reply, for when Charlotte became masterful, I felt like a child who was scolded and could not answer, except foolishly.

"Shall I go, or must I make that young kerel get the horses?" she exclaimed impatiently, making for the door.

I went unwillingly out and sought Paul, who was still keeping away from me as much as he could. I told him where and why I was going.

"Sarel," said he, "it is well; and I will go with you, for this place is now a house of abomination, where there dwelleth nothing but wickedness. They are like the children of Israel when Moses was on the Mount."

"Except that they are too lazy to get a calf," said I; but Paul would never laugh when I made a good and plain joke. I did not want him to come, and told him so.

"Nay, Sarel, I will go, and never leave you, for I see that when I am away trouble and misfortune always come to you."

"How can that be? Have I not been making money while they have despitefully used you?"

"That may be, Sarel; but this missie has come into your life, and when women come there is always trouble, and it is only I who can stop even greater trouble from coming."

"What do you mean?"

"That is just what Katrina will ask of you; she has already asked that question of her cousin, Stephen Vick, who is in the laager."

"Has she written to him?"

" Ja ; and she has also written to General Joubert
for a permit to come, and you know that Slim Piet
never refuses a woman."

My heart gave a painful thump that caused me to
feel very sick, and all I could say was, " This must
not be, Paul."

" Certainly, Sarel ; and that is why I wish to go,
that I may see the General. If you ask him to stop
Katrina, he is sure to send her, for you know how he
loves to put vrouws to baas up their men ; but if I
tell him that you want Katrina, and advise him not to
let her come, he will listen."

" Paul, you are truly my friend. Let us go to-night.
There will be moon, and the horses have had no exer-
cise since they ran from the lancers."

" Ja, Sarel ; you must tell the Burghers that you
are taking the missie to see the General to get that
money back, and they will not do anything to stop
you."

I spoke to a few of the Burghers as Paul advised.
Some of them wanted to talk of the money Andries
Brink had left, but I would not stay, telling them I
would settle everything when I came back.

Charlotte made no objection to Paul's coming, at
which I was a little sorry, hoping she might ; so we
got away quietly, and made good travelling for three
hours, when we came to an empty farmhouse, and
arranged to sleep there. The furniture had been all
smashed or removed, little but the bare walls remaining.

I could not help thinking that if old Steenkamp had
seen Charlotte lying on the floor wrapped in a blanket,
with a saddle for a pillow, he would not have reproached her with being an English missie ; though
I have seen English girls do such things almost as
well as an Afrikander, except that they are so particular about washing in the morning and changing their
dresses, while a true Afrikander girl would wear the
same clothes for a month without wishing to change
them.

Paul and I lay in our blankets outside on the stoep,

the night being very hot; but I could not sleep, thinking of the horrible news Paul had given me, and turning over all sides of the great puzzle as to why Katrina should be coming to see me. Could it be that she had heard of Charlotte? If so, then Paul must have told her, for none but he knew of my acquaintance with her.

Then I began to think on Paul's strange conduct when I came back to the laager. He had shown no surprise or curiosity, and never even asked how I escaped from the lancers, but seemed to keep out of my way, that he might not have to talk to me, and all the time kept looking angrily at Charlotte, as if he blamed her for something.

Paul was mumbling in his sleep, as he often did, sometimes speaking quite plainly. Suddenly I remembered being told that if you press on the chest of a man who talks in his sleep, he will answer any question you may put. So I made up my mind to try, for I was certain that Paul was keeping something back from me, and knew much more of many things about me than he would say. I went up carefully, and, lying down beside him, put my arm gently over his chest above where his silly secret heart lay, and began to press, at first softly, then harder. He was still every now and then muttering, as if dreaming bad dreams, and this made me press yet harder, lest the dream should stop.

All at once, with a suddenness that made my heart thump, he turned round on his side, seizing me by the ear and beard, saying, "I shall not give you the money—it's mine, it's mine!" then he struck and pushed me, and awoke, and in the broad moonlight I could see a frightened look on his face.

Before he could gather his senses, I said with great adroitness, "Why won't you give me the money?" He did not answer, but sat up and stared hard at me.

"What money?" he asked in a dazed and bewildered way, that would have deceived others not so sharp as myself. I made a shot in the dark—

"The money you took from Van der Murphy."

"Van der Murphy had no money, Paul. Andries played a conjuring trick on him, and made him the laughing-block of the laager."

"Tell me all about it."

Paul sat up against the wall and filled his pipe slowly, to give him time to think.

"After you had gone," said he, "Van der Murphy got very full of whisky, and the more he drank the more he talked of money, till at last I got so angry that I told him that he was a blower; that he never had enough to pay his whisky account, and to this day owed for the shoeing of his horses and their forage. This made him wrathful, and he took out a big envelope, saying there was a thousand pounds in it. Then a great indaba started, for you know, Sarel, how talk of money always sets the laager going. The Burghers crowded round Van der Murphy, and I saw two schelm Johannesburgers, who had been in jail for thievery, getting closer to him, trying to get hold of the envelope. So I did out of the goodness of my heart a very foolish thing. I snatched the envelope out of Van der Murphy's hand, and completed my foolishness by saying, 'Look, kerels, I have his thousand pounds, and when he is sober he shall have it.' I took it to my sleeping-place, and the schelm Burghers followed, saying it was loot-money, and that they ought to have it. But I loaded my mauser, and said I would shoot any who came near my bush. I had to keep awake all night, and nearly shot one of the Johannesburgers who came near just before dawn. In the morning Van der Murphy came, with several Burghers, and demanded his money. Now, as I sat with the envelope in my hand all night, it got dirty, for you know, Sarel, I never wash my hands, having Natal sores on them, and the wrapping got very dirty, mostly about the flap. When I gave the envelope to him, he looked at it, and cried out that I had been opening it; at which my anger rose, and I told Van der Murphy that, being a thief himself, he thought everybody else was. The schelm Johannesburgers called to him to open the envelope and count the money, to see how much I had stolen. He did this, and, Sarel, truly there was no money, only bits of paper that had been wrapped round meat-tins and whisky-bottles. Then there was an outcry too awful to hear. Van der Murphy said I had robbed him, and the Burghers pulled my little sleeping-place to pieces looking for the money, and held me down and tore my clothes off, till I thought they would have killed me; when a great thought came to me. 'Kerels,' said I, 'how do you know there was ever money in that envelope? You have only the word of this schelm Irishman, and where could he get a thousand pounds if he had not stolen it? If he had it, it was not his.' 'You are right,' said Van der Murphy; 'it was the Burghers' money — loot-money—that Andries Brink gave me to hold.' 'Burghers,' said I, 'would an oprecht and slim Burgher like Andries Brink give a thousand pounds to a man who was no Afrikander? why did he not give it to Sarel or to me?' These words struck the Burghers, and some began to tell Van der Murphy he lied, and there began great fighting; and for a long time there was tumult and division in the laager, some saying there never had been money, some that I had stolen it, or why should the paper in the envelope be the same kind as lay about the waggon of which I had charge? Others said Van der Murphy's story was true, and that Andries Brink had deceived him, which story I supported, as it took suspicion away from me. Ah, Sarel, truly money is the root of all evil, for I had a terrible time."

"Paul," said I, "I have not seen the Coetzees in the laager."

"Nay, Sarel, they went out after cattle the day you left, saying they were not lazy Burghers like the others, but meant to do their duty. They are not back yet."

I laughed much, till Paul asked me why, saying it was not right to laugh at the troubles of another.

"I am laughing not at your troubles, Paul, but at another thing. You are a clever man, Paul, and read the truth well. There was no money in the envelope. Andries gave Van der Murphy the envelope, telling him there was a thousand pounds there, hoping he would run away with it, so that there would be one wicked man less in the laager."

Paul shook his head. "That was going a long way round to stalk a baboon," said he.

I did not tell him about the Coetzees, but lay down and laughed much when I thought of them sitting on the veld opening their envelopes, and I went to sleep laughing.

Next morning we were away soon after sun-up, and in three hours reached the head laager outside Lady-smith, where the General was.

I went to him as soon as he would see me, and gave him a full account of what we had been doing, making as much as I could of the attack and capture of the convoy, and as little as possible of the lancers coming and spoiling our victory.

"Lancers?" said the General. "My Burghers will see lancers till they die. There were no lancers, Sarel. Did you see any? Speak truth."

"I saw steel shining, General, and nearly felt it as I rode. I myself did not believe they were lancers, but bayonet-men."

Then the General laughed, as if he did not care whether they were lancers or bayonets, and I thought it seemed as if he did not believe me at all, but was too tired to dispute; so I rejoiced much when the General, catching sight of Charlotte outside the tent, asked, "Who is the missie?"

"Charlotte Brink, come to see your Honour," I answered.

"The daughter of Andries Brink? What does she want?"

"She will tell you better than I. It is about a prisoner."

"Sarel," said the General irritably, "I will not see

women—not young women; they ask too much, and get it. Send her to Ben Viljoen, or Botha, or Kemp."

At these words Charlotte came boldly into the tent, looking very bright and pretty and smiling.

"Nay, General, I come to you because you are General, and know how to treat a woman."

The General smiled that great smile of his, that most people thought was a sign of anger, so fierce and big was it.

"Sit down and talk, Charlotte," said he, looking at me as if he wished me to go.

I moved towards the door, when Charlotte said, "Nay, General, Sarel must stay to hear me out in what I have to say, for the business is as much his as mine and yours."

The General nodded, and I remained standing. Charlotte, looking hard into the little eyes of the General, began, speaking the Taal, so that it sounded quite beautiful, as they say the Italian language is.

"General, two days ago a khaki captain, named Watson, was brought in a prisoner by Sarel's men."

"Ja, I know; the only thing Sarel's men have got to show for their work yet. Go on. What about him?"

"Where is he, General?"

"Why do you ask?"

"Because wherever he is, he is no use here. He must come back, for he is the only man who can read the heliograph and other messages from Ladysmith."

The General smiled, and shook his head.

"But it's true, General; I have been using him, and he is going to teach me to read the heliograph."

Again the General smiled his grim smile, and shook his head.

"Nay, Charlotte, he is verneuking you. These khaki captains are slim, and will not talk."

"Nay, General, all men are fools, and will talk loosely—when they are in love."

"And how do you know he is in love?"

Charlotte laid down her sjambok and unbuttoned

the front of her bodice, where women carry such things, and took out a bundle of letters. She carefully looked through them, and, taking one, pointed to part of it, and laid it on the table before the General.

" Read that," said she. " It is his own handwriting, and I have dozens like it."

He took it up, smiling, looked at it without reading it, and put it down again.

" I cannot read this Rooinek love-stuff," said he. " You read it. You are plainly not in love with him, or you would not show his letters. Girls only do that to other girls."

" That's it, General; I am not in love with him, therefore my head is clear. I want this man back, not to love him, but to use him, because I am in love with some one else who will be benefited."

The General turned his shaggy little eyes on me, and looked hard and smiled, while I turned hot all over, and felt very uncomfortable, yet secretly pleased.

" But how will it benefit the man you love if the captain is given you ? "

" It will help him do great things for the Burghers. The man I love is my father."

The General looked at me again, and I was moved to bitter anger; why, I know not.

" Ah, I see; but you cannot keep a khaki captain to talk as if he were a parrot, Charlotte. How do you use him, if I give him to you ? "

" General, must a young girl teach an old man ? Do you not see that if you let him come away with me he will think that I must love him much to take all this trouble, and come to see you; and he will talk the more if only to pay me, for these English are great on what they call gratitude."

The General again smiled; and I began to fear that he was only talking with Charlotte because she was good to look at, and amused him by her seriousness.

" But if he flies away, how do you catch him again ? "

"He will not fly away, General."

Piet thought a minute or two, looking all the time at Charlotte, who never took her eyes off the little piercing beads of the General. Then he spoke—

"Go away, and come again when I send; I will think what I can do." And Charlotte and I left the tent.

"You did not say anything to the General about the money the captain had," said I, when we were out of hearing of the Burghers.

She laughed. "Sarel, you are very thick; of course I talked of money to the Burghers; it is the only thing they understand. If I had not given a good reason for wanting the khaki, don't you think they would have thought I was in love with him, and therefore not to be trusted?"

"Then had he no money?"

"I wish he had."

"Why, Charlotte?"

"Oh, because"—she hesitated, as if not certain what to answer—"because then you might have it."

That speech left a very unpleasant feeling on me, for it did not sound a true reason, and I did not know how to read it. But what man can understand a woman when she will not be understood?

During the rest of the day, we rode round the Boer positions and watched the bombardment, which was very slow and half-hearted, as if the Burghers were not anxious to bring it to a finish.

Paul came with us, although I wanted him to stay behind and arrange the affair of Katrina with the General; but he had heard there was a certain predikant in one of the laagers, and he would not rest till he had found him, for he was one of those whom Paul was ever quarrelling with over Bible verses. He found him at last, and the two were soon at it, and disputed so long that Charlotte and I left them.

When we returned to the head laager the General had sent for us. We went to his tent, and found him reading a heap of telegrams with his secretary.

".I have found your man, Charlotte," said he; "but it is not so easy to get him as you think. You see, old men see farther than young missies. If I let your khaki parrot go he will think there is some secret plan against him, and he will keep his mouth shut till he finds what it is. I have thought out a good plan. You must go to Pretoria and help him escape, which will look more natural than if the door of the cage were opened for him."

Charlotte's bright eyes danced with pleasure, and the General noticed it and smiled.

"Ja, General, I will go," she said eagerly.

"Ja, you will go, and Sarel will go with you, and the wife of one of my Burghers, who is returning to Pretoria. You go to-night. When you get there, Hans Human will meet you, and will show you how to go to work; but, Charlotte, I don't think that parrot will talk as much as you think. Still, one bird in a cage more or less will make no difference, so you can try. I shall not be angry when you come to tell me he is dumb."

"General, don't you think that a young girl can make a man do and say what she wishes?"

This was a bold and foolish speech, and my heart thumped, for I knew not how the General would like being chaffed by a girl on his great weakness, and in front of me and his secretary. For once the right thing to say came to me at the time it was wanted, and, almost before the dark frown had grown on the General's face, I said—

"Why ask that foolish question, Charlotte, when his Honour knows how much you have made the khaki talk already? He thinks there is no more left for the khaki to talk about."

This was one of the cleverest speeches I ever made on the spur of the moment, as they say in English; for immediately the face of the General got as bright as it was dark when I began my saying. He smiled his ugly smile, and waved his pipe towards the door.

"Get gone," said he, coming up to Charlotte; "get

gone before you make me talk," and he put his great arms round her and kissed her on each cheek, she not objecting, but, on the contrary, seeming to be pleased, though I knew in my heart that her pleasure was that she had found favour in the sight of a man so useful and important as General Joubert; therefore I did not reproach her, though I thought she need not have turned the other cheek to be kissed as she did.

CHAPTER XII.

*I gain freedom and happiness for a Britisher, but
misery and shame for myself.*

THE train by which we were to travel to Pretoria lay
quite a mile beyond the head laager; and as it had
no regular time for leaving, but went when convenient,
we had to get on to it to be in readiness, for any time
it might go. This was the more necessary for the
reason that Mrs du Beer, the Burgher's wife who was
to accompany us, was, like all Afrikander women,
either in a great hurry to reach the train, or treating
it like an ox-waggon, that only moved when the baas
gave the word. She, having lost several trains when
leaving Pretoria, was now resolved not to miss this
one, and hurried Charlotte and me greatly. She was
too fat to ride, and there being no carts in the laager,
there was nothing for it but to walk. We agreed to
walk with her, and a great undertaking it was; for
what with her fatness, and not being used to walking,
she would sit down every few yards and cry, till I
saw the wisdom of her starting so soon. Another
great difficulty was in getting her into the carriage,
for the train had stopped in the veld, and was very
high to climb up, so that it took all the strength and
skill of Charlotte, myself, and four Kafirs to get her in.

When at last inside she wanted to get out again,
for the number on the carriage was the age of her
mother when she died, which Mrs du Beer said was
very unlucky, and a sure sign of a coming accident,
especially in war-time. But, unfortunately, there was

no other empty carriage to take us, and she had to stay, much to my after-sorrow. She had no sooner recovered her breath than she began a long and dismal story of the illness and death of her mother, and made such dreadful prophecies about the journey, that even old Paul at his worst would have been more desirable company, for most of his worst prophecies were never fulfilled, though he had great cleverness and skill in making his misses out to be hits.

It was nearly an hour before she had come to the death and burying of her mother; and just as I was rejoicing that she had made an end of talking, she started a matter even more dissatisfying.

"Are you going to be married at Pretoria?" she asked of Charlotte.

For the first time I had seen it, Charlotte was not ready with a sharp answer, but looked confused, and turned red. Mrs du Beer did not wait for yea or nay, but went on—

"I should not be married till the war be done, for cattle are so dear now, and your man will not be able to look after the farm. Besides, you might become a widow, and it is not good to be one too soon, before you know all about men; and there will be such lots of widows after the war, mostly having good farms and cattle, that you will not be able to pick a husband easily."

"But I am not going to be married," said Charlotte, when the old woman had stopped for breath.

"Then you are foolish. How old are you?"

"Nearly twenty."

"Ah, then, you are getting old, and will soon be ugly, for I see you will never be a nice fat vrouw, but bony."

Then she began a long story about her marrying at thirteen years of age, and having gone to the laager to doctor her man, who had an old complaint that had been with him since he was a boy, which complaint she had been doctoring, as nobody else could, with her own physic for thirty-eight years.

It was here that Charlotte got her revenge, for I could see that she was very wroth with Mrs du Beer for telling her she was getting old and ugly, a thing that no girl likes to hear from another woman.

"When do you think he will be quite cured?" she asked very sweetly.

"He is getting much better, and only wants a little more of my physic, which I am going home to make."

"Have you a good-sized dam on your farm?" asked Charlotte.

"Ja, very large," answered the woman, speaking as if she did not quite understand what the question meant.

"That is good; and have you a good spring to feed it?"

"Ja, we have two; one only wants opening up to give lots of water."

"Running all the year?" Charlotte went on.

"Ja," said the woman, very greatly perplexed.

"Then if you have as much water as that, perhaps you will be able to make enough physic to cure him in another thirty-eight years."

"But I do not put so much water in my medicine," said the woman, not seeing that Charlotte was sarcastic, and only jeering at her.

"Nay? Then there has not been much rain in your parts this last few years?"

"Ja; we have had good rains for four summers."

"Then must your man make a bigger dam and open up that other spring, or your physic will not hold out till the old man is well."

Still the vrouw was serious, for she did not understand that girls who have had English schooling learn sarcasm with their other lessons, and went on for long, telling how she first learned to make the medicine, and how it was mixed and boiled, taking a bottle out of her bag and offering it to Charlotte and me to taste.

Although very English, Charlotte had plainly not forgotten her Afrikander good manners, which forbid one refusing to drink or eat anything offered, for she took it, and, pretending to drink, made a very wry face, then offered the bottle to me.

"It is not too strong," said the vrouw.

"Nay; if it were, your man would not have to be taking it for thirty-eight years."

This at last made the vrouw angry, which was what Charlotte had all the time been wishing for.

"I make better physic than any vrouw in the Pretoria district," said Mrs du Beer. "My man would long have been dead but for my physic."

Then Charlotte, out of woman's contrariness, said it might be good physic, but it was the wrong colour; and a long and angry indaba began on the proper colour of good medicine, Charlotte holding out for blue and Mrs du Beer for black, till Charlotte, not making the vrouw as angry as she wished, threw gunpowder on the fire by saying, "Well, I suppose I must give way. I have only physicked white people; you have physicked Kafirs, which is why your medicine is black."

And then there was unpleasantness, which, as the end of the story will show, turned out bad for Charlotte and me; for it is a mistake to make a woman angry with sarcasm, as the longer it takes her to see through it, the longer is her anger when she does.

It was a dreadful journey, for the train being used for military purposes, it only moved on as wanted, and often went back to a station we had left an hour before; so that there was too much time for the women to quarrel together, as they did over everything, mostly on the names of the stations we passed, Charlotte always denying it was the place Mrs du Beer said it was, even with the name-board right in front of the carriage window, for she knew the vrouw could not read. At the Nigel came the crowning blow.

"This is Nigel; I lived hereby when I was first married," said Mrs du Beer.

"They have changed the name long ago," said

Charlotte, still full of contradiction. "It is Baavians' Kloof now."

Mrs du Beer made no answer, but called the guard, and asked him the name of the place.

Before he could answer, Charlotte put her head out of the window, right into the face of the guard.

"This is Baavians' Kloof, is it not?" said she to him, in a way that said plainly, "You must agree with me." Of course he did.

"The name has been changed a long time, has it not?" Again the guard said Yes.

Then Charlotte turned to Mrs du Beer,—

"Will you contradict me again? Your physic has made your eyes and memory bad," said she.

I cannot put on paper all the hard things that the vrouw said to Charlotte, for I regret to say that my late countrywomen, especially as they get old, do not say nice things when they get angry, and Mrs du Beer had a very slipping tongue. But if she was rude, Charlotte was vinegar, and said things that no man could say and escape fighting; nor would she let me stop her, but when I tried to make peace she said I of course sided with the old woman, which was not true, and she would not speak to me for an hour.

During this silence I was wondering if, after all, there was any great difference between Charlotte and Katrina; both used their tongues to hurt with, only one was a knobkerrie, the other a stinging little sjambok.

We reached Pretoria sixty-four hours after leaving Ladysmith, perhaps the longest time ever taken by a train between those places; and certainly no man ever suffered more in the distance than I did from the jangling of the two women.

When we got out, the vrouw offered her hand to Charlotte, and, I believe, would have kissed her; but she pretended not to see it, and, walking up to some porters and Burghers, said something to them. I noticed that they all began to look serious, and moved away from the carriages.

"What did you say to them?" I asked.

"I told them to take care, as the old vrouw had been nursing her man who is sick with smallpox at Ladysmith, and now she will have to stay in the carriage, for they will all be afraid to lift her out. If you go to her I shall not speak to you again," said she, thus stopping me from doing what I had no wish to do—help Mrs du Beer out, for she was very heavy.

I afterwards learned there was great trouble about that smallpox, and that they would not let her leave the train till they had telegraphed to Ladysmith to know the truth; and as this took long, it was many hours before she was let go. Even then the white men would not go near her, for there is nothing an Afrikander fears more than smallpox, except lancers.

We had to wait for some time for Mr Human—the irregular train service putting him out in his calculations—on our arrival, so that Charlotte had time to stay and look on, while Mrs du Beer stormed and abused everybody, till they put the train, with her in it, on a siding.

I was not pleased to see how much Charlotte enjoyed the unhappiness of the old woman. "That will teach her to call me ugly," was all she would say when I tried to get her to cease to look and laugh at the efforts of the old vrouw to make the railway people believe that she had not been near smallpox.

When Mr Human came, he told us that he had received instructions from General Joubert what to do with us. Charlotte he took to his house, and I went to the Transvaal Hotel.

This was my first visit to Pretoria since I had left the Transvaal, as I thought for ever; and I was a little fearsome lest the Burghers who knew me should say hard things, as they did when I went back to Prinsloosdorp. But it happened that those who knew me best were away on commando, and the town was full of strange Hollanders and Germans, who knew me not. I, however, made two great mistakes, as the end showed. First, I did not write to Katrina telling her

of my coming, which I quite intended to do, though
not until I was on the eve of returning; secondly, I
did not call on the President, for I afterwards learned
that these omissions were taken as evidence that I
wanted my presence kept secret from Katrina, and that
I feared to face Paul Kruger, after running away from
the Transvaal. But when a man has been shut up
with two quarrelling women for sixty hours, he is in no
mood to face other troubles. I was sorely in need of
rest, and hurried to the hotel.

I saw Charlotte next day with Mr Human, when I
was told all about the plans. Charlotte was to write a
letter to Captain Watson, who was with the other
officers in the Model School. It would be delivered
by Mr Human, who had the right to visit the place;
and when, after proper delay, the captain got away he
was to stay a few days in a house that Mr Human had,
then go off with Charlotte and myself, who would have
a pass for three.

Charlotte wrote the letter at the dictation of Mr
Human. It said: "I am here. Trust the bearer, and
do what he bids you. Watch for me at 10 o'clock
each morning."

There was no signature; so that if it got into
wrong hands no one would be implicated.

"But how will he know it is from you?" I asked,
seeing that Charlotte had written in a partially disguised hand.

"You have never been in love, Sarel," said she, "or
you would know that a man always knows the handwriting of his sweetheart. When I was at school at
Bloemfontein I used to write to dozens of boys in
different hands without my name, and they always
knew whom the letter came from."

Mr Human took charge of the letter, and, an hour
later, Charlotte and I went up the street by the Model
School, walking slowly on the side opposite, so that if
the captain should be on the verandah he could not
fail to see Charlotte. We afterwards learned that he
did see her, and was much cheered; but it was not

till next day we saw him, in the distance, and the pleasure on his face would have made anybody suspect that something good had happened.

A letter in reply was brought to Charlotte that day, and in it the captain wanted to know if others of his friends could be included in the escape; but this was not in the plan, and Mr Human told Charlotte to answer nay, which I could see was much against her will, for she would not write until Mr Human had shown her how impossible it was.

"If you want the captain, why make it harder by expecting too much?" said I; for I could not understand how, if she only wanted the captain for his usefulness, she should wish to help his friends.

"Don't you see, thick one, that the more I do as he wishes, the more he will have to do as I wish when I have him?" which was a clever answer, but I felt it was not the real one.

After much discussion Charlotte wrote as Mr Human desired.

Of course it would have been easy to get the captain out at once, but it was part of the plan to make the business appear very hard and tedious; for, if too easy, he might suspect a trap, which we had great difficulty in making Charlotte see. So several days were allowed to pass without anything more being done except the writing of letters by Charlotte and the captain, and there being much time to kill, Charlotte and I walked about together.

Somehow she appeared to have lost all interest in me since we came to Pretoria. She talked less to me, and became more masterful, making me do all sorts of things for her, never even asking whether I would, but saying only, "Do this," or "Go there"; and often, when we were together in some quiet place, she would take out a bundle of the captain's letters and read them to herself, just as if I was not there. If she did speak, it was only to tell me to do something, or to make some remark about my looks, or my speech, or my ignorance, till I was almost tempted to say, "If you

think me so ignorant, why do you use me so much?"
But somehow I felt afraid to say what I would like,
for she had a way of looking me straight in the face
for a long time without speaking a word, then going
on with her reading, as if she thought it too great a
waste of words to answer me.

One day we had been sitting in the park for some
time, Charlotte reading as usual, and speaking little to
me, when suddenly she looked up from her letter and
said—

"Sarel, how much money have you?"

I thought a little, and told her about fifty pounds.

"What is the good of fifty pounds?" she answered,
most contemptuously. "Is that all you have?"

I thought of the nine hundred pounds her father had
belonging to me, and wondered whether I could borrow
something in Pretoria on the security of that, for I had
got to that state of childishness when a man will do
any foolishness if he thinks it would please a woman.

"How much do you want?" I asked.

"Hundreds;—a thousand;—all that I can get," she
answered, with great earnestness.

I wanted much to know why she needed all this
money, and was framing a question that would not
offend her, as most of mine did, when she put her
hand on mine—a thing she had never done before—
and said, "Will you help me to get a lot of money?"

"Certainly," said I, too pleased and surprised to say
anything else. "Certainly, if I can," I added, for
something in her manner told me she was going to ask
a great thing.

"Oh, you can, if you are not afraid," she said.

"I am not afraid of anything," I answered hotly.

"Except your Burghers—and me. But I think you
will do this to help me."

"Of course I will."

"Say 'God's truth.'"

I said it, and we shook hands.

"Now," said she, "if you back out after saying
'God's truth,' you will go to hell, won't you?"

"Certainly," I said, though my mind went after the many witnesses who had taken false oaths in my Court, and were not yet dead.

"Do you know Coos Vorster's farm on the Krugersdorp Road?" Charlotte next asked.

I told her I did.

"Then to-morrow you must get a cart or something and drive out there. You must have a pass from the field-cornet to go out of Pretoria, and take some hammers and chisels and things to open a strong-box. I will get a horse and ride out alone, and will meet you there at noon."

I was going to ask a few questions, for the whole thing was so strange and sudden, but Charlotte got up from the seat.

"Those people are listening," said she; "talk of something else."

We walked out of the park to near Human's house, when Charlotte told me I must go no farther with her.

"What shall I tell the field-cornet if he wants to know where I am going?" I asked.

"Tell him you are going to look at Coos Vorster's house and farm; that the old man saw you at Ladysmith, and asked you to do this. But, mind, not a word about me."

Before I could ask another question Charlotte was off down the street.

I went right away about the pass. I had no difficulty, for it seems I was known better than I expected, and the few officials I met treated me respectfully, for I afterwards learned that Mr Human had told them I was up on a secret mission from General Joubert, and his name was a pass anywhere in those days. It proved useful in another way, for I borrowed a Cape-cart, thereby saving several pounds, for the lender would never think of asking payment from a commandant.

I lay awake much that night—as had been my habit since Charlotte had come into my life—wondering what the morrow's business meant, and trying hard to connect it with the money that Charlotte was so anxious to get. I had made inquiries, and learned that old Vorster was an uncle to Charlotte; that he was away on commando, and, having no wife or family, had left his place deserted, sending his cattle to another farm in the low veld.

When I reached the farmhouse, well before the appointed time, Charlotte was sitting on the stoep, eating sweets that I had bought her the previous day, for she was a true Boer girl in that matter. I also noticed another thing, which made her even more a Boer maiden. Instead of the riding-habit, cap, and gloves that she had always worn before, she was wearing an ordinary walking skirt, and a kappjie such as Boer girls wear on the farm to keep their faces nice. No one would have thought her now a girl as full of English notions as if born in London.

"Shall I outspan?" I asked.

"That depends on how quick you are. You have first to break open the door."

"Have you no key?"

"Have you no hammer, as I bade you?"

I went to the window, being the easier, and, opening it, got inside the sitting-room and opened the door for Charlotte. She came in, and took a good look round.

"I have not been here since I was a child, which must be long ago, as I am getting so old, as that cat Vrouw du Beer told me. Oh, Sarel, was it not beautiful about the smallpox!" and she sat on the sofa and laughed. Then she sprang up, and went to the bedroom, saying impatiently, "Come, Sarel, don't stand like a sheep; come and help me," as if it were I who had delayed.

The room was seemingly just as old Vorster had left it the last time he slept in it,—very dirty and untidy.

"Pull away this bed," said Charlotte.

I obeyed; and without any help from her I got the heavy wooden bedstead away from its place near the wall. There were boxes, old harness, and all sorts of cumbersome rubbish beneath.

"Move all that," said Charlotte, as if giving orders to a Kafir, and in a way that I would not have permitted from any other man or woman; but Charlotte was so different to others.

When the things were removed Charlotte sat down on the floor, which, as in all old Boer houses, was of dagga or ant-hill earth, made black, hard, and shiny with bullocks' blood. Presently she pointed to a spot where the dagga looked less smooth.

"Give me the chisel," said she; and with it she worked at the spot for a minute or two, when up came a square block, showing a hole about eighteen inches square.

I saw at once that Charlotte was looking for money, for this hole was of a kind very common in the houses of Boers who had no trust in banks.

"See what is here," said she, and I got down and felt.

The space was about a yard deep, but there was nothing there save dust and some dirty paper, and bits of buckskin in which, doubtless, money had been once wrapped.

Charlotte sat with her grey eyes fixed on me in a way she had when she was thinking deeply. Then she got up, saying, "Come to the forage-house; I remember something."

I broke open the door with a spade, and we stood inside. It was a large stone building, full to the roof with every kind of farm rubbish, from ploughs and tools to old sheep- and ox-skins, horns, old furniture, and sacks. On the rafters was a coffin, which most Boers keep in readiness. Charlotte pointed to it, saying very shortly, "Get that down."

My heart turned at the thought; but I had not the courage to say nay, and with many hurts, and much dust and turmoil, I got the cumbersome thing down, breaking one end in the falling. There was in it an old elephant-gun, very rusty and broken, and a powder-flask made of a large ox-horn. I took it up, and noticed that it felt very heavy. I thought it was full of bullets or shot.

" Break it open," said Charlotte.

With difficulty I prised out the plug that stopped the wide end, and saw an old stocking, that I knew in an instant covered money. Charlotte snatched it from me, and untied the bits of reim that bound it.

" It is money," said she very quietly, as if not at all surprised, and she poured it out into her lap. There were sovereigns and silver, and a few bank-notes, certainly not more than a hundred pounds all told.

" There must be more than this; look at those horns," said Charlotte, pointing to a heap of many score very dirty and battered ox-horns lying in a heap on the floor.

I took them up one by one, and had examined perhaps half of the heap, when I found one plugged with dirt at the thick end, and very heavy. Inside it was fifty pounds in gold. Presently came another and another. We had at last come upon old Vorster's bank, though through no accident, for Charlotte afterwards told me that she remembered as a child staying at the farm, and being whipped by her uncle for taking away a horn and throwing it into the dam. She was told that she had drowned a hundred pounds of bank-notes, which proved the truth.

As I found the horns that contained the money, Charlotte opened them by removing the plug of dry mud, and poured the coins into a Kafir cooking-pot.

When I had examined all the horns, Charlotte bade me look in several other places, but we found nothing more ; so we carried the pot into the sitting-room and counted the heap. It was mostly gold and silver, but there were many bank-notes, some of them so dirty that we could scarcely read the name of the bank, and in many cases the half of a five-pound note was pinned on to the half of a ten- or even twenty-pound note. But, making allowance for what might be lost through this carelessness, we reckoned the money at £3400.

When it was all counted, we looked around for something convenient to put it into, and I found a paraffin-tin. Charlotte tore up the bed-quilt, and wrapped and packed the money tightly in it, the whole making a very solid and heavy parcel.

While she was doing this, I for the first time put into words what had been in my mind all the time.

"Charlotte," said I, "whose money is this?"

"Mine, of course," she answered shortly.

"But I do not understand."

"There is much you do not understand, Sarel."

"Perhaps so; but did your uncle give you this money?"

"He is going to; it will be mine when he dies."

"Then you are stealing it."

"How can I steal what is my own? I thought you told me you were a lawyer?"

"Ja; it is because I have been a public prosecutor and am a law-agent that I want to know all about it. Suppose Oom Vorster says I stole it?"

"That is what he will say if he finds you have been here. Are you not a Government man?"

"But, Charlotte, I shall get into trouble."

"Of course you will if you are foolish enough to tell people you have been here."

"But do I not have any of it?"

Charlotte thought a little, with her eyes on my face, as usual when she thought deeply.

"Yes; I will give you half."

I was pleased at this, and made no more objections, for whatever I might say, this clever girl always had an answer to silence me.

"Now, Sarel," said she, when we were ready to leave, "you must wait here till four o'clock. It will then be dark before you get into Pretoria. Then you must drive straight to a store and buy one of those big tin boxes that ladies put frocks and things in when they travel by train, and put the paraffin-tin inside it. Lock it up, and drive to the house I showed you, where the captain is to be hidden, and I will be there to meet you. See how I trust you, leaving you alone with so much money, and you a public prosecutor!"

"And do I have my half when I get there?"

"Of course. You cannot take it now, stupid."

I helped her into the saddle and she cantered off.

When she had gone, I sat smoking and thinking, for it would not be four o'clock for an hour or more. My thoughts were very mixed—some happy, some not. I did not quite believe Charlotte's story as to the money being hers, though the old man might leave her some of it. Then I thought it was war-time, and old Vorster· was foolish to leave his money in this way. Besides that, he was a bad old man, and had made his wealth by robbing the Government over road-contracts, and by supplying weevily mealies to feed prisoners in the jails. Even if we took this three thousand pounds, it would not hurt him, for he must have more hidden somewhere, as he had been a Government contractor many years and spent very little. Once or twice I thought I would keep the money for myself, but I did not encourage this way of thinking, for if it were true that the old man had promised it to Charlotte, it would be wrong for me to rob a young girl of her inheritance as if I were a Government Orphan Master. On the other hand, I thought, if trouble came it would be better that I should take the blame than her, for I already was supposed to have stolen ; but if I was to take the blame why should I not have the money? But I could think of no way of getting away with it, for if I were to hide it, Charlotte was so strong and fearless that she would fight me hard. So I resolved to be honest and do my best to carry out my promise, though as a lawyer I knew such an agreement was not binding.

I made one more good search over the place, thinking that I might yet find more, it being absurd to think that a Government contractor who stood well at Pretoria should have only three thousand pounds ; but I was not rewarded. So I closed up the place, making it appear as much undisturbed as I could, and putting the paraffin-tin in the cart—a heavy job—I covered it with an old sack and drove towards Pretoria.

As is ever the case when one desires to escape notice,

and goes by back-roads and ways that have little traffic, I seemed to meet every Burgher I knew in the place, some of whom would ask whence I came. To all I gave such answers as I thought would throw them off the spoor, for my legal experience had taught me the danger of evidence such as these witnesses might be able to give should I have to deny having been to Vorster's place.

I reached Pretoria just after dark, and drove to the first store I saw open, where I bought such a box as Charlotte had described, and had the paraffin-tin put into it by the Kafirs—a task that they made very long, causing me great uneasiness, for they kept making remarks on the heaviness of the tin. But no mishap occurred, and I took a roundabout way to the house where I was to meet Charlotte. Like the clever girl she was, she was ready for me with a Kafir to carry up the box without any delay, nor would she let me do as I at first wished,—leave the Cape-cart outside while I talked with her. So I drove to the stable and returned on foot. The house, like most such in Pretoria, stood far back from the road, and was well covered in by trees and bushes, and had a wide verandah well screened with grenadilla, where we could sit and see without being seen from the street.

Charlotte had changed her dress, and looked very sweet and pink in something new, better and nicer than I had yet seen her, and a great love for her came up in my heart. We sat together on the verandah, there being no one in the place but the Kafir, for the house was one in which had lived the young Hollander clerks of Mr Human's office; but they being on commando, the place was on the hands of the owner, who had left it in charge of Mr Human.

We sat in silence for some time watching the leaves flickering in the electric light that makes Pretoria so beautiful by night. I was very happy, but all the time feeling I should be more so if Charlotte would say something about dividing the money. But she never did say what I expected, for when she spoke, after what seemed a long silence, it was to say a very strange thing.

"Sarel," said she, "how much does it cost for two people to go to England?"

I told her it came to about a hundred pounds from Pretoria.

"How many thirty pounds are there in three thousand pounds?" was her next question. I reckoned it up on the back of an envelope and found there were one hundred.

"That is one hundred months, so that three thousand pounds would last eight years and four months. How much does it cost to live in London?"

I told her I did not know, but had heard it was cheap if the Londoners did not know you came from Africa, in which case they charged double for everything.

"Are you going to England?" I asked, for these questions perplexed me much.

"Yes, some day. I want to see the Queen and the Crystal Palace—because I don't believe there is such a place—and the wax-works."

"But," said I, "you will not have three thousand pounds; half of it is mine."

"I have been counting since you were away, and I find I cannot give you half. I can only give you a thousand pounds, and you must lend me that for a little while. You will, Sarel, won't you?" and she put her hand on mine, as she did when she asked me to help her get the money. Before I knew what I was saying I said Yes. I had no sooner said it than I was angry with myself, particularly as Charlotte took her hand away directly I had spoken.

"I mean that I will lend you half my half," I said, when I had got over my surprise and disappointment.

"No, half is no good," said she with great coldness and firmness. "If you don't play fair and are greedy, I will give all the money to Mr Human to take care of."

This frightened me much, for I knew that she was

quite likely to do it, and the thought came to me that if I pretended to agree with her I might get my full share, so I told her I would let her have all.

"That is quite right, Sarel," said she; "it is much better that I should have the money, for you might be killed, or, worse still, the Government might take it from you. I heard Mr Human say the officials in Pretoria quite expected that the Government would call on them to pay up something from their savings, as the war was running away with all the money in the Treasury. And now that all is settled we will talk of something else, for the khaki captain comes here to-night."

Hearing her say this, and the memory that she had my thousand pounds and her father nine hundred, made me desperate, for I could see that unless I did something I should soon have neither money nor Charlotte; so with great courage I said what I had been wanting to say for so long.

"Ja, Charlotte," said I, "that is settled; now let us settle another thing."

"What is that?" she asked, showing no surprise.

"Do what Mrs du Beer thought we were going to do."

"I don't understand," Charlotte answered, though something in the tone of her voice told me that she was not speaking the truth.

"Let us get married," I said boldly.

She made no answer; but although she sat where the electric light could not reach her face, I felt that she was looking at me with her soft grey eyes wide open.

"Charlotte," said I, "the three thousand we have is quite enough to get married on. Then I have half shares in thirty-five salted oxen running on my cousin's place, and there is nine hundred pounds your father owes me, and I have a secret share in a Kafir liquor-canteen at Prinsloosdorp—what more can you want, Charlotte?"

She was still silent.

"Is it that you love the khaki captain?"

For the first time she seemed to hear me. "No," said she, but not firmly or as if she meant it; "but I did not know you wanted to marry me. Wait a bit till I make up my mind whether I want to marry; wait till to-morrow."

"I will wait as long as you like, if you will only agree to marry me."

She thought again for a minute, then, putting her hand on my shoulder, said very kindly, "Sarel, I have not known you long enough to say whether I will marry you; but if you do what I wish, and say nothing more about it till I tell you you may, I will marry you, if——"

"If what?"

"If I can. I can't say more than that, can I?"

I told her I was satisfied with that agreement, though I did not do as she did when I promised to help her steal the money,—make her take an oath. I thought it would be the same if she kissed me, but she made no sign of wanting to do that.

"Are you going to kiss me?" I asked.

"Yes, Sarel, when it is all properly arranged. But you must go now, for I have to change my dress. Come back at ten o'clock, when the captain will be here."

I went away, feeling not so happy as I should have liked; for I thought it strange that if she did not love the khaki captain she should want to put on another new frock, when the one she wore was already new and beautiful. It was so very much like a Boer maiden to show all her clothes to the man she wanted to marry. She had not done this to me; for though she made me buy her gloves and other women's things, she never untied the parcel while I was with her, so that often I never saw what I had paid for.

These thoughts came like a little cloud over the sun on a bright day; and before I knew it, I found myself at the door of the bar of the Transvaal Hotel, a place I rarely went into unless I wanted to see a member of the Raad or a Government official.

Standing at the bar was the brother of Katrina, Frikkie Bester, one of the most wicked, drunken, and idle Burghers in all the Transvaal. He was, as usual, drinking at some one else's expense, and, getting very boisterous, telling stories of his wondrous doings at Elandslaagte and Talana, places he never saw, for he was sent back very early for taking money out of the pockets of sleeping Burghers.

As soon as I recognised Frikkie, I did what he would have done on the sight of an enemy—got quickly out of sight, and walked about one of the few streets where there was no electric light. And this was the way of my thoughts:—

If I married Katrina, I should have to keep in idleness this schelm, for he was always seeking whom he might devour. When I was first courting his sister he was ever with us when we wanted to be alone, so that I had to give him money to go away and drink. Then he got clothes and things from me as a reward for keeping Teenie Keiser away from the house, he telling me that Teenie was so jealous of me that he would shoot me if he came and found me with Katrina; and all the time there was no such person. Then when it became a proper engagement, he came and stayed at my house free for a month, and I only got rid of him by lending him ten pounds and giving him a railway-ticket to Pretoria. Ever since I had known him, he had been as a fly on a sore place to me, constantly coming to my office when I was most busy, or sitting next me in court, and making remarks about the cases, particularly when Kafirs were being prosecuted, for he hated them badly.

The memory of all that I had suffered through this man made me resolve that I would never have him for a relation. I would marry Charlotte, and with the money that would thereby come, I would pay Katrina the thousand pounds she had insisted on my borrowing from her, and be a free man, with a wife who was not too fat to walk round the kitchen without having to sit down and groan, and who was not always saying she was twelve years older than I, and therefore able to give me good advice. Neither would Charlotte be always wanting to physic people who were well, but would buy her medicine at the chemists' in proper bottles, and not quarrel with him for giving small measure, as Katrina always did. Then I thought of Nick Smit, who had a wife like Katrina, only more horrible to look upon; and though he was a high official, he had to keep her in the bedroom or kitchen when the State Secretary or any one respectable called. Then there came up pictures of Charlotte, looking clean and pink through washing, often more than twice a-day, and wearing nice frocks that fitted her, and did not make her look like a sack of mealie-meal tied round the middle with string, as Katrina did, even when dressed for Nachtmaal in a blue silk dress that cost ten pounds in Johannesburg.

It is wondrous how things fit to help one's thoughts; for as I walked, thinking thus, down one of the quiet streets where the rich Pretoria people mostly live, I saw a young and beautifully dressed woman standing on the verandah saying good-bye to some friends who were leaving. As she stood in her white dress, shining under the electric light, a man whom I took to be her husband came up behind her from the house and stood with one arm round her waist, looking very proud. I could well picture myself doing that to Charlotte, when I ceased to fear her, but not to Katrina, for not only was she too fat round the waist, but once or twice, when I did do such a thing, she pushed me away, saying, "Don't be a fool, Sarel." The sight of so much beautiful happiness on that verandah made me sad and jealous, and I resolved that never again would I see Katrina, whether I married Charlotte or not.

It was yet far off ten o'clock, and I was getting hungry, for I had feared to go back to the hotel because of Frikkie Bester; but I remembered I had some biscuit in my haversack in my bedroom, so went by the back of the hotel to my room. The door was open, and, looking in, I saw a man lying on my bed. My haversack, and several small parcels of things I had bought, lay open about the floor.

While I looked, the man on the bed turned round. It was Frikkie Bester. He jumped up as well and quickly as he could, being very unsteady with whisky, and had his arms round my neck to hold him quiet and straight while he was calling me in English, which he always spoke instead of the Taal, of which he said he was ashamed.

"Good old Sarel! dear old chappie!" he kept saying, pulling me nearly over, for I am not a very large man. "I heard you had come, Sarel, and I waited for you. I have borrowed a collar, Sarel," and I saw that he had tried to put on a new one; but as he could only fasten the back button, it stood out from his neck very stupidly, and the more so, as he had the old and dirty collar still hanging by one end from the front button; nor would he allow me to remove one or the other, being in that contradictory stage of whisky when a man says everything is all right.

It was in vain that I tried to persuade him to go away. He clung to me, and insisted that I should go down to the bar and drink with him. So, as the people in the hotel were opening their doors to see what the noise was about, and one old Burgher told me I ought to feel shame for being drunk, I went with Frikkie, which I should have had to do in any case, unless I wanted him to fall down the stairs and break his neck; for, like all Boers, he was not used to them, and when full of whisky always would go down backwards, because he said looking down made him giddy and feel stupid; but he looked much more stupid the way he would go.

Arrived in the bar, he called for whisky, inviting the four or five Burghers and Hollanders there to drink with him.

"Who is paying for them?" asked the barman.

"Commandant Sarel Erasmus here, my brother-in-law."

"I am not your brother-in-law," I answered angrily, but not because I had to pay for the drinks, which I quite expected.

"But you soon will be, Sarel, and a good brother-in-law;" and he took my hand and put it into the hands of the other Burghers, saying, "You know Sarel; he ran away with the fine-money from Prinsloosdorp. Good old Sarel! Fill up again, boys; Sarel has plenty of money."

"You are a liar, and you are drunk," said I in great wrath, trying to get away; but Frikkie caught hold of me and tried to put his arms round my neck.

"He says his brother-in-law is drunk, and that I am not his brother-in-law; but I shall be, Sarel, when you marry Katrina. Good old Katrina! weighs two hundred pounds, Katrina; champion fat woman of Transvaal, Katrina."

"Again I say I am no relation of yours, and never will be," said I, at last shaking Frikkie off.

"What! not marry Katrina after stealing her thousand pounds?" and he was beginning to tell the Burghers about that much misunderstood business, when I could stand no more; but taking up a bottle from the counter I hit him a hard knock on the side of the head, and he fell on to the floor, groaning and crying.

The men drank up their whisky and went away.

"You had better take him up to bed," said the barman.

"Never," said I. "He is nobody to me; I only know who he is," and I did as the other Burghers, and left.

I walked quickly away towards the house where Charlotte was, my heart thumping hard with anger, and altogether feeling very ill and unfit, for I was not quite satisfied whether, if I had killed Frikkie, I had now sufficient friends to secure my discharge should trouble come of it.

When I arrived in front of the house it was not yet ten o'clock. There was no light to be seen inside, so

I walked quietly up through the palms and oleanders towards the verandah, and presently, by the light from the electric street lamp, saw something.

Charlotte was on the verandah in a white dress, and a tall man was holding her with his arm. The sight made me step from behind the bush. At the sound of my foot on the path the two started apart.

"Is that you, Sarel?" came the voice of Charlotte, very softly and sweetly, for her voice was more like an English than a Boer girl's, and particularly her laugh, which had only music, and no harsh croak and gurgle in it.

I made no sound or answer.

"See what it is, dear," I heard her whisper, and the man, whom, by his tallness and straightness, I knew to be the one I had seen on the verandah of the Model School, stepped off the stoep and came towards me. I believe that if I had had a revolver I should have killed him as he came, so angry was I at what I had seen and heard. For a moment there passed through my heart a quick thought that even without a gun I might so injure him that Charlotte might not want to marry him, especially if I spoiled his face. But the thought went away as quickly as it had come, for he was a big and strong man, and carried his hands low in front of him, as men do who are ready for danger and know how to use their fists. So I stepped out, saying, "It is I, Sarel."

"Come up, Sarel; we have been waiting long for you," said Charlotte, which could not be true, as it was even yet not the hour fixed for my coming. But in a moment my anger was cooled, for as I got upon the verandah Charlotte took me by the hand and led me into the sitting-room, the man following. Still holding my hand, Charlotte presented me, saying, "Captain Watson, this is Commandant Sarel Erasmus, who has done so much to help me and you."

The captain shook hands, saying how glad he was to meet me, and how grateful for all I had done, and spoke as if he meant it. He was a fine-looking man, just the kind that young girls fresh from school always admire most, and pick out in pictures as the men they will marry; and when I had had a good look at him, and felt how much bigger he was than I, a sad conviction came over me that after all it was the man Charlotte wanted, and not his usefulness at reading the heliograph.

So deep was my grief that I had not noticed that Mr Human was also in the room; neither could I listen to what he and the captain were saying to me about the escape, and the plans for the future. I had no eyes or ears but for Charlotte, and I could only watch her soft grey eyes as they followed the captain wherever he moved, never once looking at me as I sat in misery on a couch in the darkest corner of the room.

When we had drunk coffee, Mr Human said it was time that we went, and soon after we left the captain.

As we got into the street, Charlotte came up to me, saying in her masterful way to Mr Human, "Go on in front; I have to talk to Sarel," and he meekly obeyed, as men always did with Charlotte.

"Sarel," said she, taking hold of my arm, "I do not love silly jealous men. Why are you jealous of the captain?"

"Charlotte, I saw something on the stoep."

"Of course you did," said she, quite unconcernedly. "You saw him kiss me, I suppose? Is it very wonderful that an English captain should kiss a girl who he believes has got him out of prison, and especially when he loves her? Some men have more love and courage than others."

"But if you do not love him, why did you let him kiss you?"

"Sarel, you are a fool. Would you have me say to the captain I am not in love with him, but with some one else, and so spoil all our plans? If you have no brains yourself, why should you think others have none, too?"

These words made me happy again, and I kissed

Charlotte boldly, which she did not resist, though she seemed surprised.

"Now," said she, quickening her walk to catch up with Mr Human, "if you are again a fool I will have nothing to do with you, for I have no use for fools," and before I could frame an answer, she was walking beside Mr Human, holding his arm, and chatting and laughing as if nothing of any importance had happened.

I was wishful to go with them into the house, hoping that perhaps Charlotte might have other things to say to me; but she said "Good night" at the gate in a way that forbade any such hope, and walked away, saying to Mr Human, "Tell Sarel about to-morrow."

Mr Human did say something, but I had no ears for him; my ears and my heart had gone into the house with Charlotte. So I said good night before he had made an end of talking, and for an hour walked before the house, till the police came and asked me what I did and who I was, walking to the hotel with me, as they said, to make sure that my story was true, but, as I knew well, that they might get drink.

It was not till they came up to me that I remembered Frikkie Bester, and for a moment I got a great schrick, thinking he might be dead, and that they had come to arrest me. But they made no mention of him; and when we got to the hotel the barman made my heart rejoice by telling me that he had doctored Frikkie, and sent him home very much cut, but not hurt. So I gave him a sovereign, told him to give the policemen drinks, and went to bed.

CHAPTER XIII.

Reveals the selfishness of a woman's love.

JOHN BUNYAN, Sir Walter Raleigh, and I are striking examples of the blessing that prison-life may become to those who know how to use and value it by thinking out, properly and fully, thoughts that have stayed but a short time in the heart during freedom; for when such finished thoughts are put upon paper, they become of value to our fellow-creatures.

Since I have been in the jail at Pietermaritzburg, many things that heretofore I thought little on, or else were exceedingly great puzzles to me, have come back to me in their proper truth and fulness. For example, it was not until I have had time to ponder on the strange happenings of the past year, that I saw one of the great advantages of living in England. I have been told by Englanders that it is quite possible for a man to live there and not know or be known to other men living only a few miles away,—a thing hard to understand and believe by one living in a country where you know every farm within a hundred miles, and are related by marriage or cousinship to every second man and woman in South Africa. I have in my ignorance pitied such people in England, thinking that, if it were true, it showed how unsociable and unfriendly Englanders were to each other. But a thing that happened at Pretoria made me wish that we Afrikanders were more like the English in this matter, and did not know so much of one another's goings-in and comings-out.

The morning after my serious talk with Charlotte, and my resolve to take her for my wife, I went to Mr Human's house early to see her, for I was quite restless and unhappy away from her. She was, as I feared, gone to the cottage to see the khaki captain with Mr Human; and on the way thither I met them returning, when Charlotte said I must go shopping with her, which I knew meant that I should have to pay for all she bought. But so long as I had her away from the khaki, I did not mind what it cost me.

We had been in two stores, and were going into a third in Church Street, when who should suddenly stand in front of us but the old vrouw of the dreadful railway journey, Mrs du Beer. Before I could get into the shop she stopped me.

"So you are not married, Sarel Erasmus. You are waiting for Katrina Bester, I suppose. Charlotte Brink," the wicked old woman went on, speaking to Charlotte, who was looking in the shop window and had not yet seen her, "do you know you are taking away another woman's man? You ought to be whipped; but what do you expect from a girl who would tell the porters I had smallpox! Katrina Bester will be here presently, and she will spoil that pink face for you."

"What business is it of yours?" I asked, not knowing what to say, and feeling very sick.

"It is all my business. Katrina is my second husband's half-cousin, and it is my right to see that no girl in the family is made a fool of by a thing like you."

Charlotte had stood very cool and amused, her grey eyes passing all over Mrs du Beer, and staying long on the old woman's big and ugly boots.

"Mrs du Beer," said she with politeness, "you are very drunk, and I can see that the smallpox has made your feet swell. Why do you not go back to the hospital before they miss you? Come on, Sarel; if the police see us talking to her they will send us to the lazaretto," and she turned away.

The old woman stood speechless during Charlotte's

talk, her mouth open, as if the words had frozen in coming out; and we had gone several yards down the street before she recovered her voice, when she screamed, "You pair of Rooinek spies! Look at them! Stop them! Here, Burghers, catch them; that girl says I have smallpox. They are spies; I saw them at Ladysmith."

The word "smallpox" made the people in the street stop and look frightened, for they could not quite understand whether it was we or she who had the dreadful disease; so nobody did anything but look from her to us, and we could have got away easily; but Charlotte's anger was stirred by being called a spy. She turned back, and walked boldly to the old woman.

"You wicked, old, ugly thing, how dare you say that! It is you who are the spy. You have brought smallpox to kill all the Burghers, and you call me spy because I found you out. Keep away from her, Burghers. Look at her feet; they are swelled already," and while the crowd were looking at the old woman's feet, Charlotte walked away, the people making a path for her as if she was a smallpox ambulance.

Long after we had turned the corner we could hear the shrill voice of the old woman trying to satisfy the crowd that her feet were only of the size usual in her family, and were no sign of smallpox.

When we had got into a quiet street, Charlotte said very earnestly, "What is this about your marrying Katrina Bester?"

I had expected this, and for once was ready with my answer.

"Katrina Bester I have known since I was a child, and she is as fat and old and ugly as Mrs du Beer, who would no doubt much like to have me marry Katrina."

"Old, fat, and ugly, is she?" said Charlotte.

I did not give her time to say more. "You have such a sharp and clever tongue, Charlotte, that I don't wonder that the old woman said things to hurt you."

"She did not hurt me; what she said made me glad," and she left me to puzzle what her saying meant, for that she was pleased at something I could see. "Now go," said she, "and come to the house to-night, for I think we must leave to-morrow. The Burghers may set importance on what that old cat said about our being spies, and we shall be watched, which will make matters bad for the captain," and with that she ran to the house, without waiting for me to go as far as the gate.

As I walked away, a great sadness came over me— first, because of the way the khaki was keeping Charlotte away from me; and secondly, because of the words of the old woman about Katrina. I was afraid to think what would happen if she should come, for I feared that Charlotte believed what had been said about my going to marry Katrina, for young women always think that men are wanting to be married to some other girl, which shows that they are all jealous and afraid of one another. Then what did she mean by saying she was glad? Did it mean that she was glad to have an excuse for not marrying me?

As I walked aimlessly down a quiet and nearly deserted street, I came to a respectable drinking-bar to which, in the old days, I used sometimes go to find certain Government officials who used it. It was open, though most such places were at that time closed by order of the landdrost, and before I knew where I was, I found myself drinking whisky with a kerel who knew me.

After a time, and just as I was about to leave, there happened one of those things that, as I have often had cause to remark, change the direction of our paths. Two policemen came in and ordered the bar to be closed, so the barman invited us all into his private room, saying it would not look well if a lot of us all left at the same time.

The police sat drinking a long time, I having to pay for their liquor. They finding I had come from Lady-smith, I had to tell them all about the war, which kept them there so long that my complaint began to be bad, and I fell asleep.

I was awakened by the barman, who told me it was already night, and that I must go home. I went outside, but had not walked far before I felt really ill, and knew that the whisky I had drunk a little of must be poisoned. But after I had rested, by lying behind a banana-tree in a private garden, I got up, feeling very full of a strange desire to go to Charlotte, and, once for all, settle the question,—me or the khaki. I would begin to act,—not meekly, as I had done, but as a man having the right to a woman because he was going to marry her.

It was nearly eight in the evening, and about the time I had decided to go to Charlotte. So I called at the house of Mr Human, who told me he had sent a messenger for me already, as the captain must be got away that night. This pleased me much; for as the train left at ten o'clock, there was little time for Katrina to come. I hurried to the hotel to get a few things I had bought, and particularly a uniform. My clothes had grown so shabby and dirty that Charlotte said she would not let me walk in the streets with her. So I went to a Jew's store, and having bought a nice suit of clothes that, though rather big, were cheap, he showed me a beautiful uniform, which he said was just the thing for a commandant. It had been made for the chief sanitary inspector of Johannesburg, but did not fit him. I thought it looked too rich and full of colour for me, being blue and green; but the Jew persuaded me. "It may save your life," said he, "for if you get captured, the British will think you are one of their great officers, and while they are finding out what uniform it is, you can run away." So I bought it, and decided that I would put it on to travel with.

I got to my room and changed, and was paying my bill, when the barman gave me a great schrick.

"There is a lady asking for you," said he.

"What name?" I asked, getting the words out with great difficulty.

"She did not say; but she is with young Frikkie Bester, and is rather fat."

My heart gave a great thump; but I knew that I had to be cool, and act as if in a very serious position, as I was.

"Is she here?" I asked.

"Yes; somewhere in the hotel."

I took out a five-pound note, nearly the last I had, and gave it to the man.

"I don't want to see her," said I. "Keep her here as long as you can, and tell her if she asks again that I have sent a messenger to say I am coming here at eleven o'clock. Do you quite understand?"

The man laughed. "I have been porter in a Johannesburg hotel; you can leave me to manage it," and I went off almost happy, though, as I walked to Mr Human's house, I kept glancing behind to see that I was not followed, and I hurried so much that I arrived quite breathless.

Charlotte and the captain were there. He was dressed as much like a Boer as they could make him. They had tried to make him look like a German, as the pass he had described him as a German artillery officer going to Ladysmith; but he looked so much like an Englishman, that they made him change into an old Boer suit, but still he looked more British than Afrikander, particularly when he tried to smoke, for he was not used to a pipe and strong Boer tobacco, and at that time there was only bad leaf to be got in Pretoria.

When Charlotte at last ceased to look at the khaki and noticed me, she said, "What is the matter, Sarel? you look ill and worried," which, I have no doubt, was true.

"It is the food at the hotel; I am not used to it." As I said this I saw a strange smile on the face of the khaki that made the blood rush all over my body.

"Perhaps you do not feel well enough to go to-

night," said he, in a tone which I interpreted to mean,
" I hope you will not come."

" Whether I am well or not I must go, for I have
to look after a lady," I answered, putting as much
feeling and meaning into my voice as I could.

" Why did you not think of that before you drank
so much whisky?" said Charlotte, in a most unfriendly
manner.

My anger, which had been growing stronger the
more I looked at the khaki and saw how plainly
Charlotte cared for him, now got hold of me, and I
answered hotly, " I am quite as well able to look after
you as the khaki, and better; and I am going to do
so properly."

There must have been great meaning and dignity
in my words, for Mr Human came to me and told me
to be calm and quiet, and lie down on the sofa and
rest. I pushed him away, saying I did not want rest,
as I had been sleeping all day, at which I saw the
khaki again smile and look at Charlotte.

This made my anger burn. " Yes, I will stay,"
said I; " but the luggage stays with me," and I looked
meaningly at Charlotte.

She came to me, in her wondrously smooth way,
and, putting her hand on my shoulder, said, " Sarel,
you are not drunk; you are ill. You have been worry-
ing too much about me, and can hold out no longer.
Sit down," and she pushed me gently on to the sofa
and sat by my side.

I could hold no longer, but put my arms round her
and kissed her and nearly cried. She turned very red,
and looked at the captain, but did not push me away,
but told me not to cry, so kindly, that I could no
longer be angry, but resolved to sit quietly on the
sofa, while Mr Human and Charlotte made pre-
parations for leaving, as the time was getting late.

I must have fallen asleep, for I was awakened by
Charlotte telling me the cab had come.

I got into it with difficulty, being weak and giddy
after all the heart trouble I had gone through.

The first thing I saw was the tin box; and the thought of what was in it made me feel happy, and I spoke nothing on the journey to the station. The train was waiting, and we went straight to a reserved carriage without causing much remark, though I noticed that the Burghers, who were on the platform in numbers, looked very hard at my uniform, thinking I was a very high German officer. To help the deceit, I walked with my head well back, and struck my heels hard on the platform, jingling my spurs, which much amused Charlotte and the captain.

I sat in the corner nearest the door, the captain and Charlotte sitting at the farther end, so as to be away from the eyes of the Burghers as much as possible, for, with their usual love of handsome uniforms, they came and looked at me as they slowly passed the carriage.

We were shaking hands with Mr Human, and the train was slowly moving out, when I saw a commotion near the entrance-gate, and looking up, I saw Katrina, Mrs du Beer, and Frikkie Bester hurrying towards the train.

Immediately the blood rushed to my head, my heart thumped, and my stomach turned deathly sick, and I slipped on to the floor of the carriage just as I heard Frikkie Bester say, " There he is, Katrina," and I felt a hand, which by its hardness and bigness I knew was Katrina's, clutch my hair and pull so hard that I could have called out in my pain, while her big voice screamed, " Stop the train ! he has my thousand pounds and another woman."

I heard and knew no more, but passed into a blissful sleep of death.

When I again saw the light I was sitting on the floor, the captain holding me up, and Charlotte putting water to my mouth. I got up with great difficulty, and spoke no word, although they both asked if I felt better now, for I wanted time to frame what I should say when they asked about Katrina.

They let me remain quiet for some time, till I put my hands to my head, for I could almost still feel the big fingers of Katrina in my hair.

"Did she hurt you much?" asked Charlotte.

"Who?" I answered, still further to gain time.

"That woman who said you had stolen her thousand pounds."

"I do not remember; I was ill. Was it Mrs du Beer?"

"No. Mrs du Beer said she would tear my hair; but it was the other woman who pulled yours. What did she mean about your stealing her money?"

"What did Mrs du Beer mean by what she said about you?" I was still trying to put off explanations.

"Katrina seems to object to your leaving her," said the captain.

"Ja; she always does," I answered, quite unthinkingly.

"Why? Has she any right to object? Is she your wife, for instance?" the captain went on, speaking as if very much interested, and determined to get the matter cleared up.

"God forbid!" I answered. "She wants to be my wife, and has persecuted me for years. She is my cousin, and often lives in my house with her aunt."

"Poor creature! She seems very fond of you."

"You promised to marry her, did you not, Sarel?" Charlotte broke in.

"Do you believe what that wicked old du Beer woman says?"

"Nay; Katrina said so herself, and her brother also."

"I would make a thousand promises to escape a woman like Katrina," I answered boldly, seeing it was useless to try to make Charlotte believe I had not promised marriage, for all women are hard to convince when they get this notion into their heads.

"Yes," Charlotte went on; "but what does she mean by saying you have stolen her money?"

"I have no money," I said; and then I looked straight and hard at Charlotte, who turned red and looked away through the window, where she could see nothing, for it was dark. I noticed, too, that the captain seemed surprised at this sudden alteration in Charlotte's manner. He looked inquiringly at Charlotte, then at the tin box, which was standing on end in the middle of the carriage.

"Mrs du Beer said the money was in that box," said the captain.

My heart gave a thump, and Charlotte turned round quickly—

"Arthur, how can you know what she said, for she only speaks the Taal?"

I noticed that she called him "Arthur." Before she had only called him "Captain Watson." In a moment a thought flashed through my mind that she had got this money for the captain, and did not wish him to know anything about it.

"It doesn't require to know much of the Taal to understand what a woman means when she points to a box and says, 'Daar is de gelt.' You forget I know German."

"If I had money that did not belong to me I should give it up," said I, again looking hard at Charlotte, for something told me that if I kept on the subject of the money she would get frightened, and I should get my share without trouble, for I could see she was fearful lest the captain should know the truth as to how she got it.

"You are stupid people to listen to what a silly old woman says, and I am also stupid for listening to what the other one said. Give me something to eat," said Charlotte, skilfully turning away the subject, which I could see was getting very disagreeable to her, for she had not reckoned on ploughing such a deep furrow when she put her hand to the plough.

Then she told the captain about our first meeting with Mrs du Beer, and the scene in the street at Pretoria.

The captain laughed much, saying he could now quite understand why the old lady should be so spiteful. "It was a very feminine revenge she took," said he, and this started Charlotte on asking whether English women would have done such a thing, and if they quarrelled as Boer women do, and many other questions, in which I joined, for it kept the talk off dangerous subjects.

The captain made one or two attempts to get back on to the track; but Charlotte and I were too much for him, and we kept him off.

I had noticed that, after a few stations had been passed, the stationmasters always came to our carriage when the train stopped, and gave a good look round, as if counting us. Sometimes they asked to see our passes, and they always looked hard at the tin box. When this had been done several times, the captain remarked upon it.

" Do they suspect me, do you think ? " he asked.

This was a good excuse to put him off the spoor, for I had no doubt that Katrina had sent a telegram down the line asking that we be watched.

" I have no doubt they suspect you," said I; " for any one can see you are no Boer, and you will talk English when we stop at stations.

" But what does this pass say ? "

I read it. It described him as Captain Brandt, going to Ladysmith to take charge of the signalling.

" Then why do they look so hard into the carriage ? "

" It is Sarel's uniform," said Charlotte. " They think he is the German officer. My people will go a long way to see fine clothes."

Although the captain laughed at this, I could see he was not satisfied; and to keep him amused, I told him about Katrina's parting speech to me at Prinsloosdorp, at which he laughed heartily; and this encouraged me to tell him all I could against Katrina, secretly intending that Charlotte should be the more convinced that I cared nothing for Katrina. I laid great stress upon her physicking me, so that I might be fit for fighting, saying, " It must be a strange kind of love that makes a woman do her best to get a man killed."

" Perhaps she has high ideas of the duty of men," said the captain.

"That is it; all she thinks men are for is to make money to give to their vrouws. I think the vrouw should do something when she has money of her own," and I looked at Charlotte again, who appeared not to hear, but called the captain to look at some buck running in the distance, which neither he nor I could see, though I pretended I could, to oblige Charlotte and keep the captain off disagreeable subjects.

We made a good and quick run into Natal, the only thing noticeable about it being the regular visits of the stationmasters to look into our carriage.

The adjutant and private secretary of General Joubert were at the train to meet us, and I was told that I had to go right away to the General. There was a spider to drive us to the head laager; and I noticed that the adjutant looked specially after the tin box, which he saw to being put into the cart.

"Does the General know about me?" asked the captain of me.

"Of course. We Afrikanders are not altogether fools," said the adjutant, who was always very bitter against everybody who was not a Boer; and I feared that the captain might say something in his anger, but he kept very quiet.

When we reached the head laager we had to wait some time before going in to the General, as Charlotte had disappeared. She presently came from behind the General's tent, and we went in.

"Well, Charlotte," said he, after looking close at the captain through his little half-shut eyes, "you have done your work well." Then to the captain, "How did my kerels treat you in Pretoria, captain?"

The adjutant translated, for Slim Piet would never let Englanders know that he understood their tongue if he could disguise his knowledge.

The captain replied that he had very little to complain of.

"Neither will you if you treat us properly," said the General.

My heart began to thump, for I was in fear lest the

General should go on to make the speech he had made
to me and to all who were going to help him, for he
was very fond of it, and let it out very often. I knew
that if he said anything about helping the Boers to the
captain, there would be trouble; for though I had not
been told all the story of how the captain was got
away, I had heard that when it was explained to him
that the General thought he would help the Boers, he
refused to leave till matters were put right. But Piet
Joubert was well called " Slim Piet," for he knew how
to read men, and what to say at the right time. He
even knew how to handle women, though he would
never take advantage of his great skilfulness with them.
I could have kissed the General with joy when I heard
him say, " Good-bye, captain. All you have to do is
to put yourself in the keeping of Charlotte."

The captain looked as if he would say something,
but the General gave him no time, but waved him
away.

Then he spoke to me, looking me through and
through—

" So, Sarel, you have brought money back. That
is bad, for the vrouws want all the money while their
men are away."

I became very frightened, and knew not what to say,
so I answered—

" General, money is not made easily in the Transvaal
now."

" But I hear it is, Sarel, though I never before heard
it was easy to get money out of a vrouw."

Then I knew that Katrina had done as I feared, and
I felt very sick and bad at the heart and stomach, the
more so as the General had his little eyes fixed on me,
and kept putting back the smile that would grow.

" Why did you take Katrina's thousand pounds,
Sarel? Do you not know that even in war-time men
do not rob their own people ? "

" General, it was years ago. She lent me a thousand
pounds to buy cattle, and I have bought oxen with
the money."

The General let out a long "Oh!" and thought for some time. Then he spoke, and his manner was very different.

"You say it was long ago, Sarel, and that you have bought cattle with the money?"

"Yes, General."

"Then why does she say you stole it?"

"Jealousy, General. She saw me in Pretoria with Charlotte, and this is her wicked way of vengeance."

The General lay back in his chair, and laughed his funny quiet laugh that made little sound.

"Sarel, I begin to think I am getting old and foolish. Of course she was jealous; I forgot about Charlotte. Where are the cattle you bought with the money?"

"With my cousin in Natal."

"Ah, that's good. If they are in Natal my Burghers will get them, so I can tell Katrina that the Government has her money. That will do, Sarel," and I went out, feeling like a man who has been pulled out of a river in flood just when he thought he must drown.

I went to the tent where the adjutant had taken Charlotte and the captain to have food. As I entered, I could see that the two had been having serious words, for Charlotte's face was red, and there were tears in her eyes. They were quiet for some time after I entered; then the captain said very seriously—

"Sarel, I am not at all satisfied about that money. It is no business of mine how you came by it, but it is my business to know that Charlotte has nothing to do with it. She now tells me that there is money in her box, but that it is yours."

I saw, as in a flash, that after this I would, if I were clever, have all instead of only half, or even the thousand pounds that Charlotte had cut me down to.

"Yes," said I; "the money is mine."

"Then how came it in Charlotte's box?"

"Because there was no other way to carry it."

"Then will you oblige me by taking it away? I

don't like her to have the risk of carrying so much money that does not belong to her." The captain pointed to the tin box, which had been brought to the tent.

"But I have nowhere to carry it," I objected.

"A thousand pounds does not require a waggon, or even a box of that size. Open it at once, Charlotte."

Charlotte, who had been standing as one uncertain what to do, slowly took a purse from her bodice, produced the key, and kneeling down, opened the box. The paraffin-tin was there just as I had put it, except that the rest of the box was full of women's clothes. Charlotte tried to lift the tin.

"He cannot take it now; it is too heavy," said she.

The captain also tried to lift it.

"Is all this money?" he asked sternly. "There is much more than a thousand pounds."

"There is three thousand," said Charlotte.

The captain got up and looked gravely at me.

"Sarel," said he, "unless you tell me the truth about this money, I shall go to the General. There is something more than either of you will tell me, and I will not be mixed up in anything shady. Is the money really yours?"

There are some men that you cannot easily lie to, and the captain was one.

"Part of it is mine," I answered.

"And the other?"

"Mine," said Charlotte, looking very pale and agitated.

"Yours? Where did you get so much money? Tell me truthfully all about it."

"It is mine, given me by my uncle. Sarel knows. Don't you, Sarel?"

I could see that Charlotte was losing the great coolness that before was always with her in time of trouble.

"Yes, captain; it is all right. It is Charlotte's."

"Then how came you to claim part of it?"

"Only a thousand of it is mine. I had nowhere else to carry it, so put it in the box."

"Then that is the thousand pounds the woman claimed."

"No, no; it is my own."

The captain had a hard look on his face, showing me he was not believing either of us. He made no further remark, and got up as if to leave the tent.

Charlotte sprang up, and, throwing her arms round him, said, with her voice all choked with tears and emotion—

"Don't go, Arthur. I will tell you the truth. It is all yours and mine. I got it so that we could go away together, as I know you are poor. Don't go to the General," and she clung to him, sobbing, and showing herself as weak and fearful as before she had been strong.

The captain sternly put Charlotte away from him, holding her at arm's length so that he could see her face.

"Tell me all the truth, Charlotte. If this money is yours, where has it been?"

"Sarel can tell you; he helped me get it."

"It's all true, captain," said I; "her uncle gave it to her."

"Did you see him give it to her?"

"No; but it's all right."

Charlotte broke in, clinging to the captain and kissing him, "Arthur, it is all right; don't ask so many questions."

Seeing her kiss him, and call him by his Christian name,—which English girls only do when going to marry a man,—made my anger rise, and I cared not what I said, so long as the money did not go to the captain.

"Captain, I will tell all the truth. We got this money from her uncle's farm, where it was hidden in the forage-house, while he is on commando. I am to have half of it for helping Charlotte."

She turned to me, and in a low and bitter voice, said in the Taal—

"You miserable schelm! now you shall have none

of it." She turned to the captain. "Yes, Arthur, I took it; but it will all be mine some day. But give it to the General to keep for me."

"That is the best thing to do, Charlotte. Then he can find your uncle, and, when I know the truth, you can perhaps take it back."

I was too full of just wrath and disappointment to speak, for not only had this wicked girl made love to me and promised me marriage, but now that she had got her captain, she threw me away, and robbed me of the share of the money that I had hurt my conscience by helping her steal.

She was still hanging on his shoulder, sobbing, so I went out of the tent, and smoked several pipes to help me think what I had better do; for if I had lost the girl, I did not see why I should lose the money also.

As I walked and smoked, I thought out a great plan by which I might get the money to my laager. Once there, I could contrive to get hold of at least half of it.

I went back to the tent, where Charlotte and the captain still sat like lovers; but I pretended to take no notice.

"Captain," said I, "I have thought out a plan that even you will see the righteousness of. If we leave this money with the General it will all go to the Government, and neither old Vorster nor Charlotte will ever see it again."

Then I told a story I had invented, of how money was left with the General and never seen again.

"Vorster is in the commando next to mine, so we can take the money with us and find him, and he will say whether Charlotte's story is true."

Charlotte looked surprised, and inclined to say something; but she remained silent.

"Are you sure Vorster is there?" asked the captain.

"Yes, unless he is killed, and then the money would be Charlotte's without further trouble."

The captain made no answer, but still looked unconverted, so I drove in another nail—

" Did you not see how the adjutant looked at the box ? He is the man who stole the money I told you of. He is a great schelm, and would do anything for money."

This was not true ; but I remembered that the captain had said to me when he first saw the man, " What an evil face ! " and I find that it is always easy to make a man believe that he is right in his dislikes of another. So I kept on telling bad stories of General Joubert's officials, winding up very cleverly, as if I were address- ing a landdrost in a case wherein I was very anxious to get a conviction.

" The case is very simple, captain. Here is the money. Charlotte says it is hers by inheritance, and, as old Vorster has no relations but her, this may be true. We can get the only witness who can settle this question by going to him. You say, make the general the judge and leave the money here. The general has not better means of finding out the truth than you have ; and what is most serious is, that he is a man who will not take any trouble, but leave the matter to his adjutant, who will do anything to keep the money for himself. If you have any interest in Charlotte, you will protect her money by doing what I advise."

After a pause the captain said—

" There is sense in what you say, Sarel, and I agree ; but remember, it is on your assurance that we shall find Vorster. If we do not, the money goes to the General."

" That is quite right and fair, and I also agree," I answered.

Charlotte had, during our talk, been sitting quietly twisting the loose twine on her riding-whip.

" What do you say, Charlotte ? " I asked.

Then she said a clever thing—

" I am content to leave it to you two, who have to take care of me. I know that Sarel is right when he says if you leave the money we shall never see it again, for these Hollanders cannot help taking what is not their own."

Charlotte got up, and went to look at a waggon that had just arrived in the laager; and I felt that she went away so that she might not have to talk on the subject.

When she was quite out of hearing the captain came nearer to me, and, speaking very quietly but with great seriousness, said—

"Sarel, let us properly understand one another. I know that you think you are in love with Charlotte, and I am sorry for you, because she was mine long before she knew you existed. She has used you for her own purposes, and we are both, I hope, duly grateful to you for what you have done. But I know that your silly jealousy won't let you look at things sensibly; and as jealous men generally do very foolish things for the sake of revenge, I don't suppose you will be any different to others. But I want you to understand that I am not a bit afraid of you, and that I don't mind going back to Pretoria. In fact, I am half sorry that I have come, for there is such a thing as paying too high a price, even for liberty. Of course I would naturally rather be among my own people than shut up in jail; and if you help me through I shall not forget you. But if you play traitor,—well, you will never forget me. Do you quite understand?"

There was so much devil in his face and manner that I could not but well understand; so I promptly told him that I would do nothing to hurt him, but everything to help him, at which he smiled in a way that reminded me of Piet Joubert, there was so much meaning in it. I offered him my hand to shake, but he did not take it.

"No," said he, "we will not shake hands till it is all over, for I'm sorry to say I don't altogether believe you."

This was such a bold thing to say to me, who could do so much to hurt him if I wished, that I felt there was truth in what he said about not being afraid of me or of going back to Pretoria; and I began to feel towards him as I did to Andries Brink, for men always feel when another is their master. So, although

I was very angry when he refused to shake hands and said what he did, I made no sign, but answered, "You are quite right, captain," and I secretly planned to do nothing that would make him suspect that I was determined to have my share of the money, and to show him that an Afrikander could be quite as slim as a Britisher.

Charlotte came back soon after, and stopped our further talk, for which I was not sorry. I then went to the adjutant to arrange about my return to my commando.

"You need not trouble about the captain," said he, when I began to ask questions. "The General has told the girl what is to be done, and she has all the plans."

"When did the General tell her?" I asked in amaze, for he had certainly not said anything of the kind to her in my presence.

The adjutant laughed.

"Don't you know that when a woman makes up her mind to get in first she always gets there. She saw the General once before you, and once after."

CHAPTER XIV.

Shows how a Dopper would comfort the heartbroken.

WE had some trouble about horses before we could get away. Those we had left, being good, had disappeared, Paul having sold or exchanged them for food and clothes. Although there were plenty of spare horses in the laager, they had cost us nearly five pounds apiece before we could persuade the oprecht Burghers to forgo their right to the next call on them. The money we had divided into three equal parcels, which we carried in our saddle-bags and haversacks; our other things, with Charlotte's now numerous wardrobe, being put on a pack-horse, led by a Kafir.

We reached the laager after six hours' easy riding, during which I talked very little, not feeling in the proper spirit to speak with either Charlotte or the captain, for I had a special grievance against both. Those two kept together as much as the path would permit; but when they began to talk, I generally silenced them by pointing out that scouting parties of either side might be within hearing, and it would not be well for us to meet them with so much money upon us, for war-time made men very keen on gold, and ready to suspect it everywhere.

When the laager came in sight, I thought it was deserted. The tents and covered places were nearly all gone, no Burghers or horses were in sight, and a broken cart lay where the waggon full of stores had been.

As we rode up to the large tent, Paul and two or three of the oldest Burghers came towards us.

"What is this, Paul?" I asked with authority. "Where are the Burghers?"

"Sarel, you now see an abode of peace : only godly men are here now. The sinners and strife-makers have betaken themselves to the worship of the golden calf."

"Stop this Bible language, and tell me in the plain Taal where are the Burghers."

Paul made no answer, but, having helped Charlotte out of the saddle, was beginning to strip the horses.

"Call a Kafir and come and answer my questions," said I angrily.

"There are no Kafirs, Sarel; all have gone."

I began to get really angry, for Paul spoke as if he were pleased that the commando had gone, while Charlotte stood, with laughter in her eyes, watching the old man as if she too enjoyed the disaster.

"Come into the tent," said he, "while I tell you all the story."

We all went in, and over some jam and sardines— all the food left in the laager—Paul told how, when he returned to the laager, after having made great trouble with the predikant, with whom we had left him out- side Ladysmith, he brought with him a waggon-load of stores, which he had not time to examine before starting on the journey. When the cases were opened, it was found that they were mainly full of women's clothes and things bought by the Rooineks in Johannes- burg, — such as soap, blue, clothes-pegs, and other useless things, the cases being loot from the Johannes- burg stores, and sent down without examination. The only thing of use to the Burghers was ten or twelve cases of whisky, which had somehow not been seen by the Hollanders at head laager ; and in a very short time the Burghers were all in a bad way, and for several days did nothing but drink and play cards. They had no money, but used the buttons of their clothes for counters, meaning to redeem them with the money I was to bring back. But on the fourth day came a Burgher from head laager saying I had been sent as prisoner to Pretoria to be tried by court-martial. Then the Burghers revolted, for they would have no one for commandant in my place; and the food being all gone, they broke up into small parties and went off to plunder farms that the Kafirs reported were unoccupied, while some went over to a Free State commando that was said to be making much loot. Within a week, the only Burghers left were Paul and seven old men who had internal complaints, and large families at home, and were therefore not wanting to fight.

"But how have you lived?" I asked, when Paul had finished, which was very long.

"Like Elijah in the desert, we have been fed by the ravens."

"Who were the ravens?"

"The Kafirs living in a few kraals down by the river. They used to bring us a little mealie-meal and Kafir beer, so that we might not burn their kraals. We also found a cow, but the Burghers used to quarrel as to who should milk her; so she wandered away, and often we had no food for a day or two."

I asked why they all stayed if they had no food.

"But don't you see, Sarel, it is great to have Burghers who will listen while you read and preach, and are too weak from hunger or too well filled when food comes, to dispute your interpretation of Scripture? If I were only sure of the ravens, I should like to be always on commando."

"But why do not the other Burghers leave?"

"They like being on commando where they can be at peace, and pray for the strengthening of the arms of those that do the fighting."

While Paul went to find something to make a bed for Charlotte, the captain began to talk seriously.

"I must be going on," said he; "but before I go I want to know whether I have to carry this money with me. When can you find Vorster?"

The strange change in the affairs of my laager had

quite upset my plans, and, as usual when in trouble, I wanted time to think what I should say; for I always did my thinking and plan-making in the Taal, which is not so quick a language as English, which I used only for speaking. So I said I would go on to the next commando and bring Vorster back with me, and would start to-morrow. This appeared to satisfy the captain, and we prepared to spend what proved a very happy evening.

I have said that a piano was in the tent; and Charlotte found that it could be played if she were careful not to touch certain notes. The captain also played and sang English songs about love, and he and Charlotte sang together, till the Burghers came and sat outside the tent, and smoked without talking, except to say that it was so beautiful that it made them think they were at home in the farm sitting-room singing psalms, they felt so good. I also felt very happy, yet miserable; for I could not help thinking that all this loveliness was for the captain, and not for me. I had not heard Charlotte sing before; and if it were not that Paul had almost converted me to his belief that there were no girl angels, I should have thought that Charlotte was singing in heaven. But the wickedness of Paul had deprived me of feeling such happiness.

We sat listening to the music till very late, and Paul began to get angry, for he cared only for slow, drony singing such as they have in the Dopper church. But what made him most impatient was that the only candle was getting short, and could not last more than a quarter of an hour, which was not half the time he would require to read the Bible to the Burghers and make his night's prayer. As the two at the piano made no sign of ceasing, and I would not do as Paul wished—ask them to leave off—he did it himself, and not very politely.

Charlotte was for going on with the music, but the captain got up and left the tent, making an excuse that he could not understand Dutch prayers.

"You had better stay, captain. I will translate as I go on, though it will be slow work, and I fear the candle will not hold. I would pray in English too; but I fear it would not be respectful to the Lord, as my language is not good and prayerful in that tongue."

The captain made a polite excuse once more and went away, but I could see that Paul was angry, for when he came to his prayer, he made special supplication for Rooineks, setting forth all their wickedness as the reason.

Charlotte had once warned Paul by saying, "If you go on like that I shall tell the captain what you say;" but he took no notice, and was going on, when Charlotte got up off her knees, blew out the candle, and walked out of the tent.

Paul, who never prayed with his eyes closed, saw what had been done, and immediately began to use language against women that made it improper for him to continue to pray.

So he got up and went out to find Charlotte; but she was away in the veld, talking with the captain, nor did they return till long after we had been lying under our blankets in the shelter of the thorn-bushes.

Next morning we had nothing for breakfast but coffee without sugar, and sardines without bread or biscuit; and Paul made a longer prayer and Bible-reading, to make up for it and the profane interruption of the previous night.

When it was over, Charlotte came to me and whispered—

"You must go to-day to find Vorster. Of course I know you will not find him; but while you are away I will make plans and all shall come right. Take old Paul with you."

This fitted in with my own half-formed plan; so I hurried up Paul, and, telling him I would explain everything while we rode, we went off.

When we were well out of sight of the laager we halted the horses in a kloof, and as we sat and smoked in the shade of the trees, I told Paul the whole story of my affairs with Charlotte, from the time we left the laager to the return from Pretoria. I told him everything, keeping back not even my love for her.

The old man listened without a word, and never before had I so long a talk without being interrupted or preached at by him.

"And what think you, Paul?" I asked, when I had made a finish.

"Sarel," said he solemnly, "you have had a great and awful escape from danger. Suppose you had been foolish enough to marry a girl who would blow out the candle while you were praying! Man, but it is worse than President Burgers going to fight Kafirs before and without a Bible-reading. Nothing but trouble would have come of it, Sarel. When she did that my anger was great; but now I am glad, for it has revealed her character to you and to me, and proves that all the unchristian thinkings I had of her were just. Better have twenty fat Katrinas than one Charlotte, Sarel."

"But what about the money, Paul?"

"It was wrong, perhaps, of Charlotte in taking it; but having taken so much trouble over it, and had so many schricks, I think it is but right that you should have all you can of it. Besides, I know that Oom Vorster made it by selling his land to Rooineks, and it is but just punishment that he should make no profit out of bringing the stranger into the land. We must get back and get that money, Sarel."

"But Charlotte may have made a plan," said I, remembering her parting words.

"Whatever plan may be made by a sinful woman like Charlotte must come to naught, Sarel. We are nine to one. Let us go back and tell the captain plainly that we want the money, and that if he does not give it up peacefully—well, as I have said, we are nine to one, unless the other Burghers are afraid to fight."

I did not like this plan at all, but having told Paul everything, I was helpless if he got the other Burghers to side against me; so I could do nothing but agree.

After a good sleep, to kill the time and make it appear that we had been long looking for the commando that held old Vorster, we cantered as fast as we could back to laager, to make our horses look done up.

We had been away but four hours, yet in that time there had been great happenings. First there was no sign of Charlotte and the captain; but knowing how fond they were of walking away together, I took no note of that. I did, however, expect to find the Burghers lying asleep within the tent, but they were not.

Pinned on to the tent-pole was a piece of foolscap paper with my name written on plainly in pencil, and underneath it a small carefully folded note addressed in the handwriting of Charlotte to her father. I opened the folded sheet addressed to me, my heart thumping hard, and something telling me that strange news was coming. It was a letter from the khaki captain, and being in what is called in English an educated hand, I found it very hard to read, but in time I made it out to run thus:—

"*Commandant Sarel Erasmus.*

"DEAR SIR,—By the time you get this, Charlotte and I will have left the laager and be on our way to the English lines. I am writing you thus fully because I feel that the apology and explanation I have to make ought to be put into a more lasting form than spoken words. During your absence Charlotte has told me the whole of her story, which includes her connection with Andries Brink, who is her stepfather; how she has been used by him as a decoy to procure information from both sides, and the whole of the truth about the money. I have forgiven her because of the motive which prompted her to take what did not belong to her, for I can see that she looks at these things very differently to an English girl; and, for the same reason, I forgive her the peculiar and complicated deceit she has practised to secure my release. It is all so new and unexpected that I can hardly yet make up my mind as to how far I am justified in allowing myself to be a party to the business, for as an English officer I naturally object to have my liberty secured for me by my friends promising that I shall help the enemy. But that is a matter on which I shall be guided by my superior officers. I also hesitate to blame either you or Charlotte, for, as I have said, you appear to look at everything from a standpoint so different to that of myself and my countrymen that I cannot hope to make my meaning clear. I therefore express my sincere regret for anything I may have said to hurt your feelings, believing now that your motives were entirely friendly. I also regret that Charlotte should have found it necessary to make a tool of you by playing upon your affection for her; but I am satisfied that she would have done the same to me had our positions been reversed, and I suppose her conduct is condoned by the proverb, 'All's fair in love and war.' Of course it is impossible for me to allow her to take any of Vorster's money. I therefore have hidden it in the piano, and I trust to your honour to take the necessary steps to see that it is restored to its owner. Charlotte joins me in asking your forgiveness for the deceit played upon you, and hopes that you will have nothing more to do with Andries Brink, who is a dangerous and unscrupulous man, and only using you for enriching himself. He is not in the service of either side, and your connection with him can only lead to disaster. Charlotte asks that you will somehow deliver to him the accompanying letter, which is to tell him that she is going to Durban, where she will remain with her aunt until we are married."

When I came to this, I could read no more aloud, but did what any man who has a heart and true feelings of affection would,—I sat down and wept bitterly; for although I had felt ever since the captain came out of tronk that it was him and not me Charlotte wanted, yet I was kept up by a secret hope that in the end she, being an Afrikander girl, would come to her duty, and choose me rather than a stranger. But I had not reckoned on her English education carrying her so far away from true justice and patriotism. Now that the truth had come, and the hope I had clung to was broken, I was a finished man; and the pain was the more because the thought that she was with the khaki made me want to love her harder.

Paul sat on the ground smoking and watching me cry, saying no word, which made me angry, for I wanted him to preach at me, to give me something else to think of; for when a man has pain in any part of his body he will not feel it if he be hurt somewhere else. At last his hard looking at me made me speak.

"What think you, Paul?" I asked.

"I am thinking what awful rinderpest and other new diseases a young ox may get through mixing with strange cattle," said he.

"What do you mean, Paul?"

"I mean that before the Rooinek women came, a young kerel never cried because he could not marry the girl he wanted. When she threw dirty water at him, he saddled up and rode to another farm where there were daughters. I suppose Charlotte wants a man with a nicer farm and more cattle than you have. Ach, Sarel, but you should have stayed when you took the Government money, and not run away. If every official who took money did as you, we should have all the Hollanders from Holland in the Transvaal. If you had but been brave and kept in the country, you might have married Katrina long ago. She is a real Boer girl, and not half British like this Brink missie; and then she is big and fat, while Charlotte is only a child."

"Paul, a man does not now take a wife as butchers buy oxen, by weight, unless he wants a vrouw too heavy to move off the farm."

I said this because I had heard that Paul's first wife was too heavy to move off her chair, and never left the house from the day she was married till the day she was buried on the farm.

"It's a great thing, sometimes, to have a wife too big to travel, Sarel; but bigness does not always keep a vrouw from running after a man when he does not want her. Katrina weighs two hundred pounds, but she moves about."

I again cried, not at the sharp and cutting answer, but because it reminded me of the wondrous difference between Katrina and Charlotte.

The old man went on praising Katrina, her fatness, her cleverness at mixing physic, and her people.

"She will have one of her father's farms," said he, "and a hundred head of cattle, and what more can a man want?"

"Paul," said I in anger, "you are a fool to think that men have not feelings in these matters. Have you never liked any one so much that you cried when you lost them?"

"Certainly; I liked all my wives and my children, especially the girls, and my fine after-oxen. Man, but when they died from rinderpest I cried hard as you do now, for they were worth twenty pounds apiece, and I could not get two like them for less than thirty, for the price of cattle was up. But you can get another girl, and one with more cattle; for you see, Sarel, you don't now know who Charlotte's father may be, and certainly you would get no cattle from Andries Brink, for does not the captain say what I told you, that he is a schelm."

"Don't you know, Paul, that a man can love a girl so much that he will take her without cattle?" said I.

"There is such foolishness; but the father of one of the two has to keep them. Look at Dantzie Vook and Jappie du Preez"—and the old man gave me the long stories of a dozen cases where the sons had married girls without cattle, and had come to sorrow. "All this," he went on, "has come about since the Rooineks have set the example of marrying a girl because they like her looks better than those of any other girl. But, Sarel, it is foolishness, and in the old days a kerel who did it would be tossed on a wet bullock-hide."

" That may be right in some cases, Paul; but when a man likes a woman, it is her he wants, not the cattle: they can come afterwards. It is Charlotte I want, not cattle."

" But if you have lost the girl, that is no reason why you should lose the money, Sarel," said the foolish old man, when I had given up trying to explain to him that love was above oxen.

He went to the piano, where the captain said he had hidden it, and for the first time I noticed that the piano was loose, having been taken to pieces. There was no sign of the money. Paul and I pulled the piano to small bits, and looked everywhere besides, but there was nothing but some of the paper and rags it had been wrapped in.

" The captain is false. He has taken the money in spite of his fine words," said Paul at last, when we had looked in every likely and unlikely place.

" Nay, it is those godly Burghers of yours," said I; and I was right, for never again did we see them or the money. They must have seen the captain hiding it, and have gone off with it directly he was away.

" Sarel," said Paul, " you see what comes of making a child of yourself over a woman. She has fooled you and made you think there are no other girls in the world fit to marry, and robbed you."

" It's false, Paul. It's your thieving Burghers. I expect they have taken it to build you a kerk that you may preach to them—with my money, Paul."

" Ja, Sarel; it is your money, for now you will have to account for it to Oom Vorster."

I broke down again and cried, for I saw there was truth in the old man's words.

" You are very unfortunate with money, Sarel. First you speculate unwisely with the thousand pounds you borrowed from Katrina; next you lose two thousand of the Government money at Prinsloosdorp; then you are verneuked out of your fair share of loot-money by Andries Brink, and his girl runs away with the money you honestly earned by robbery; and the worst of it is, that though you have never had any of it, you will have to give it all back. The captain will see to that."

This was so true that I could not answer, but hastened to defend Charlotte, for I did not like to hear Paul speak of her as a thief.

"If she was clever enough to get money and verneuk me out of my share, is not she the sort of girl I should have for a wife?"

This argument, I thought, would confute Paul on his own ground.

"Ja, Sarel; but what is the good of a vrouw who can get money, but runs away with it? Katrina lent you a thousand pounds; Charlotte robbed you of two."

Then he went on to point out that Charlotte was a strange woman according to Bible ideas, and that the Bible was always against such, as they were the cause of the undoing of many men. He told me about Jezebel and Jael, and other Bible women who were not good, but said nothing about those that were, they being mostly in the New Testament, which Doppers pay small regard to, using only the old. He of course got on to his great quarrel with the people of the Dutch Reformed Church at Rustenburg, where he had been put away from his deaconship for making trouble with the vrouws by saying there were no female angels. "If there were," said he, "you would be sure to read of them in the Bible," and on this he badly refuted a young predikant who had not been taught this, but relied on a picture in a family Bible, wherein Adam and Eve were being turned out of the Garden of Eden by female angels. But Paul had made a great study of this subject, and was victorious over the young predikant.

Then the women got tar and feathers, and waited

for Paul to make a feathered angel of him; but the predikant interfered and stopped them. So, instead, they waited on the road by which Paul rode to kerk, each woman having a water tortoise under her apron; and as no horse can bear the smell of this creature, and Paul's was no different, he bolted the moment he smelt the tortoise, and threw Paul, breaking his leg, which was why he left that church and went back to the Doppers, where all the congregation are predikants and the vrouws are not so particular whether they will be angels or not.

I got a little comfort from this long discourse, although Paul did not mean it. He was enlarging on the harm women can do to men, particularly when they are young and educated at Rooinek schools, like Charlotte.

"See how doubly she has harmed and hurt you, Sarel. First she fools you into believing that you may have her for wife; then she not only throws you away, but makes it that you cannot go back to the woman who does want you."

"How so?" I asked joyfully.

"If you ran away because you had Government money, how much more will you run now that you have the money of an oprecht Burgher like Oom Vorster; for it is nothing to take Government money, but foolish and wicked to take the money of a Burgher."

Instead of making me unhappy, this did just the opposite; for now I saw that if Katrina wanted me she would first have to pay the three thousand four hundred pounds, and as I could not live with her till she had done that, and made me safe from having to go to prison, I should have to live out of the Transvaal, and Katrina was too patriotic to do that.

These thoughts cheered me a little, and helped to resign me to the lòss of Charlotte; and when Paul suggested that we should go to Andries Brink's place with Charlotte's letter and try to get the nine hundred pounds he owed me, I quite agreed, for there was no food in the laager.

We waited all that day to give the seven Burghers a chance to come back, as Paul foolishly maintained they would, though I knew better, and next morning we left the laager, as it proved, for ever.

CHAPTER XV.

Reveals a plan for the capture of a traitor.

ONE of the disadvantages of being an educated man among ignorant people is that they cannot understand one, and much sympathy is lost, and more anger created, at the inability of the ignorant to see things in a proper light. I have always been careful not to cause annoyance to others by letting them see my superiority, and only in my letters to the papers or to the Government did I make a habit of using big words. Although I wield both English and Hollands with great fluency, I only use in my ordinary converse words that are within the comprehension of lower intellects, a practice that grew upon me when public prosecutor; for it is not often that educated people get into court, unless it is Germans, who make bad witnesses, because they will talk too much, being the reverse of Scotsmen, who say too little.

As I have shown, Paul was quite unable to understand my great grief at finding my affection for Charlotte sown on barren soil. Love, in its noble and inspiring form, as practised in England and in stories and plays, has no meaning for a Boer, who looks upon it as foolishness; and Paul could know nothing of it, for he was first married at sixteen years of age, and, as he lost each wife, took others quickly, not having even the trouble of seeking them; for he was always well off with cattle, had two good farms, and stood well in the kerk, until his foolish doctrines and his jealousy of predikants caused trouble. So high did he stand as a marrying man, that all through his district he was looked upon as a safe stand-by; for, somehow, it was felt that he would frequently fall into widowership, as he did, and his next wife was fixed upon by the vrouws, who were always correct in their guessing. Thus it came that, women being much after him, he held them in light esteem; and there is a story that he once put one of his wives to help the Kafirs draw the plough as a punishment.

When the predikant rebuked him for making his wife a beast, Paul was ready with a scripture verse from Ecclesiastes, which says a man has no pre-eminence above a beast.

"That may be true of some men," answered the predikant, "but the Bible does not say that a woman has no pre-eminence."

This was the only time that Paul was defeated out of the Bible, and on a verse of his own choosing. And it was this that started him as a hater of predikants, except those that were young and not so good at argument as he; then he was fond of them.

But though highly educated on all that concerned the Bible and the management of kerks, both of the Dutch Reformed and the Doppers, and particularly on the history of all the predikants in the country, who were his special study, Paul was an ignorant man, and unable to understand what I meant when I tried to express my finer feelings.

As we rode away from the laager I gave a last look round at the deserted place, and a lot of sad thoughts came over me, for I could hear the voice of Charlotte singing as she did only two nights before, and I could see all the crowd of Burghers of whom I was com-mandant. Now the place had become as Sodom and Gomorrah, and the words of Shakespeare came to me: "Farewell, a long farewell, to all my greatness!"

I said this out aloud to myself, remarking to Paul in what is called irony, "I have not many to see my greatness."

"And a good job, Sarel," answered he. "It is

better that a man should have no one to see him when he falls into a dirty sluit, for he looks foolish while getting out."

"But I have not fallen into a sluit," said I, being the more angered because I secretly felt that I had.

"No? Not fallen? Not even if you have lost your commando, and got four thousand pounds in debt, and all over a missie who doesn't want you? Nay, Sarel, it is the only ending to a man who listens to a vrouw before he is married to her; and all your trouble comes of this Rooinek way of getting a wife. A man who goes wife-finding in the new way is like a Boer who sets his heart on having a trek-ox that is dearer than he can afford. He rides over often to see it, watches it pulling in the trek-chain, talks about it to everybody, counts his money, thinks all his own span is bad because that one ox is not in it, gets unhappy, and sits all day thinking and drinking coffee; but when he has bought the ox he puts it with the span and thinks no more about it. You should have married Katrina and inspanned her early; then you would not now be hungering after a pink missie, who is no good for pulling, and this punishment would never have come."

"But I am not punished," said I, not that I believed what I spoke, but because I hated to think that the old man was right.

"If you are not, you soon will be. What is General Joubert going to say when you go back, and Ben Viljoen?—'They that are first shall be last;' 'The wicked prosper but for a moment.' Ah, Sarel, but you do make the Bible come true; yet you never want to listen when I read all the evil that comes to the unrighteous."

I could not answer, for, being of a very quick intelligence, I could but see that there was much truth in Paul's sayings.

"But what must I do, Paul?" I said.

"You have come to wisdom at last, Sarel. This is the first time you have sought advice of the only man who can give it. While you have been wasting your thoughts and your heart on a girl, I have been planning everything. The time has come, Sarel, for you to be a man and not a mouse, for you dare not go back to Slim Piet with your hands empty; you must take back something."

"And what will that be?" I asked, in great wonder.

"Andries Brink. He is a great schelm, and no oprecht Burgher. I did not want the captain to tell me that; I knew it all the time. We will make him prisoner and take him to the head laager, and all your foolish failures will be forgiven."

I was too astonished to speak. Paul, as usual, tried to read my thoughts, but mistook them.

"You have a chance to obey the Bible now, Sarel. You can't visit the sins of the father upon the child, but you can punish the father for the sins of the daughter,—that's real good Bible religion, Sarel."

Paul spoke with such seriousness that I grew frightened, for I knew Andries better than he did, and I was not going to fight a man so strong and clever.

"Paul," said I, "it is easy to say any man is a schelm, but you must have proof. We do not even convict a Kafir till we have heard at least part of the evidence."

"You are yet a calf, Sarel, or you would not need me to tell you that Andries is all that the captain says he is. Has he not always had his Kafirs in our laager, spying out? I knew them. He is a traitor, and I would shoot all traitors, even if they were my own children."

These discomforting words made my heart thump, for Paul spoke them so savagely.

"But you believed in him once, and was angry with me because I did not."

"Sarel, again you do not understand. If you are going to catch and saddle up a fresh young colt running loose, do you go up to him shaking the bridle? No, Sarel, you may be a public prosecutor, and know how to convict a man when you have him in tronk without bail, but you do not know how to catch him first."

As I had never told Paul all my full knowledge of Andries, and my doubts, I was anxious to find how much he knew, so I said—

"Paul, it would be foolishness to catch Andries for a traitor if we could not prove it. What do you know against him except that he had Kafir spies in our laager?"

"I know that no man can serve two masters, and that is what he is doing. I know, also, that he has a Kafir running for him who was running for Scotty Smith, the great horse-thief, years ago, and I judge a driver by the cattle he chooses to inspan."

"How long have you known all this, Paul?"

"Ach, Sarel, when a young kerel sets his eyes on a girl he thinks everybody else is looking the same way. What do you think I was doing while you were being fooled, but trying to find why she was fooling you. You forget that I have been in the veld seventy years; and though my eyes are not as good as they were from the print of my Bible getting worn, yet I never see a spoor without wanting to know what animal made it."

"And do you know the animal you are after?"

"Ja, Sarel; he is a big biting chameleon, and I am going to mark the place where he sits and change his colour to red."

This talk was so bold and unlike Paul's usual discourse, which was always for peace, except when he was reading of smiting the Amalekites hip and thigh, that I began to feel sorry that I had agreed to come; for if he acted as he talked there would be trouble, as I feared that Paul would be no match for a slim kerel like Andries, and secretly hoped he might not be. Still, I was in the dark as to how he was going to work, so I said—

"Paul, if Andries be all you think, he should be finished; but how will you finish him?"

"When you go out to shoot a buck or a baboon, can you say where you will finish him? You must first put him up, then shoot as near the heart as you know how. We have first to find our baboon."

" But we are only two," said I.

" And he is only one."

" Ja ; but he has the eyes, ears, and scent for danger of a herd of buck and a troop of baboons."

" Then must we stalk him with more care," answered the old man ; and as we rode he unfolded to me the plans which he had worked out in the quiet days and nights when the commando had left the laager.

We were to go to Andries' place, and, by certain cunning ways that Paul had planned but did not then tell me, we were to get him to come alone with us to my old laager. Then, when he was so far away that there was no fear of any of his Kafirs helping, we were to say " Hands up ! " and take him prisoner to General Joubert.

This, in a few words, was Paul's plan, but he not being like me, clever, and trained to seeing the weak places in a case, was not prepared for my searching questions.

" Paul," said I, speaking as if addressing my old landdrost father-in-law when he was extra hard to convince, " let us suppose, for the sake of argument, that Andries comes away as easily as you seem to think, and that we get him to the head laager. Are you satisfied that Piet Joubert will be as convinced that Andries is a spy as you are ? for, you know, he is very hard to convince."

" Ja, Sarel ; you may well say that after that whisky business of yours."

I passed this over without reply, for I knew that when Paul said spiteful things like this it was because my arguments were too much for him.

" Further," I went on, " how do you not know that all the signs that look so suspicious to you are not part of the cleverness of Andries, and used to deceive the British, for if he has deceived you, how much more easily will he deceive the stupid British ? "

This pleased the old man, for he answered—

"It may be so, Sarel; but, as you say, I am hard to deceive, and though he might throw dust into the eyes of the khakis, he could not do it with me."

I used many more good arguments, which Paul could only answer by saying, "You do not know all that I know;" but he would not unfold all his plans to me, and though I had the best of the argument all through, I gave way, and consented to go on, on the agreement that we were not to attempt to arrest Andries unless we were both quite satisfied that the evidence was strong against him. All the time a secret feeling told me that Paul's plan would come to nought, as I hoped it would, for my heart was with the British and my money with Andries.

. . . .

"So the only two oxen in the herd that have escaped the rinderpest have come to my kraal," was the remark with which Andries Brink met us when Paul and I rode up.

"Nay, Andries," answered Paul, as he dismounted and stood looking at Andries without offering to shake hands; "it was not rinderpest, but a scourging wind that drove them away. Evil-doers cannot face the scourging wind of righteousness," and he looked at Andries in a meaning way that that slim kerel could not but notice.

"Don't do any blowing here, Paul," said Andries, pretending to laugh. "I have had one big blow already. What have you come for?"

I did not want to tell Andries the bad news all at once, but let him have it gently; but the fear that Paul would say something foolish before we were ready caused me to make haste, and, without waiting to eat what he had on the table for us, having seen us half an hour away, I signed to him to follow me to the bedroom, which he did, Andries being ever quick at seeing signs that were meant for him.

"I have a letter for you, and I fear it is a scourging wind," I said, handing him Charlotte's letter.

I filled my pipe while he read it, and watched his

face. To my surprise he only smiled,—a real, natural smile, and not such as men put on to make it seem that they are not angry or upset.

"Clever girl, Charlotte," said he. "Sarel, there was a lot of money put into that girl's education, but it was a good investment."

Paul came into the room just then. Andries looked at him as if to say "Go away," but the old man was not good at taking hints, and sat down. So Andries changed the subject by asking if we had seen the khakis going over the ridge. We had not, but Paul said he had, for he would always rather lie than take a reflection on his dulness.

"I say they are Boers in khaki," said Andries. "Go to the ridge opposite and tell me what you think, Paul," and the old man, all unsuspecting, went out to look for what was not to be seen.

"What was the message she gave you?" Andries asked, when Paul was gone.

I was surprised, for I had none, and told him so.

"But, Sarel, this letter is written as a blind to the khaki captain. She is pretending to run away with him, that she may get among the British and be even more useful to me. Surely she told you as much in private?"

Then I saw that Andries did not realise how great a blow had fallen upon him.

"Nay, Andries," said I, "it is no blind, but all truth; she has gone away for ever with the khaki, and they will be married."

"You are a fool, Sarel!" said he with real anger. "Are you also blinded by the slimness of a girl?"

"I was," said I sadly, "but my eyes are now open," and I began to tell Andries the whole story of the part I had taken with Charlotte, from the going to my laager and the interview with General Joubert to the journey to Pretoria, with all that happened there.

Andries listened with great interest, laughing much when I described the sjamboking of young Van der Merwe and the terror Charlotte made in the laager.

He also laughed when I boldly, and, like a man, told
him that I loved Charlotte. I have found that men
are ever different to women in this matter; for while
you have but to tell a woman you are in love with
another to make her friendly and serious, a man always
laughs and turns it to fun, as if it was a foolish thing
to love anybody.

"Ah, Sarel," said Andries, "that is Charlotte's cleverness. She makes all the men love her, so that she may
use them as she did you. I shall soon have the khaki
captain coming to tell me how badly she has treated
him."

The only part of the story that made Andries really
serious was that about our taking the money from old
Vorster's farm. Immediately he began to interrupt,
which he had not done during my talk, and asked
many questions. When I told how the money had
been taken in the end by Paul's pious Burghers, I could
see that he was of Paul's way of thinking, that Charlotte
and the captain had gone off with it.

"Sarel," said he, "you do not know men and women,
leastways not my daughter. She has Hollander blood
in her, and is not likely to go leaving four thousand
sovereigns in the veld when she could have them for
the taking."

I was thinking whether I dare show Andries the
letter of the captain, wherein he gave good reasons
for not taking the money, when Paul came in at the
door.

"So you are no Afrikander, Andries, but a Hollander
by marriage. I could see it all the time; and you
have a daughter who is not your daughter, but you
use her for wickedness."

"Go slowly, Paul; go slowly," said Andries, looking
as if he had great work to keep down his anger. "How
long have Afrikanders not been allowed to marry the
widows of Hollanders?"

"Who was she, and where did she live?" demanded
Paul, in his blunt rough way.

"Not behind the kraal wall," answered Andries,

making the reply that Afrikanders often make to people who are rude and curious.

I could see that the old man was going to make trouble by his foolish questions, for he in his ignorance did not know that the great cleverness in cross-questioning is to keep the person questioned ignorant that he is being made to commit himself,—an art in which I excelled, as many a witness who thought himself slim could prove with sorrow.

While I was contriving to turn the subject away cleverly, Andries spoke—

"As you are so deep in the secrets of Piet Joubert, Paul, I wonder he did not tell you all about me. Perhaps he was afraid of your slippery tongue."

Instead of answering wrathfully as I expected, Paul said very quietly—

"Even Piet Joubert cannot tell what he does not know; and he doesn't know you."

"He seems to know my daughter. Do you think Piet is going to tell his business to every old Taakhaar?"

Now, although Paul had once been a Taakhaar Boer and a Dopper, he had long ceased to be one, cutting his hair twice a-year so that he might not be thought one.

"Who do you call a Taakhaar?" he asked, in great wrath.

Andries got up and went to the cupboard, taking out a bottle of whisky.

"Now, Paul, we'll soon prove it. If I am a Hollander I should keep and offer you gin and not whisky, and if you are no Taakhaar you will drink whisky with me," and Andries poured out three big coffee-cups of whisky.

I could see that Paul was at first for not drinking, and I would rather have had none, particularly as we had had no food yet, and whisky is not good for men whose stomachs are empty; but I would much rather suffer through drinking than have Paul and Andries quarrelling; so I sacrificed my better judgment, and, taking up a cup, looked towards Paul and said, "Health."

Paul still hesitated, till Andries said—

"Ah, so you are a Taakhaar after all," on which Paul snatched up his cup and emptied it.

"That's right; but let's make sure," said Andries, pouring out more.

Paul did not hesitate this time, but drank thoroughly, and by the time we had all eaten, his tongue was running freely, and he spoke so friendly that no one would have guessed he had evil thoughts towards Andries.

Now there is a thing that many otherwise good and sensible people, and especially women, do not understand when they reproach men for drinking too much. "If you know that two or three glasses are enough to make you merry," say they, "why do you not then stop?" Such people do not understand that when a man feels the better for two or three soupies, he sees things very differently, and thinks that he can drink yet more; and he generally does. This was the case with Paul; for, when I saw how fast and loosely he was talking and drinking, I tried to stop him, but he only replied that he was no calf, and could drink as hard as any Hollander.

Then he asked Andries all about his family, where his farm was, how many cattle, and all those questions which old Boers ask of strangers without offence, though Englishmen always get angry when so questioned. Andries gave answers which I could see were not always consistent, and were made to put Paul off and confuse him, for Andries was quick and sharp with his tongue, but said rude and cutting things with a laugh that made a slow-thinking man uncertain whether it was meant to be rude or only a joke. And so it was with many of his answers. Secretly I was pleased that Paul was showing his true feelings, for it would prevent my having to warn Andries as I had intended; for, as I have said, my heart was with the British, and I was more than ever anxious to get my money from Andries, and his help to join the British, for I had quite resolved not to go back to the Boer commando. I had thought I might persuade Paul to my way of thinking; but I now saw that, in his ignorance, he was prejudiced in favour of his own people. This was shown by his remarks as the evening went on, and more whisky was drunk by him. His questions got ruder and more pointed, and several times I thought Andries would get so angry that he would show it; but he did not, only laughed and joked with Paul, and pretended to agree with or to misunderstand his questions.

I regret very much that my tiredness, and the heat of the evening, made me very sleepy, so that I do not recall very clearly all that was said. But I do remember that just as I was dozing away, with my head on the table, not wishing to show rudeness by going away to sleep, Paul was saying very hard and bold things of Andries, who, instead of showing anger, only nodded his head and smiled. So, seeing that they were friendly, I, with a good conscience, gave way to sleep.

CHAPTER XVI.

Tells of the triumph of Samson over the Philistine.

I HAVE noticed, among other great peculiarities of the English that make them so different to us Afrikanders, one thing very particularly, and that not only in their talk, but in their books and newspaper writings. It is their obstinate refusal to confess like men that they know fear. How often have I heard young Rooineks, fresh come to the country, boasting of being in danger, such as in crossing a river in flood, or going close to a smallpox ambulance, and even playing cards during a thunderstorm, and saying they were not frightened. Now all this is vain boasting and unseemly, for it is natural and religious for men to have fear, as the Bible often shows ; and for a man to proclaim that he knows not that godly feeling, which is given us that we may keep out of danger, is to confess himself a blasphemer. We Afrikanders are much more honest in this thing, for we are not ashamed to declare openly when we are afraid ; and there is no phrase more often on our lips than, " I got a bad schrick," which means, " I had a bad fright," a thing no Rooinek would say, his vanity and ignorance of the Bible preventing him from being truthful in such matters. We have seen how dangerous such foolishness may be in war-time, for again and again, if the British had been more fearful, they would not have had so many of their soldiers killed.

As one who knows what danger is, through having heard my parents and old voortrekkers tell of the terrible calamities that befell them in the veld from Kafirs, lightning, and wild beasts, I am not ashamed to say that I freely own when I feel fear, not having become arrogant and boastful through my close contact with Rooineks.

Therefore do I not refrain from saying, that when I came out of my sleep — which, as I afterwards learned, was about midnight—I suffered the terror that comes to a man when he finds himself in darkness and knows not where he is or what has come to him. I do not know what awakened me, but my first knowledge was that my heart was thumping so hard that it gave me pain; and when I would put my hand to my side to ease it, I could not move. I was lying on my back, on what seemed to be a hard smooth floor, very cramped and stiff; and the fear that filled me made me break into a hot and then a cold sweat, and feel as unhappy as if all the woes I had ever known were crowding into my heart at once. Again I tried to move, but my arms were stiff at my sides, and my legs straight and moveless. I tried to open my eyes, but they were stuck close, and I could feel flies and things with many legs moving over my face.

My first thought was that my internal complaint had at last become real, and that I had been buried before I was quite dead, a thing that I have known to occur in the land. Next, as I could feel the air moving, I thought I must be paralysed, as my grandfather was for a month before he died, lying, as I was, stiff and moveless, except that his eyes were open and fixed on me in a way that would have made my conscience unhappy if I had ever done him wrong. I tried to speak, but my tongue clave to the roof of my mouth; and again a great fear and trembling came over me. I tried hard to remember some of the good things the predikant used to say when I was once really sick, and I even tried to recall the best of old Paul's godliest sayings and Bible-readings; but the fear that it might be too late for them to be of any use confused my mind, and I could think of nothing except to wonder where Paul was.

After making several strange noises in my efforts to speak, I cried out, " Paul! Paul! "

Immediately came an answer, in a voice so unfamiliar that it added to my terror for a moment or so.

"Sarel," it said, "I am in the Valley of Ezekiel, and am all dry bones. Are you also dry bones?"

"I do not know, Paul, for I am in darkness, and cannot see or feel," I answered.

"Shake yourself and hear if you rattle. I have tried, but cannot even shake. I can feel the wind that passed down the valley of dry bones. I fear the Bible words have come true, that our bones are dried and our hope is lost. We are cut off. Oh, Sarel, how often I have warned you of this, but you would not heed."

"But we can talk," said I, my fear now fast going on finding that I was not alone.

"Yes, our tongues are loose; but why cannot we move our bodies? My arms and legs are dry bones, and my throat is parched as in the days of the great drought before Kimberley was made. I lay then two days in the veld, just like this."

"But how came we here, and where are we, Paul?"

He made no answer, but I could hear that he was struggling as if to free himself from his stiffness. I also made an effort, having no longer any fear that I was dead or buried alive, though I could not understand my eyes being closed so tightly.

At last, in my struggling, I discovered something. I could feel with the ends of my fingers that the sleeves of my jacket were sewn to my sides with sack-thread. I told Paul what I had found, and soon he felt the same.

"This is not the work of Bible things but of mendevils," said he; "it is that schelm Andries. Ach, Sarel, why did we not do what we came for, and take him prisoner instead of drinking his whisky and being friendly? You would drink, Sarel."

This made me angry, for Paul had drunk six soupies to my one, and this I reminded him of.

"But, Sarel, what has come to our eyes? Are you, too, blind?"

I told him I was.

"Then it is a judgment upon us for not using our eyes to discover the wickedness of schelm Andries. Ach, Sarel, if we do not use our good gifts they will be taken from us, as they are. Have you flies and creeping things on your face?"

Then a thought came to me which I put into words.

"You are right, Paul; this is the work of Andries. It is birdlime we have on our eyes; I can smell it, and at first I thought it was a death smell, but I remember seeing the birdlime in the kitchen."

Paul sniffed hard. "You are right, Sarel; and it is the work of that devil Andries." And then he fell to abusing him most violently, as only Paul could when truly angry.

It was all clear to me now. Andries had waited till we were asleep—having no doubt put sleeping stuff into the whisky—and then had stuck our eyes, and sewn our legs and arms together, just as Scotty Smith did the sheriff who went to capture him and fell asleep under Scotty's whisky; only he was put into a cattle kraal. We were still in the house, but I knew not in which room. Presently I heard a match strike, and smelt tobacco.

"You are smoking, Paul," I said.

"Smoking, Sarel? It is not so bad as that, is it?"

Before I could explain that I meant tobacco-smoke, I heard a quiet laugh that I knew to belong to Andries.

"Nay, kerels, you are not smoking yet, but you ought to be," said he. "You are both verdomde schelms, and I have you condemned out of your own mouths. I think I shall set fire to the house and leave you to burn."

I would have said something to smooth Andries; but before I could frame it, Paul, as usual, was the first to speak, as he ever was when he had an improper thing to say.

"Now I know you are a schelm," he shouted. "You would burn us, would you; take this stickiness off my eyes and let me see what the devil looks like."

"You have seen enough, Paul; it will do your eyes good to have a rest."

"Ja, I have seen enough. I have seen your schelm Kafir Mabaan. I knew him of old. What does an oprecht Burgher want with a Kafir who has a spell for making cattle follow him?"

This Mapaan was one of those Kafirs who can make any beast follow him, which was why Scotty Smith set such store on him; for Mapaan was famous through the land for his cunning with cattle and horses, having stolen thousands, and been in jail many times.

"I always have the best oxen in my span that I can get," said Andries, "and when I find I have got a bad one I get rid of him."

He said this in a meaning sort of way, and I knew that if I had had the use of my eyes I should have seen that he was looking hard at me.

"You have not had me in your span, you schelm," answered Paul, with foolish boldness, for if he did not fear Andries for himself he had no right to endanger me.

"Yes, I have," said Andries. "An ox does not always know his owner. I have had my work out of you; but now I know from your own mouth that you are a bad ox and a foolish one, who does not know when he is well off, so I am going to turn you out of my herd."

I was fearing to hear Andries say something of the same sort about me, when there came the sound of horses' feet. I heard Andries move quickly away, and felt by the cool air that a door had been opened and shut, and I thought we might be alone; but I resolved that whatever foolish things Paul might say in his wrath, I would be discreet in my answers, for Andries might be listening, as he was before.

" Has that schelm gone away, Sarel ? " asked Paul.

I told him I did not know, thinking that might make him careful in what he said ; but it did not, for the old stupid began again—

" I expect he is listening, Sarel ; and I hope he is, for I want to tell him other things."

Just then we could hear Andries' voice calling a Kafir, out by the kraal.

" What does he mean by getting rid of us ? " I asked, for I did not like that remark.

" Doing as the old Boers in the Colony used when they wanted to get rid of a Kafir,—give him a good taste of the sjambok, and five minutes' start before they fired a handful of loupers after him," answered the old man, quite cheerfully.

I was thinking and fearing much the same thing, but I dared not put it into words, so I answered safely, lest Andries might be listening—

" You could not be surprised if he did that after the hard things you have said of him. You would not say such things if you had had your life saved by him as I have."

" No, Sarel ; neither have I been robbed by his daughter and made to look foolish."

" I deserved to be made to seem foolish, for Charlotte is a slim girl, above all Afrikander missies, and no man need feel shame for being made to look foolish by a clever woman."

Paul's answer was, of course, full of bitterness against women ; so, lest he should say something more unwise to anger Andries, I cleverly put him off by saying I had found how to untie my sewing, which was not true, but it answered my purpose, and made Paul cease abusing, and writhe and struggle instead to loosen his stitches.

I had contrived, with great difficulty, to get into a sitting posture, and had moved to that part of the wall where I guessed the door to be, and I was leaning against it, when suddenly it was opened, and I felt myself pulled backwards into another room, for I could dimly see that it was lighted. I heard Andries speak to some one, as he helped me to my feet and led me to a chair.

"Take this," said he, putting a cup of whisky to my lips. I was fearful about drinking, but deemed it wiser not to refuse, so I drank, and soon began to feel better.

"Now, Sarel," said Andries, "let us have a plain talk. You are a fool in many ways, particularly in letting Charlotte and the khaki run off with that money. But I am going to give you one chance more. You must go back to the commando, get more Burghers, and catch another transport convoy."

"Andries," said I, "it is you who are foolish. I cannot do that, for I am finished with my people, and have no commando now, and go back to head laager I will not. Let me stay here and help you, or go to the English."

"You are of use to me only as a commandant, Sarel, so you must go to the English; but it is as a prisoner you will go, and that means St Helena or Maritzburg jail."

This was not what I expected; and I began to see that firmness is not always wise, however much it may be praised by those who have never tried to be firm when it meant St Helena.

"But, Andries," said I, "you are so slim, and have such a hold over the Burghers by that clever loot-money trick, that you can yourself go back and get as many Burghers as you want."

"Nay, Sarel; if you knew more of the world you would know that a clever conjurer never repeats the same trick before the same audience. That answered well at the time, but they now know how it's done."

"How do you know?"

"It's my business to know. By the same means I also know that if you have the pluck you can bring off one more trick, and, by God! Sarel, you must do it. I may tell you that things have not been going well with me lately. The last lot of cattle I sold were retaken by the British, who are beginning to ask questions about me, and the speculators who buy from me are getting shy. If what you say about Charlotte is true, I am finished, and I can see no way of coming out without your help."

"Neither can I without yours," said I; "so suppose you open my eyes."

"Ja; I think it will help him to see wisdom," said a voice that sounded familiar.

Andries went away, and returned with warm water and a towel and washed my eyes, while other hands cut the stitches that confined my legs and arms.

When at last I opened my eyes, they lighted on a strange thing. There stood the khaki captain who had taken me prisoner and made me take the oath of allegiance; but he was no longer in uniform, but dressed like a Colonial farmer. Immediately at sight of him my memory came back to me. I saw the horse-market on Marshall Square, Johannesburg, and this man, standing with a whip, showing off the horses that an auctioneer was selling.

"How do you do, commandant?" said he, laughing.

"How do you do, Kelly? How is your baas, Mr Burton?"

"So you know him, Sarel?" said Andries.

"Ja; he is Fred Kelly, once clerk to Burton, the Rand auctioneer, and no khaki captain."

"Irregular corps commandant," answered Kelly, still laughing.

"Ja, very irregular," put in Andries, who went on. "You have not time to kiss and be brothers just now, Sarel, for you must first decide about going back to the commando. The captain here has brought bad news, and unless you can get sufficient Burghers to hold up a convoy he knows of, we are all finished. If you do this, we shall make money enough to get out of the country to Delagoa Bay; then we can go to Holland or Germany and wait till the war is over. Now, hurry up; Yea or Nay? Holland or St Helena?"

My heart was thumping so hard that I could not frame words, which would have been to gain time; but just then the voice of Paul sounded through the door. It seems that he had rolled along the floor, and had got his head by the crack at the bottom, and had heard everything.

"Say 'No,' Sarel; say 'No!'" he shouted. "Tell the verdomde schelm to be damned. Be a man, Sarel; he wants our Burghers that they may be shot down. Andries, you are a schelm, and your daughter, and your wife—all of you."

Andries looked at Kelly and smiled; then opened the door, and looked at Paul lying on his side, with his ear against the floor.

"Paul," said Andries quite calmly, "you are a very rude old man, and if you use language like that I shall report you to the Dopper elders."

Paul replied by a volley of abuse, which only made Andries and Kelly laugh. They let him go on for some time, when Andries turned towards me.

"Now, Sarel, have you made up your mind? Never mind this old idiot; he can't help you one way or the other. You have to pull your own load this time."

"Andries," said I in great perplexity, "you know I have no commando, and if I go back what chance have I of getting another? Already General Joubert will have heard how I have fallen to pieces. It is too difficult a thing you ask me to do."

"If it were easy I should not want your help. Any one can do easy things: it needs men to do hard ones. Say you are afraid, then I shall know what to do."

"And what is that?"

"I shall take you to the nearest British position, saying I have captured you, and that you are the commandant who stuck up the convoy. That will give me a chance to get through, and help to patch up my character in their eyes."

"But you surely wouldn't treat me like that, Andries, after all I have done for you without pay?" I objected.

"You are a nice one to talk about what you have done for me. If I had been the fool you take me for, I suppose I should have been on the way to the head laager by this time."

I could not think of a proper answer at the moment, and Paul came in to prevent my explaining and making things easy.

"Ja, Andries," said the foolish old man; "but for Sarel going to sleep over that whisky of yours you would have been tied up by this time. We have found you out, you schelm."

I hastened to explain to Andries that the plan was not mine, to which he replied that he was quite satisfied that I was not capable of it.

"We should have tied you up, but we should not have blinded you," Paul went on.

"I think you have all the pluck," said Andries, quite friendly. "I think they made a mistake in not making you commandant. I am going to open your eyes, and perhaps you can see the sense in what Sarel cannot."

Paul made no reply, and Andries got water, and, having pulled the old man into the room, washed his eyes free from the stickiness; but he did not cut the strings that tied his arms and legs.

As in my case, the first thing that Paul saw was the so-called khaki captain, and immediately a great look of anger and surprise came over his face.

"Oh, you pair of verdomde schelms!" he shouted. "I know you. You are not Kelly; you are Johann Smit the gun-runner, the scoundrel who took rifles and a machine-gun to Magato, and taught the Kafirs to fight white men. Sarel, we are in nice company. If this is Smit—and I can never forget him, for he out-spanned at my farm three times when he was gun-running—this other schelm is Sailor Robinson, the Johannesburg thief. I have never seen this Robinson before, but the description fits. See if Andries has lost a middle finger on the left hand."

I remembered that such was the case, though it was only the first joint that had gone, and as Andries always kept his fingers closed, it was not easy to see.

While Paul was saying all this, Andries and the man I knew as Kelly looked at each other and smiled.

"Ja, Oom Paul," said Kelly, "I remember you well. Your vrouw made the worst coffee in the district, but she never asked too many questions. Do you remember when I hired your little buck-waggon? It carried through a hundred guns, Paul, and there was your name on the board, so that Magato could know who the kind Boer was that helped him get guns through."

"I'm afraid, Paul, that after this you will not be inclined to go into partnership with us in the scheme we have in hand," said Andries, speaking now for the first time in English, and with a sarcasm that was most annoying.

I cannot put on paper what Paul replied. He used up all the offensive words in the Taal, and the worst that he knew in English, and threw them all at the two men. He was sitting on the floor, with his back to a low Dutch chest of drawers, and as he threw out the words, not being able to use his arms, he swung his head frequently against the top drawer in his angry excitement.

"Paul," said Andries in his irritating, cool, and polite manner, "I wish you would not spoil my furniture with your wooden head; I must stop it," and he went up, opened the top drawer a little, then pushed Paul's long hair inside, and, closing the drawer, locked it, making the old man a prisoner.

"Now, Paul, if you had not kept up the dirty Dopper custom of not cutting your hair, this would not have happened," said Andries, and he and Kelly had a good laugh, though I thought it very cruel, especially as it did not stop Paul's tongue, and said so.

"We can put his tongue in instead of his hair," said Kelly, and for a time I feared they would do it; but they seemed so amused at the angry abuse which the old man continued to use, that, fortunately, they did not act upon the suggestion.

These humorous ways of Andries in treating his prisoners were so like those told of the great Scotty Smith, that I began to wonder whether, after all, this might not be he, for he had not been heard of for some years. If so, then there was no saying what horrible things he might not do, from baking us in an oven to tying us naked over an ant-hill or burying us up to our necks in the cattle kraal,—all of which atrocities had been perpetrated by the great highwayman and cattle-thief, though there was the very comforting memory that he always sent his Kafirs to let the victims free when they were nearly frightened to death.

There was one story about him that had always seemed very terrible to me; and from the moment I began to suspect him I could not get it out of my mind, the more so as he had talked of setting fire to the house. Many years ago, Scotty had caught a man who had put the field-cornets on to his track. This man had very big ears, for which he was well known throughout the land. Scotty took him to his stable and nailed one ear to the manger; then, giving him a sharp knife, left him, and set fire to the place, telling the Boer that he could get free by leaving one ugly ear behind. This the poor man did, and I have since seen him with only part of his ear left.

The contemplation of these horrors, which came crowding on my memory, so choked my brain and heart that I had no ears for what was going on between the others in the room. When, after a whispered conversation between Andries and Kelly, the former came up to me and took me by the arm, I was dazed with a nameless fear, and thought that at last my end had come. But he only led me towards the door and then out to the back of the house, where the horses were being saddled up by a Kafir. Andries bade me mount, and I did so. In fact, I dared not refuse, so great was the terror this wicked man in-

spired in me. I had ever felt towards him that meek-
ness one always feels in the presence of strong and
masterful people; and there was now added to it the
fear that he might be Scotty Smith, and would do to
me any of the horrors he had done to those who had
stood up against him.

We had ridden some distance from the farmhouse
before I missed Kelly, and was brought to remembrance
by his cantering up.

"I have taken his knife, so that the old chap will
have to pull his hair out by the roots," said he; and
the two laughed, while the story of the ear-nailed
Burgher in the burning stable again came to my mind
and filled me with unhappiness and apprehension. I
glanced several times back at the house, expecting to
see flames and smoke, but was rejoiced that none
appeared.

I now began to collect my senses and think more
clearly, for during the past hour I had been confused
and dazed. I noticed that neither Andries nor Kelly
seemed to be prepared for a long ride, having only
their saddle-bags, rifles, and bandoliers, but no haversacks for carrying food. Then, again, it was, as near
as I could judge, about two o'clock in the morning,
and bright moonlight. I inferred from our starting
so early that Andries was anxious to get away from the
farm, expecting unwelcome visitors. I asked him once
where we were going, but he replied flippantly that he
had been invited to breakfast with General Buller; and
when, after a little waiting, I again asked what he was
going to do with me, he answered shortly, and with
much unfriendliness, "You'll see in good time." So
I held my tongue and rode in silence, hoping to learn
something from the talk of the two, but they said
nothing to enlighten me.

After an hour's ride, when dawn was well advanced,
Andries pulled up by some stones in the centre of a
smooth, flat, grassy hill, that gave a good view of all
the country round. He took his field-glasses from a
case and sat in the saddle, looking long in a southerly

direction, while Kelly dismounted and drank whisky from a flask, inviting me to drink also, which I did.

"We will give him an hour," at last remarked Andries to Kelly; and he too dismounted, and lay on the grass.

Then the two talked together in a way that satisfied me they were expecting to meet a Kafir messenger, for they pointed to one very large square boulder, about the height of two men and wide enough to shelter a man on horseback.

"You are sure he knows that is the stone we mean?" asked Kelly.

"A Kafir never forgets a place he has seen once," answered Andries, and we sat and watched the sun rise,—a thing that English people are so much given to talking and writing about that I often wonder whether they have a proper sun in their land.

We had been sitting thus idly for the greater part of an hour, when I noticed that Andries' horse was straying away some distance. Andries got up and walked towards him to bring him back, when there came the small sharp crack of a mauser rifle, and a cry from Andries.

Kelly and I looked in the direction the sounds came from, and saw Andries running, with his head and arms forward and stooping low. He ran to the big stone I have mentioned, and threw himself flat beside it, just as another crack came, and a bullet struck the ground only a yard to one side of him. Kelly and I immediately crawled behind the stones against which we were sitting, and asked one another what it meant.

"It's that schelm Paul got away," said Kelly. "What a fool I was to forget the rifles."

"Who could let him loose?" I asked.

"The Kafir, I expect; yet I saw him ride away before I left."

"Throw me your whisky-flask," shouted Andries. "I am hit, and feel bad."

Kelly took off his flask and carefully stood up, stooping low behind the stones, which were only about a yard in height.

"It's too far," he said to me ; and he spoke truly, or the distance between the big boulder where Andries lay and us was quite thirty yards. While he hesitated, Andries called out impatiently, "Come with it ; stoop low and run hard," but Kelly did not move, and I could see great fear upon his face.

"You go, Sarel," said he ; "you are smaller, and will make a lesser mark." But fear had got hold of me.

"For God's sake hurry, man !" shouted Andries.

Kelly swung the flask by the strap, and it fell about midway the distance.

Again Andries shouted to us to run, but neither of us dared obey, for we both knew that if the man behind the mauser were Paul, he could not help hitting any one who ventured out, for the shot came from a heap of stones less than a hundred yards away. As if to remove any doubt that we might have, there came a third crack, and we saw the flask spin several feet from where it lay. It had been hit and pierced by a mauser bullet, which also struck a stone beyond the flask, splintering it to dust.

There was no doubt left in my mind that the shooter was old Paul; but I said nothing, for I feared they, believing this, would tell me that he would not shoot at me if I tried to reach the flask, on which I was not so certain, as I had no doubt the old man was angry with me for leaving him, though I could do nothing else but obey Andries.

Kelly loaded his rifle and laid the muzzle over the stones in the direction of the shots. At the same instant a bullet struck our stone, and the crack of the mauser arrived at the same moment.

"Whoever he is, he has got us fixed," said Kelly. "This is going to be a waiting game. Our only chance is to exhaust his ammunition."

He put his hat on the end of his rifle and moved it above the stones, but no shot came.

"He's too old a bird to be caught that way," said he; "we must wait. How goes it, Andries?"

"I think my hip-bone is smashed," answered he, as coolly as if it were the merest trifle. "I think it must be old Paul du Plooy. Serves us right for not finishing him. Is that you, Paul? What do you want to leave us alone?"

We waited, but no answer came. Then I shouted several times, but only silence followed.

"We are in a very tight place," said Kelly, after a long pause. "We have no idea where the old schelm is; while he can see us, and the ground is so smooth that a rock-rabbit could not leave these stones without being seen. We must wait patiently till dark."

"That will be a long time; for though the moon does not rise till near eight, it will not be dark enough to cover our movements in the meantime, for we must be on the sky-line to a man lying on the edge of this flat. And what about eating and drinking?" I asked.

"All our drink was in that flask, and unless you have something in your pockets we are foodless."

"Then we *are* in a tight place," I replied, "for I have nothing. But are you not expecting some one to come to this spot?"

"Yes; one of Andries' messengers was to be here by sunrise, but he can now no more get to us than we can get to him. Can't you talk this old rascal over? We can't stay here for ever. Something must happen."

I shouted out, "Paul, don't shoot! I am coming to talk to you," though secretly I resolved not to expose my body to any such risk.

Still no answer came. I cautiously raised my hat over the stones, but no shot came.

"He is too slim," said I. "He knows no Boer would be foolish enough to show his head like that." Twice again I shouted, but I might have called to the lonely veld.

The suspense and anxiety became great as the time passed slowly on. There was also another thing happening. It was yet full summer, and terribly hot. The sun had risen on the side on which we lay, and, having no shelter, we began to feel its discomfort. But it was not so much the heat then, as the recollection of what it would be a few hours' later, when we should begin to be faint for want of food and water. The thought alone was awful.

"If he means to kill us, why does he not get round to this side?" remarked Kelly. "We cannot see him, as he can keep below the ridge and pick us off as he likes."

The same thought had occurred to me, and my explanation was that Paul's object was to make us suffer the pains of uncertainty and hope, and, just as we had begun to think he must be gone, he would shoot us. At the same time, I had a secret belief that the old man would not include me in the slaughter, but would be content with giving me a schrick in punishment for my not standing up more for him.

"Paul, I'll put my hands up and let you take a thousand pounds if you will let me go away; my leg is broken," was Andries' next cry. "Go out to him, Sarel; he won't hurt you."

"Will you hurt me, Paul?" I shouted; but only silence followed, and we drew ourselves up into small space and tried to sleep.

The morning passed and the sun got high, scorching us badly. It was just past noon when we heard a noise as of some one walking over stones. We dared not look out, for it might be only a trick to make us expose ourselves.

A minute later a Kafir appeared; he was the messenger Andries had expected long ago. He looked about him surprised, and then, spying Kelly and me, came towards the stone. As he stopped before us the rifle cracked again, and a bullet cut the ground near his feet. He threw himself flat beside us.

"Has he water?" shouted Andries, his husky voice showing that he was beginning to suffer from thirst. The Kafir turned his bottle up to show that it was empty. Andries let out a cry of pain and anger, the first he had made.

"Did you see any one when you came up?" Kelly asked of the Kafir, who replied that he had only seen our horses loose, but that an hour after dawn he had seen khaki scouts, who were scattered so wide over the country that he had to lie close, and this it was that had made him late. I gathered that he had been sent by Andries to watch for any Britishers who might be coming in the direction of the farm; but though I much wanted to know why Andries had so suddenly left his place, I was afraid to ask in the presence of Kelly, and he showed no wish to talk much, as men in danger do not waste words except to swear, and Kelly did not even do that.

Meantime we could hear, by Andries' small cries and groans, that he was suffering much from his wound. Once or twice we called to him to know how he fared; but his reply was not clear, and plainly caused so much pain that we refrained from troubling him.

The sun passed slowly towards the Drakensberg, but no sign or sound came from Paul. We tried to get the Kafir to go out and see if the old man was still on the watch, but he refused; and no threats would make him even put his head from behind the stone. "If I go, I shall be shot; if I don't go you say you will shoot me; what matters if I don't move?" said he, and he lay on his back and smoked calmly.

We were hoping that when it got fairly dark we might make a run for it, but there were two objections to that: first, Andries could not move; secondly, our horses had disappeared, having, no doubt, gone to a hollow in the direction of Paul, where they would find water. I could not help wondering whether Andries had been carrying his money in his saddle-bags, for if so, Paul would get it.

Then I began to think how marvellously things had worked out for the old man, who not only probably had the money of his enemy, but had got him completely at his mercy. I could see him, in fancy, sitting behind a big boulder, with his rifle ready, aimed in our direction, pointing through a little scanze he was certain to have built, while he searched the Scriptures to find verses to fit the occasion, and tell him what Joshua would have done; not that he needed to find out, for he already knew all the bloodthirsty and vengeful verses from beginning to end.

It wanted about an hour to sunset, when we were startled by a shout of " Sarel ! "

I knew it was Paul, and answered; but I would not show my head over the stone.

" Give the two rifles and bandoliers to the Kafir, and tell him to bring them to me," came the same voice from behind the stones.

" Ja ; do it," shouted Andries, but very feebly. " Take my revolver too, and Kelly's."

Very reluctantly, the Kafir got up and collected the guns, but neither of us dared look out to see what he did with them, but we heard him throw them heavily to the ground.

" Come out, Kelly," was the next order.

Kelly hesitated.

" I am not shooting you," said Paul, with a stress on the " you " that made me feel very uncomfortable, for there was great and deep earnestness in Paul's voice, that showed me he had been reading much about Joshua.

Kelly went towards Paul, and I gathered courage to spy cautiously, with my head well on the ground.

" Lie down on your stomach," said Paul.

Kelly obeyed ; and the old man, carrying his mauser ready, felt him all over to make sure that he had no hidden weapon.

" Now you come out, Sarel." I got up with difficulty, for my limbs were stiff with lying so many hours in one position. " Go to Andries, and see that he has no more revolvers," said the old man, pointing his rifle at the big stone to cover any movement.

" You need not worry, Paul," said Andries faintly; " I know when I have lost a game. I'm finished."

As Paul came towards the stone, Kelly made a movement, and in a moment Paul had sent a bullet within a foot of his legs. " If you stir till I tell you I'll shoot both your legs through," said he, carefully reloading his rifle.

" Well, Paul, your end is up now," said Andries, who lay on his back, looking very sick and full of pain.

Then this strange man burst out laughing, looking up at Paul. I looked too, and nearly laughed, for all the hair was singed off the old man's head.

" Ja ; I am no Dopper now, Andries. You did not leave me a knife to cut it, but you left my matches, so I fired myself free. Man, but it was a dirty trick to play on an old man. Where did I get you ? "

" On my hip-bone, Paul. It's all smashed."

" Then I shall not have to kill you, for you will, for the rest of the time, be a light to the Gentiles. You will carry the brand of Cain always. Old Coos Swannepool had his shin broken when a young kerel, and he walks with sticks to this day. How much money have you, Andries ? I heard you say you would give me a thousand pounds to let you run. You can no longer run, so I'll take two thousand to let you ride."

At that moment Paul turned round suddenly, raised his rifle, and fired. Kelly rolled over with a howl. He had quietly crawled to where the two rifles were lying, and had just got hold of one, only to find that Paul had removed the magazine.

" He deserves it as much as you, Andries ; and now you two schelms can limp through life together. I don't know that it wouldn't have been more merciful to send the bullets through your heads instead of your legs, but you will be better exemplars to the wicked as you stump along," was all the old man said.

Paul's bullet had taken Kelly along the calf of his leg and above the knee.

" Why did you not do this before, Paul ? " Andries asked sadly.

"I wanted to give you time to think over your wickedness; and for myself, I did not want the sun to go down upon my wrath. I was for shooting you at first, but I thought that as you had robbed me of my eyesight I would take away your hearing. Was it not bad, Andries? I once lay all day in an ant-bear hole, with Kafirs waiting for me, to die of hunger and thirst. I could not see them any more than you could see me, but the thought that they might be near enough to assegai me was awful, Andries. I had no Bible with me in those days, and could think of nothing but the pangs of death. Did you have many pangs, Andries?"

"Ja; all up and down the leg."

"You would have had worse pangs, Andries, if you could have known what I was thinking all the time that I was not shooting. I was searching the Bible to find what Joshua would have done with you. I read nearly all Kings, Joshua, and Judges, but I could find no case that quite fitted yours. I don't think there could have been schelms so bad as you in Bible days. So, after reading all things that were done to the heathen and Philistines and Amalekites, I couldn't think of the proper thing that would fit you in a Bible way. The nearest I can get it is that you and that schelm Kelly are the Philistines that got Samson. I am Samson, for you bound me in a strange way as the Philistines bound him; my hair is off, and though I burned it myself, it is the same as if Delilah cut it; and you put out my eyes, and made me make sport for you. I could not pull your house down as he did, but I did what Samson would have done if he had not got hold of the pillars,—I have burned it."

I saw Andries smile, and I knew the reason. Paul went on—

"I have not been able to make up my mind whether your girl Charlotte is Delilah. It looks very black against her in many ways; but even if she were, I don't see that Delilah was punished in any way. If Charlotte marries that Rooinek captain she will be well punished, for the Bible is quite as much against women taking husbands among strange men as it is against the men who take strange women. The thing is what to do with you. If it had not been summer, and the grass green, I should have set fire to it as you lay with your hurt leg; and it would have happened to you as it happened to the Philistines' mealies when Samson sent the fiery foxes into the fields. But that would have destroyed your paper-money too. How much have you, Andries?"

"I have five thousand pounds, Paul; and I shall give it you with pleasure, as you have not destroyed me as you might have."

My heart gave a great thump.

"Don't forget that nine hundred pounds of it is mine, Andries," said I.

"I have not forgotten it; and if Paul is the honest man I think he is, he will give you the nine hundred, and half what remains."

"Certainly I will," answered Paul. "Let us have the money now."

Andries, with great effort and many groans, took from his inside pocket a wallet, and, taking out a piece of paper, handed it to Paul.

"That," said he, "as you can see, is a deposit note from the Natal Bank for five thousand pounds. All my money is there, and if you go to Maritzburg and show the manager this, he will give you the money."

I was very disappointed; for though I, being educated, understood all about cheques, there still lingered some of that dislike of paper-money impressed upon me by my late father-in-law.

"This is not money," said Paul, who I could see was, like myself, very disappointed, expecting to see gold, or at least bank-notes.

"Neither is a Government order money till you take it to the bank, is it?" replied Andries. "Sarel understands it; don't you?"

"Ja," answered I; "but why not give us a proper cheque?"

"I thought you said you understood," replied Andries. "Every man who is not a fool knows that cheques are only given for small sums. When a man wants to give all the money he has got in a bank, he doesn't give a cheque; he gives up his deposit note, which is the same as a transfer of title that you get when you buy a farm. Is not that so, Sarel?"

"Ja," said I very foolishly, not wishing to appear ignorant before Paul.

I took the paper and read it.

"But this is in the name of John Wilson, not Brink," said I.

"Sarel, you are very simple. Do you think that in war-time I would put money in an English bank in a Boer name? They only know me in Maritzburg as Wilson."

I knew that this sort of thing was often done on the Rand, where men have banking accounts in different names; so, although I did not like it, I told Paul it was all right.

"But have you no gold or bank-notes?" Paul asked.

"Only enough to carry me out of the country. You wouldn't have me stay here and go on helping the British, when you could make certain of me getting out of the way, would you?"

I stood up for the justness of this; and though Paul was for taking the money when he saw that what Andries had in gold and notes came to nearly five hundred pounds, he at last gave way to me, and let Andries keep it.

"And now," said Andries, "you have quite finished me, Paul, so I must get away if I do not die in the veld. I know a farm two hours from here where I can lie till I can ride, and then I shall get to Delagoa Bay and go to Germany. This money will be just enough."

Paul stood thinking deeply.

"I don't know that I shall be doing righteously in letting you go, Andries; but if we took you, as we should, to Piet Joubert, you are so slim that you might turn even him to do your will, and Sarel here has not done so much for me that I should share with him the glory of capturing you."

"I want no glory, for I am never going back to the head laager," said I; for now, having the money, I felt courageous and independent.

"Just so, Sarel," said Paul reproachfully. "A young ox that breaks often out of the kraal will do it again, and is best got rid of. You are no Burgher at heart, Sarel; you have been spoiled by a Rooinek woman. It is always so,—it is Scripture. You know how I told you once you were as Moses, and I Joshua—well, it is all working true, Sarel; you are on the top of the mountain, and will never come down to your people, so I will go and finish the work you have begun so badly. The only pity is that you are not dead, Sarel."

"But you can tell the General I was shot, and he will make you commandant."

Paul stood leaning on his mauser, and thinking hard for some time.

"Yes, Sarel; that is best for you, and best for me. It will put a bar between you and Katrina."

I had thought of that, and secretly rejoiced that the old man agreed with me.

"Tell the General that I shot many khaki officers before I was killed, and you must be careful to say that it was lyddite, and that I was behind a very big stone. He particularly told me not to get into danger, and I would not have him think I was so foolish as not to get under cover."

"Nay, Sarel; I will tell Piet you are dead by lyddite, but I will not lie about officers, for does not he read all the Rooinek newspapers that give the names of all the killed? If he should ask where you killed khaki officers, he would find that I lied. No, Sarel; I will not do anything that Joshua would not have done. I will help you by saying you are dead; but what about the money, Sarel? How will you get that if you be made prisoner?"

"It will be all right, Paul," said Andries. "The British do not take away a prisoner's money, but keep it safe for him. But I don't think he will be taken prisoner, for it is easy for a man who knows Natal like Sarel to get safely through to Maritzburg."

"Then as soon as you get in, go to the bank and get the money, Sarel, which you must hide in a safe place till you can send me my share. And don't forget, Sarel, that a thousand pounds must go to Katrina. You may rob the Government, Sarel, but you must not rob a Boer woman. Let me look at the money-order to see that it is all right."

I handed him the deposit note, smiling as I did so, for I knew the foolish old man did not understand such things, but in his vanity he pretended that he did. He looked it all over very carefully.

"It's a small piece of paper to carry so much gold," said he, "but it's a Rooinek custom. It's quite right, Sarel; the figures are quite plain. Now, remember what I have said. You send me my half, and a thousand besides for Katrina, and I'll give it to her. Have you any message to send her?"

"Nay, Paul; tell her I was dead before I could speak about her."

"Right, Sarel; I will do it faithfully, soon as I can get away off commando. But, Sarel, if they should find you are not dead, what shall I say?"

"Say it was Katrina's medicine that saved me. That will make her quite happy, for it will make her greater than Mrs Van den Berg."

Paul sent the Kafir to catch our horses, which had wandered over the veld. While they were coming he went up to Kelly, who, it seems, was not so much hurt by Paul's shot.

"I ought by right to finish you," said he; "but it is better to make you a limping example to wrong-doers. Have you any money on you?"

"Only a few sovereigns," answered Kelly, taking out his purse, as a man fearful of more danger.

Paul took it.

"You must now fight Andries for half that he has if you want more. I am glad that I can say I have shot a gun-runner. I hope you will die soon," and the bloodthirsty old man got on his horse.

"Good-bye, Sarel," said he, shaking hands. "The old ox is the best in the span after all. My interpretation of your dream was the only proper one, Sarel, for Moses is now dead and Joshua takes his place. It is right it should be so, for you have worshipped the golden calf, Sarel. Get away from these schelms as soon as you can, and while you are with them, keep them in front of your mauser, or they will have that money-order again. Good-bye, Sarel; good-bye Andries, you schelm!"

"Wait a bit, Paul," said Andries; "I should much like to know one thing. How did you get your hands free from the sewing?"

"It was all through the Bible, Andries; the wisdom of the righteous availeth more than the cunning of the wicked," and the old man cantered off.

"What does the old devil mean?" asked Andries of Kelly.

"I have been puzzling over that all the time I have been lying on my face," answered Kelly; "but I think I see it now. Just as I was leaving, he called me back and asked me to put his Bible into his inside pocket. I unbuttoned his coat and obliged him, but I don't remember fastening it again."

Andries burst into a long, loud laugh. "Kelly," said he, "it's time we retired from business when we are done down by a Dopper."

CHAPTER XVII.

*Shows that there are exceptions to the Afrikander
motto, " Alles zal recht komen."*

THE first thing that Andries did when Paul was out
of sight was in keeping with all his acts from the first
day I had known him. He proved himself an adroit
deceiver. Getting up, he walked briskly round the
stone, slapping his leg and extending his arms as one
who stretches himself after a drowsy sleep, whilst I
looked on in amaze.

"I thought your hip was broken," said I, in surprise.

"It was while Paul was here; now he's gone, I
find it is only bruised."

"Then you were pretending all the time."

"No, Sarel; I was feeding the old man's vanity.
If I had not made him believe he had got home with
his first shot he would have peppered us till there
would have been no occasion for shamming. Did he
get you, Kelly?"

"There's not much sham about mine," said Kelly
sadly. He pulled up his trouser leg and showed where
the bullet had travelled, along the outside of his calf
and out at the side of the knee, making a ploughed
furrow as if cut with a blunt thick knife.

"We have all been hit low down, Sarel—hit below
the belt; but you Afrikanders don't see any disgrace
in it. We call it cowardly, don't we, Kelly?"

This was the first time I had known Andries dis-
sociate himself from Afrikanders.

"It's time we made a move," said he, "for we are

more likely to die of hunger than of wounds. Can you ride, Kelly?"

Kelly said he would try. We shouted for the Kafir, who was lying asleep in the long grass, and sent him to fetch water and catch the horses.

"Put down that rifle, Sarel, or you may hurt us," said Andries.

I handed it to him, remarking that probably he wanted the money-order also.

"No, Sarel, I never take back a free gift. The old man spared our lives, and deserves some reward. I should advise you to get into the bank before closing time," said Andries in his laughing way, that generally meant there was great meaning behind.

"That is what you must show me to do," I answered.

"I am going to, Sarel. I have had plenty of time to-day to think out plans. Let's get Kelly into the saddle and be off."

With great difficulty we got the lame man on to his horse, collected the rifles and revolvers, and sending the Kafir on in front on foot, we followed at a walking pace.

I tried once or twice to draw from Andries some statement as to his plans, particularly with regard to myself; but he was in no mood for talking, and gave me such short sharp answers that I held my tongue and reined in my curiosity, well knowing that I could not make him speak if he had no mind to. So we rode almost in silence, taking a direction that would bring us, as well as I could reckon, somewhere by Estcourt.

It was just on sundown when we turned up a deep and narrow kloof, riding with difficulty along a Kafir footpath, that I could see was but new and little used. Presently, on a flat part of the side, we came upon two old tents, and, by the portable forge, picks, and shovels and similar things, I knew we had struck the camp of one of those men called prospectors, who search for gold and other minerals, living out in the veld, and generally among mountains such as these, for many months quite alone, or at most having a Kafir to help them.

This camp proved to be that of Mark Capper, a famous Natal prospector, who has found nearly all the places where coal is now dug in Natal, and many other things, some good, but mostly only promising. I had heard a great deal of him and his cleverness, and his hatred of men, when I was living with my cousin in the Newcastle district. He had been a sailor, an officer on a mail-boat, but had come to Natal many years before. He had spent nearly all his time out in the wildest part of the country, sometimes seeing no white man for a year.

He was standing at the door of the least ragged tent as we rode up,—a spare man with sharp features, fair face and blue eyes, and long grey hair that curled under the biggest and broadest smasher hat I had ever seen. His cord trousers were fastened up below the knee with straps, after the fashion of the railway navvies I remember in Cape Colony as a small kerel. They were the first Englishmen I had seen; and until I grew up and went to the Raad I believed that all Englishmen dressed like navvies, with cord trousers strapped up, a strap round their waist, and a grey shirt open at the neck showing a lot of hairy chest. This was what Capper looked like, and the sight of him took me in a flash back to the days of my childhood.

He looked hard at us as we dismounted, and when Andries went up and put out his hand, Capper seemed to remember him suddenly. "Sailor Robinson, by all that's holy!" said he. "Where the devil did you spring from? I thought you were in tronk, or dead long ago."

Then he looked hard at me.

"What have you got here? a London postman or a Natal police superintendent?"

"Allow me," said Andries, with mocking politeness: "Commandant Sarel Erasmus, of General Joubert's Holy Terrors—Captain Kelly, late of the Durban Irregulars."

"Boers and Britons,—a funny mixture. What has happened? Is peace declared? I saw some khakis the other day; so did my Kafir. He bolted, and they chased him over the Basutoland border. I suppose they want to employ him at ten pounds a-month. I wish you chaps would get this business finished. All the Kafirs in the country seem to be working for the British army at Johannesburg wages, and I can't get a boy. The one they scared away I only kept because he had escaped from jail somewhere, and was afraid to leave the camp. But come inside and tell a fellow what you graveyard deserters are up to."

"You may well call us graveyard deserters. We have all been within a foot of it. Kelly here is limping still. Haven't you got something to rub on a wounded leg?"

While Andries was saying this we followed Capper into the tent, and sat down on the stretcher-bed and a stool or two, while Capper knelt down at a packing-case on end that served as cupboard, and began looking for something.

Next moment Kelly gave a yell, and jumped nimbly from the bed where he had been sitting.

"Snakes! snakes!" he shouted, and pointed to a big puff-adder curled up on the bed.

Capper looked round in the most unconcerned manner.

"Oh, he's there, is he? I haven't seen him all day, and wondered where he had got to. Mind you don't hurt him."

"You still keep a menagerie, then?" remarked Andries.

"Yes; only a few. I've that gentleman on the bed, an iguana—a beauty five feet long, only he eats my fowls and their eggs, and frightens a little buck that comes and looks me up occasionally. Then I've a crow with a broken leg, a tiger-cat—a bit shy, and this fellow here," he held up a basin containing a large striped mouse. "They are a sight better company than most humans in this country. They've got more brains, and don't use them to do you down."

"But they are not much good for eating," remarked Andries. "Why don't you rear something to kill?"

"Never killed a thing in my life except fish. The river's full of them, and they're so tame that it seems cowardly to haul 'em out. It's too much like humbugging an infant, and I haven't the heart to do it."

This talk did not hold out much prospect for food, for which we were all hungry; and I was thankful when, after giving Kelly some Dutch droppels to put on his leg, Capper brought out bread and tinned meat, which, with some cold sweet potatoes, made us a good meal.

"What's your game now, Andrew?" asked Capper, as we ate. "Thieving as usual, I suppose?"

"No chance, Mark; too much competition."

"But you generally managed to get a look in with the crowd. You haven't come to steal my mine, have you? or has the commandant here come to annex it for the Transvaal? "You had better look sharp, because there are plenty of other thieves with their eyes on it."

"Been done down again, Mark?"

"Yes; do you remember that thing I had in Zululand, the last time I saw you?"

"The gold-mine you were going to make twenty thousand out of as usual? Yes."

"Well, the syndicate of respectable leading citizens did me down. They liquidated the company, repegged the claims in the name of a relation of the chairman, and forgot to put me in. I went down to Durban to talk to the head conspirator, but when he heard I was in town he bolted. He is a patriot now in one of the volunteer corps, so if you come across him you might send a bullet his way. I suppose you could arrange it for me; or have you better business on?"

Andries laughed. "All the professional murderers I know are engaged on one side or the other, and I've been doing too well myself to take on fresh business in a retail way."

"I daresay this would be quite as honest as anything you have on, Andrew."

"My last game is up, and I am going to start a new one."

"Why not try something honest?"

"Too late, Mark. Twenty years in South Africa doesn't give a man a training for a Sunday-school teacher, and I can't say that your example is very encouraging to a man smitten with honesty. You have been honest enough; but you are still grafting hard, and getting grey at the job, I notice."

"Quite true, Andrew; but I haven't to change my name so often that I forget my last. By the way, what is your name this time, Andrew?"

"Andries Brink. You see I always stick to the same initial for my Christian name; and Andries is very near Andrew."

"What is your particular line of swindling just now?"

"Commission agent in the cattle-dealing business. Back to my first love, you see. I wonder what the fascination is that makes a man cling to the game? I suppose it must be the spirit of my old Border ancestors prompting me. I was riding a stolen horse the first time you met me, twenty years ago, and to-day I'm riding one with another man's brand on. Funny, Mark, but I always seem to run up against you when I'm laying off a fresh course. I was going up-country to get an honest living the first time we met, and now I'm starting afresh."

"But not on a straight course, Andrew."

"No, Mark; not so long as there are fools asking to be robbed, and other fools anxious to help me. That's one of the disadvantages of having brains, Mark. You are too anxious to bring other men up to your own level. Now this gentleman here in the variegated uniform was a professional suppressor of vice,—a public prosecutor,—but in less than a month I have made him one of the best wholesale cattle-dealers in the country. Haven't I, Sarel?"

The blood rushed to my head, but before I could frame a proper answer, Capper remarked—

"I don't suppose a Boer wanted much teaching in that line, but I never heard of their stealing one another's cattle. You must have been lifting from natives or Englishmen."

"The commandant is a British subject, Andrew; aren't you, Sarel? You see, I have educated him thoroughly and quickly."

"Been keeping school, eh? I thought you must have been in jail, as I have heard nothing of you for two or three years."

"Not in jail, Mark, but nearly as bad. I have been imprisoned in towns, trying the virtuous citizen tack. I married a Hollander widow, and took her name. She was educated, and horribly civilised; had a splendid daughter, sharp as a needle. I think I married the mother for the sake of the daughter. I took a horse-breeding farm on shares with a sleeping partner, but he woke up one day and wanted to know too much; so I left him and what was left. Then the wife died, and the war broke out. I got an introduction to Piet Joubert as an oprecht Natal Burgher who could be useful to him in Natal, and I got to windward of the British at the same time. Lord, Mark, what fools there be in high places! I did very well for some months; but, after all, I was knocked clean out by an ignorant old Dopper, who smelt out my game, while the slim Hollanders and British staff-officers and Intelligence Department were eye-dusted. He put a bullet into Kelly, and only missed me by a hair."

"Kelly? Isn't that the chap who got caught gun-running up north, and landed in Pretoria jail?" asked Mark.

"Not Pretoria, Mr Capper—Pietersburg. Always select a country jail if you have to put up at one. You can always leave them when the accommodation doesn't suit you."

"You are a pair of beauties. I wonder what my Natal friends would say if they knew I was entertaining you? How is it none of the Transvaal crowd have spotted you?"

"I didn't mix with them, Mark. My educational work with the Burghers was done by correspondence and a private secretary—that girl I told you of. Man, but she was smart," said Andries.

"How many rascally games have you had a hand in since you came to this country?" asked Capper.

"I was reckoning up only to-day, Mark, having a little time for quiet thought. First there was illicit diamond buying at Kimberley,—the short-cut to wealth and respectability or the breakwater; contractor to the troops in three native wars,—profitable, but requiring too much handiness at cooking accounts; slave-dealer, otherwise native labour agent,—profitable, but dirty, and opposed to my early religious education. Then illicit liquor-dealer on the Rand,—most profitable, but dirtiest business of all; and, grandest of all, purveyor of arms to the native races. I was reckoning up to-day, Mark, that more than half the rifles owned by natives in the Transvaal and Natal have been supplied by me at an average of a tenner apiece. That means a lot of trouble coming for the whites presently. I was in hopes that they might use them against the Boers, but I see no prospect of that. You see, Mark, I'm still a Britisher at heart, although I have funny ways of showing it. I'm a good man spoiled by contact with inferiors. I've given them my virtues, and taken in exchange their vices——"

"And cattle," Capper put in.

"Yes: I'm sorry to say that the old Adam has been sorely tried in the presence of good Boer herds; but in the long-run it is as well that I yielded to temptation, for it was part of my system of education. Few Boers ever met me without being the worse for it in property and morals, for I helped to sow the seeds of race hatred that has brought about the war, and will end in the absorption of Boerdom. That is where my patriotic British sentiment is fed up. What I don't like is the knowledge that I have helped to spoil a promising race. The Boer to-day, Mark, is only what men like me have made him. I am the only Britisher hundreds of Boers had ever seen, and they judged all that came after by me, and put a guard over their horses and women, and sat on the stoep with a rifle till the Rooinek was well off the farm."

"You have been a scoundrel all through, Andrew. I wonder you call yourself an Englishman," said Capper.

"I don't, my boy, except among Englishmen who don't know me, and Afrikanders who do. Don't start preaching, Mark. You ought to know by this time that I'm the victim of disposition, climate, and vanity. I can't bear that any man should go away with the idea that he is smarter than I. A man in a country like this has to begin by impressing people with his smartness, and he keeps it up so long that it becomes second nature. I can no more help doing down a greenhorn, whether he's a Johnny-come-lately or a Boer from the Woodbush, than you can help picking up a new specimen of rock. And you know, Mark, that in this country a man is esteemed for what they call slimness, but which in the old days at home we should have called damned rascality. Look at the fellows at the top of the tree now. How many of them would be out of jail if they were at home?"

"Don't get me on that tack, Andrew," said Mark. "You know I'm a prospector, and every prospector's religion is to believe that a financier is a rascal. Let's talk of something else."

"Well, Mark, perhaps you're right. I have no right to throw bricks. God knows, I've never missed a chance to do another man down; but I'm like you in one thing—I've never killed anything. I've never had a revolver out of my reach night or day for twenty years, but I've never pulled the trigger. A man who can't go through this country without shooting is no good here. It's brains that do the trick, not bullets.

I don't say that the temptation to shoot isn't often great, but I've put my brains against temper, and the lives I've saved that way entitle me to the V.C."

By this time Kelly was falling off to sleep. Capper turned the snake out of the tent, and helped the wounded man to lie comfortably on the bed. I lay down on the ground in my blankets, the spare tent being, as Capper said, too full of insect lodgers for white men's accommodation; and while Andries and Capper smoked and talked over old times, I passed into sleep.

We had an early breakfast, said good-bye to Capper, —who seemed the strangest, kindest, and most contented Englander I had ever met,—and started off on what proved to be my last ride with the man who, in the short space of a few weeks, had marked my life.

"Now, Sarel," said he, when, after riding two hours, we came in sight of what turned out to be Estcourt, "I'm going to do you a last good turn. Take my advice. Ride in to the commandant and give yourself up, telling him truthfully who you are, and don't forget to make yourself out as big as possible. The bigger they believe you, the better they will treat you. After a little delay they will send you to Durban, where you will be put on parole, which means that you will have nothing to do but spend your money and wait till the clouds roll by."

I did not like this, and said so; but Andries stopped all my objections.

"You cannot go back to your commando," said he; "and if you are caught without surrendering, it's jail, and perhaps a bullet. Be a man; face the music and go in boldly, telling them you have been a Burgher on compulsion, and are sick of the war."

"But don't you come in with me to say a word for me?"

"Well, no, Sarel; I am not popular at Estcourt. The commandant there has been making inquiries about me in a very unfriendly spirit, and I don't care to meet him. I am going through to Delagoa Bay."

He stopped suddenly, and, turning in his saddle, looked long and anxiously behind.

"It's too late, Sarel; I find I must go with you. Now don't be a fool; do what I've told you, and bear me out in anything I may say."

I looked behind, and saw six or seven khakis riding towards us.

"Come on," said Andries, leading the way to meet the picket. Kelly and I followed, my heart thumping hard the while.

When about fifty yards off, the leader of the khakis called Halt! and we stopped while he came on.

"Who are you?" he asked.

"Boer commandant come in to surrender, sir," answered Andries.

The khakis came up closer, looking hard and curiously at us.

"Which of you is the commandant, and what uniform is that?" he asked, evidently much puzzled; for he was a new-comer, and not having yet seen a Boer, was unable to understand us, like most khakis, who expected to find us black, or at least covered all over with hair, as one of the Tommies told us later.

Andries very respectfully explained that I was Commandant Sarel Erasmus, who had grown tired of fighting, being made a Burgher against my will, and that he had persuaded me to surrender.

"And who are you?" asked the captain.

"Inspector of Transports and Guide attached to the Sixth Division. This is my assistant, Mr Kelly."

Andries said this with wondrous self-possession, and the captain evidently had no doubts as to its truth.

"You must come in to the commandant," said he; and we rode in to Estcourt, the captain all the time looking at us with surprise and pleasure written largely on his face, for it was, as I afterwards learned, his first day on duty, and to capture a Boer commandant was a great thing.

There were camps of regulars and irregulars all round the town, and, as we passed through, the

Tommies and volunteers swarmed out to look at us, my uniform causing great surprise and many strange remarks, that showed me the British soldier knows no uniform but his own; for some said I was German or Russian, and one that I was the Japanese attaché. Nobody took me for a Boer. If any one of us was suspected it was Andries, though he looked more like a prosperous Natal farmer; while Kelly was got up like a young Englander newly come to the country, with white riding-breeches, leggings, and white collar and tie. Altogether, the Tommies were vastly puzzled, and I think disappointed, at which I was secretly joyful.

We were taken to the commandant, who sat at a desk in an office just as if he had been a clerk at Pretoria. He was very polite; but, like everybody else, much concerned and very curious over my uniform, about which he asked many questions, such as, "Was it the mark of a commandant?" "Did my Burghers wear one like it?"

When I told him the truth about it he seemed very much amused. After further talk I was taken away to a guard-tent, leaving Andries and Kelly with the commandant. I had no thought then of saying good-bye, for I did not know that was the last I should see of him, and that he was passing out of my life as unexpectedly as he entered it.

I remained in the guard-tent two hours, the Tommies coming past in twos and threes all the time, and looking in at me curiously, always with some remark about my uniform. The Jew who sold it to me knew something when he remarked that it would puzzle the British, and give me a chance to run away while they were inquiring about it.

At the end of the two hours I was taken to the train by three Tommies with fixed bayonets, and travelled to Maritzburg, where there was another interview with a commandant, more questions about my uniform, and a long wait, which ended in my being told I was on parole until further orders; that I was to call at the office and report myself every morning, and not to go out of the town or change my lodging without giving notice.

As soon as I was free I went off to the Natal Bank and presented my deposit-note.

Then came the crowning and farewell blow given me by that schelm Andries.

The clerk took it, looked it over back and front, and, in a puzzled way, said, "Yes."

"I want the money," said I; "I'll take it in notes."

The clerk laughed quietly, and went away to the back of the desks. When he returned he asked me to follow him, and took me to a room where the manager sat, who asked me my name and where I got the note, and many other particulars for which I was not quite prepared, though I answered discreetly, telling him that the money represented my share of a partnership with Mr Wilson.

"I'm afraid," said he, "that you have been made the victim of a joke. Mr Wilson had an account here before the war, but it is now closed; and even if it were not, this paper would be valueless to you." And he explained what a deposit-slip meant.

I left the bank, dazed and angry with Paul for having spared Andries' life, and angrier still that he did not insist on taking the real money that he had on him. So confused and upset was I, that I found myself drinking whisky in a canteen, and a number of khakis asking me all about my uniform, before I fully realised what I was doing. I stayed at the bar longer than was wise, and spent more money than I should have, for all I possessed was twelve pounds. How I was to live in a place so expensive as Maritzburg I did not know; and I walked around the place looking for a cheap lodging, filled with bitter thoughts of Andries, and thinking how wise was my late father-in-law in having nothing to do with banks and paper-money.

But my troubles were not to end with the loss of my money. I was sitting on a seat outside the Law

Courts, when a young man came up and very politely told me he was a newspaper man, and wished to interview me.

I had suffered so much from newspapers in the Transvaal that I became fearful, and said nay; but the young man talked on so much, and I spoke so little, that I was like one who is photographed without knowing; for next day, when I went to report myself at the commandant's office, I was sent into the office.

"I see that you are a Natal Burgher," said he.

He said this so seriously that I felt there must be something more in it than appeared; so I replied very discreetly that I had not said so.

"No, not to me; but you told a newspaper man so," and he handed me a Maritzburg paper and pointed to an article marked with a blue pencil. It was headed, "The Latest Capture," and was as follows:—

"The monotony of khaki that pervades the city was agreeably broken yesterday. Parading Church Street, at a deliberate pace that gave full opportunity for inspection and admiration, was a young man arrayed in a uniform whose identification puzzled the authorities on service sartorials. Imagine a blue mess-jacket, intended for a warrior forty-five round the chest, enveloping in its flabby folds a thirty-four inch measurement, the numerous green braid frogs and facings suggesting the adornment of a lady's zouave jacket. Sleeves bedizened with the broad gold stripes of a sergeant, cuffs of a mail-boat steward, and green collar and bright gilt buttons the size of half-crowns, trousers a shade of brighter blue than the jacket, very narrow, but broadly striped with green. A small, sharp-featured, close-eyed face with incipient moustache and shaggy black beard, half concealed by a wide-spreading smasher hat. This gaudy and original get-up covered the five-foot-six personality of Commandant Sarel Erasmus, late Public Prosecutor of Prinsloos-dorp, and, later, Chief of General Joubert's flying column of Taakhaars and Reimschoons, who were responsible for the sticking up of the convoy at Bokmans Drift.

"Our representative found the commandant sitting on a bench outside the Courts of Justice, smoking a big cigar and looking preternaturally thoughtful. The gallant commandant recently surrendered at Estcourt, and is now on parole. He was at first a little bit shy, having all that fearsome prejudice against Rooinek journalists that is characteristic of Transvaal officials, but with a little encouragement was persuaded to talk. As becomes the wearer of a uniform that would shame a Portuguese field-marshal, the commandant has been a ferocious warrior; but owing to the fact that he is also a Natal Burgher who was kidnapped over the Border, and made to fight against his conscience and his late neighbours, he considerately tempered his native ferocity with mercy. His fame as a fighter secured him the goodwill of General Joubert, who, despite his reputed slimness, was no match for the ex-public prosecutor, whose long experience of the criminal classes of the Rand enabled him to spot the undesirables who had attached themselves to the Boer forces. The commandant suggested to the General that he should be given a commando with the right to select his men. The General fell into the trap, and Commandant Erasmus enlisted the cream of Transvaal rascaldom, whom he kept out of mischief by taking them on an imaginary looting expedition in the peaceful and deserted regions at the foot of the Drakensberg. When at last they grew fractious, he arranged that they should meet the pick of the British and Colonial scouts, with the result that there is now no commando. The commandant is anxious to obtain some well-paid staff appointment, where his peculiar knowledge of his late countrymen, as he calls them, would be of value to the British; but the authorities do not appear overwhelmingly anxious to avail themselves of his services."

"Is it true that you were a Natal Burgher?" asked the commandant.

"Yes," I answered, not certain whether it would be to my advantage or not.

"In that case, Mr Erasmus," said he, "I fear we must cease to treat you as a prisoner of war on parole, but as a rebel."

My heart gave a great thump, and did not cease paining me till I found myself, among fifty or sixty other Natal Burghers, in the jail at Maritzburg, awaiting trial as a rebel.

It is strange how it often happens that the thing done for the best proves in the end to be the worst. In saying that I had been a Natal Burgher to the newspaper man, I foolishly thought I should do myself good by showing that I was loyal and friendly to the British. I did not know that the Government had begun to make very careful inquiries about Natalians who were fighting on the Transvaal side, nor did I then understand that it was wrong for a Transvaal Boer who had been living in Natal to go back. In talking the matter over with other rebels in the jail, they pointed out that I was not a Natalian, being only a visitor; and this made me happy until Jack Bosman was caught and brought in. He was a law-agent, and knew a little law.

"How long were you living in Natal?" he asked.

"Just over a year," said I.

"Are you sure?"

I could not answer, for so many things had occurred since I left the Transvaal that I had forgotten how much time had gone.

"But I hear you applied to be put on the list of voters for the Newcastle district. Is that so?"

I had forgotten that my cousin had persuaded me to do this, so that the Transvaal Government could not get me if they wanted to prosecute me over the money mistake at Prinsloosdorp. I told Bosman this.

"Then you are a finished man," said he, "for that shows you were a Natal Burgher, having given up the Transvaal."

This broke my heart, and hope died.

And now began a terrible time of suspense and weary waiting, made worse by the hostility and jealous spitefulness of the other prisoners. The word had gone round that I had surrendered after doing no fighting, and had offered to give the British particulars of other rebels. All sorts of unfriendly and untrue things were said of me, till I soon had scarce any one to speak with save the warders; for when new prisoners came in they were warned by the others to have nothing to say to me, as I was a spy put there to hear and report anything that might be said against the British, and thus make it hard for them at their trials. My money, too, had been reduced to about five pounds; and I could foresee that unless my trial came on soon I should have to eat prison food instead of being able to buy my own, as I did now.

I wrote several letters to the commandant and others who I thought had influence, pointing out the mistake that had been made in treating me as a rebel, setting out my sad story in full, and exposing the perfidy of Andries Brink. But I got only a formal acknowledgment and the suspicion of the other prisoners that I was reporting their sayings, and my lot became even harder.

Then came every day disquieting rumours of what was to be done to us, followed by news that would raise our hopes or throw us again into despair. The other prisoners found pleasure in telling me only bad news, keeping from me anything that was cheerful. They knew well how the war was going on both sides, though how they got their information they would not let me know, so that I could only guess.

Another thing that hurt me much was the feeling that I was quite alone and friendless. There were few of the other prisoners who had not visits from relations or others, who brought them food, money, books, and clothes. But I had no one. When I tried to make a friend of the predikant by telling him I was a God-fearing Burgher who had been a deacon, he seemed to suspect me, asking why I had ceased to be a deacon, in a tone that sounded as if he knew of something to my discredit, for he said one day I was like many people, inasmuch as I only took up with religion when it suited me.

It was very annoying to see Burghers not half as religious as I getting pineapples and peppermints sent them, while I got none,—a thing not wise if intended to prove religion profitable, for it made me more irreligious than the worst; and my indignation grew strong when I saw these same Burghers take out the cards they had hidden beneath their beds, as soon as the predikant had gone, and often using their Bibles to put under their plank-beds to make them higher.

At last, when all my attempts to make friends with the predikant had been repelled by coldness,—he even accusing me of hypocrisy, a thing I have ever been opposed to in others,—my vengeance was gratified.

It happened that the Burgher who used to play the harmonium at the Sunday service hurt his hand and could not perform. I, being the only other Burgher in the prison having musical talent, said nothing about it, and the hymns had to be sung without any accompaniment. The natural consequence was that the singing fell into a long-drawn drone after the style loved by Doppers. Now the same wing of the prison was filled with military prisoners, and it being Sunday, they were all in their cells, with nothing to do. They could hear the singing plainly, and all joined in, keeping on one note all the time, and making such a hideous noise, as of bulls and people in pain, that the governor of the jail had to be sent for to stop it.

We heard that this business grew into a story, told by a prisoner released that week, that the Tommies had disturbed and broken into the chapel service of the Burghers, and there was great indignation, especially in the pro-Boer papers; and the jail governor, and commandant, and predikant had to assure the public through the papers that the thing was greatly exaggerated. But the pro-Boer papers said where there's smoke there's fire, and that the hushing-up of the scandal was in keeping with the traditions of British rule in South Africa.

But the sweet part of my revenge came through the foolish words used by the predikant, who wrote to the papers denying that there had been any attack on the chapel. "It seems," wrote he, "that the soldiers were only imitating the noises made by the Burghers who could not sing." This brought trouble for the predikant, who did not again come to the jail, but sent another, who was in many ways his superior, and appreciated me.

Meanwhile I would secretly laugh when I thought how all this trouble had been caused by my refusing to play the harmonium.

It is a terrible thing for an Afrikander to get into prison, seeing that he is less fitted for the life than Englanders and others who live in towns. In the whole of his life, an Afrikander probably never spent two following days between four walls, except when sick. For such a man to have to spend months and even years in a space no bigger than a cattle-kraal is abominable cruelty that should be practised on Kafirs only. Before a month had gone there was not an Afrikander in the jail who did not look five years older; and even I began to show signs of the cruelty of my treatment, for I kept careful note by watching my face in the only looking-glass, which, the other Burghers never using, I had all to myself, they not caring how they looked; and most of them would say they were ill on Saturdays when bathing-time came round.

One day, in the sixth week of my unjust detention, when my last half-sovereign had been spent on food and my name was down on the list of those to receive prison rations, I received a great schrick, only of a joyful kind. The warder called my name, and took me to the little room at the entrance-gates, where prisoners saw their friends.

"Who wants me?" I asked.

He was a surly warder, who never spoke to prisoners

except to growl at them for doing something innocent, and he made no answer, except to push me into the room.

Any anger I felt against him was suffocated by what I saw.

Sitting on the only chair was a lady, dressed beautifully all in white and pink, with a big picture-hat and a lovely sunshade all bright red. So tall did she seem in her long frock, that I, who had never seen her but once out of riding or short skirts, did not recognise the girl Charlotte in this beautiful full-grown woman, who stood up as I entered.

I rushed at her and took her hand; but before saying a word to me, she, still holding my hand, turned on the surly warder in the same masterful way that she had turned on the Burghers that day she visited the laager.

" Do you know how long you've kept me waiting? Nearly half an hour. I'll report you to the commandant."

The warder made no answer.

" I don't believe you took my message," she went on.

" But he must have, or I would not have come," said I, anxious to appease the rising anger of the warder, who went outside and stood near the door, as if to listen to what we said.

" That brute has been starving you, Sarel. I can see it in your face," said she.

" It's not want of food I have been hungry for, but friends," I answered.

" I only knew a week ago that you were here, and I came up from Durban as soon as my aunt could come with me. But how did they catch you, Sarel? and how long have you got?"

I told her I was not caught, but surrendered; and that my trial was not yet, so that I did not know how long I should get.

" Then I am not too late. How much will it cost to get you out?"

" We are not in the Transvaal, Charlotte, and I

don't know the prices, or even if there are any," I answered.

"But surely a public prosecutor can get himself off? I didn't know they could put officials in prison. They never did it in the Transvaal."

I tried my best to explain how different things were in Natal; but it is ever foolish to explain law to a woman, and Charlotte was like all of them.

"Who will be landdrost? I will go and see him, and tell him that it's all wrong about you, and that Andries Brink led you astray."

"There will be no landdrost," I explained, "but a judge—a Rooinek judge that they are going to import from England—and he would not see you."

"But I speak English beautifully; and how could he not see me if I went to his house?"

"It would be useless, Charlotte, as I am going to plead guilty."

"What's the good of that, you silly? Never say you did a thing. People always say they are not guilty. It's not lying. I read that in a book only the other day. I'll bring it to you. It's a beautiful story about a young man who stole money and went to jail."

"Charlotte," said I, "you are a woman, and cannot understand these things."

"Then if I can't understand, I won't try to get you out. Didn't I get Arthur out of Pretoria when they said I couldn't?"

"Yes; but that was different,—the Government helped you."

"And why shouldn't this Government help me? I have seen the commandant. He is even nicer than General Joubert, and I'm sure I can manage him."

"Charlotte, I tell you things are different," said I, almost angry that she would not see reason.

"Of course things are different. If they were not, it would be easy to do everything when you had done it once. It seems to me you want to keep in prison."

"Yes, Charlotte," said I sadly. "Now that I cannot

have you, I don't see much happiness in being outside these walls."

Charlotte looked at me with her eyes wide open, in that surprised and silent manner that always made me feel that she was too astonished at my words to answer me.

"You must not talk to me like that. I am engaged to be married," said she after a long pause, and very coldly.

"Then why do you come and try to get me out of jail if I must not talk to you?" I asked.

"I suppose it's because I had something to do with getting you here."

"Did Captain Watson tell you to come?" I next asked, secretly resolving that if she said Yes I would not let her do anything for me.

"No; he is away fighting. But he will know as soon as he gets my letter, and he will help to get you out, for he says you are more fool than knave, and have been the victim of Andries Brink. He knows all the British, and is sure to know the judge who is going to try you."

"I don't want him to do anything," said I.

"Don't be a fool, Sarel. You are only jealous, but you have no cause to be, for I should not have married you even if I had not met Arthur. You ought to be glad that he is not jealous of you, for he might tell the judge to make it hot for you."

"Why do you talk so hard and cruelly now that I am in trouble?"

"But I must be truthful, Sarel; that's in my agreement with Arthur. I have been causing so much trouble and wickedness by lying and deceiving people, that I'm not going to do it any more, even though Arthur may not find it out."

"But you once said you would marry me."

"Yes, if I could. Don't you remember I was very particular about that? But I never could marry you, least of all now that I am going to marry Arthur."

"Then you deceived me," said I sternly.

"Yes, that's true; but I was a deceitful girl then. I didn't know any better, and I didn't know Arthur objected to lying women. He hadn't been teaching me to be honest long then, as we didn't see much of one another. Besides, what about your deceiving Katrina?"

"I didn't know you then, Charlotte, and I didn't know any better."

As is ever the case when a woman gets a clever answer, Charlotte got angry.

"If you don't promise to marry Katrina, I won't do anything to get you out of jail," said she spitefully.

"Then if I don't get out, how can I marry her?"

This would have been a sufficient answer for a man, but not for Charlotte.

"But you won't be here more than ten years, and you won't be too old to marry when you come out. You will be only about forty."

"Charlotte," said I, speaking very seriously, "would you like to be compelled to marry me?"

She shook her head.

"Then why do you want to make me suffer by making me marry some one I do not like?"

"But it's quite different with men," said she. "It's much worse for a girl to be disappointed than for a man. They can always keep away from home if they don't like their wives; but a woman can't."

There was no answering such foolishness, so, with a sore heart, I changed the subject.

"Charlotte," said I, "this is the only shirt I have. Won't you buy me some? And I want socks and lots of things."

"Certainly," said she, very cheerfully. "I was going to tell you how dreadfully shabby you look. What do you want?"

I told her, and she made out a list. By the time it was finished the warder told her she could stay no longer, on which she put out her tongue at him, being very angry with him for keeping her waiting.

When she shook hands I noticed that she kept her

head back as if fearful that I should kiss her, and hurried out of the room, saying she would come again soon.

Next day there came for me a nice bundle of clothes and other things for comfort that I needed very much. I became the best-dressed prisoner in the jail, and I noticed that the female friends of the other prisoners would look at me, and sometimes gave me sweets and fruit. This, with my smart appearance, made the others jealous, and I became more unpopular. But somehow, now that I knew Charlotte was thinking about me, this did not trouble me as it used, and I spent much time in planning revenges that, owing to my superior intelligence, were generally successful and undetected.

A few days after, Charlotte again came. When I got to the visiting-room, I found her laughing and talking in a most friendly manner with the surly warder, who was on gate-opening duty. She had brought him a tobacco-pouch with his initials worked on it, making this surly man as pleased as a child. He showed his pleasure by leaving us quite alone, and making the time of our being together much longer than the rules allowed.

Charlotte was very bright and cheerful, the reason being that Captain Watson had sent her an engagement-ring, which she showed me before even asking how I was, or if I liked the clothes she had sent. She made me examine it, making a great fuss lest I should drop and lose it.

"It cost twenty pounds," said she. "That shows how much he must love me."

"How do you know?" I asked.

"Oh, I took it to a shop and had it priced."

This made me lose a lot of my love for her, I forgetting that a girl would wake up a dying man or woman to show her engagement-ring, for in this matter the Afrikander girl is quite as bad as Rooineks. However, she was very kind, and told me all that people in Maritzburg were saying about us rebels, and what ought to be done to us, from shooting to banishing us and taking our farms.

"It is fortunate you did not marry Katrina after all," said she, "for it would be bad for her to be a widow without a farm, for no one would marry her."

"You are very anxious about Katrina," said I. "You never were before."

"Ah, Sarel, you do not understand. When a girl is engaged she always feels sorry for girls that are not," answered she. And then she made me examine the ring again, and said that I should never be able to give Katrina one so good, because Arthur had told her this was the very best he could get.

Each time that she came, which was twice a-week, it was ever the same,—little about me, much about herself and Arthur, till I began to hate him more than ever. But I misjudged her; for though she talked little about my affairs while with me, she was thinking of them while away, as was proved by a lawyer coming and saying he had been retained to defend me, but he was not to say who was paying him. I knew it was Charlotte's work, and guessed that Captain Watson was finding the money, though when I asked Charlotte she pretended ignorance, hinting that as Andries Brink had safely reached Delagoa Bay, he would not forget what he owed me. But I knew him too well to give him credit for such thoughtfulness.

My having a lawyer pleased Charlotte much more than it did me; for, being one myself, I knew exactly how little they could do, despite their fine and encouraging talk. But Charlotte talked as if I was free already. Even when I told her that the lawyer had advised me to plead guilty, and rely upon the address to the judges and the extenuating circumstances that would be urged on my behalf, I could not convince her. All she would say was that I did not know what would happen, and that if the lawyer had not been a good one, Captain Watson would not have chosen him, thus forgetting herself and letting out her secret, as women always will if you contradict them, and pretend that you do not believe they have any secret. She talked so cheerfully every time she came, that at last I began to feel there might be something in what she said; for although a man pays no attention to a woman's opinion when it is against his secret wish, when her ideas agree with his he believes in her; and so it was with me and Charlotte. I had a secret feeling that in the end something would happen in my favour, though I could not say what.

And so the time passed slowly. Charlotte came once, and sometimes twice, a-week, always bringing something good to eat or to read or to wear, and telling me all the most cheerful news, and paying for my food that was sent from the hotel.

At the end of nearly six long months, I was taken with the first batch of prisoners to Ladysmith to be tried, my case coming on on the third day. I was not a bit surprised when I looked round the court, to see Charlotte sitting there eating chocolates. She had come up alone, I heard from my lawyer, and had been sitting in court for four days waiting patiently for my case to come on, and sending many notes to the lawyer, reminding him not to forget this or that, which annoyed him very much, as he was busy with other cases.

Mine did not last long. The principal evidence was all admitted by me, and had not to be called. My lawyer made a moderately good speech, in which he laid great stress on the fact that I had been forced to join the enemy, and had come in as soon as I could.

The judge president, however, made much of my being a commandant, he not knowing that a commandant is not master of the Burghers, and cannot do as he likes, as my story plainly shows. He told me I had done a wicked thing in robbing the convoy, saying nothing about the share Andries Brink had in it; and the sentence was one year's imprisonment, two hundred and fifty pounds fine, or, in default of payment, six months more.

I heard it without showing any fear, or even crying, for it was much less than I had secretly feared.

I heard after I was taken from the court that Charlotte said very rude things to my lawyer, calling him a fool and an idiot because he would not say what she wished him to. It was all spoken in open court, too, and the police were ordered to put her out; so that I did not see her till next day, when she was allowed to say good-bye before I was taken back to Maritzburg.

She was still very angry with the lawyer and the judge, and with everything and everybody connected with the trial, down to the policeman who had put her out of court, and even me for pleading guilty.

"Well, Charlotte, it's all over between us now," said I, after we had shaken hands.

"It was never anything else, was it?" she replied, wondrously cool.

"But I had thought there might have been something," I answered sadly.

"That's where you were foolish."

"Didn't you say the captain was away fighting?"

"Yes."

"Suppose something happened to him, wouldn't you want to marry again?"

"Certainly not," she answered firmly. "I should never want to marry anybody else, not if I lived a hundred years."

"But, Charlotte, how can you say now what you might want to do, say, five years hence? We all change much, you know."

She thought for a moment, and I felt I had for once said something she could not answer; but she was clever to the last.

"Then if I cannot tell what I shall feel in five years' time, what about you? How do you know you will want to marry me then?"

"I shall never change, Charlotte," said I.

"Neither shall I." She thought a moment, and then gave me her hand. "No, Sarel, I have done you quite enough harm in getting you into jail. I'm very sorry I should have been such a deceitful girl, but it's all over now. I'm not going to deceive anybody again;

that's why I won't tell you I would marry you. Let us say good-bye," and she kissed me quickly on the cheek.

Before I had recovered from my surprise she was at the gateway of the courtyard, through which she passed out of my life for ever.

. . . .

In a few weeks I shall be again free. The news came as suddenly as most of the great events in my life have. The governor of the jail sent for me, and told me that the two hundred and fifty pounds fine had been paid by friends, and that I would be released at the end of the twelve months.

I had one letter from Charlotte about nine months after my conviction. It was from some place in England, and told me about her marriage to Captain Watson, and was mostly full of a description of what she wore and how she looked, and a few words expressing a hope that I would write some day to tell her I had married Katrina.

I wrote directly, and was able to tell her that Katrina was married to a cousin, making his third wife and the step-mother to sixteen children.

I told her also that old Paul du Plooy had returned to his farm in the Woodbush, where, as soon as I became a free man, I should follow him, to explain in person why I had never paid either to him or to Katrina the proceeds of the deposit note.

THE END.

AFRICASOUTH PAPERBACKS